The Kithseeker

M. K. WISEMAN

Book 2 of the Bookminder Series

Xchyler Publishing,

an imprint of Hamilton Springs Press, LLC

Penny Freeman, Editor-in-chief

http://www.xchylerpublishing.com

1st Edition: August 21, 2018

Cover Illustration by Egle Zioma

Titles by http://www.pennyfreeman.me

Interior Design by The Electric Scroll, http://www.electric-scroll.com

Edited by Penny Freeman and MeriLyn Oblad

Published in the United States of America

Xchyler Publishing

THE

KITHSEEKER

Chapter One

The very act of breathing felt different to the mage, as soon as he'd lost his Gift. Eyes newly opened to the bleak reality found themselves stung by the acrid smoke of fire and spent magicks. Even the faintest whisper of sound: harsh and tearing at his ears.

Anisthe of Vrsar, war mage of legend and counselor to kings, lay unmoving amongst the wreckage of what had only earlier that day been his grand foyer. And though he'd done so countless times since the duel's conclusion, he delved once more into his soul, seeking for the thread— any sign that his powers had survived the battle.

The result was the same: Darkness. An empty, yowling hole where his Art ought to have been. A shuddering seized him, building from the toes, blossoming upward into knees, arms, leaving him quaking all over.

Incantate.

A fate worse than death for a mage.

How dare she. How dare that little minx curse me so. Even as he gave in to the angry venting, Anisthe could not help but feel a grudging admiration for the tactical move.

Liara. His *aurenaurae*. Daughter-in-magick.

And I with no magick . . .

The shuddering became a wracking cough. It forced Anisthe into motion. He had to get out of there, away from the smoke which threatened to finish him. Bewildered, for it was the first time in memory that he had to deal with the elements as a mere man, Anisthe crawled forward toward the door. For the briefest of moments, he was tempted to stop and let the suffocating air take him.

But no. Even miserable, begging for death's quiet kiss, self-preservation kicked in. He couldn't die. Not if he wanted Liara to live.

Oh, and he wanted her to live. Aurenaurae. Made of magick. No discomfort would keep him from such power. He'd meant his words to Nagarath and to Liara. His was a temporary state. He would get his power back. And then? He was coming for her.

Hindered by his heavy wizard's robes, Anisthe's knees caught in the fabric. He tripped and fell hard onto the tile floor. A sharp pain and loosening sensation informed him he'd just cut his chin.

"Damn you, Nagarath. Damn you to the furthest circle."

He could not be mad at Liara. No. Her, Anisthe admired. But he certainly could be angry with Nagarath. Life-long enemy. Destroyer of everything he had held dear. And the person that Liara had chosen over him.

"Viper. Blundering, lucky fool!"

Reaching, Anisthe grasped double handfuls of his robes and, writhing where he lay, pulled them up over his head. The yards of cloth muffled his struggle briefly before coming clear, a bedraggled half-burnt pile. Another thing Nagarath had ruined.

The last was misplaced blame. It had been Liara herself that had thrown him into the fire with an aura strike. But, as there was no one to correct the thought, the former mage allowed his anger to best him. It gave him purpose in the wretched, stinking air, his mortifying, average exist-ence. Gathering the armfuls of his robes, he stumbled to his feet and careened towards the door.

Ash and smoke swept past as the air in the long room changed current. Turning quickly, Anisthe only had time to see the door open at the end of the hallway. A man's figure rushed out towards him. The mage did the only thing he could think of. Dropping his robes, he stretched out his arms to incant, shouting hoarse words of gibberish.

For a moment, as the magick gripped Liara, the only thing solid in all the world was Nagarath's warm hand in hers.

And then, reality. Daylight. The Limska Draga valley snapped into bright focus as Liara's spell folded in on it-self, returning her and her companion to safety. Away from warring magicks and hard truths. Away from Anisthe with his cruel lies, his groping, grasping spoliation of her promised apprenticeship.

As if sensing her descent into terror over what they had so narrowly escaped, Nagarath squeezed Liara's hand. Grateful, she tightened her grip in return, joyful in the re-minder that her mage was not about to let go. He cared for her in spite of all.

The black gates of Dvigrad stood before them.

Home. Such as it was. Place of bad memories, Liara had grown up amongst its people, only to be banned from dwelling within its walls. Had it only been nine short months? So much had happened since.

Behind those high walls Dvigrad had sat empty for nearly two months, its citizens slain by the hand of magick.

The mage had murdered her people simply for sharing her birthplace. She had lived alongside them for the first sixteen years of her life. They had given her protection within their walls. The devastation reminded Liara of the lengths to which Anisthe would go in order to get what he wanted.

And yet, fleeing to the desolated town was still a better option than Nagarath's castle of Parentino. That Liara herself had destroyed. There the damage was as much emotional as it was physical. Not forty-eight hours had passed since she had abandoned the home of her protector and mentor. She had turned to Nagarath's archenemy in selfish service to her own ambition. Atop it all, poisoned by Anisthe's calculated lies, she'd returned to sabotage the catalogue book in Nagarath's library, knowing full well that the broken magick would, in turn, tear through every spell in the collection on its next use, catching the caster in the blast. Vrsar's war mage had orchestrated all, making certain that Liara would have no one to whom she could return, no ally upon which to call—save for him alone.

And Nagarath had still come for her.

Heartfelt as they had been, Liara's apologies outside of the war mage's seaside home had been but a bandage over a gaping wound, something she feared would be redressed as soon as was practical.

She slid her gaze sideways, still holding the wizard's hand, assessing him as she felt the last of the teleportation spell's lingering sparks let go its weary travelers. If he felt even half as terrible as she did at present, he did not show it. Nagarath's mouth was set in a straight line, his eyes probing the fortification before them, the trees alongside the path. Ready for any sign that their abrupt return had caught anyone unawares, his free hand strayed to where his wand lay concealed within his robes. Ever the protector.

Liara, for her part, was merely glad that her spell had not left her retching into a ditch this time. But then, she'd been doubly careful with her sorcery. The spell of instantaneous travel was, by default, not easy on the body. Her own treachery at Parentino aside, the wizard's duel had taken much out of her friend, enough so that it had been her magick, and not Nagarath's, that had returned them to Dvigrad.

Liara's heart lurched as the mage's fingers slipped from hers. Nagarath moved forward, his long legs taking him towards the city gate, towards safety and rest. Bereft of Nagarath's steadying hand in hers, her battered and bruised lifeline, Liara jolted into motion behind him.

Clenching the hand that Nagarath had let go, knowing his brief abandonment to be one of practicality, Liara blinked back illogical tears. It was nonsense to think that the mage would hold her hand forever. But his withdrawal left her feeling numb. Not knowing what else to do with herself, Liara folded her arms tight around her and simply waited for the mage to perform his magick on the gates of the outpost.

And waited.

The uncomfortable pause grew long while Nagarath's spell flickered beneath his outstretched hands. He'd splayed his fingers across the worn wood of the gates, foregoing his wand. Liara couldn't hear his words clearly enough to tell whether the trouble was with the mage or the gate itself. She moved to help.

A dull *thunk* reverberated in the quiet forest as the heavy bar on the other side of the door shifted at last. With the loosening of the latch under Nagarath's spell, something within Liara loosed as well, things she'd hoped to keep from the mage. The day's pain, heartache, her fear, all came crushing down. It set her lungs to burning, her eyes to smarting as Nagarath pushed open the gate with his failing magick, as he stepped even further away from her. But the worst of it? A guilty apprehension, setting twin waterfalls cascading down her cheeks.

Liara found that she had to look away lest she burden the wizard with her unchecked tears of remorse. *I haven't the words for him. None that I could bear to have him hear. Not today; not now.* Avoidance over apology. After all that had occurred over the course of the previous day, Nagarath's kindness could very well shatter her again.

Kindness. Had she reached the limits of his kindness? Had she any herself?

Or am I merely a selfish, desperate, and reckless wretch?

"Liara?"

Liara gave a furious scrub to her stained cheeks before turning back to the wizard. Luck was on her side, and his attention was on the silent buildings that rose on either side of the street, his academic distance keeping her safe. But then Nagarath made his way back towards her, and she had to try not to see the limp in his gait. The mage continued, "To the folk here, I stayed a stranger and so know very little of where anyone lived. Where is Piotr's home?"

Piotr. Dvigrad's apothecary. Of course.

In leaving Anisthe, Liara's heart had emptied of the terror he induced. The pressing realities of Nagarath's condition rushed to fill the vacant space. Anisthe's magick. Her magick. It didn't much matter who'd caused which lacerations on her friend's nose and jawline. There was no need to lay claim to which hex inflicted the trickle of fresh blood sneaking down the mage's temple or had blackened his eye.

Choking on the lump in her throat, Liara pointed a shaking finger towards one of the side streets. With eyes averted, she caught him up. "This way."

Liara felt the mage again slip his hand into hers, Nagarath gifting her with his weary, encouraging smile. Such trust. He was going to destroy her with that trust.

The first thing Anisthe noticed upon regaining consciousness was wetness on his cheeks. Tears. Evidence of his own weakness. Furious, he blinked them back.

A familiar face pressed close to his. Domagoj. Trusted servant and individual whose advancing figure had startled Anisthe into using magick he no longer had.

"Domagoj." Anisthe searched the man's face. He found compassion, worry, but no alarm. The air was cleaner, too, carrying a hint of spice. They were in the kitchens.

"I await your instructions, sir." If the servant understood what had befallen his master, he tactfully made no mention of it.

"Where are the others? Is it just us?" Anisthe made to rise, noting with some surprise that the softness he lay upon were his own much-abused robes.

"Scattered. Fled at the enemy's urging. He left with the girl, and I could not stop them." Domagoj hung his head, half apology and half obeisance.

Anisthe drew himself into a seated position, frowning. Domagoj. Who had been with him since his Habsburg days . . . before that, even. In ten years, he'd seen the lad grow from a skittish child to a solid young man, one who'd traded subjugation for subservience without losing the natural grace afforded his kind. Anisthe had always felt the youth to be trustworthy. But then, a well-kept dog was generally loyal.

A pity that the wizards of the past had tried to quash the fey rather than embrace their prodigious talent for the Art. Granted, without said persecution by man and mage, the cultures and lore of fairies, naiads, satyrs, and sirens might have survived the ages. However, though only half-mer himself, Domagoj would have had little use for Anisthe's promises and protection under such circumstances. The war mage would have been bereft of his convenient protégé and the rarer magicks he afforded.

Still . . . Anisthe was without his powers. And so he was touched but also wary. Curs could turn on masters.

He opened his mouth, but the thanks stuck in his throat. "Get me a fresh change of clothes and implements to make myself presentable."

"Sir." Domagoj rose, regarding him hesitantly before taking his leave.

Anisthe fingered the hem of his robes, thoughtful. It was quiet. Still nighttime. Early morning, technically. But no alarm had been raised. Interesting.

He looked up into the dark rafters of the kitchen. The building still held. That was good. He'd constructed it with enough magick that it well could have come down on their heads when Liara smashed his pendant.

Incantate. Not possible.

The empty void inside begged to differ. It threatened to swallow him whole. Eyes staring unseeing at the hem of his robes, Anisthe tried to master himself. Domagoj had seen his tears. Dear gods.

The silver runes that lined the edges of his cloak spun and twirled, a dizzying dance of nonsense. Anisthe could feel himself falling, and he tore his eyes away from the magick. A cold sweat broke out on his flesh, leaving him gasping.

Incantate.

Waiting in the darkness with naught but his frantic thoughts, Anisthe debated the wisdom of rising to his feet. He was mostly certain that the book he'd had Liara steal from Nagarath still lay in the front parlor, forgotten in the flight of the mage and his librarian.

He indulged in a weak chuckle, feeling ever so slightly like his old self again. To think that they might have left him the one thing that could lead him back to Power once more. *Very like Nagarath, after all.*

With a short hiss of breath, Anisthe gingerly gained his feet, surprised to find nothing further hindered his progress. He felt . . . normal. It was disgusting. And he vowed that under no circumstances would he allow himself to get used to such a pathetic state.

"I am a mage. I was born to it, by the gods, and I will regain my place." The words gave him strength where Power failed. Invigorated, plans flitted through Anisthe's fevered brain.

Domagoj had stayed. And so the former war mage still had magick at his disposal, after a fashion. Having had a taste of her power, a whiff of her signature, they might monitor Liara's movements. Meanwhile, he could finish his research—that which had required the book from Nagarath's library. Research that took on new importance that morning.

With a jolt, Anisthe realized the grim truths that Nagarath and Liara were likely confronting at present. They might have triumphed there, using Anisthe's own Power against himself to render him incantate, but they would have to face the consequences of Liara's actions. The library at Parentino: reduced to rubble. The collective work of the lifetimes of countless mages burnt to ash by the backfiring of the powerful spells that lay at their center. It was a wonder that Nagarath survived at all.

The girl was truly treacherous. And angry. Deeply angry—something Anisthe had recognized, had tried to use. Perhaps, if he worked fast enough, she would still come to see his side of things. She had the heart for it, the nerves of steel that it took to hit one's enemy at the point sure to cause the most damage. And here he was admiring her again in the midst of the wreckage she had left him.

The front hall: that damage belonged to Nagarath. Anisthe quickly crossed through the space, barely seeing the shattered front door and smoke-darkened walls. The hexes and trickery of his enemy had left their mark.

His eyes were on the parlor beyond, drawn to where the real battle had transpired. Stained with the soot and stink of wizardly warfare, the room mirrored his defeat. Anisthe imagined he could again hear the soul-piercing whistle of his magick as it was torn from him, siphoned through the broken pendant in Liara's outstretched hands. So cold. So clever.

Anisthe's heart lurched.

The book! Where is it?

"She took it. Vixen. Thief!" Anisthe half-ran, half-leapt across the long room. He'd foolishly imagined that the artifact had lain forgotten in the violence of the wizard's duel. Mistake upon mistake! Despair blossomed in the darkness, and he fell to scrabbling about the half-burned tatters of his ornate curtains. With a shove, he added to the disarray, knocking aside a decorative table and sighing in relief as he espied the small codex.

Excitement twitching his fingers, Anisthe opened the cover reverently. He possessed, perhaps, the sole surviving specimen of Archmage Cromen's collection. With no magick and naught but this one book in hand, Anisthe still held all the cards. The cut on his chin twinged again, the slow smile creeping across his face coming unbidden. Triumph in the face of defeat.

"Over there. In the war mage's house."

The damning sentence echoed in the early morning quiet. Soft footfalls soon accompanied the disembodied pronouncement, and Anisthe moved to hide himself in the shadows.

Slinking about in my own home like a burglar. Loathing renewed its attack, and Anisthe started forward, stopping as a restraining hand held back further movement.

Domagoj had returned. A finger pressed to his lips pled for silence.

Glaring at his servant, for he took no orders from one such as he, Anisthe shook off the suggestion, stopping a moment later as more voices drifted in through the open windows.

"Had it kept up much longer, I was going to find a way to douse my home as a precaution. Fire and light like a real battle raged. Not just some chimney gone bad, but a real demonstration of hell-fire here on earth."

At last, Anisthe had a view of the speakers, though he doubted they could see him hidden within the dark interior of the window. A small grouping of a dozen men and women stood clustered as people do when facing a crisis.

"Watch your words, fool, when you speak of the devil." Anisthe saw one man hastily crossing himself and imagined the speaker wore the trappings of clergy. "We're to wait until the guard arrive now that the danger of fire has passed."

"So you believe that he's still there, Father?"

"The mage could well be anywhere with his blasphemous art. Such are the ways of his kind. But, yes, I do believe him to still be there. His servants reported as much."

"Servants. Slaves, more like. More victims of his unholy powers."

"But what can we do?"

"At present? Watch and pray; return to our homes. The doge has been in talks with France. He has men who have been trained in these types of conflicts. You and I can only fight with what weapons faith has given us but they . . . they have been blessed with so much more."

A dark chuckle followed the priest's statement. Another speaker chimed in, "Hex-breakers. I've heard of them. Pit like against like."

Anisthe looked to Domagoj in the dark. Had the mighty Republic of Venice turned to magick itself for help? That would be novel. But then, the rumors from the rabble were often grossly exaggerated.

"Shouldn't have tolerated his type this long. Habsburg sympathizer." This last came accompanied by the grating sound of a nose and throat being cleared, followed by the soft slap of spit hitting pavement. A generous gob, insult and curse. From his hidden place, Anisthe made to jump forward once more.

"Come. There is little you can do against their weapons at present." Domagoj's whisper cut through Anisthe's seething concentration.

He hadn't known his hands raised, wand at the ready, until his servant called him back to himself. Another narrowly avoided mistake. Would he ever not immediately jump to magick as a solution?

Growling, Anisthe rounded on his servant. "You stayed. When you could have slit my throat and claimed all for yourself. So why run now? Stand your ground, magus."

"To what end? There is nothing for us here. Your Power lies elsewhere, does it not, Master?" Domagoj was quiet in his reply, though it was hard to miss the curl of his lip, even in the dark. "Our best move is in discovering that Power before it is lost to us. And then there's Liara to think of."

Liara.

"Her safety and ours—far more important than this pile of stone and tile. We can hide amongst the Artless until you have recovered your strength."

Anisthe eyed the simple attire that his servant held out to him. Plain and plain. He had not known he'd had such bare trappings in his possession. Recognition dawned. He had not. These were Domagoj's clothes or, more likely, some other servant's whose name he had not bothered to note. So, he was to flee into the night in the clothing of one who had betrayed him to the soldiers of the Republic?

Ah, but I have the book—the true story of the woman who cheated death itself and her wicked stepmother who had ensured as much via her magick mirror. Khariton's Mirror.

A twitch tugged at the corner of his mouth. Anisthe's smile returned. His magick would return as well, once he unearthed the mirror of the most powerful mage who had ever walked the earth.

Chapter Two

With his legs shuddering beneath him, Nagarath clutched futilely at the air with his free hand. It was a reflex he hadn't realized he'd acquired through years of wielding a mage's staff. Inwardly, he admonished the instinct and the longing it prompted. *Stop it, fool. You're not an old man yet. Not at twenty-nine.*

But he felt old. He felt every inch the stooped, decrepit man that he'd become. Thank the gods at least his memory—and magick!—was sound in spite of the double thrashing he'd received within the space of a day.

Luckily, the high walls of Dvigrad kept the streets dark at that hour. In the crisp and cold early morning, Nagarath's aborted motion would look like a shiver. Liara hadn't seemed to notice. Her eyes were on the path ahead, stone like the buildings and just as empty.

Nagarath's injuries proved trying. What had been troublesome and inconvenient in Vrsar had become nigh unbearable. They had left Anisthe defeated and incantate. But Nagarath knew his own danger. He, too, could push himself beyond his ability to fully recover. Granted, with the extent of his injuries, such might already be out of reach.

Liara's *progenaurae* had both strength enough and knowledge of the hexes meant to kill a man. But Liara's entrapment of the spellbook in his own library had caused his most grievous injuries. No man ought to have survived the catalogue's explosion. The spell of the book connected to hundreds of other codices and scrolls; the unravelling of the magick had meant the unmaking of all. And with Nagarath standing at its center.

Over and over Nagarath had asked himself: How had he not died? How?

Nagarath stumbled, his hand jerking free of Liara's. His arms wrenched as he found the edge of a building to grasp, but he hadn't the strength to hang on. Slowly, he slid into an ungainly heap, twisting as he fell so that his back might take the brunt of the impact. A shoulder glanced hard against the wall, forcing a gasp. His vision sparked stars. Blackness threatened.

Liara knelt at his side, placing her arm about him, supportive and solicitous. She didn't say a word, merely watched him closely, her eyes asking their questions.

"I'm fine," he said.

And then his leg twinged. The sharp pain led him to cry out. His hands went to his screaming thigh, though there was little they could do. The ache was internal and without definite source. It wavered, then was gone.

A clammy wetness clung to Nagarath's brow, and he passed a shaking hand across his forehead to clear it away. Sweat. Not blood. Not that that was any relief. His right leg refused to respond to the command to stand. His left grew numb. In that moment, panic took him. It grew as Liara tried to help him back to his feet, and he had to say it, had to say aloud, "I can't."

Her pause and silent inquiry drew neither patience or sense from Nagarath. Not with his legs refusing to work. He barked, "Liara, just leave me for one second."

This forced her back. Hurt confusion pooled in Liara's eyes.

Nagarath braced himself, pitting his back against the wall to try to gain leverage. But his legs would not obey, did not appear even to hear the call of his will. Reaching up behind him, his hands brushed the rough stone of the wall. Only two of the fingers on his right hand fully registered the sensation. So that, too, was growing numb. The realization summoned a sort of madness within him, and Nagarath let go of what little progress he'd made. He slumped back to the ground.

Again, Liara crouched at his side. Her hands hovered near but did not touch him. He could see that she shouted, her face white with fear. But Nagarath could not hear her over the buzzing in his head, over the bright heat of the magick he summoned from his soul.

Heedless of the girl and thinking only of the spells he could no longer do should he lose control of his fingers, Nagarath lay where he had fallen and concentrated on his Art. Sending the resultant spark through his body, he catalogued each hurt and its cause. Patchwork sorcery. Sloppy but effective. For he could not—could not!—lose his fingers, his hands. His legs? Damn his legs, he'd get to them or he wouldn't. They'd stopped hurting. What he couldn't lose was the magick.

Nagarath closed his eyes and whispered the words of the only working he was capable of at the moment. Relief swept through him, leaving him chilled. With his quick hex, he'd learned enough. And it was enough simply to know that the loss of control was temporary, an internal hiccup blocked by swelling and aided by—ironically enough—magick's sluggish refusal to move through him as it ought.

The conclusion cascaded through his psyche, a tumble of knowledge first learned under the tutorage of the old Archmage and later made rote through study of his library.

Nagarath remembered Liara, and his eyes regained their focus.

At his scolding, she'd retreated. At Nagarath's use of the Art, she'd grown practical and merely waited, a mage in training. But she was sullen, having worked through her fear and read his petulant non-response for what it was: deep selfishness.

"I can't move my legs," he blurted, not knowing what else to say.

What have I done? Liara's hands flew to her mouth. As though that could stop the choking cry which escaped her.

At last, the true cost of her treachery revealed itself: Nagarath not dead but crippled and broken. And this after he'd rescued her, gave all. And for what?

Liara had known something was wrong when Nagarath had inquired after Piotr's home. Terse and unlike himself. *Known something was wrong? Idiot. Think of what the man has been through!*

But she didn't truly know what her mage had suffered. Until then, Nagarath had been battered but strong. Somehow impossibly resilient. He'd given her strength, support. Invulnerable in spite of all. Someone to be believed in. But reality began to bite back, bleeding on the ground, and very much real. Horror shook her.

Liara's hands fluttered back to her sides. Useless. She didn't even know how to help him. Useless and powerless and her wizard lay on the ground, needing her help.

And not wanting it.

And can you blame him? More mental self-flagellation. Not humility; not pity. Punishment. Self-loathing. If he wouldn't give it to her, she would. And so Liara lost her turn to speak.

"I do believe it temporary. Merely my body reacting to extreme weakness—magick included. It is eliminating the extraneous, putting its efforts where they are most needed, most useful. It is such as I would do myself, had I the strength and the power at my behest." More verbose, more like himself he might be, yet still Nagarath did not move to sit up. Liara found it unnerving and looked away. Coward.

The mage continued, "I'd venture to say that it's a good thing."

This last got Liara to look back at him sharply. Likely as he'd intended. She found strength in the quiet sparkle of his eyes. Mischief even in the dire moments. Her heart eased, and Nagarath smiled, adding his usual unnecessary details. "It means the magick is doing what it ought. My bones and muscle and humors are all working in concert to make certain that my last worthwhile act on this earth is not merely having given Anisthe the beating he'd been owed for over two decades. It is . . ." Nagarath trailed off, his eyes far away. "It is a unique situation. Perhaps you might be persuaded to chronicle this malady and recovery, provided we can find the implements of writing?"

"But first we get you inside."

"But first we—well, yes. Of course."

Nagarath's calm impracticality had cut down Liara's fear. Her guilt remained, however. And that made her hesitant as she asked, "I'm sorry, but I don't think I can move you without the aid of magick. Am I allowed to—?"

Nagarath's response was a mute smile, his hand outstretched.

Had her heart been able to bear the arrogance, Liara would have been happy with how close her spell landed her patient next to Piotr's bed. Nagarath was able to scrabble onto the low pallet with ease.

Within moments, his breathing became regular and deep in sleep, which left Liara with little to do save watch over him until daylight crept in through the window.

Soon she found other ways to make herself useful. Dvigrad's thief was back. It was but the work of a morning to stock the apothecary with all that she and the wizard might need in the short term. She even discovered a bit of crockery that would do for scrying.

Nagarath slept through it all. Slept for two whole days, in fact, peaceful until Liara discovered the mage sitting upright in bed. Heedless of his surroundings, he looked intently at his battered and shaking hands, his useless weak legs. She felt certain that he did not hear her approach and so fled with the sound of his broken sob in her ears, clutching a sack of cellar-sprouted potatoes to her chest.

Liara's retreat took her back to where the mage had fallen. A retracing of steps, she wished she could go back further still, back to before she'd betrayed him. Even if such were possible, would she not make the same mistakes? Fall prey to Anisthe's lies through her same, bitter arrogance?

Not anymore. She'd changed.

That, too, was thought without action. Mere wishes.

Well, Liara had discovered how dangerous her wishes could be. Had she learned from it?

Picturing Nagarath, alone and in pain—pain of heart, of soul—Liara took a deep breath, calming herself. What was done was done. Now was the time to make up for it. Now was the time he needed her. More than ever.

'Yes, before you ask . . . I trust you.' Words spoken in earnest outside of Anisthe's home. A promise made by a man who'd risked his life to save her. How dare she flee when the time, the opportunity, for reparations had come?

Cowed, Liara made her way back to the apothecary's.

There she discovered the mage yelling at a chair.

"Ah. Liara," Nagarath broke off his tirade, turning to eye Liara's latest acquisition.

Don't you, 'ah, Liara' me!

Taking quick stock of the situation, Liara dared a scold, "Why aren't you in bed?" Her eyes darted to the mage's legs.

"Still numb. But, look. I've managed a solution! *Hm'shiik'* . . . No, that way. *That* way, you oaf!" Nagarath bellowed at his chair as it shuddered into motion, tottering briefly before obeying the mage's command to carry him across the small room to the fireside table.

Liara jumped back, hugging the wall in her surprise.

Wooden legs slipping and scrabbling like a chicken's, the enchanted bit of furniture did as good a job tipping the mage about as it did moving him to where he wanted to go. It simply was not designed for such. But Nagarath, of course, pressed on. Heedless of the shortcomings of his remedy, he seemed to be enjoying himself. Liara allowed a frown to cross her face, quiet disagreement over Nagarath's way of handling things.

Not to mention worry.

Two days—two days!—of uninterrupted rest and her mage was worse. Not better. Not as he had reassured her. For if he could bespell a chair to carry him about the apothecary's home, surely he had the power to bring back function to his legs? Even from where she watched in the doorway, Liara could tell that the malady of his legs appeared to be spreading. She could see the change in the wizard's fingers as he tried to cast. Trembling and arthritic.

" 'Why are you not in bed.' I take it that my recovery efforts disappoint you?" Nagarath's hard look told Liara he did not at all appreciate the silent judgment that resulted from her scrutiny.

Mortified, the shiver of Liara's guilt had her holding back new tears. "That's not what I meant. I thought maybe you were truly feeling better after resting for so long."

Hurrying past the apology that could not quite seem to find its voice, she met the wizard at the small table, doubling back to fetch the white willow bark she'd found in one of the abandoned homes. A peace offering. And good, common sense. Gruffly, Nagarath nodded his approval.

At length, he flicked his gaze to hers. " 'Resting so long.' How long was I out?"

"Two days."

"Two—! Two days." Nagarath lost his disinterested peevishness and gawked at her. "You kept watch over me for two days. Did you sleep? Eat?"

Self-conscious, Liara moved to fetch plates and the makings of a simple meal. She'd all but forgotten to eat. And in her fretting, her useless hand-wringing by the mage's bedside, sleep had come only when she'd exhausted herself in fighting it. This punctuated by her endless errands around Dvigrad.

Covert raids of the homes of people she'd known, paths that had purposely never taken her near the church. Fetch and carry—*no, thieve*—that was all she was good for. With each rummaging of a silent cottage, Liara had recalled something of those who had lived there. Pain amidst pain; each memory of loss an echo of her fear for Nagarath. She'd done her best to avoid it, walling off her heart. St. Sophia's, the place that had been her home, the site of Father Phenlick's death—she could never again return there. She did not dare.

Through her tears, Liara saw Nagarath lurch forward and, heart in her throat, she moved to catch him. *Useless hexed chair.* But rather than saving the wizard from a collision with the floor, she instead found herself wrapped in a tight hug.

"I make a pretty poor patient, don't I, magpie?"

"I'm sorry."

"Hush. It's done. Over. And I know," Nagarath soothed, "the healing is hard. For you more than me. And shall take more than a willow bark tincture."

Liara could not help herself. The wizard's goodness was catching. She leaned back to look him in the eye. "Potions work? Are you sure you're recovered enough for that, Nagarath?"

"As neither of our magick is going to help the other at present, it's a start." Nagarath answered her smile with one of his own. He moved to make himself useful. That is to say, getting himself thoroughly in Liara's way, a surer sign of recovery than strength of sinew and spell. "I'd venture that a good bit of tea is always reminiscent of warmer times and memories."

Liara could not agree more.

Chapter Three

"Scrying again?"

Nagarath felt the magick retreat into the shallow pool of his Art, the words of his spell faltering under Liara's interruption. With a glare, Nagarath fixed his eyes on the young woman newly returned from scavenging the empty village. Impertinence and cheek. She was doing it a'purpose. She had been all morning and half the day before. Small incursions, excuses to prevent his using his Art for anything save to heal himself.

Softening, Nagarath inclined his head, instruction that Liara deposit her findings over on the table by the window. She meant well, even if she was wrong. "Did you not say, just yesterday, that you wished there were a way to know Anisthe to be safe?"

"Keep him safe," Liara corrected. "Safe and far from us."

"What is it you want me to do, Liara? Chain him up for the next two and a half years until you gain autonomy?"

"I want to forget! I want you to forget about him. Stop peeking in on his life and look to yours." Liara wavered, her eyes darting from Nagarath's chair to the mantle that held his as-yet-unused wand. "Please."

"Liara. This man relied upon his Art for every last thing. We left him broken, adrift. He is defenseless if . . ." Nagarath hesitated. He disguised his unease by urging his chair forward towards the door. It didn't much matter. Liara's arch look informed him that she was not in the least put off. She'd keep at him until he told her the truth of why he was so intent on scrying the former mage.

Tell the girl. Guilt hammered at Nagarath's tired soul, and he opened his mouth to continue. Secrets from Liara were as good as lies. Everything he hadn't told her at Parentino had, in the end, worked to hurt her. And his inaction had led her straight into utmost peril at the hands of his enemy.

"So, he's in danger." Liara's words robbed him of the opportunity to speak first and gain her trust.

"We would only know that for certain if you would not keep interrupting my spellwork, Liara."

"But there's something. You've seen something." Liara sat, her eyes alight with the fearful urgency he'd hoped to sidestep.

"Heard something. Soldiers," Nagarath said. "Venetian and from farther up the coast. None of Dvigrad's postees. Anisthe neatly sidestepped them, taking to the woods. Nobody who knows firsthand of our involvement in—"

"Soldiers!" Breathless and shrill, Liara's shocked outburst sparked an answering tremor in Nagarath's heart. In the silence that followed, both recalled their last encounter with Venetian soldiers, though each memory was far different from the other. An unprovoked attack on Parentino following the violent demise of Dvigrad's citizens, Liara had known the men sent from the doge to protect the valley—having lived alongside them within the town. Nagarath only remembered their screams as they'd fled from his magick.

"Anisthe has been left with no power. There is little they can do to him on that account, should they bother looking for them. As I said, our learning of the soldiers is a lucky happenstance of my eavesdropping but not, I believe, any real threat to the man." Again, the quaver in his chest persisted and tempted Nagarath to say more. Liara was right to worry about soldiers—and her not even having overheard what he had through his scrying.

But I haven't the whole picture myself. Am I to hurt her anew, posit betrayal by Dvigrad's priest? It is not my place to tarnish the memory of the man who raised her. And all based on half-scried words and surmise.

He shut his mouth, shaking his head and looking back to his hands. Raw scrapes and cuts crisscrossed the pale skin. Scrying—indeed all magick—hurt. Time might heal, but it would leave scars. Nobody could fault him for not improving faster than his battered body.

"I do not believe Anisthe has fled persecution from Venice, per se. He has gone for his own reasons. Ones related to the Art, I would suspect."

"Why do you think he left?"

"Demons take the man! How am I to find out if you keep interrupting me each time I try to learn such answers?" Nagarath looked pointedly to the scrying dish, his ire up at last and ready to do battle with his ward.

Liara's own eyes followed to the fireside table. "Everyone in Vrsar knew Anisthe for a war mage. Surely his reputation would pique the interest of the doge's men. And now that he has no magick . . ."

"He has no magick, Liara, yes. And whose fault is that?"

Liara darted her eyes downward. Her whisper barreled into him, "Mine."

"It is a risk to leave your progenaurae incantate, is it not?"

He waited. Liara did not move. She left his searching gaze unmet.

"The man does not know how to function save as a wizard. Twice I've witnessed him reach for the lost Art on instinct."

At last, Liara matched him glare for glare. "It is dangerous, for he'll just keep searching for a way back to the magick. He'll keep at it; he'll keep on trying and reaching until either he is a threat to us once more or he—"

"That's a risk that I am more than willing to take, considering all that could have happened. Would you have had it otherwise?" *Talk to me, Liara.* "Would you remain prey to Anisthe's designs while you worked out for yourself a less dramatic exit from his influence?"

Silence. Nagarath could feel Liara's tension. But she kept her fire to herself, locked in the stubborn set of her jaw.

Caution abandoned, Nagarath let the words bite. "Anisthe is cunning, he's intelligent, and he's perfectly capable of ensuring his own safety for the next two and a half years. Most especially while I am allowed to keep my eye on him, ready to step in should he find himself in danger. Beyond that, I don't think either of us cares what happens to the man. Am I correct?"

A quiver shook Liara's shoulders, and Nagarath saw what had seemed the girl's implacable bitterness for what it really was. She was shaken to the core. At a loss for words, worried his next sentence would further shatter her,

Liara surprised him when she managed a deep, calming breath.

"But he is up to something, else he would not have left his home so readily."

The statement drew a smile to Nagarath's tired face.

"Anisthe is always up to something. And so, short of going back to Vrsar and taking him captive until you reach the age of autonomy and are free of your life's dependence upon his own, this is the course we must stay. Believe me, Anisthe has no intention of imperiling himself needlessly. . . . The only one who ought be worried is that companion of his—that servant."

The last was muttered mostly to himself. Nagarath knew all too well the perils of being an expendable in the war mage's life. And while it comforted him to know that Anisthe was not wholly on his own in his incantate state, it alarmed him to think Anisthe might still have such a loyal ally that they would have to reckon with.

"I wish we knew what he was up to, though." Liara sighed, seating herself close by but not too near Nagarath. The startled cat still had her guard up. "But then, I suppose we'd know that if, as you say, I stopped interrupting your scrying."

Because you're working yourself too hard. Nagarath supplied the unspoken reproof for her. And she was right. Blast it, she was right. Like so many other times before.

Nevertheless, Liara repeatedly shied away from any mention of her potential involvement in scrying Anisthe, leaving the task to Nagarath. But, equally, it was difficult for her to even sit through mention of the mage's name. The realization had him darting his eyes to the table in shame. He was not the only one with deep wounds in need of healing.

Nagarath had hurt Liara, too—pushed her into using her magick against his. And then expected her to rebound merely because he needed help. *Just because I think it would be good to talk about what happened doesn't mean she's ready.*

Eyes back on the bundle of goods Liara had gathered for him, Nagarath welcomed the distraction. Already he espied a few of the items he had so desperately sought while held up in the home of Dvigrad's apothecary. There'd be time aplenty for apologies and explanations. But later, once the physical damage had been addressed.

Recovering his strength had gone poorly so far, the wizard's duel taking far more out of him than he'd have thought—the magicked, spindly-legged chair being but one shortcut to get him through the day. Mentally, he was still sharp as ever—*thank the gods!*—but as for full recovery? That would be a long road and with no certain conclusion at its end.

Sorting through the herbs and poultices that Liara had fetched from the abandoned homes of her kinfolk, he was reminded of half a dozen pressing ailments. For instance, numbness in the last three fingers of his right hand persisted. He still clung to the hope that such was temporary.

Piotr's apothecary, a small country outpost with winter-thinned supplies, had proven useful but had fallen short of expectations. Thankfully, Liara's former neighbors had practiced some basic witching in their homes—though they never would have admitted as much. Fennel hung in various doorways throughout town; a surprising little jar of very fine yarrow oil; each gave him apt replacements for some of the spell components that had been destroyed when Parentino fell.

Still, if there's the slightest chance that some of my things survived in the wreckage of Parentino . . . Nagarath still held on to hope that he might have the opportunity of returning to the tumbled stones of Dvigrad's twin fortifications one day soon and seeing what they might glean from the wreckage. "Thank you, Liara."

A silent nod was her rejoinder. The fire had gone out of her and stayed out.

He continued, wistful, "Still no bitterroot?"

"No, sir. I'm s-sorry." Guilt lined her every feature: her pale face paler amongst its tangle of long, black hair, her otherworldly gaze crystalline with apprehension, and her determined mouth a mere dark gash across her face for the tumult of emotion.

Nagarath made certain that he had an untroubled smile affixed to his face before he spoke. "Not a problem at all. It was a vain hope. I'll be better without it, in the end. I do appreciate all that you're going through to help me acquire what poor Piotr seemed to lack amongst his stores."

Dash it all, Liara. Come back to me. Smile still pasted to his face, Nagarath urged the chair forward with a mere thought, clutching the herbs he would need for his afternoon elixir.

Already ahead of him, Liara hoisted the waiting pot over the fire. She then turned to busy herself by clearing away the implements of the mage's magick from his fireside table so that he might have the space needed to mix his components. A sharp gasp tore from her lips as the scrying bowl slipped from her fingers. She lunged as the earthenware vessel shattered on the hard floor just out of reach.

"Liara! Leave it. Please." Nagarath's barked words stopped the girl shy of gathering the sharp fragments into her hands. Tears dotted her reddening cheeks, and he almost softened. Almost. Enough was enough. "Find another bowl. Just don't cut yourself. We don't need two invalids, after all."

"It was an accident," Liara whispered. Nagarath narrowed his eyes, testing the claim and wondering why she'd even said it. "I'll go find another bowl."

Immediately Nagarath felt the pang of regret. Through his paranoia of Anisthe he'd misjudged her. Yet again. His apology was as absent as hers, however.

Nagarath reminded his apprentice of the basics. "Flat. Shallow. Dark. And with a metallic sheen, if you can get it. Perhaps something from the armory." Her education had not yet begun—too much had happened, too much remained unspoken—but he was adamant that she learn the proper way of doing things. That was how Archmage Cromen had done it and, Nagarath's slovenly habits aside, that was how he would teach magick himself. "Oh, and Liara?"

The lilting question arrested her movement. He waited for her to turn her gaze back on him.

No more tears. Good.

"If you please, I cannot quite reach the lip of the cauldron from this chair." Nagarath gestured with the fragrant bundle of herbs, ostensibly meant for yet another of his healing tinctures. Could he have simply lobbed them in himself? Certainly. He renewed his smile—this one genuine—as Liara approached.

Their fingers brushed as Liara accepted the bouquet of vegetation and added it to the steaming pot of water. Pain stabbed through Nagarath's heart as Liara then shied away from the accidental touch.

"I'll go find you another bowl so you can keep scrying Anisthe." Those words managed, she was gone in a trice, the sweet smell of the steeping herbs mingling with the bitter remorse rising in Nagarath's throat.

Oh, you broken thing. He raised a hand, closed his eyes, and remembered the euphoric moments of victory but days before: The early morning coastal air, heavy with salt and the tang of magickal warfare. *'I'm awful. I'm bad . . . and evil . . . and awful.'* Liara's words, intermingled with her sobs, cut through that quiet darkness.

He'd comforted her, reassured her. And gained her smile and trust back. Where had it gone?

Shattered like pottery. *Like Anisthe?*

Shuddering, his mind's eye again saw Anisthe fall to the ground, the war mage screaming as his magick was torn from him. Fellow student of Archmage Cromen, Nagarath had known Anisthe nearly all of his life, had spent years cleaning up his messes, an ongoing apology to the world for his friend. Or was it penance? Or merely an enforcement of right over wrong? And did that excuse the terrible thing Liara had inflicted upon her progenaurae? Incantate. Magi hell.

More images racked him: An amber pendant, dangling from Liara's hand, a crack marring its perfect power. Expensive curtains in a long, richly decorated room, going up in flames as lightning from Anisthe's spells set them afire. Liara's luminous face and delicate fingers, burning with the light of the very Laws of Magick. This after he'd thought that all was lost.

Nagarath backed out of the memory. Truly, his pain went far beyond anything physical. Or even the magickal. Such wounds wearied the heart. If he could get Liara to open up to him, perhaps the two of them could lean upon one another and heal those broken parts.

In his mind's eye, he could again see Liara's pale cheek resting gratefully in the palm of his hand, leaning into him and pouring out her heart. Raw. Truthful. The dark and blasted doorway of Anisthe's once-grand home loomed in the background. Pre-dawn birdsong on the breeze. A new life, unshackled from secrets and terrible pasts.

Opening his eyes, the conjured image faded. The hand that had held Liara steady shook in the dim light of Piotr's abandoned home. Mangled and bruised like the rest of him, he wondered if that hand could again rekindle the magick it had known.

Chapter Four

There is a horrible brightness to a guilty conscience. Liara found herself laboring under such as she ran through Dvigrad's streets, intent on the barracks and its armory. The fog under which she had sat for days had lifted, and she could more clearly see the homes she had invaded, pillaged for their comforts and provisions. Survival or not, she could feel the ghosts of Dvigrad's former inhabitants shaking their heads at the fey girl who once again ran roughshod through their midst.

With her observation, Liara's shame shifted, making room for sorrow. She found she had ample space in her weary heart for both burdens. She slowed her steps and let the memories surface.

That one was Tomislav's. Liara passed the home recalling how, when she was about seven years old, she had tripped going up the stairs near the north gate with a basket of apples. Tomislav, stiff with rheumatism, had stopped to help her pick up every last one.

Zarije's house. *Old Woman Babić,* Liara made the mental correction with a grim smile. She hurried past, hoping to escape the unpleasant memories that hung like mist about the darkened home. That woman had been instrumental in having Liara expelled from the town. But hadn't she, also, made certain that the newly orphaned Liara had an extra *kolač* at every holiday during her first year as ward of the church? At least, that's what Father Phenlick had claimed.

Liara dodged the memory of the priest as though it were a whip.

More homes; more facts bubbling to the surface. Like words to a spell, Liara lost herself in reciting her story of each neighbor whose home she passed, as if in doing so she might discover the magick that could bring them back.

There, Zvonko with his deep singing voice. And next, Ante who everyone knew cheated at cards.

And there, Danica had lived with her parents. Plump and pretty Danica, two years younger than Liara herself and sweet on Krešimir.

My Krešimir. Liara recalled another memory, one from outside Dvigrad's walls. A sunny riverside rock, Krešimir's goodhearted laughter, and an ill-conceived spell leading to a mess of horridly pink oak leaves. The last time she'd seen him. The last time she would ever see him.

Sorrow slowed her steps and blurred the stones of wall and street behind a fresh veil of tears. Liara turned back towards Ante's house. To reach the barracks, she'd have to pass the church. If thoughts of Krešimir could catch her thus . . .

"A week. What could have happened in a week's time?" Her argument came in vain, and she did not veer from her new path.

For, following her heated argument with the mage, before Liara had even known about Vrsar or Anisthe or any of the dark secrets of her past, she'd visited the church. Confined to Parentino for weeks, with only her fears as testament to what had happened in Dvigrad, she'd had to see it for herself. The night she'd left Parentino, she had come to Dvigrad, had gone first to St. Sophia's.

And the horror of it led you straight into the darkness. Liara found voice to explain away her unnamable reluctance.

Much could happen in a week's time, she well knew.

There were dozens of homes in Dvigrad. Liara had found one bowl useful for scrying in one of the houses, perhaps she'd find another without much effort.

Liar. Coward. Her conscience pounded in her ears. Liara ignored it. She ducked into a low doorway and peered into darkness. Finding nothing, she moved to the next. And the next. The result was the same each time: more tears and empty hands. She backed out into the glaring brightness of the day. There would be no hiding from the past, from the truth of what she must face.

Perhaps Krešimir's house . . .

No, not there. *Never there.* Shivering, Liara hugged her arms close about herself and simply ran. She ran, as if in doing so she might outstrip the ache in her heart. Careening around corners, up and down narrow alleyways, she made the stones of Dvigrad ring with her footfalls—anything to defeat the silence. And then, having exhausted herself, and drowning in her own heavy breathing, Liara slowed and found that her troubles were right there, waiting to catch her up. Her guilt, her shame, her fear. It had a name. It had a voice. The Laws of Magick tied her, her life—her very survival—to his. Anisthe of Vrsar.

'I killed your sorry little town. I killed its messenger.'
—It was Liara's fault. All of it—
'You were mine to claim from the beginning. Mine.'

—The blame as sure as if her own hand had been in it—

'I will find a way to get my power back. And when I do . . .'

Anisthe's parting words. For all that Nagarath had dismissed them with the curl of a lip and nary a tremor to his voice, Liara knew better. Anisthe was cunning. Nagarath was well aware that, for Liara's sake, they needed him safe. Safe but harmless. But that had never been how Anisthe had lived. He'd find a way back to power by whatever means necessary.

And that terrified her. It scared Liara how well she seemed to know his black heart. Her progenaurae and, considering her own dark actions at Parentino, tied to her in more ways than magick. Anisthe would always remain a sobering reminder of what she was capable.

And Dvigrad stands as silent testament to the worst that magick can do.

Liara turned her tear-stained face skyward. And was startled to see where her fears had driven her.

Of course. Of course she would find her way to St. Sophia's at the very moment she needed Father Phenlick most. She could see him in her mind's eye. Wizened and worn. Ancient beyond count—or so he'd always seemed to her. And constantly hiding his bemused smile under his far more proper glower of warning.

What he'd think of her after her actions in Parentino, in Vrsar, Liara quailed to imagine. She was half tempted to slink away. She'd passed beneath the shadow of the steeple, felt the worst of it. But . . .

You raised me better than that. Pausing and doubling back to stand before the imposing doors of St. Sophia's,

Liara placed her hands on her hips. For he had raised her better. Caught thus, Liara found herself unprepared for her shouted words of the next moment.

"I thought I was doing right, you know. I thought Nagarath had hurt you—had murdered you. And with you trusting him and leaving me to his care—it hurt to think it." New tears chilled Liara's face. She let Father Phenlick see them. He'd dried so many when she'd been too little to know to hide them.

"It hurt so bad that I wanted to hurt the wizard back. I needed to make up for what—" She choked and started over. "—for what I lost. And I know, Father, that violence isn't the answer. But wizards are different. They're powerful and don't always play by our rules."

Turning 'round, Liara sat upon the front step, wishing desperately for an answering voice, an assurance that her heart had been true, if misguided.

"You're right, though. I was dishonest, leastways to myself." Her answer had come sooner than expected, and she leaned back into the rough wood of the door. The sun had warmed it. Squinting, Liara stared up into the sky, a late-winter arc of pale blue edged by the teeth of Dvigrad's buildings and walls and ringed by the barren branches of the forest beyond.

"I lied when I told Anisthe that I hadn't meant to kill Nagarath when I sabotaged the catalogue book. And I'd be a fool to pretend that Nagarath doesn't know the truth of it. I knew it wrong, even if done for what I thought were the right reasons."

Liara allowed herself to be swept away in the flood. She could not have stopped the honesty if she tried. She was drowning. She was freed. Her tears no longer tasted of salt. Rather, she believed they carried within them the purity of a summer's cleansing rain. She turned her face to it, feeling real for the first time in perhaps weeks.

"So how do I face him? He who rescued me, when he was on the brink of death himself—injury done at my hand! How do I face him when I don't even want to look at myself?"

Sympathy, sister of kindness, prodded Liara's heart. She bent her head in stubborn refusal to be soothed. This time, her tears loosed groundward, tiny spots darkening the paving stones of the church steps.

"It was easy to take his hand, to accept his kindness while Anisthe lay behind us. A common enemy. But here? I'm the enemy. I've taken Nagarath's regard and thrown it in his face. I suspected the worst of him, and instead of finding out the truth of it, I punished him for the lies that Anisthe had fed me."

There. She'd told all. Closing her eyes, she let the waves die to stillness. Unforgivable she may be, but her unburdening to Phenlick had freed a part of her. More importantly, the confession was safe. Nagarath was bound to his chair and unlikely to be anywhere save Piotr's at present.

More guilt passed over her at the thought. *I'm the reason for that, too.*

And even then, he'd tried to mask the fear in his eyes; hidden much of his pain behind jest and joke. She'd even welcomed the mage's long-winded explanation.

Something to do with the *nervus* system, he'd said. Some conflict between body and the Art and how the two were healing from their separate injuries, each stealing from the other. Not learned in anatomy as Nagarath was, it had made little sense to Liara. Her main impression had simply been that, once Nagarath regained his full magickal strength, he could address the rest of the issues that plagued him.

She smiled in spite of herself. Nagarath always made everything seem so easy. Goodness, it had all seemed effortless when they'd left the terrors of Vrsar behind. Simple words of apology, explanation; the straightforward taking of a hand and going home . . .

Love is easy, Liara.

Bolting upright, Liara listened hard for the voice.

Also, it can be infinitely hard. But love is always the right way.

She waited, stock-still. But Father Phenlick did not again speak within her heart. But then, he did not have to. Liara completed the lesson herself: "You've hurt Nagarath badly enough, Liara. Don't continue to hurt him now."

Liara's own heartache eased as she again pictured the kindly face of her priest, her . . . friend. Until his death alongside the rest of Dvigrad, Liara hadn't even known she'd had anyone she might call such. And she'd certainly have never suspected that there might be some truth to her calling the town her home.

No, that last was an overreach. Parentino had been her home. And a place with magick and wonder, laughter and love. Even considering the betrayal that she had brought to it.

Liara's pulse quickened. There was something she could do for Nagarath. She could bring Parentino to its wizard. She could pick up the pieces. Surely not all had been lost. Nagarath had survived. And had done so with the presence of mind to arm himself for battle with his one-time friend.

That's what I'll do. I'll return to Parentino and rescue what I might. Liara smiled up at the heavens. Happy tears sprang to the corners of her eyes. Fetch and carry. She'd do far more than that for Nagarath. She'd give him his life back. She'd give him Parentino.

And yet . . . Though the corners of her mouth wanted to signal relief from her guilt, Liara's heart remained heavy. Again, Phenlick's memory prodded at her, a gentle reminder that her reparations could not be mere deeds. And neither could they be little more than a safe confession to a dead man.

Liara would have to talk to Nagarath. About all of it. Maybe not tomorrow or the next day. But the truth lay out in the road in front of her. And in that, in looking at it straight on, unshrinking and secure in her heart's wish, Liara found the peace she'd sought.

Glancing up at the mute bell of St. Sophia's, thanking George Phenlick's still-silent ghost, Liara stood and moved from the shadow of the church building. Before she could talk to Nagarath, before she could return to Parentino and rescue what she might, she had work to do.

A quick turn down the alleyway to the north brought her to the barracks.

Liara tried the door of the armory and found that it opened with ease. She peered about the long, dim room, picturing men playing cards and making outrageous boasts. In the seventeen years since her birth, the Limska Draga valley had seen little action. The trappings of the guard sent to protect the town from further magickal aggression were solid and simple. With a little imagination, a shield might well make a good scrying vessel. "Right again, Nagarath."

Although it is ridiculously oversized for our purposes. Liara huffed, hoisting one of the less battered specimens. It would have to do. Hurrying back before she lost all the strength in her arms, Liara nearly laughed out loud as she wound her way back through the alleyways and past the silent houses, imagining the strange looks she would have gotten from their inhabitants. *Still Dvigrad's queer, outcast magick girl.*

Strengthened by resolve and the newly found peace in her heart, Liara flew back to the apothecary. With a quiet smile, she presented the shield to the mage.

Nagarath leaned forward over the metal, testing it with his hands. "This is almost perfect, Liara. A bit overdone, perhaps—I had in mind a bowl or platter—but we'll be able to see everything," It rocked gently on the table, a consequence of the protruding pattern on its front. He frowned, and Liara felt her heart sink.

A scrying vessel had to be level and stable, so as to keep the surface of the water as still as possible. Liara had been so caught up with the inside of the shield that she'd overlooked the difficulties the outside would produce.

"Liara, if you please. I need you to repeat after me. Oh, and hold your hands just so, along the edges of the shield so that it sits level, as I am holding it now." Liara approached, copying Nagarath's pose with her hands. The mage instructed further, "You'll find that you need to press downward a bit once you begin the spell."

"I'm not scrying, am I?" Liara felt her face go white with fear. Cringing, she remembered too late that there had to be water in the bowl—to the brim and still as glass—for such a spell of spying to work. In her terror, she had forgot the most basic of principles. On its heels, a wave of guilt swept over her. Not wishing to see Anisthe was no excuse for not helping.

"No, Liara."

Liara's relief was somehow worse than the guilt.

"*Tsiref hiik esh.*" Nagarath's words cut through further thought, and Liara repeated after the mage, emulating the inflection while drawing deep from the well of her Art.

"*Tsiref hiik esh.*" Under the application of the spell, the metal dish glowed lilac and grew hot to the touch. With a gasp, Liara nearly pulled back, lest she be burned, but conviction took over, and she instead bore down upon the shield. She was rewarded by thin rivulets of smoke which curled up around the edges. The steel seemed to settle beneath her fingers, ceasing to rock on its wooden stand.

Ending the spell and freeing herself, Liara stumbled backwards. Nagarath gently grasped her elbow to steady her. A quick glance informed her that her magick had worked. The shield sat upon the small table, level and secure. Or rather, it sat partially sunken into the table, scorch marks ringing the edge where it had burned itself into the wood.

"What did I . . . ?" Liara breathed, giddy and a little dizzy in her triumph.

"You changed the border between the ending of one object and the beginning of another. 'Joining with fire', if you will. Magefire."

Liara looked sharply to Nagarath, finding that a dazzling smile awaited her. "But . . . I suppose we ruined the table?"

Smirking, the mage nodded. "You suppose correctly. But then, have you ever known me to be all that careful with furniture?"

But it's not our furniture. Her short-lived burst of excitement ended. Liara looked about the small room. Piotr had kept a tidy home. And now it was strewn with the clothing from half a dozen other houses, dry goods from any number of neighbors, and cutlery from Zarije Babić herself. Never mind Nagarath's magicked, mobile chair and the soldiers' shield now permanently burned into the fireside table.

"They're not coming back, Liara."

"I know. But . . ." But she wanted it to feel as though they might. Rather than like two vagabonds had holed up there in a time of desperation, mixing what had so carefully been kept apart, bringing disorder to the last things that her people had touched before magick took their lives.

"Liara, I'm ill."

This time, Nagarath shut his eyes to the reality he was trying to confess. It was enough that he'd tried at all. "I don't want to have to give up on Anisthe. I don't want you to think I care so little about protecting you—"

"What do you need?" Liara did not care that she'd interrupted him. She'd hardly noticed that her hands had clasped his.

"I need your regard and trust, Liara."

"You have it."

"If I tell you that I trust you still and do not feel that you believe me—that you question that very statement . . . then I do not have your trust."

And just like that, he had exposed her very heart. "It's just so hard to accept you have forgiven me for everything I did, everything I said and believed."

"I can trust you without forgiving you. Though it doesn't mean that forgiveness is not on its way. We both have hard roads ahead of us, even if we were to peacefully live out our days here. I'd like to at least begin the healing and acknowledge that we both have to do our part."

Each do their part. Escaping the thought, Liara moved to fetch the water needed for the scrying spell. It took her three times crossing the room to fill the large shield. As she did so, she wondered if Nagarath assumed she was staying to watch this time. She wanted to help Nagarath, to support him and show that she was there with him in all things. But for all that, the very thought of seeing Anisthe's face again twisted at her guts, knifing her until it hurt to breathe. She let the words out in a gush, "I cannot scry Anisthe. I cannot. Seeing his face would . . . I can't."

Nagarath regarded her for a moment and then seemed to turn his focus inward. "You don't have to stay, Liara. I understand."

Chapter Five

Anisthe watched the steady rise and fall of Domagoj's chest as he slept, hating him.

The former mage had come to subsist on a steady diet of envy since it had become too dangerous for him to enter town. He sheltered beneath resentment, keeping dry through enmity.

And despair kept him from the solace of sleep. He'd thought himself weak—pathetic even—upon awaking in his home in Vrsar. However, in the subsequent few days, things had become ever so much worse.

Anisthe was cold. Anisthe was hungry. He'd been forced to flee into the wilds with naught but the borrowed clothes upon his back and hide, certain he would be betrayed, while his servant had gone back to claim what else they might safely carry.

That Domagoj had returned at all kept hatred from becoming a knife in that sleeping back—that and Anisthe needed him. Anisthe. Who'd never needed anyone. Wanted, certainly. But confidence in someone? Utter dependence? Never!

And with his current beggared state, he couldn't even feel that humiliation properly.

Domagoj shifted in the late morning light. Soon he would wake and feel Anisthe's eyes upon him. Soon he'd breathe deep and sit up to stretch muscles cramped from sleeping on dew-damp ground and stare his accusations at the war mage for not resting as he ought.

Anisthe resented that too. Silent judgment but never outright confrontation. If he hadn't known better, Anisthe would have thought Domagoj resented the lack of opportunity to turn the knife on his master.

But the oriaurant is a dog, still. Anisthe's lips curled at the crude observation. The rare smile startled even him. Even bitter, he reveled in the satisfaction of his superiority, surprised to note he could feel thus, considering.

An Art-less mage. And yet he held power over an oriaurant. The aurenaurae—the other side of the same magick coin—had eluded him. Liara—his Liara—had left him ruined. But Domagoj, adopted son and servant, had remained. Somehow Anisthe still had the trust and regard of a half-fey cur of a man who had, perhaps, more power in him than anyone save Liara herself.

"An aurenaurae versus a half-man/half-siren. That's a contest I would dearly love to see," Anisthe muttered as he rose to his feet to fetch more wood for the fire.

Though dawn had given way to broken sunlight hours before, the air was chilled enough that the few moments away from the center of camp brought new discomforts to the mage. Fighting a shiver, the rough edges of the kindling's bark bit into Anisthe's fingers as he hurried back to the fireside warmth. More reminders of life as it would be for him, should he prove wrong about the mirror.

Anisthe's hands were quicker than his mind. Questing through his pack, he breathed easy once more as his fingers closed around the cover of Nagarath's book. In his head, he replayed the spells Domagoj had done—at Anisthe's urging and careful instruction. It galled him that he could not have performed such himself.

Still, the mirror, the power, was in Spain. And Khariton's rival—though freed from his own prison—remained, as he always had, in Albion. There was little chance of interference from England's Archmage. The man had never roused himself beyond the archipelago in over five hundred years. Powerful Merlin might be, but he was as lazy as Parentino's wizard.

Anisthe indulged in another smile—half-grimace, but satisfying nonetheless. That was why Domagoj had stayed on. It was why the oriaurant would never leave him. There was ever so much more to magick than power.

And, subsequently, why I need him more than I'll ever let on, Anisthe mused. His eyes lit on his servant-cum-apprentice. The time for rest was over, and he'd missed it. An already brisk wind freshened. Anisthe could feel his anxiety sharpening along with it. Domagoj's tentative arrangement with one of the ships at harbor had depended upon whether the *Bura* commenced its blow that afternoon or the next. Such a strong northerly wind could force an early departure.

And Domagoj still had not acted upon his master's orders, so far as Anisthe was aware. No matter the winds, nor the doge's soldiers, Anisthe was not about to leave for Spain without providing clear signs for Liara and Nagarath. He'd lost his aurenaurae for more than seventeen years. He wasn't about to lose her again while he chased a cure for his incantate state.

With that resolute conclusion, Anisthe rose and began kicking dirt over the fire. Seconds later, both he and Domagoj were choking on the cloud of dust and ash.

Scrambling to his feet, the dressing down Domagoj gave his master was not near as silent as expected. "What in the gods . . . ? You madman. Are you daft? The cloud from this will be visible from town," he spat between violent coughs.

Anisthe backed away, brushing embers from his clothing and trying to look as dignified as he might, considering. "That's the hope."

"Why?"

Anisthe faced down Domagoj's bulge-eyed disbelief with careful calm. He did not want to have to call the oriaurant on his having not done what Anisthe had asked—such was still a dangerous line. "We need the rumors of our movements to reach more than the ears and eyes of the soldiers. I want that dock buzzing with news of our departure toward Ragusa."

"Breadcrumbs."

Anisthe nodded. "Breadcrumbs. Enough to force the girl close. Endanger her, yes, but not so much that Nagarath takes us from the reach of our—your—magick."

"You're evil."

"I'm just a concerned father is all," Anisthe purred. "You know the truth of it more than anyone."

Domagoj's answering look was unreadable, and Anisthe smiled inwardly. Keep the oriaurant hungry, keep him close. Incantate Anisthe might be, but he was known for keeping his promises.

Another gust of wind tore through the small clearing. Impatient, Domagoj snuffed the last of the campfire with a hurried hex. "Come on, then. I've left a few tell-tale signs for Nagarath to scry, even if they don't make it as far as the house. We miss this boat, we miss them all for a week. And I, for one, am sick of sleeping in the woods."

~*~

"Tra'shuk." Liara materialized into a startled group of pheasants. With a shriek, she raised her hands to her face as the birds exploded up out of the low brush in a rush of feathers, beaks, and angry cries. But they were more interested in escaping the unexpected witch in their presence than they were in attacking her. Liara was left in relative peace to give her surroundings a better look. A moment later, she wished she hadn't.

Parentino lay in a tortured heap. The mage's tower leaned precariously over what remained of the grand building. The roof itself sagged and, in several places, had broken open onto the floors below. Courtyard trees, winter-barren, were blackened and peeling, as if a fire had caught hold of them.

Or, was the appearance merely that lent by Nagarath's spells of protection? Liara knew from experience that the mage had enchantments upon enchantments laid about his home—insurance against uninvited guests as well as a bid to remain unnoticed by any passerby. Piotr himself had believed the wizard and his ward lived in a hut in the heart of the forest rather than the twin fortification of his own town of Dvigrad.

Perhaps when Liara crossed the wreckage of the outer wall, the whole would come together before her eyes as it had on her first day under Nagarath's protection. Perhaps . . .

Liara's brief hopes were dashed as, stepping over the boundary to the dilapidated castle, the destruction seemed to grow even more complete to her tear-dimmed eyes. Up close, she could see that patchy snow had melted and re-frozen, incorporating wind-blown ash until, in a mix of grays and blacks, it had filled the new haphazard crevices and cracks in the half-tumbled fortification like some form of dispiriting mortar. Ice clung to the shadows, scowling frigid refusal to bend to the warming sun's command. Liara wondered if, once spring fully took hold of the valley, the melting snows and ice might bring the rest of Parentino down with it.

Picking her way gingerly over the rock-strewn courtyard, Liara noted wide swaths of the cobbled path were fully papered over. Peering closer, she saw snatches of spells, fragmented histories. Bit of pages, books of Parentino's library, ground into the walkway in a treacherous tangle of nonsense. She wondered if any of the power remained in them and chose her steps carefully. Thus hopping and leaping through the ruined pathway to the castle's kitchens, Liara found herself with no breath to spare for despair and no energy for tears.

Even so, Liara felt her legs go numb as she came face to face with the darkened outer door which led to the kitchens. How many times had she entered with expectations of cheer and warmth, even in the midst of any number of her heated arguments with the mage?

What's done is done. Nagarath needs you to be a repentant woman, not a mopey child, Liara. Thus fortified by her own no-nonsense scolding, Liara entered Parentino with a defensive spell cast and more magick ready on her lips should the stones prove to be less solid than they appeared.

Steeling herself, Liara whispered the words that would call her witchlight into being as she gently opened the broken door. By the light of her magick, she could see little damage beyond some blackening and chipping of the stones. The fireplace looked as though it was falling in on itself. Turning, she could see that the same fire which had scorched the trees outside had marked the table where she and Nagarath had spent many a meal.

Hurrying past the memory, she crossed into the great room, noting with some surprise that the flames which had tortured the courtyard and adjacent kitchen had not marred the main living spaces. There, crumbled masonry accounted for the whole of the damage.

New patterns of daylight marked the well-trodden floors, the inside finding itself newly acquainted with the out through a roof gone permeable. The slanting sunlight looked like gashes to Liara's remorseful eyes, and she lingered little in the familiar space.

She turned and found that the tapestry that had once hidden the library door had been rent in two. Though St. Jerome and his lion still stood guard over the entrance, the tear had divided the figures. The image warped painfully under the strain of separation. Feeling foolish for having thought that she would need her witchlight in a building sun-pocked as it was, Liara snuffed out the spell.

The library itself lay unreachable, blocked by stone, wood, and worse. The balconies which had ringed both the second and third stories had come crashing down. Shelves had been blown to pieces. Splinters of the heavy wooden beams had been woven into fantastic shapes, a barricade Liara could never hope to remove.

But she had to see it. Had to. For still she held on to faint hope. It could not all be gone. Such defied belief.

Liara took a deep breath and reaffirmed the strength of her shielding spell. The bubble of magick around her flashed its protection. She approached the impenetrable obstruction, peering through a low gap.

The same cracks that slashed the walls of the rest of the fortification marked what remained of the library. Wreckage of the room's contents lay not in piles, but bent in twisted agony. This was no mere trick, no easy illusion.

Liara's breathing came in sharp gasps, but she could not look away. Her fingers again felt the smooth page of the catalogue, the rippling sensation as the binding gave way beneath her violent pull—the fight going out of the book. She'd understood the principles behind her trap for the mage. But she hadn't fathomed the awesome power. A cold shiver broke over her skin.

Liara looked upon theory made real, and she realized, at long last, the dignity with which Nagarath wielded the Art. Her graceless mage. How dare she aspire to such— even if she wanted it so and felt her insides burn with the power. She backed away in silence, eyes darting over the whole and learning more about magick—about herself— than ever before.

Liara had her answer. There was nothing left to save. Pages and parchment scattered and burnt. The bleak barrier across the library's entrance seemed to bleed ink and magick. It made her heart hurt to look upon it.

They had been her friends, these books. Boring, boisterous, and broken in turns. She'd known them by name. She had labored over each to mend their hurts. Through them, she had grown into knowing her wizard.

Or so I thought. For Liara had then turned on Nagarath and turned her back on the collection. Worse even. A week prior, she'd not even spared a thought for these extra casualties of her pique. The precious treasures given over to her care—they'd been weapons. They'd been curses in echo of her own. Overcome, Liara looked away.

Every book—*every* book—in Nagarath's collection had been ripped asunder when the catalogue, the master book, exploded. They were all connected by magick. The Laws were inflexible. And, in this instance, cruel. When the parent died, so did the child.

A quiet whispering at Liara's back had her whipping around in alarm, a shield of magick snapping into brightness around her. The whole place was coming down! She'd die here, crushed by her own betrayal at last. And Nagarath would never know. He'd wait for her to come back. Again. And when she did not, he'd go looking for her and die out on his own, injured as he was. And—

The words of the traveling spell would not come to her. Paralyzed by fear—for Nagarath far more than herself—Liara stood frozen. And thus it was that she saw the source of the slippering, soft sound that was clearly not the building crashing down around her.

It was a book: one of Nagarath's special collection that required chaining to a bench. Not due to their value, oh no. After all, each of his books was valuable. Rather, the chained collection required restraint lest they simply hop away on their covers, complaining and threatening in their bookish language.

And it was exactly why Liara had not bothered to catalogue them in the first place.

That particular specimen struggled and snarled for freedom, pinned beneath a long wooden beam. The rest of its companions lay unmoving.

"You poor thing." While she had long hated Nagarath's most antagonistic set of codices, her heart went out to the book. Jammed open, the lonely volume was attempting to close itself, its pages tearing with the effort.

Hesitant, for she was in no way certain she could move the heavy beam—*never mind that it could cause the entire pile to collapse*—Liara knelt and tried to see if there was a way she might unlock the book from its chain. With a sharp intake of breath, she felt the blood turn to ice in her veins.

Crumpled from the book's struggles, the illustration on the open page was marred and distorted. But wholly recognizable to Liara.

It was a near identical copy to that on the frontispiece of the book she'd stolen for Anisthe.

"Mmm— Nm—" Squinting, Liara tried to sound out the foreign words which captioned the picture. It was strange. In all the dialects and alphabets that Nagarath had drilled into her, this one seemed familiar yet foreign. She did not know it.

The translation did not matter. The picture was the same.

And so the book was coming with her.

"You lucky thing, you." Murmuring, she glared at the book as it gave one of its classic snarls. Did it not understand she was there to help? "I really don't like you, you know that?"

She ran her eyes along the length of the beam. It did not look as though it was holding anything up. It was, in fact, just the top half of the bench to which the books were chained, a sort of whimsical decorative cornice.

The spell to remove it needed no words, merely magick guided by thought and gesture. Both Liara and book sighed together as the heavy beam shifted to the side.

"Come on then." Liara slammed shut the book and tucked it under her arm. The books were annoying, but they did not bite. At least she was pretty sure they didn't.

Flashing her magefire at the lock and chain, Liara gave a tug. Nothing happened. The lock held firm; the chain merely glowed back with a magick all its own.

"Blasted, paranoid wizard." Grinding her teeth at Nagarath's idea of security, Liara hammered at the chain with half a dozen spells. Each produced the same lackluster response. The book stayed firmly attached to the wooden bench.

The wooden bench! With a wicked smile, Liara placed her free hand on the dusty beam, throwing her magick at it. Not an elegant spell, but it did the trick. A large chunk of wood came free. More importantly, it came away with lock and chain still safely doing its duty in its midst.

Heart thumping with her discovery, Liara turned for one last look around Parentino, *"Tra's—"*

Nagarath. You came for more than your needs, Liara. Quickly canceling the spell of traveling, she turned her attention back upon the castle's great room. The wizard was not returning. Not in his condition, not with what he'd have to see. Such would be far too cruel. But what to take? The books were gone. What had survived which Nagarath might value? Did she even know him well enough to venture such a guess?

What matters to you, Liara? She decided to start with the easier guess, eyes following a shaft of sunlight that lit the corner next to the caved in and darkened hearth. Nagarath's *cindra.* Knocked off its pegs, the long-necked lute lay in the bright circle of illumination almost as if Liara had been meant to find it. Her heart in her throat as she lifted it, she found little more wrong with it than a hairline crack, likely caused by its fall or possibly even something that had already been there. Even the tuning pegs seemed to be in working order, though one squeaked gentle protest under her exploratory fingers. Without hesitation, she took the instrument.

Emboldened, as much by the sign as by the fact that the castle hadn't fallen in on her, Liara tried the stairs. Solid enough. Hurrying, she made her way to the mage's workroom, feeling the increased lean of the tower in the way that the steps no longer fit together as they ought. In some places, the climb was almost sheer, with little room for more than her toes on the treads. The whole effect was dizzying, and Liara gained Nagarath's sanctuary well out of breath.

The walls were crooked. Very crooked. Though the whole workroom had been knocked off its foundations, most of what was within had been broken by a more mundane enemy: gravity. Still, Liara shifted through broken bottles, bent and torn spell components, hoping to salvage what she might. The open sky—once touted as a feature by the careless mage who'd ruined the actual ceiling—had become a true detriment. Birds had scavenged the workroom. The elements had had their way at long last.

Her thoughts turned to the birds, the wind, and the rain. Liara wondered if there might be added consequences to the Limska Draga valley from her destruction of Parentino. Already there had been a violent loosening of power upon the place. What if the creatures which had made off with or ingested Nagarath's spell components suffered for it or were altered in some way?

Her concerns were interrupted by a small miracle. Nagarath, that inconsiderate, absentminded mage of hers, had made off with a fair number of his notebooks. And there they lay, some on and some next to a shelf by a mouldering chair.

Something he'd pointedly asked her to not catalogue, due to their contents and his tendencies for their use, the journals were saved by the mage's quirk of humor. Liara hurried to gather them into her arms, depositing them with the rest of the tidy pile she intended to bring back to Dvigrad. Again, sentimentality reined over practicality. It was quite possible the wizard would have no use for any of those things, but she had to try.

Bending, Liara tried to bundle the whole mess into an old, careworn cloak. A shiver bolted through her as she knelt. A vibrating set in, the very stones of the room seeming to reverberate, though Liara could not hear it. It made her bones hum.

Magick.

Magick filled the room. Greater than any she had ever felt, foreign and yet containing a thread of familiarity. Keeping her eyes down and her movements small, lest she expose herself to . . . to whatever caused it, Liara steeled herself for a hasty defense and escape. She tried to convince herself that to abandon the castle to this new menace was not cowardice. Again, the feeling of familiarity pressed at her, drowning out the words of magick in her mind, like a song whose words she could almost remember.

Nagarath. For Nagarath. The wizard's name broke the spell that had been cast over Liara's heart, and she whispered the word of the Green Language which had brought her to Parentino, throwing her violently back to Dvigrad's town square.

Dropping the rescued bundle of objects onto the ground, Liara ran for the apothecary's, seeking Nagarath.

The mage lay face-down upon the floor, his magicked chair overturned a stride's length away.

Chapter Six

"Nagarath." Liara knelt swiftly at the mage's side. The lacerations which he'd gained from the catalogue's explosion, indeed every dark bruise and stain, seemed highlighted in his abnormally pale face. He did not move at the sound of his name.

Gulping back the lump that rose in her throat, Liara gently grasped the wizard's shoulders, thinking to turn him on his back. The motion shifted his dark robes to the side, revealing a long, wooden staff with a knot at its top. Without hardly looking, Liara knew the knot contained a stone—reddish, unremarkable, yet magicked. It was a wizard's staff she knew nearly as well as the face of he who owned it.

Still, Nagarath did not move.

"Nagarath. Your staff. The one you'd lost . . ." Crying, Liara reached for the powerful artifact, stopping short as habit aborted the movement. Nobody was to touch Nagarath's staff. Ever.

How had it gotten here? She knew he hadn't had it with him before.

The words to the unknown song came back to Liara in a rush. The power in Parentino, so familiar, so strong . . . it came from the cinnabar stone in the mage's staff. The memory of the magick quickly faded, leaving the room as dark, as bleak, as Liara's fear.

Adrift, Liara sat back on her heels, knowing she should act, but uncertain as to how. The mage's staff again caught her eye. Separated from its master, the artifact looked to her as broken as the man next to whom it lay. There was a wrongness, a sadness to it. Impulsively, Liara clasped the staff, gingerly lifting it and placing it back down in Nagarath's open hand.

There. Something done right. Useless gesture as it was—like closing the eyes of a dead person—it eased Liara's heart to see Nagarath reunited with the staff once more. It looked . . . normal, almost as if nothing would again have been right without it.

Nagarath's eyes snapped open, and he jerked into wakefulness with a garbled yell.

With a scream of her own, Liara fell backwards, all elbows and wrists. In the dim light of the apothecary's home, she could imagine that the stone atop Nagarath's staff glowed red for one brief moment, the mage's skin responding with an answering illumination.

"Ha-y'k shel ha Olam shinah. Ha-onah hekh'reach avad li. Has'kerah ha n'tiyah k—" The words wheezed out of the mage, stopping abruptly as he thrust the staff from him with a mighty yell.

Still frozen in fear, Liara watched as Nagarath slumped back and emitted a shuddering groan—alive but clearly shaken. Eyes rolling in his head, he searched the room from his supine position, his gray gaze alighting on Liara a short moment later, his hand inching along the floor to rest itself atop hers. Beads of sweat dotted the wizard's otherwise pale forehead, glittering drops amongst the dark marks of violence that marred his face.

"Liara." Her name was an exhalation. "It was you who put the staff into my hand."

"I'm—"

"Thank you." Gingerly, Nagarath rolled up onto his side. He seemed exhausted and yet humming with life, with Power. Liara could feel it through the mage's fingertips, still lying against her own. She could sense it in her own aura without even trying.

"Fool that I am." Nagarath's focus wavered, and he wheezed the words. "A near fatal mistake, that. And one even a novice ought to know."

"You tapped into your own life force to summon the staff." A tremor betrayed Liara's incredulity. "Why?"

Her question did as much again in rousing the mage as the magick had. His hand slid out from beneath hers, and he moved to rise. "We must run. And quickly."

Nagarath's voice sounded stronger. He reached for the overturned chair, eyeing the cinnabar staff with mistrust. After the briefest of hesitations, he shook his head and scrambled up into his bespelled chair, barking orders all the while. "Cloaks and packs. Leave the spell components. We'll scrounge what we can along the way. And food. We'll need food."

"Nagarath." Liara jumped to her feet and attempted to insert herself between the mage and the seven tasks he was attempting to accomplish from where he sat.

"Nagarath. Just stop it. Why do we have to run?" Fear made her outburst shrill. It got his attention.

The chair wobbled to a halt, and Nagarath's piercing gaze reflected his own tension back at her. "They are coming! Vrsar's soldiers are coming to Dvigrad."

Liara glanced to the makeshift scrying bowl.

Nagarath read the look. "Yes, I saw the soldiers headed our way. And little more than that. We have, at most, an hour or two if we wish to avoid them altogether."

"That's why you needed your staff."

"Well, I couldn't find you, and I was in a hurry. Where were you?"

Liara was not used to such a direct question from the wizard, and she squirmed, thinking of the dead castle with its dead books. She opened her mouth to reply. Nagarath had already moved on. He waved off her non-answer with a frown and shake of the head. He urged his chair to the other side of the room and pointed with a finger here and gesture there. Liara ducked as articles of clothing whizzed past her head.

"But leave Dvigrad? You—we—can't! I mean, you can't even—"

"I do a lot of things that cannot be done, Liara. It's part and parcel with being a wizard."

As he spoke, Nagarath urged his chair into motion. Eyes on his staff, the mage winced as an uneven portion of the floor sent his seat spinning sideways. Pitching forward, he caught himself on the table's edge, breathing hard.

"I'll get—"

"DON'T touch it."

The barked warning stopped Liara in her tracks. The light and roar of magick drowned any other thought in her head.

The staff came to life under the mage's touch. He required no words or gestures to call upon its power. Red like the last rays of the evening sun through a low bank of clouds, white like lightning, the stave's magick arced through the room. In answer, Nagarath's own aura flickered and flashed. Call and response.

It was impossible for Liara to tell which was the master—mage or staff. For a brief, horrifying moment, it reminded Liara of Anisthe's amber amulet, herself at the center of a sorcerous storm.

Nagarath seemed to grow, to fill her vision. Crimson fire and pearl-white luminescence mirroring the blood-red scrapes and cuts on his pale, narrow face, the mage stood as straight as the staff in his hand.

As quickly as it had begun, the storm ended. Blinking the stars from her vision, Liara gaped at the wizard. "You're better!"

Nagarath swayed and righted himself. "Somewhat. Yes. On my feet, at least."

"Why didn't you—" Liara withered under the mage's silent, glowering response. She hid from further reprimand by hurrying to the bed to fold and pack the clothing that the wizard had collected with his magick.

"Just shove them in any old way, Liara. Time. Time!" Nagarath edged Liara aside, grasping handfuls of cloth and cramming them into the two packs. "At this rate we'll be having dinner with the soldiers sent to kill us! Piotr's hearth will be warm"—Nagarath doused the fire with a hex— "the evidence of our having camped, as will all this disarray—" Another spell straightened the much-altered chair into something akin to normal. "They'll be close on our heels, and that's only if they stop first at Parentino. And Anisthe has left Istria—Liara, are you even listening?"

Liara was and had. What they could take from Piotr's was pitifully small. She'd left two small armfuls by Nagarath to be jumbled with the rest. Her brain buzzed with spells. Had she anything at all in her memory that could serve the mage? Make packs lighter or paths more sure?

Nagarath, she could see, was cheating. Packing allowed him to use the bed for support. He relied upon the staff in the moments between.

How are we going to do this? Liara swallowed her protest. And it was up to her to ensure they both survived.

Liara made her escape the second she was able, calling back to Nagarath some sort of nonsense about fetching warmer cloaks. The mage's protest followed her, and she paid it little heed. Liara had finally remembered the book with its puzzling inscription.

Ice cold pinpricks assaulted Liara's face. Rain. Perhaps it would be snow by nightfall. Even healed to the point of walking, Nagarath's journey would be perilous in such weather. Perhaps they'd do better to bring warmer clothing. One could not keep oneself warm with books. An instrument did not make for good shelter.

'Anisthe has left Istria.' Good. Good riddance.

Ah, there it was. The ability to lie to herself was intact, at the very least.

Wondering if any of the mage's notebooks had any tips on weather-working, Liara squinted up into the graying skies. Walking and thinking, she almost toppled Nagarath. Grabbing the shabby bundle of salvaged goods, Liara hurried to explain, "I was fetching some—"

"—warmer cloaks, yes. Well, you'll find it much warmer down coast," Nagarath dismissed Liara's words before they were halfway out of her mouth. But, even desperate and distracted, he remembered to add, "Thank you."

Liara hadn't realized she had been waiting for the twinkle in his gray eyes to return. He was feeling better. Even if the mage didn't know it himself.

I swear, sometimes I think he likes being the invalid. Following the mage down the winding alleyways which hugged the western wall of the town, she let her fingers trail over the stones. Saying goodbye. If they were going to leave like this forever, she needed more time.

A lump formed in Liara's throat, and she shook her head to dispel the sentimentality. *Save your tears for Phenlick and the rest, Liara. Old stones are just that.* Still, she liked to think that the town would come to miss having folk roam its streets, climb its steps . . .

Perhaps someday— Liara stopped as Nagarath abruptly came to a halt in front of her.

Dvigrad's southern gate.

Beyond it: an unnatural silence.

Liara's fingers itched. She called upon her magick.

'Oh, so you'll defend your enemy to death?' Mocking words from a week—a lifetime—ago.

If that's how I must protect the mage, yes. Liara waited in silence, her heart thumping so that she feared it might give them away to the men who hunted her and the wizard.

Somewhere in the wood, a bird chirped.

"It's safe. We go," Nagarath whispered.

Liara kept her eyes on the surrounding woods as the gate to Dvigrad swung shut behind them. Her throat was again thick with unexpected remorse. Not daring a look lest the tears gathering at the edges of her eyes spill over, she instead listened as Nagarath cast his spells—one of protection, one of Godspeed—over the empty town.

Whoever happened upon its stones would find peace and contentment.

Liara hoped it would, some day, be her.

Nagarath trudged on, not sparing any of his breath for conversation as he picked his way across the rocky terrain. Liara wisely held her questions. In some places, as in Parentino, icy patches held their ground and threatened the safety of passersby. Both Liara and the wizard picked past these pitfalls, lest a footprint give away to their pursuers the direction of their flight.

They headed north, in the opposite direction of Parentino. Not the most clandestine of movements, but that way lay the river. Gaining its banks, they would cross and follow the ribboning line towards the coast and away from the two abandoned settlements of the Limska Draga valley. Hopefully, they could avoid the soldiers who would, inevitably, expand their search upon gaining Dvigrad. Vrsar was large enough that they might lose their pursuers altogether and find opportunity to learn more of Anisthe's aims.

The two of them had their magick, though Liara did not yet fully trust Nagarath's fantastic recovery. They had the advantage of time. They would have to take their chances that the patrols would march first to Parentino, taking to the road rather than the river.

At her side, the wizard made full use of his staff—not for its magick, but for the stability it offered his steps. Liara admired his doggedness and held her tongue still further.

But soon the tower of Dvigrad was obscured behind tall trees, and the way grew tedious. Their late-morning start had left Liara and Nagarath with less time than they'd need to gain the coast before nightfall—especially considering the wizard's condition.

Mid-day gave way to afternoon, gave way to twilight. And still the mage pressed silently onward, seeming tireless, his magick ever at the ready in case of ambush. Tension followed in his wake, and Liara did her best to avoid losing herself to it.

Soldiers. The conclusions they would draw from finding Dvigrad bereft of citizens. But then, there was no sign of violence, no easy mark of magick at which to point and say: "See? It was wizards that did it."

Oh, but there is. Memories of what Liara had found in St. Sophia's upon her first return to Dvigrad rose up in argument. But would those artless men know the black marks for what they were? 'Round and 'round the worries chased each other through her mind, gaining her nothing, for they fled fast as they could.

At length, Liara decided she must become the voice of reason and beg a halt. The stunned look on Nagarath's face told her he'd hardly noticed the hours passing. And just like that, the vitality bled from the mage's face, fading as quickly as the setting sun.

Liara hurried to set up camp.

It wasn't much. Nagarath had packed with a longer journey in mind—one involving inns, buying passage to save their tired feet. But trees don't care to exchange money for shelter, a river does not charge for its water or even require use of a mug. Cloaks became makeshift tents. A simple but serviceable meal was laid out.

"Do we risk a fire?" The dark, more than the cold, pressed in on Liara, though the chill in the air threatened to take hold before dawn.

"But of course, Liara. Provided you can set up the proper wards for us. I'm so spent that I could not scry at present, never mind secure us for the night." Nagarath bundled his cloak behind his head as he spoke, stretching out his long legs before a fire which did not yet exist.

He was asleep before Liara could coax him into eating anything. She was left with the dismal company of her fears and the first—the *only*—watch the thin night would have from the two fugitive wizards.

Chapter Seven

The clouds that had witnessed their flight covered the moon. Every night sound gave cause for alarm. But Liara's protective spells held firm.

She distracted herself by thinking of her progenaurae. Dark thoughts for a dark night.

'Anisthe has left Istria.' Not Vrsar, but the region itself. Folded in amongst the rest of his concerns, Nagarath had let loose the cryptic statement and never elaborated further. Liara had been left to wonder on her own. Why had Anisthe left? Was it from the same persecution that had forced her and Nagarath into hiding? No, the war mage moved with purpose. Nagarath had said that Anisthe faced no immediate peril. Not with him having no magick.

But wasn't that precisely why he'd be in danger? The first defense against the claim of witchcraft was to declare yourself as having none of the power. The second was to use it to escape.

Liara buried her head in her hands, wanting to scream at the sleeping wizard. That wouldn't get them anywhere. Nagarath knew the danger. Her worries were his, so far as she could tell.

And that's where shame made entrance. For Liara's concerns were not Nagarath's. The evidence of it lay heavy within her pack. She had gone to Parentino to find something for the mage and instead came away with something for herself.

In fleeing Dvigrad as they had, she'd lost the opportunity to tell the wizard of where she'd been and what she had discovered. Then, with each passing hour, the weight of her secret had set Liara against herself. Shame and incredulity. She could see the book's woodcut image, its sharp lines drawn in her mind. Surely guilt had played tricks on her eyes. She'd hauled a broken book over rock and muddy path for no reason other than fear giving lies to her inconstant heart.

Compromised, that's what she was. True, she could not have borne to see Anisthe's face through the scrying dish. Equally true, she wanted to know more of him. But then perhaps that's what her discovery of the chained book had been all about. Answers. Something she could look to and say "It is done with."

Carefully Liara unearthed the book—still with its length of chain and bit of wood. This last she had managed to cut further with her magick. It now resembled a terribly impractical bookmark. Liara had stuck it at the point she wished to go back to later.

A log on the fire popped, sending a shower of sparks up into the dark sky. Somewhere in the woods an owl sent out its midnight call, but otherwise, nothing moved or gave further noise.

Liara turned to the page she sought, the book meekly obeying—perhaps it was shocked by her presumption. That or the injury done by the collapsing shelf was telling at long last. *Can books die?*

Sidestepping the horrid thought, Liara fixed her attention on the ruined pages. The image was as she had feared—had hoped. Confirmation. Condemnation.

The book trembled beneath her gentle touch. The movement seemed to bring the inked drawing to life. Eyes darting to the still-sleeping mage, she did not bother whispering her own command for silence.

The scene was of a richly decorated room, perhaps that of royalty. To one side, a woman in chains struggled against two armed men, her eyes on a large mirror across the room. A man with a sword, imperious and grand, was gesturing in the midst of all. "Take her away!" he seemed to say.

But it was the mirror itself that drew the eye. Somehow.

For though the peril to the woman was great and the men in the room of import, all seemed small beside the mirror. Plain and plain, the glass seemed to steal focus.

"A magick mirror?" Liara guessed at the meaning. She still could not decipher the inscription beneath. She peered closer, jumping back as the book snapped shut, growling at last over the unasked-for scrutiny.

Even with the book closed, Liara imagined she could see the inked drawing within. Her mind stuck on it. It was the same illustration, identical to the frontispiece in the book she'd stolen for Anisthe. What could it all mean?

"Where did you get that, my little magpie?" Nagarath's voice made Liara jump. She let out a screech as the book slipped from her hands. When had the mage woken?

The fire had burned low under Liara's neglect. She watched, numb with embarrassment, as Nagarath moved to build it back up. The mage returned, gathering the fallen book and sitting by her side once again.

"Why, this is—this is one of mine!"

Nagarath examined the book, heedless of its snarling complaint. Laid upon the wizard's lap, the cantankerous codex opened, rifling through its own pages before slamming shut. A bookish equivalent of "pfft."

"I don't understand."

Something in Nagarath broke, crumbled before Liara's very eyes. She had to rush past it, having already cried these tears. "I took precautions. I did not enter until I thought it safe. The building—some of it, anyhow—is sound. I was able to go most places save for the—" Liara choked on the word, and pain paled her face.

It didn't matter. Her mage knew.

Liara moved to gather up the wrapped cloak that held the rest. "There's more."

"More?" Nagarath's gaze jerked towards the jumbled collection.

Liara loosed the folds on the cloth, revealing the—

"Telescope! My telescope! Well, half of it. And my cindra. And— Oh, Liara! You have gotten my notebooks." Tears dotted the mage's cheeks. He wiped them carelessly away with the sleeve of his cloak.

Liara tensed in spite of herself. In another lifetime, Nagarath would have hugged her. She could sense him fighting it now. But such was to be expected. This was all that was left. Archaic treasures of untold worth. Gone. Rare compounds to perform powerful sorcery: ground to dust and left as nesting for birds. Liara had spent countless hours repairing Nagarath's library. But she could only return to him a sorry handful of books.

"Apologies, magpie." This time he didn't even bother using his sleeve to wipe away the new tears. His hand came away wet and marred the cover of one of the Cromen notebooks. "I'm thankful. I am."

Nagarath took a shuddering breath. "But, too, I am angry with you."

There it was. Liara winced.

"Dangerous and dumb. The castle—"

"You needed spell components. You couldn't even walk! And the books—how could we leave the books, those that survived, even if we were to stay in Dvigrad? Animals. Weather . . ."

"—they'd have ruined what was left," Nagarath thundered. Anger bested him and he continued. "And if you think I care for you less than I do a book or a jar of . . . of bat wings, you're much mistaken!"

Liara found herself holding back an utterly inappropriate laugh. With surprise, she could see that Nagarath was doing the same, his ears having caught up to his incensed outburst. She ventured, "Bat wings, Nagarath?"

The mage opened his mouth and then closed it, shaking his head. "I'm all out of sorts now. Your fault, too."

Contentment fell over their quiet camp. Two fugitives in a late winter wood, on the run from the authorities, and they had found occasion for mirth. *I care for you, as well, Nagarath. Very much so.* Liara could feel the sentiment bubbling up inside. Nothing was stopping her from saying it aloud. And yet she feared to break the silence. For in it she had found Nagarath's forgiveness. Liara hadn't realized it could feel so warm, so comforting. She basked in it, safe once more within the firelight of her friend's regard.

"I do wonder one thing, Liara. Considering how you have always felt about this particular collection of mine, I am surprised you went through the trouble to bring the one all this way." A sideways glance from the mage told Liara he felt no such thing. She would have to confess all, right there and then.

"I had to, Nagarath. Look—" Liara jumped back with a startled yelp as the book tried to elude her touch, snapping at her with its end sheets. "I—stop it—"

Nagarath let her struggle a moment longer, helpless as he was with laughter.

"Look, I can't—couldn't you just—?" Liara addressed the book. "You weren't being this horrid a moment ago."

Leaning forward, Nagarath put forth his request in a slithering, soft tongue. The book shivered, whispering back its answer.

"Why didn't you teach me that?"

To his credit, Nagarath seemed more embarrassed than guilty. "Um, they did not wish to talk to you. They're . . . kind of set in their ways. And, shush."

They both listened intently as the book made its case. The mage frowned. The book ceased its movement. Liara sensed her wizard was getting nowhere in the negotiations.

Nagarath tried putting his inquiry another way. A pause, and the book snapped its answer—more growl than sibilation.

"How dare me? It wasn't me that got you blown up!" Nagarath was indignant. "You rough, old thing. Open I say." Both he and Liara watched and waited as the volume fell still, then pushed its cover open with a short hop. The pages slipped by, the book slowing as it neared the injury done by the fallen beam.

"There. That's the page. The bench's awning had fallen onto it, holding it open."

"This is very old, Liara." Nagarath peered at the mangled text.

"I know that image, Nagarath. Sure as I know every stone and street in Dvigrad. It's the frontispiece of the book I stole for Anisthe."

Nagarath blinked his surprise, turning his attention to her. His gaze offered Liara as much scrutiny as he'd lent the book. "A book of fairy stories? Anisthe wanted a book of old folktales?"

"Is that what this is?" Liara leaned forward, examining the image with renewed interest. "Whatever was a book of fairytales doing in your bench-bound collection, Nagarath? I thought those books you found valuable . . ."

"While most libraries chain their most valuable books to prevent thievery, clearly you've surmised that my reasoning for the restraint was for far different reasons."

"Yes, but—"

"Anisthe and fairy stories. Why is it that the two things I dislike most have found themselves in an unlikely friendship? Of course, I shouldn't be surprised that those detractors of magick's reputation should fall in together."

"Nagarath. I am being serious."

"As am I." Nagarath pinched the tip of his nose, lost in his contemplation. The habitual motion ignited fire in the still-raw wound that crossed its bridge, and he winced, quickly stopping.

Nagarath leaned forward, translating as best he could the old-fashioned speech beneath the image. " 'Behold the

Mirror of The Einatus Praecantator! It has seduced our Queen and forced our Princess into exile. Take her away, this Fairest in the Land, and search the snows for our beloved Daughter.' My apologies, Liara. You will now doubly believe I neglected your education, but I hadn't any idea that I had any books in my collection that used such an old alphabet."

"Einatus praecantator?"

"Sorry, *einatus* is another term for the well of Power that a mage holds. It is the wizard's term for 'soul.' *Praecantator* is merely a very formal, very archaic way of saying 'Archmage.' I could see why this might have a draw for someone like Anisthe, had such stories any truth to them." Nagarath's questing fingers again reached for the tip of his nose, his brow furrowing in thought.

Liara wasn't sure where the mage went when his eyes lost focus and he considered thus, but she took the opportunity to bring the book over onto her lap and examine the page more closely.

"But, Liara, presuming it all true, we don't have the faintest clue about this mirror unless we know what Anisthe knew. This book is an index. The entry for this story"—he leaned over, flipping forward a handful of crumpled pages—"was three pages long, if that. And all that survived is this half-ruined illustration and nonsensical caption."

"Snježana's Tale." Memories made cautious entrance into Liara's heart. Warm nights before the fire, a woman's voice crooning tales meant to beg obedience from a girl bent on magick. Liara gave vent to a strangled sob. She hadn't known she had such memories. Father Phenlick certainly hadn't indulged in fairy stories.

"The princess with snowy white skin and lips as red as apples," Nagarath's deep voice chased away the heartache, returned Liara to the present. "Which would make Anisthe interested in the source of the queen's power, the mirror once held by the mother of Snow White."

"Step-mother." Liara shut the book and scrubbed at her tears.

"Depends on the telling." Nagarath waved away the correction. "Yes, I know the story."

Liara looked sharply at the mage. Something in his face, a shadow she could not name, had fallen between them. Another secret, perhaps, or half-remembered moments from his own childhood. The old stories were designed to frighten, to warn impudent children through the most powerful magick of them all: imagination.

No wonder the wizard did not believe such tales had any truth in them.

"Such an Anisthe thing to do. Fixate on an impossible task. Going off after some whisper of a dream, devil take the rest of us."

Nagarath seemed suddenly to realize his words had not fallen solely upon his own ears, and he looked to Liara. "He'll be fine. He has a knack for it. Truly. But we must be certain of his intent before we leap to any conclusions. It could well be some elaborate prank. But if not . . . then we must think. If he will not think, we must. I must."

Her mage looked tired, and for an instant, Liara regretted having ever found the book. He was right, Anisthe was a grown man. And grown men took care of themselves with or without magick. Her own safety was not in peril so long as Anisthe valued his. And when had the war mage ever endangered his own skin unnecessarily?

"Liara, I'm going to spend the rest of my life chasing that mage. Cleaning up his messes, protecting the world from him, and growing old myself from the efforts. The world does fine on its own!"

Liara let him vent.

"And it's not as if he can do anything truly terrible while incantate. Let him chase all over, looking for some magick artifact that does not even exist. Cannot we just . . . ?" Head bowed, Nagarath wound down at last. At his elbow, the book flopped closed, providing added finality to the subject.

"What else do we know?"

Liara almost missed the mage's query, soft as it had been spoken. "We, um, I—I don't know much more about the book he has. I had description enough to use—" She cleared her throat, all of a sudden finding it hard to breathe. "Enough to use the—" Forced to clear her throat again, Nagarath seized the opening she'd left.

"Enough to use the catalogue."

There. It had been said. The memory lay between them, the wound torn wide open.

"And?"

"And nothing. I never read the book. Anisthe snatched it from me as soon as I returned. The description he'd given me was obscured enough that I didn't see the story for what it was."

"But it did not appear that he had any particular plans."

"I don't know. At the time, I was so angry, I could think of nothing else."

Nagarath grunted, opening the book. He reached out to grasp the edge of the page that held the drawing.

"What are you doing?"

"We do not need the rest," Nagarath spoke through gritted teeth. His other hand he'd placed upon the inner crease, ready to tear free the needed page.

"Stop." Liara covered the open book with her arms. "You'll hurt it!"

The mage stopped, jerking his hands back off the page, a curious expression on his face. "Hurt it?"

"Yes."

"It's heavy," Nagarath cautioned. "Most of what is there is useless to us."

"I don't care. I'll carry it."

Again, that strange smile upon Nagarath's face. He seemed to be measuring her. For what? For having, in some respects, come to Anisthe's aid with the finding of the codex? *I'm on your side, Nagarath. Just . . . just don't hurt another book. For me.* Liara let the plea die unspoken.

Nagarath looked away first, his eyes on the sky through the canopy of trees. "Come, the day arrives."

After a quick breaking of their fast, Liara made preparations for the second leg of their journey, requiring not one but three attempts at getting her magick to effectively clear all traces of their having camped in the clearing. Nagarath sat to the side and merely watched, saving his strength for the journey ahead.

It also kept him from rummaging through the items Liara had rescued from the broken castle. He both did and did not want to know, though he had some idea of the extent of it. Nagarath considered his tears, the manner in which his heart had hitched in his chest at the sight of the Archmage's words within the old books.

Nagarath had, of course, thought the loss of all worthwhile, having saved Liara from a terrible fate at the hands of his enemy. But the sting of his sacrifice had persisted deep within his soul. He had other treasures, worth tucked away in distant corners of the world. Far flung collections gathered dust under the custodianship of trusted friends. But those belonged to a past he'd long left behind. Perhaps they were merely the memories of others whom he'd chosen to preserve.

He risked a glance to Liara. How had she known? How had she dared Parentino to give him something of his own back to him? The telescope. That would have to stay, a curiosity for whomever found it. And the cindra.

His fingers itched to page through the journals. Cromen's notes. Anisthe's notes. His own. Amsalla's. These were the irreplaceables. Not the spell books, nor the catalogue that had connected them all. One could always design new spells, rediscover histories.

What's more, it meant something to him to learn that Liara understood the value of the personal. This last rang home more when he saw her lift the cindra from the folds of his old cloak.

"This we take." Her eyes begged him to agree.

He sighed. "Yes, this we take."

They set off towards the coast, silent in their trek, even as the day grew noisy with each new chorus of forest creatures.

Spring had already begun its work in the deeper sections of the woods. The first shoots popped up through the soil, tiny green heads waking at the call of warmer days and brighter sunshine. Squirrels and birds chattered in the trees above, no longer merely darting from here to there as quickly as they might, but stopping to enjoy the unhurried thawing of their world. Buds swelled on branches, radiant as a woman carrying her first child.

Nagarath liked to think it an omen. New beginnings.

With the turn of the seasons, however, the ground had grown treacherous. Nagarath found every hidden branch, overturned every soggy stone half buried in the slop of fallen leaves and rotting bramble. On more than one occasion, Liara flung a steadying arm his way, concern clouding her face.

Slowing his pace, Nagarath leaned heavily upon his staff once more. He gripped the old wood, sucking in the power greedily. The pain that had begun to regain ground made a quick retreat.

Ha-onah hekh'reach avad li. Has'—

Nagarath beat back the words with his mind. Adjusting the pack on his back, he strode forward, daring Liara to challenge him. He watched her questions surface and then fade, prompting a surge of guilt. What he was doing was wrong. *But necessary.*

He and Liara resumed their grueling pace through the forest.

"This staff . . ." Nagarath cleared his throat and began again. "I had mentioned that this staff once belonged to Archmage Cromen of Tours de Merle—that's in the south of France, Liara. He gave it to me upon his passing. Penance and absolution for my friendship with Anisthe and my involvement in his affairs. The cinnabar stone buried in its haft holds near infinite power. I—I should not be using it as I am."

"Why are you telling me this?"

"Anisthe cannot have this staff. Cannot. Understood? He cannot know its secrets. Nobody can." Nagarath leaned heavily upon it as another tree root reached out to catch his foot.

"But why—?"

"Because someday, this will be your burden to carry. And, incantate though he is, Anisthe will always pose a threat. In some ways, he is more dangerous than ever. This staff cannot protect itself. Quite the opposite, in fact. It is like that mirror we seek. An artifact of incredible power and remarkable tenacity for finding its way into the hands of someone who might seek to put it to use. This staff . . . this staff ruins whomever holds it."

"Penance."

Nagarath nodded. "You've heard it working on me when I've dared tap into its power. I resist. But it is so very strong."

"Then why not leave it buried?"

"You've seen how it has saved us already? No, it could not be buried and forgotten."

Turning her eyes to the path, Liara seemed to lose herself in her thoughts. The wall between them rebuilt in a matter of seconds. He could almost hear her blaming herself.

"This long predates you, Liara."

"I know."

"And if it is anyone's fault, it is mine."

Her sharp intake of breath told Nagarath that his confession had cut Liara's heart. So be it. He had to begin the mending, even if it meant bleeding out for a time, else their travels would be long indeed.

"Then, your staff is why teleportation to Vrsar is not possible."

"Precisely." Nagarath corrected himself. "My ailments make it impossible. Had I the strength, I could witch us anywhere within twenty leagues, though we carried any number of artifacts blessed with the Art. It would take some time to do the calculations, of course, but it would be possible. What I lack is the strength. And so, ironically, we walk."

"Thank you for telling me." Liara did not look at him. But her avoidance spoke of depth of feeling rather than lack of it. "Whether you felt you had to or not. Thank you. Trusting me is different than saying you trust me."

Trudging by the girl's side, exhausted from their harried flight, Nagarath felt a spark of hope take hold. Liara had changed, indeed.

"Hsst—"

This time the restraining arm thrown Nagarath's way was one of warning rather than support. He could feel Liara's electrifying tension. He heard it a moment after her: the soft murmur of men.

Raising his staff, Nagarath called to mind a few preparatory spells. Shielding. Concealment. Defense. Attack.

Liara shook her head, wriggling her fingers. They blurred in the forest air.

The girl has figured out an obscurity mask. Clever magpie. Nagarath knew the illusion for what it was. Not perfect invisibility—such was beyond magick's ken. But the spell would render the two of them hard to see. With it, they might slip past the patrol of soldiers now visible through the trees.

Provided they could stay silent. Which is why, of course, a moment later, the book in Liara's pack decided to make all the noise it could.

Chapter Eight

Flecks of salt water danced across Domagoj's cheeks. He stood at the ship's rail and imagined himself one with the sea. Immersed in its power, the effect intoxicated. In Vrsar, he had swum within the sun-warmed waters of the Adriatic. He had felt the awakening of his mer magick. But never before had the blue-green expanse stretched around him in all directions.

At least, not since he was a small boy. Domagoj shivered. He jerked his hands back from the wooden balustrade. After ten years in servitude to the mage who had rescued him, the ghosts of his childhood still haunted every ship on the wide waters.

Nearly sixteen years had passed since Anisthe led him to shore. Domagoj had never looked back. He hadn't the daring. For even though the men who had snatched him from his mother were likely scattered or even dead, the memories remained. The nightmare of his childhood had been burned into his soul as indelibly as the thin white scars which crisscrossed his back.

Domagoj cast his eyes over the blue-on-blue horizon. No one on that ship wielded a whip. Had that instrument of punishment made an appearance . . . With a shuddering breath, Domagoj escaped the thought, turning to see if Anisthe had come up on deck as he had promised he would.

A part of him wished the incantate would not. In his absence, Domagoj might simply leap into the sea. His departure would likely go unnoticed until it was too late to bring him back in.

"Leave all behind. Come closer to the sea's embrace."

The siren's call still sounded within his heart. That which led men to their death whispered a lullaby to Domagoj. It fed his magick. Too, it fueled his anger.

Liara stood in his way. Domagoj hated her more than he despised every sailor on the Adriatic. The past could bring pain, certainly. But it was the future which threatened. He'd seen her power firsthand. He understood why Anisthe wanted her so. An easy jealousy, it overran Domagoj's senses and called sparks of magick into his vision. Liara, the interloper. Anisthe's new favorite.

From the corner of his eye, Domagoj saw his mentor emerge onto the deck. He talked with a sandy-haired sailor, a youth perhaps a couple years younger than Domagoj himself.

Liara's age. The observation came unbidden to Domagoj's embittered mind. He narrowed his eyes at the two conspirators. Anisthe insisted that he needed the man. Something about getting a spy aboard Liara and Nagarath's vessel or some such nonsense. Anisthe grew more and more fearful that, in his quest for power, his enemy might avail himself of the opportunity he had been granted and whisk Liara away to somewhere outside Anisthe's reach.

"Nothing is out of your reach, magus—with or without the aid of magick." Domagoj kept his praise to himself.

Leaning casually on the ship's rail, Domagoj turned his back upon the sparkling waters. He watched Anisthe's new over-eager pet climb into the rigging. Waiting until Anisthe looked his way and held his eye, Domagoj gave a short jerk of his head. A sudden gust tore at the ship. The sailor cried out in surprise. He managed to hang on to the line by one hand. A very close call.

Smiling, for he hadn't even needed the gesture to call the wind, Domagoj strode forward to meet the mage.

Incantate. Bah. The mage relied upon him, true. But Anisthe must realize that Domagoj needed him as well. Liara would not—would never—take his place in the war mage's life.

"Ho there! Who's out there?"

Liara could see movement through the trees. The doge's men. The evening sun, a heavy orange ball sinking behind the trees, illuminated the soldier's quarry—them.

I don't know what I'm doing. I don't know what I'm doing. I don't— Her spell of concealment faltered as Nagarath grabbed her arm. Quickly turning and throwing out a hand of assistance to the mage, Liara prepared to run.

But Nagarath did not move. A low droning reached Liara's ears, and she then saw that the wizard's lips were moving along with the sound. He used a magick in a language she did not know. The revelation somewhat astonished her. The stone atop his staff caught the waning light.

The world went dark. Silent.

Liara had the sense not to scream, instead waiting and watching as her senses caught up with her. The air had changed. They had come indoors. But where?

Nagarath released her hand and moved towards a window, peering out through gauzy curtains. He stayed well to the side of the casing to see and not be seen. The cinnabar stone cast a faint red glow upon the mage's pale cheeks and colored some of the gray hairs peppered in with the black before fading into stony dullness.

Liara didn't even feel nauseous; such had been the power of Nagarath's magick and his skill in wielding it. She looked around. Her knees buckled as she realized where they were.

Anisthe's home in Vrsar.

Nagarath crossed the room to her in two short strides. The fainting sensation left her slowly; words were beyond her reach. She waved him off.

"I'm sorry, Liara," Nagarath whispered. "The only path open to us was one where we would not be seen."

Why? Why here? Logic did not factor in it. Liara simply did not want to be in that place. Ever again.

They had materialized in one of the unused workrooms in the upper story, a corner space above the receiving room below.

"Why?" Liara managed to rasp out the solitary word.

"I'm sorry," Nagarath repeated. He moved back to resume his sidelong look out the window to the street below. His cool practicality helped her to cut through her irrational fear and become useful once again.

Anisthe was gone, fled on a ship across the sea. What had she thought they were doing by following him? Going on a fun little adventure? Seeing the world?

"What do you need me to do?" Liara sidled close to Nagarath, staying out of sight from the street and keeping her voice low.

"You know where he would have kept anything of importance."

Liara almost argued the point. However, while Anisthe had not entrusted her with any of his secrets, Liara had been, well, herself. She had made her clandestine explorations of the house, and the spaces she had not directly explored—such as the mage's personal workroom—she had conjectured. Liara led the way.

"Do you honestly think he left anything in here that would be of use to us?" Even as she voiced the question, Liara knew her answer. According to Nagarath's scrying, Anisthe led them a'purpose. He would know they would come to Vrsar, to his home. Doubtlessly he would also have left some sign for them to follow.

That or he'd have left a trap.

But, no. Aurenaurae. Anisthe won't wish any harm to come to me. Anisthe would hardly extend such protection towards Nagarath. But then, he wouldn't risk her safety to take a shot at his enemy.

"Drat," Liara said as they entered Anisthe's ravaged library and adjacent workroom. The one who had destroyed the war mage's things had understood the magick.

Liara could practically hear Anisthe's bitter vow: if he could no longer use the artifacts of his Art, nobody would. The incantate had burned and tossed the contents of every shelf, table, and nook. The scattered ashes of journals and spell components lay strewn about the floor and crunched underfoot.

"Liara, I think we should move on. There is nothing—"

"Shh." Holding up a hand for silence, Liara stopped to inspect the large table that hulked in the corner. She leaned in close to the worn wood, marked by the ravages of endless spell workings and recent attempts to destroy his work. "Are you looking at this with your eyes or with your Art?"

"There is nothing left to see through magickal means, Liara. Any remaining signature would have been destroyed alongside Anisthe's power."

Never underestimate Anisthe. Liara waved Nagarath close. "I'm alive. There's enough magick left to satisfy the Third Law. He didn't just magick his pendant. Cups, plates, everything . . . it imbued his whole home. The shadow of his Art remains."

Liara stepped back, waiting as Nagarath looked—really looked—at the war mage's table. She knew he saw the magick.

The signature was so muted that one wouldn't notice while staring directly at it. But, out of the corners of the eye, the observer could see the faded spectrum of spells and incantations. She refused to flinch. She would not let on how it bothered her to stand amongst such reminders.

The whole of it was like looking into the center of a storm, one that had bled the color from all that it overshadowed, leaving only pale specters in its wake. The mage's work table stood at the convergence.

Lines of text had been burned into the wood of the table. Blacker than black to Liara's magickal sight, the words were as indecipherable as those found in the snarling book.

"Can you read any of this?"

"This is old. The language, I mean," Nagarath's observation came almost reverently. "And see how it sucked the life out of the surrounding magick? The words themselves had that power. Based on what happened here, I would say that Anisthe got the translation right."

"But he has no real power."

" 'Tis an invocation to Kerri'tarre. The words possess the magick, not the speaker." Nagarath read the name aloud for Liara's benefit—more importantly, nothing else. Kerri'tarre, the Einatus Praecantator of whom their book had spoken. "Or in modern parlance, Khariton."

Liara's sharp intake of breath betrayed her knowledge. But then, having been given free reign of the world's most complete collection of magickal books, how could she not? Who, besides Merlin himself, was a better known magus in the history of the Art? Khariton would have had the power and knowledge—and skill—to potentially bind his soul to an artifact such as the mirror.

And so, the stories—this one, at the least—were true. Liara trembled at the thought. She suddenly wanted to be anywhere but there, staring at those black words and the even darker truth they proclaimed.

Ludicrous as it seemed, Anisthe truly was after the mirror—the mirror that held the last of Kerri'tarre's immeasurable power. His discovery of it would put Liara in graver peril than ever before. Even Nagarath would not be able to stand against Anisthe, most likely, should he gain Khariton's magick for himself.

"But why go to Ragusa?" Nagarath first broke the silence. He turned away from Liara so that he leaned on the table. He'd gone back to pinching the tip of his nose. Deep thought. She wondered if it actually helped. "Why not to where the mirror actually is?"

"Where is it?"

Nagarath turned back, a sheepish smile on his tired face. "Not Ragusa."

"But . . . ?"

"But nothing. The mirror has been lost to legend for hundreds of years. Goodness, there are fairytales built up around it, after all." Nagarath shrugged. "But the Archmage never travelled this far east. Our best chance lies in Spain."

"Which is impossibly huge."

"Agreed, which is why—Aha! Ragusa might help us after all." Nagarath shoved off from the table. He summoned his magelight and sent it to hover over a patch of ashes that marked the floor near the hearth. With his wand, he drew lines within the soot. "Spain. France. There the Italian Peninsula with its various states, Rome at the center of all. And here we are, up near Venice. Ragusa southward, there. Easy trade route point from Venice. We shall be able to book passage with a bit of luck. Their own Republic, we can ask our questions with little fear. Unless they, too, have taken a sudden dislike to mages. From the walled city"—the wand followed the coast, darted across the expanse of sea, and stopped near the Kingdom of Naples' southern tip—"it is a relatively easy hop over to Messina. But the doge's reach is limited. Once we reach Cagliari"— Nagarath tapped the uneven island he had drawn to the west—"we will be out of Venice's sphere of influence and can be more public with our inquiries. Yes. So long as we stay ahead of Anisthe, we have a chance of ensuring it is us, and not he, who get to Khariton's Mirror first."

Nagarath swept the whole of his map into the coast of Spain and then turned back to Liara, his brief excitement dimmed. "Liara, I—I have to ask something of you. Something you won't much like, I fear."

Liara's inclined head bade him speak.

"I must find us passage on a ship."

That was fine so far as Liara was concerned. She'd known they'd have to leave that way.

He continued, "I can defend myself, even in my current state—"

"And I can defend myself," Liara countered. Her pulse quickened in fear.

"No need as yet. There might be when we leave, but this is merely preparation, arranging passage and testing the streets for rumor or worse. Far better that only one of us risk getting caught while we have the opportunity to stay hid."

Does he know how terrible it will be to wait—alone— in this nightmare of a place? Does he? Liara pleaded silently, though she knew the mage's plan to be the logical one. He understood what he was asking of her.

"Here." Nagarath rummaged in an interior pocket of his cloak. He produced two coins and passed one hand over the other. He murmured quick words of magick. "*Na sha q 'ue.*"

Handing one to Liara and pocketing the other, the wizard ducked down so that he stood face to face with her. "Should anything happen to me, you will know of it. And I you. The words are 'I, Magus' and the charms are bound together. I do not anticipate trouble but—"

Liara waited in vain for him to complete the sentence. In the darkness of Anisthe's wrecked workroom, it seemed to her that Nagarath's piercing gaze held other thoughts, unreadable and all the more terrifying for it. Whatever barrier that had grown between them seemed to come crashing down for a brief instant.

Liara turned away first, finding safety in the coin in her hand.

Freed, Nagarath leaned more fully upon his staff and pulled his hood up over his head. He would be using magick, of course, once he left the house, but it made Liara's heart easier to see him take the added precaution. "Oh, and Liara? Your spell work in the forest earlier? Wonderful concealment spell."

And with that, he was gone. Liara waited until the door had closed downstairs before giving in to her shivers of fear. She stood at the window for the entire hour he was gone.

The coins proved to be an unnecessary precaution. Liara breathed a sigh of relief as Nagarath's familiar form came strolling through the shadows, back to Anisthe's house to claim her.

Still, she whispered a quick, "*Atsmi'i,*" before the cloaked figure came too close to the building, gladdened when the charm signaled Nagarath's close proximity.

He entered with wand drawn, his hood thrown back. "Liara! I— Is everything all right?"

He did not seem panicked so much as puzzled. And a little annoyed.

Liara blushed. Nagarath had not felt his charm's activation as she intended. To him, it seemed more a cry for help than a gatekeep's challenge. Her explanation earned a distracted grunt from the wizard as he put his wand away and performed a quick examination of the burned out front hall in which they stood.

"Ragusa?"

"Soldiers are everywhere, as anticipated. But we are in luck. The ship's captain I spoke with had meant to sail yesterday but held off, believing the north wind would soon be shifting. Too big a blow to otherwise cast off. As predicted, the breeze lessened within the short time I was negotiating passage. They sail within the hour and will take the sculptor and his boy."

Funny weather, that. Liara quirked a smile, certain that luck had nothing to do with it. "The who and his what?"

Nagarath looked down the empty street, nervously searching for any sign that their departure had been noted. A simple glimmer had him and his apprentice looking like two peddlers. The guise would not avoid suspicion or scrutiny for very long. Luckily, the moon hid behind a veil of clouds, giving Nagarath an easier time of the spells.

"You know that I truly hate you sometimes, yes?" The darkness of Vrsar's streets and Liara's pack partially concealed her face from him, but Nagarath could have sworn he saw the glitter of good humor in his apprentice's eyes.

"I have known that many long months, my dear. Haven't you discovered that I tolerate your hatred extraordinarily well?"

A snort. But no rejoinder.

Setting off, Nagarath gave one last look to Anisthe's home. The once grand house, resplendent with gardens, greenhouses, and gables, stood a shattered husk. Windows gaped at passersby, and the door hunched crookedly in its frame, as if to challenge all who dared enter. It did not look menacing so much as tired. So very, very tired. It wouldn't be long before it toppled over. One could only hope that its owner was far more robust.

Liara had already run ahead, eager to leave the broken memories behind her.

Nagarath hurried to catch her up. "Just don't let them put you to work on the ship, Liara. After all, as a sculptor's assistant, I would hate to have you developing the incorrect callouses. And if they get too close a look at you once we are aboard . . ."

"Why couldn't we just use magick?"

The old argument.

"Voice down, please, if you are going to talk so. We cannot because it is not a good long-term solution. I need the rest, and you need the practice before we can attempt something as involved as that. These precautions are so that, when my simple glimmer fades—"

"Then let me practice!"

She had a point.

"Fine. You practice."

Nagarath stopped in his tracks to face the girl. It was so strange to look at Liara. Hair bound up under a cap, stockings and breeches where a skirt would normally be. Knowing her as he did, he was not fooled. He wondered if anyone else would be.

"What? Here and now? What if I mess it up?"

"Then we get captured, tortured, and we don't ever have to worry about what Anisthe is getting up to these days." Nagarath impulsively reached out to grab Liara's hands. "I would not let you try if I thought there was any real danger of failure. Have I not told you that you are a most excellent pupil?"

Liara's eyes grew wide under Nagarath's compliment, a reaction more visible by her face free of her dark hair. She quickly mastered herself. "Fine. Tell me what to do."

They claimed they traveled from inland, refugees from a town farther up the valley from Dvigrad. It would give them an excuse to inquire more about Vrsar's fugitive wizard, should his name arise.

Nagarath would do the talking while Liara maintained the enchantments about them. Simple glimmers, the magick would enhance the faces she and the wizard presented to the men of the docks.

The hexes, though laid upon themselves, worked on the mind of the beholder to enforce whatever lies she and Nagarath told them. If Nagarath said he was a sculptor, an observer immediately marked the callouses and intelligent-yet-far-away-dreamer cast they imagined would be associated with the type. If he claimed Liara a boy, she most certainly looked a boy.

A complex combination of several enchantments, Liara found herself expending much of her concentration on maintaining their disguise. It left few idle thoughts to contemplate the morality of her actions. Nagarath also had her weave in an additional hex, one that would serve to erase any significant memories of their encounter with Artless folk as soon as they were gone from sight.

He surprised Liara in allowing such blatant interference with others' senses. Nagarath had waved off her concerns, explaining that the spell merely capitalized on what people did naturally: forgot and moved on from encounters deemed unimportant.

To her, the line seemed fuzzy, and Nagarath bent the truth to fit their needs. But then, had she not asked the mage for a way to enhance their disguise via magick?

And there was the rub. Did not all mages use of their power cross lines with regards to the Artless? She had once likened use of magick to using one's height to advantage. The comparison seemed simplistic now. She wondered if she would grow to learn more uncomfortable truths before she had completed her education.

But is not mere physical disguise also dishonest? 'Round and 'round her thoughts went, distracting Liara from Nagarath's dockside inquiries. The looming wall of the dark ship, the wooden outcropping jutting from the shore, the grunt and mutter of men taxing midnight-stiffened muscles as they trudged back and forth with their heavy burdens—it all began to blend together, the next much like the last.

Liara strove to rouse herself from her thoughts. *Come, Liara, you've had your fair share of sneaking back in Dvigrad. Where are your skills now? Just because you've magick does not mean you must disappear into it.*

"—all the way to Split. Yes, that would be more than welcome. Thank you."

Liara attended just in time to hear Nagarath's quiet words. Rousing herself from her out-of-the-way place in the shadows, she followed the mage down the docks, surprised at his rapid gait.

The city of Split. Liara's shudder almost shook her from her magick. *Isn't that within Venice's rule?*

As if in answer, Nagarath slowed to allow her catching up and bent to her ear. "They plan on making a stop along the way. Some merchant was eager to latch on to our luck."

"But Anisthe went to Ragusa."

"Understood. But it is as close as we are going to get today. Even with your assistance in our disguises, I fear that my inquiries over the war mage might have roused suspicions. So, to Split we go."

"Oh." Liara felt a twinge of guilt over her perverse eagerness.

"Don't you worry, my dear. The weather oft changes with a north wind." Nagarath indulged in a playful smile. "Drop the spells, Liara, quickly. Ho there!"

This last was directed to the ship before them. Liara did as she was told—startled out of her enchantments as she was. What game did the mage play at now?

An answering hail came from topside. The ship strained at its moorings, eager to be off on its run. Sailors stood alert at their posts. Liara wished she had paid more attention to the negotiations which had led up to that moment.

"Come aboard, friends. Come aboard." Helpful hands assisted Nagarath and Liara up the gangway. However, it seemed to Liara that less friendly eyes assessed them upon embarkation. Freezing in place, wholly self-conscious, Liara waited while the brief assessment was completed. She slumped in relief with the extended invitation: "There's little room here for anything besides the cargo, but you can stow your belongings—and yourselves—below, provided your money is as good as your word."

"It is." Nagarath tossed the sailor a small purse.

"Then welcome." The man spared from his duties for taking the payment gave a half-smile and, with one last look at his two strange passengers, was off to ready the ship for departure. The breeze freshened on pace with the coming of day. With any further delay, Liara and Nagarath would have missed their chance to leave Vrsar so soon.

Liara froze in place as barked orders rang out. Though they had indulged their passengers during their negotiations and greetings, the sailors spoke another language amongst themselves. Rounded tones rolled through the air, foreign yet faintly familiar.

"Men of Spain. We are doubly lucky for our find," Nagarath bent close to explain. "Come. Let us put our belongings below and leave the sailors to their tasks."

Liara followed meekly. There would be time later for questioning the mage. At present, her eager eyes roved every line and board. Her ears strained to puzzle through the various shouts from the sailors. It set her heart racing, and her blood thrilled to the adventure.

Ducking his head to enter the cramped passage which lead to the berths, Nagarath looked back at her. A brilliant smile crossed his face. Liara responded with one of her own, gladdened that the mage enjoyed himself and that the forced undertaking was not as big a burden as she feared.

Chapter Nine

Nagarath found himself ill-prepared for the delight that sea travel would spark in his land-bound librarian. The first portion of their journey secured, Liara flung question after question at him during their first day sailing down-coast. Her uncustomary enthusiasm alone made it almost worth the inconvenience of pursuing Anisthe across the known world.

The crew met most of Liara's observations with amused smiles—none least as the girl's knowledge of their language had come from Nagarath's books. Her initial attempts to communicate were overly formal, halting, and came colored with many an unconscious blush. The effect? Charming.

Undeterred, Liara reverted to her Italian when all else failed. Soon she held her gaze to the water, proclaiming her staunch beliefs in the existence of merfolk in both languages, a notion which the sailors encouraged. And, though Nagarath wanted to correct her, it occurred to him that as they were currently on the hunt for a mirror only spoken of in fairytales, it could well all be true. Terrible as it might be, Anisthe might know something of magick which he did not.

Unfortunately, while Liara was entranced by the sea and the magnificent ships that rode it, traveling upon the open water proved to be another matter for her. Seasickness deprived Nagarath of his assistant for much of their short voyage south.

Despite Nagarath's many talents, he could not cure Liara's nausea, had he even been up for the attempt. It was probably for the best. They could not risk their cover.

"A very dismal lack of magick," Liara lamented, riding the bow of the ship. She discovered that by keeping a weather eye on the horizon she could limit her vertigo. Nagarath feared she would be sunburnt beyond recognition by the time they reached the next port of Split.

Still, Liara generally stayed out from underfoot, and her green-tinged innocence seemed to lift suspicion from the two runaway wizards. A platonic fondness for Liara—their "Lookout," as the sailors called her—could be found from bow to stern. Nagarath was content to closet himself in their cabin and read, merely watching from afar.

That said, he had to call Liara down into the cabin when, upon the second day, it had become clear to him that the sailors had formed their own opinions as to the identity of their passengers.

"Liara, a moment of your time, if you please." Nagarath let his cryptic words hang in the salt air between them.

Liara's eyes darted to the mage's person, alarm springing quickly to her face.

Nagarath smiled, noting the concern. "Words best left for below, I'm afraid."

He let go the rail and picked his way carefully back towards the hatch, feeling Liara follow him. For all that the conversation he intended was of a nature different than she feared, she was right to be concerned. The deck's near constant pitch and yaw was wreaking havoc on his still-mending bones and muscles. If he could have but used his staff to aid him in his moving about—but, no, that would have led to an even more serious problem of disguise than the current one.

Below deck, he had an easier time of it. The close walls allowed him to grab hold as they made their way to their cramped cabin space—a converted storage area at the fore of the ship. Ducking the sprit, the large wooden beam that cut through the narrow apartment, he let Liara shut the door behind them.

They sat facing one another, practically knee to knee. His thoughts were slow to untangle themselves, and Nagarath's instinct was to avert his gaze. *No need to be embarrassed, you fool. She's her and you're you. Just as always.*

The words still rang in his ears. Insinuations overheard on deck had given rise to a new and disturbing feeling: shyness. Nagarath wondered if he ought to share with Liara what had been said or if he should simply demand that they change their cover story. But, no. Better for her to hear the gossip from him, rather than come upon it without warning.

"Liara," Nagarath began, then stopped. He had to clear his throat. "Liara, I think we might have to change our story."

Liara's responding look was an education in itself.

"Oh." Nagarath struggled to find the words. "I take it you are aware then of how tenuous our cover has become."

"You mean, none of these sailors have believed for one minute that I'm a boy?"

"Er, yes." Nagarath wilted under the girl's amused glare.

"If I thought their eyes so easily fooled, I'd have never gotten on this ship." Sighing, Liara shook her head. "I thought you knew how transparent our story was."

"Yes, well . . . I knew that if we supplied them with one so decidedly dumb, their sordid minds would be so busy constructing other wild untruths that they would never hit upon the real one," Nagarath admitted.

Again, that funny smile from Liara.

" 'Other wild untruths'," she echoed, arching an eyebrow. "I'm eighteen in June, Nagarath. What they're thinking isn't all that big a mystery to me. If anything, the clumsy denial that we're a man and woman traveling together unchaperoned is making the whole thing worse."

Nagarath felt his cheeks redden. "Exactly. So, what do you propose we do?"

This time, Liara had the grace to blush.

"All right. We shall let the sailors say what they will say. I am sure they believe, with our hasty departure and not-overly-particular aim in port, that we are running and are likely to protect us should no one step forward with the kind of silver that loosens tongues."

Nagarath cocked an eyebrow. "No past lovers to worry about? No distant kith nor kin that might object to you traveling with the likes of me?"

Liara giggled. "None as such. No. Only the one we're seeking—though we both know that Anisthe would never approve of our little escapade."

"It's settled then." Nagarath moved to rise, then stopped short. "Oh, do not let your hair out of your cap as of yet. We might still need to fool the eyes upon the shore when we arrive in Ragusa."

"Ragusa? I thought the ship was going first to Split."

"Ah, but the Bura wind, she is fickle." Nagarath indulged in a grin. "I do believe I overheard one of the men aloft suggesting they skip that port and send the goods to the merchant's contact in the walled city. If they stop in Split for one shipment, the blow from the north could delay departure and spoil the rest."

"You're wicked." Liara's eyes sparkled. "Teach me."

Nagarath sat back down. It seemed he had a cure for seasickness after all.

"Land ahoy. Look there, Mir."

The call rang out somewhere above Liara's head as she clung to the line of the ship's rail. She turned at the name the Spanish sailors had come to use for her. It fit. So far she had spent every possible second of their three-day voyage on deck, staring at the horizon. She had impulsively given Krešimir's name as her own when coming aboard. The sailors had shortened it, a play upon their own *mira*.

Krešimir. Thinking of him, of Nagarath's words to Liara in the cabin the day before, she wondered. Did Krešimir count as a lover? Not particularly. They had been friends since childhood. And while she had harbored hopes—and had, at times, been certain he felt the same— the last time he'd walked away from her, no such promises were made. And then he had died, cut down by Anisthe's magick with the rest of doomed Dvigrad.

Not sparing a glance aloft as the lookout gave the cry again, Liara darted eager eyes over the horizon. *Best to look forward, rather than back.*

A thin whitish line snaked between blue sky and azure sea.

And that was all.

Liara waited. And waited.

But after a fair piece of watching that thin line, nothing further materialized. They were as far away as ever. Had they stopped? Perhaps they needed a fresher breeze, a turned tide in order to get nearer the walled city-state. At her sides, Liara's hands itched to try her recently learned magicks.

The thin band upon the horizon grew, if only slightly. It stretched farther in each direction, losing some of its paleness in the green-brown of forest and rock. How far from shore were they?

Looking for someone to answer her questions, Liara turned around and found Nagarath had come to join her. He stood with eyes shaded against the sun's glare and stared at the unmoving horizon.

Only his face, unlike Liara's, was one of rapture. He spoke before she could open her mouth. "Amazing how quickly the land falls behind a ship and how slow he is to rush and greet us upon our return. It is as though he's sore about our having spent time away. The sister sea and brother earth do not always get on as they ought."

Liara let her eyes be drawn back to the teasing white line so far away. "That'd be family for you."

"Ha!" Nagarath let loose one of his booming laughs. "Well said, magpie. Well said. Come, we have at least a few hours until we are close to land but the deck is about to be a very busy place. I am sure our hosts would rather we be out from under foot."

Liara eyed the horizon. Did it already look closer? She believed it did. Maybe.

The ship began its change of course. True to Nagarath's word, sailors scrambled to and fro, over rigging and deck, hauling lines and whistling orders. Liara felt the shifting breeze dart over cheekbones, arms, and legs. Giving vent to the resultant shiver, she moved to follow the wizard below and out of harm's way.

A banging on the door to Liara and Nagarath's cabin roused each from a shallow rest. The wizard had his wand at the ready in the space of a breath. Liara reacted with necessary calm and decorum. Granted, it helped that she hadn't a wand of her own, else their steward might have found himself at a sticky end.

As it was, Liara called her answering 'hullo' through the door with shaky voice.

"If you please, m— Mir," the sailor's greeting came muted by the wood. "You'd asked to see the city as we came about."

While true, Liara hadn't thought her remarks noted. What else had she said while aboard?

"We're rounding about. Come up to the forecastle and see a true sight."

Exhilaration rushed through Liara, heating her cheeks and setting her hands a'tremble. Nagarath's amused smile told her that she needn't ask. She was off before the mage could rethink his position or indulge in any number of cautionary speeches.

Ricocheting through the narrow passage and up through the hatch, Liara reveled again in the freshness of the sea air. The sky rang a brilliant blue, the water foamed and danced, the ship creaked and sang. And Ragusa? Ragusa topped it all.

Unlike Dvigrad's relying upon Venice for protection, Ragusa chose a far different solution. They bartered in politics as skillfully as they did oak and spices. The city was sometimes Venetian, sometimes Ottoman. Their fortifications made them nearly impregnable—and autonomous. The great white-gray walls had even withstood the devastating earthquake of thirty years prior. They would stand forever.

Liara stared, wide-eyed at the magnificence before her. It dwarfed grand Vrsar. Even with its massive towers and ramparts, countless red tile roofs could be seen within, one growing higher than the other, the whole of it topped by more gray stone pinnacles and spires. The city seemed to carry within it a pride, a confidence which dismissed having surrounded itself by such protections.

Already Liara's vantage of what lay within the walls quickly fell behind the stone and rock of the city's defenses. The fortifications loomed, dwarfing the ship's masts as the sailors scrambled to bring the vessel about. And then the scene changed again, the port coming into sudden view as they rounded the wall to enter the harbor, a jostling of ships and more buildings rioting to gain Liara's attention once again.

"Oh!" Liara didn't care that she gawked. Coming to stand next to her, the sailor who'd gone below deck to fetch her nodded his agreement.

"A sight indeed, Mir." Flashing a quick grin, he teased, "Mayhap you'll abandon your sculptor and stay with us after seeing sights like these?"

"I heard that." Nagarath's growled complaint preceded him up the ladder. "Trying to steal my assistant from me, are you?"

He came to stand at Liara's back, placing a protective hand upon her shoulder. It made her glad for the biting breeze: it hid her blush under wind-ruddy cheeks.

Nagarath leaned close. "So, Mir, you like Ragusa?"

She nodded, not trusting herself to speak. Something flipped inside Liara's chest, an anxiety she could not readily name. The reality of how far away from home she and her mage had come began to sink in. *It's him and me against the world now.*

Entering a forest of swaying masts, the ship slowed. The tang of salt-air carried within it the colorful and sometimes ripe smells of civilization. Liara and her companion were left to their own devices as the sailors all but forgot them in the coordinated dance of docking a merchant vessel. The sound, the teeming of traffic on the shore past the piers, was invigorating.

Liara could hardly wait to be off amongst it. To lose herself in such a crowd . . .

Again, the odd sensation stirred within her chest at the idea of the crush of people throwing her closer to Nagarath.

That's what I've needed. Not stammering apologies nor a slow mending of a broken companionship. But a forced mutual experience. Liara shook off her uneasiness, waiting for Nagarath to finish his hushed conversation with the ship's captain. He returned to her but a moment later, his brow darkened with annoyance and a rapid pace that belied his newly mended limbs.

"Come. Our subtle weather manipulations had extraneous consequences. The captain must now contract for more cargo and load it, but that's all the time we will have," Nagarath said under his breath as he steered Liara towards the gangplank. "I must be off to find my man."

"Your man?"

Nagarath's annoyance grew, and his answer came curt. "Yes. This ship's preferred route is south and east before they turn westward, toward our destination. Preveza is the best I can believably do."

It was with himself that Nagarath was angry, not her. He confirmed it as they gained the shore. "As I said, the captain needs new cargo. I'd like to have the next port be another of our choosing—which means I must find some poor merchant both wealthy and naive enough to accommodate my spells. Someone who will later come to his senses as we are carried off to sea—taking our magick with us—and wonder why on earth he has sent a terribly large shipment of his wares in a terribly large hurry. Luckily the money is real. There are some lines even I will not cross."

"It's . . . It's all right, Nagarath. We haven't a choice if we are to gain any lead on Anisthe."

Nagarath spoke over Liara's attempt to absolve him of his guilt. "The comfort is that, Anisthe having come this way, he will have had to go as out of the way as we. And, he likely has had to stop in Split and Corfu. I just wish these men would take money over merchandise. That way we could be ahead of the man for certain."

Liara paused, her attention diverted to the newness of her surroundings. Nagarath was unsympathetic.

"If we want any time at all sniffing out his activities, we had best be moving. I hate not knowing more of his movements. Liara, if you could stay close, please."

Briefly lost to her own distractions, Liara hurried to match Nagarath's long-legged stride. She was ashamed to admit that his plans to magically manipulate their transport made her queasy—doubly so when he'd mentioned Anisthe in the same breath.

Liara repeated her consolation to herself: they must stay ahead of Anisthe. Never mind that he would do the same if he were able.

A quick walk along the docks provided them with their dupe. True to the wizard's prediction, a casually unguarded discussion of their travels—and a less nonchalant application of magick—attracted the attention of a vintner.

"Did I hear you say you are sailing directly to Preveza, sir? Preveza. Not Corfu." Thin, twitchy, and overeager, the gentleman approached, his eyes as hungry as his waistline. Simply looking at him made Liara nervous, and she shrank towards Nagarath instinctively.

"Preveza." Nagarath inclined his head. "Provided the money is in it, of course." He ignored Liara, helping her to blend into the background by his mere dismissal of her distress.

Head buzzing with the hexes Nagarath whipped up into the salt-air around them, Liara quashed her scruples and tried to be as aware as she could. His efforts absorbed the mage. It was her responsibility to keep an eye out for trouble.

"Corfu does me no good, you understand. If your vessel alights there and the wind shifts, my merchandise will wither and die before it can go where it ought."

" 'Tis that ship there." Nagarath pointed. "We are merely passengers and have no say in our captain's choice of ports along the path to our destination—"

"Thank you, sir," interrupting the mage's niceties, the merchant jumped at his change of fortune.

Nagarath leaned close to Liara, sharp eyes raking the teeming dockside. He whispered, "Come. The spells are at their best if we stay close to him. But not so close as to expose our game to the men aboard our ship. As it is, they will likely find it odd that such an eager merchant is approaching with an agenda so similar to our own."

"Then what are we to—"

"I would like to try scrying Vrsar's mage." Nagarath straightened and began to navigate the crowd.

The mage's spells were giving Liara a headache. An unhealthy fog, the hexes pressed upon her own aura, and she gripped Nagarath's elbow to steady herself. Far from the delicious experience of being alone in a crowd with her wizard, Liara found herself assaulted by the babble of too many foreign languages at once, strange smells of unknown origin, and the heavy guilt she felt in her chest whenever she spotted their merchant as they navigated their way towards the ship.

Liara's discomfort redoubled when, a dozen or so yards later, she confirmed that the prickle that tickled her neck and lived in the back of her mind was not all magick-based. They were being followed.

"Nagarath . . ." The mage did not respond. Liara tried to look around without turning her head. Nothing stood out. Nobody came rushing forward to exclaim: "Me! I'm the suspicious person following you."

The thrumming of Liara's nerves replaced the hum of Nagarath's magick. The ship loomed ahead, comfortable—and also dangerous, now with the mage engaging in his dubious spells. Even so, she longed to rush aboard, passing up the vintner, and escape to the peace of their cramped quarters. Seasickness began to look all the more pleasant.

Especially as Nagarath veered off into an alleyway, tugging Liara along.

She tried again. "Nagarath . . ."

The mage's jaw tightened, drawing his reddened scars white. His gray eyes sparked a warning, and his magick dipped and wavered.

But he had to know!

"We're being followed," Liara gave voice to the fear at last. She whipped her head around to check behind. She and her mage were not the only ones to duck out of the docks by that path.

The feeling of being under scrutiny faded. She whispered, "Never mind."

Nagarath grunted his acknowledgement, gently guiding her to an even narrower and darker street. Here the buildings rose up in severe columns, pressed together by the sheer need to fit into the precious real estate close to the docks. Liara's nose informed her that they'd closeted themselves near an inn, and her stomach churned—both in hunger and in complaint over its recent sea-bound abuse.

"Ah, perfect."

Liara felt Nagarath pull away from her. She turned and found the mage crouched before a shallow puddle. Hemmed in by the cobbles and set beneath a gutter, whose casual drip of water Nagarath now thoughtfully diverted, the water shimmered before dying to stillness under the wizard's outstretched hand.

"Keep watch, if you would, my magpie," Nagarath spoke without looking up.

In silence they waited, Liara turning 'round so that she might espy and therefore prevent anyone coming upon them unawares. And also to keep herself from seeing the war mage's face. Her skin prickled as the icy whisper of the wizard's incantation met her ears.

Coward. She let the scolding sink inside her chest, thinking instead of the strange sensation of being followed and waiting for its return. The irony of their clandestine scrying coupled with Liara's own immediate fear of being watched was not lost upon her.

The soft words of magick whispered against the close-pressed walls as Nagarath found his quarry and shifted his spell to match. Liara tried to close her ears to it. A perverse eagerness to learn of Anisthe's whereabouts knifed through her. Part of her wanted to know; a part of her wished to see. Curiosity. A love of danger.

Liara moved to approach Nagarath, cautious lest she disturb his puddle-gazing.

A slipping, sighing sound rang against the stones. Liara whipped her head back up, her eyes searching the mouth of the alleyway in time to see a man ducking out of sight. Heart hammering, she gave a shout. Nagarath had a restraining arm flung her way before she could take a step.

"Come. Let us not throw ourselves after danger, Liara. This way."

"But there was a person. He saw you—"

"Peering into a puddle?" A smile tugged at Nagarath's lips. "I hardly believe that to be against the law anywhere. Perhaps I was looking for some dropped object."

"But—"

"Until there are soldiers with Venice's insignia bearing down upon us, I refuse to be put in a position of unnecessary worry. Our more pressing concern, I fear, is getting ourselves back to our ship before they decide that cargo is more precious than passengers."

"And Anisthe?"

The smile that had been playing about Nagarath's face disappeared in a fast-moving frown. Darkness fell over his brow as he answered, "He is ahead of us. Left yesterday evening for Corfu. Also, he all but confirmed for me that he is, indeed, seeking Khariton's Mirror."

They returned to a ship and crew eager to be off. The hold was full, the sea and sky indicating a fortuitous swell. And not one of Nagarath's design, he was quick to explain to an arch-eyebrowed Liara. It was likely that the crew would make very good time and profit on this run. Lucky Mir and her lanky companion were welcomed aboard with smiles and good-natured expressions of curiosity.

Nagarath gave up nothing, returning to their berth to rest his tired bones and rebuild his Gift as best he could. Liara watched as Ragusa's white walls rapidly fell behind them. And even when it had gone, leaving nothing but dark surging water so far as the eye could see, she looked on, feeling as though she had lost something along the way.

A strange misgiving haunted her. A tension lay at the back of Liara's mind while she stared at the distant horizon, much like one finds on a summer's day when the air crackles before a sudden turn in the weather.

Anisthe. Father-in-magick.

Her thoughts would not leave him be.

Where are you, Anisthe? Her heart called out to him over the open water, somehow believing that, where she could not scry him, her connection to his life via her Art might suffice. Silence. Nothing.

Her thoughts rebounded back to Ragusa, to the magick she dared not attempt and Nagarath's thoughtful silence on the topic of her reluctance. It heartened her to think that the strange sensation of having been followed had not come from the incantate mage. For a moment, she had considered the possibility, wild as it was. Hadn't it been magick she'd felt? A part of her was still unsure. And that uncertainty bothered her. In fact, it had followed her aboard.

Or maybe it's something I've carried with me all this time.

Glancing around nervously, Liara marked that she was unobserved before plunging her fingers into the pocket that dangled from her belt, reaching in to pull out that which preyed upon her mind. Dull and oval-shaped, smaller than an egg, an amber pendant lay in the palm of her open hand. The chain, affixed via a small metal bail, slid free of the pocket, glinting in the sunlight before her fingers could capture its length.

Anisthe's symbol of power.

Turning it over in her hand, Liara inspected the amber pendant. It didn't catch the light as it ought.

The defect was not due to the large crack which riddled the stone, Liara was certain. Rather, there was a wrongness to the object, some menace even the sunshine shied away from. A wary watchfulness; the darkness of black magicks.

The last threads of Anisthe's magickal signature hung about the broken artifact like mist in the morning. To Liara, it felt as if that same mist hung about her heart. She waited, still, for the warmth of Nagarath's steadfast sunshine to burn it away.

Anisthe. Her progenaurae. She dare not scry him. She hated and feared the man. And yet she was curious, excited even, at the thought of him. He was fire; he was power—even now. He was every bad thing, and yet she could not let go.

And she had kept his amber pendant, the very last of the mage's magick. She stared into its depths. *Toss it over the side and be done with it. Be free.*

Free. She scoffed. Liara could not be free for two years hence, per the Laws of Magick. They were immutable as Fate herself.

Liara pocketed the bauble, her hand closing around it as she recalled the searing white-hot power that she'd loosed when she tricked Anisthe into pulling upon his Art, saved within the broken artifact. She had used those same Laws to save herself, to save Nagarath, from the war mage's cruelty.

And, though it was a very Anisthe way to look at things, Liara had to admit there were ways around every rule. Tricks, even in magick. Cheats.

Liara's drifting thoughts came back to her now, dragging in their wake a new possibility. Jerking her hand away from the pendant as though it burned her, she considered the idea, breath coming in excited hitches. If anyone besides herself, besides Anisthe, was versed in the Laws, it was Nagarath. Perhaps they might not have to wait two years for her autonomy. Perhaps they might not have to chase Anisthe across the seas in some ill-considered quest for a mirror that might not even exist. Perhaps she could take her mage home for the rest and recovery he deserved. Let Anisthe chase his rumor. Let him do what he would. The world was not hers to save from the likes of him.

Liara nearly ran headlong into the wizard in the narrow passage outside their quarters. Swaying as the ship played with her balance, Liara found Nagarath's hand on her arm, steadying her.

"I am such a dolt . . ." she breathlessly began her explanation.

"In." Nagarath half-guided, half-pulled her into their cabin. "Sit."

The intensity with which he regarded her stole the rest of Liara's words away for one long moment. Belatedly, she realized he was waiting for her to continue.

"Oh, yes, sorry. I might have saved us this whole ordeal." Eyes downcast, Liara trembled, fearful that Nagarath's blazing scrutiny might soon turn to ire. "Chasing after Anisthe, I mean. I was so—" she gulped "—so concerned with what he was doing that I only thought of that. Instead of thinking how I—you—we—might fix things."

"Fix things?" The wizard softened, coming to sit by her.

Liara nodded, dutiful pupil giving recitation. "The Laws of Magick Creatio bind my magick to his. Or, in my case, my life to his. Until I reach the age of autonomy in two years.

"But I've been considering. What if there were a way to cheat the Laws?" She rushed past the dark knitting of Nagarath's eyebrows to explain, "After all, I'm still here so the thread of magick that binds me to Anisthe . . ."

Liara faltered, withering under Nagarath's glower. He looked positively forbidding—doubly so in the small quarters with nowhere for her to shrink to. "Surely someone has writ something on how to circumvent them, change them even."

Something seemed to break within Nagarath's face, some stunned combination of horror and pain. Liara darted her eyes over the mage, alarmed—what had happened? The nervus system again? Here on a boat in the middle of the sea with naught but her wits and . . .

Before she could open her mouth, before she could react, Nagarath had risen and was gone. That he slammed the door behind him was not lost on her, though it might have been another pitch of the ship that had done it.

Liara sat unmoving for a long time afterward. She felt ill. And not just from the heaving of the ship. Somehow, she had managed to hurt him. Deeply. But how?

Find out. Liara rose on unsteady feet, feeling the movement of the ship more than ever. Since when had the seas been so rough? As if in answer, the small room heaved sideways, catching her on the bowsprit.

Arms flung out to right herself, Liara wondered at the vibrations palpable through the rough wood. A tension, an energy filled the air, almost like that of magick. Heavy. Dark. Menacing as the cloud which hung about the pendant hidden within her pocket.

The door to the cabin swung open, Nagarath bracing himself against the frame as the ship rolled again. Frightening though his face had been before, something in his eyes spoke of a graver unease. He managed to rasp out, "Liara, I would like that you should come up on deck, if you please . . ."

Chapter Ten

Nagarath lurched past Liara, intent on his bunk. Freeing his staff that, until then, had been wrapped in his discarded cloak, he overbalanced and fell against the wall with the next heave of the ship.

"Nagarath!"

"I'm fine." Nagarath did not look fine. "Get up top."

Hesitant for but an instant, Liara gambled and thrust a hand in the wizard's direction. He clasped it gratefully, leaning on his staff with the other. Together they hurried up the surging staircase and into chaos.

For a moment, Liara wondered if they'd somehow made landfall during her sulk below deck. Sailors ran and shouted, their preparations much the same to her eyes as those for coming into port.

But the air was wrong. Just as in the cabin, the atmosphere crackled with tension.

The seas had turned angry. The water churned, dark with pointed white peaks that looked like teeth. Reaching up, the waves snapped at the edges of the heaving ship. For the first time since their embarkation, Liara watched, mesmerized, as water leapt skyward, baptizing the deck and making footing hazardous.

Come up on deck? Why ever would that be a good idea? Liara turned her question to Nagarath and saw her answer over his shoulder.

"Come. The captain has asked that we shelter in the quarterdeck until we either outrun or ride it out." Gallantly, the wizard tried to block Liara's view. But there was no concealing the grim promise which darkened the sky to the south.

Never in all her tender years had Liara seen such a cloud. Charcoal and shot through with streaks of near-indigo blackness, the bank seemed to boil, roiling across the heavens towards them. Unremittent. Inevitable. There was no outstripping such a storm. Already the first sheets of rain sluiced down, an advancing curtain cut through by sharp knives of lightning.

Liara felt numb. Cornered. Doomed. She had no need to panic. The storm would shatter the ship as easily as a child might a toy. Careless weather. Already the waves were mountains. How much worse would it be when the storm truly caught them up? What would an ill-placed bolt from above do to sails and mast?

Still, Liara made her way toward the cabin in uneven steps—alternately fast and slow as the ship's roll demanded.

Nagarath believes we can outrun it. Nagarath knows what to do. The disparate conclusions of comfort clashed within Liara's heart. She turned her attention to the mage's staff the moment he shut the door behind them.

"You can calm the storm," she breathed—more like, another buffet knocked the wind from her lungs.

"That was my hope," the answer came, not from Nagarath, but from an unknown individual who sat in a dark corner of the ship's quarters.

Nagarath and Liara turned in alarm, the mage raising his staff protectively.

The sailor strode forward, his gait easily matching the increased pitch of the ship. Familiarity surged within Liara's breast. That shirt and vest; the slouched hat, pulled low. The man who had followed them in Ragusa! It was he who had witnessed Nagarath's clandestine scrying of Anisthe.

"A rumor followed you back aboard." A grim smile accompanied the sailor's statement. Having essentially hid the rest of his face, the expression chilled Liara. "Captain wanted me to see to the truth of it, if there was any."

The man slowed his steps, keeping his distance, and presented the large book he had tucked under his arm.

It snarled.

Liara felt the hair on her arms prickle.

More than she felt indignation over the violation of her and Nagarath's privacy, more than fear over having been discovered as wizards, Liara felt anger. Something in the insolence of the man's stance rankled her. Cocksure, alongside his obvious fear and respect for his passengers' powers, there, too, was something personal to the confrontation. She wondered at it.

Her thoughts ran back to Dvigrad, to Vrsar, and the devastation magick had wreaked in each. The man who stood before them had a personal vendetta against wizards. Liara could feel it even at twenty paces distant, in the midst of a wild storm at sea.

Another wave rocked the ship. The floor dropped out from under Liara, setting her to flying. Flinging her hands up over her head, she braced for impact with the wall of the cabin. And instead found strong arms steadying her. She looked up into the face of the sandy-haired sailor, noting eyes blue and dark like the heaving seas outside. The surprise in those eyes confirmed that he knew his disguise had slipped.

"Liara!" Nagarath, too, had lost his footing, falling hard to his knees.

Adrift in her shock, Liara had little to offer him in the way of assistance. Her limbs had all but given up. She leaned heavily upon him who had caught her, the sailor having dropped the precious book of magick. Some distant part of her brain signaled the automatic desire to pick the poor codex up and smooth its much-abused pages. Anything but to be in the here and now of the storm. Anything.

"Liara. Can you hear me?" Through the confused buzzing of her racing thoughts, she heard Nagarath's voice turn sharp. "Get her to a seat, man. She's white as snow."

"I'm fine," Liara managed to croak.

"She is shaken but unhurt. We'll still put up in your town if that is your demand. Just, please spare us. She's as safe as you can make us, master." This last was given as a mild threat. Liara knew the man who held her steady would not harm her. Did the mage?

"My gift, at present, is much occupied." Nagarath paused, making sure that Liara focused on him before continuing. She did her best to meet his gaze. "But, certainly I will do what I can."

He left before Liara could recover herself. Door banging shut behind him, the frigid watery blast that swirled through the cabin in the wake of his departure had the same effect upon Liara's limbs as smelling salts. She pushed away from the sailor, stumbling a bit with the rocking of the ship. His face crumpled in concern, but he did not stop her.

A ghost. She was aboard a storm-besieged ship with a ghost. It was the only explanation.

Her thoughts must have betrayed her. The man spoke, gifting her with a crooked smile. "No, I'm not dead, Liara."

"Dvigrad," she blurted, unable to say—to think—anything else.

"I was in Vrsar, awaiting response to Phenlick's letter."

Liara stood regarding him, still distrustful, unaccustomed to hope. What he was saying was impossible. That he was there before her—to even say it: impossible.

If she named him, it was over. Her heart . . . it couldn't take being wrong. Not about this.

He smiled, this time warmly. With it, he broke the spell between them.

"Krešimir." Liara let the tears spill freely from her eyes then, not caring that she could no longer see him, for Krešimir—her Krešimir—put his arms about her once more.

"Hush. I've got you safe, Liara," he whispered. "This time, I won't let you go."

Another blast of thunder set Liara's teeth to rattling, and she closed her eyes to the sound.

"No." As predicted, Liara's heart tore itself in two as she pulled away from him. But she had to go. She had to help. What one mage might accomplish—

The door banged open, an invitation by the elements, a challenge from the wizard at the other end of the storm.

"Stay here," she cautioned, magefire flaring at her fingertips. Sparks of violet and sapphire, they matched the lightning's arcing blast. She redirected the storm's fury even from there within the ship's cabin. Blinded, Liara made her way to the open doorway, staggering with the pitch and yaw of the ship.

Krešimir lived. Even this shocking discovery, that which had drained her limbs of strength, robbed her tongue of speech, was buried under the eagerness with which her Art met the weather's fury. Liara grasped the lintel as another downdraft sent the ship skipping sideways.

Who are you? Liara raised her gaze to the black skies, seeking the heart of the spell which drove it.

The magick within the maelstrom was a match to hers. It did not feel like anything else she'd known, no. But the heart behind it, that she understood. Wrath and envy, pride and arrogance.

And that, Liara could conquer. Her heart eased as she spotted Nagarath—or, rather, his magick—glowing in the prow of the ship. The enemy mage was before them but the storm was still behind. Nagarath would only be able to do so much from his position.

Soaked within seconds, Liara almost missed Krešimir's restraining hand on her arm. The wind snatched at his words, carrying them away so that she had to lean close to hear him.

"No, Liara, it's not safe."

Neither is magick. Instead, she said, "This storm, it isn't lessening. If anything, it is getting worse."

"Still—"

"Lash me to the rail, then. I don't care. Just get me up there, and I can do something about this." Exasperated, Liara pulled away from Krešimir's touch to point up to the aft end of the ship.

Hands slipping on the rain-slick ladder, what she knew of weather-working spells raced through her mind. It was appalling how little she knew. No matter. She was committed.

"You there! All hands!" the barked command cut through the gale, and Liara turned to see Krešimir disappear into the chaos of scrambling crew. She turned back to her own efforts, resolving anew to be of use. Splinters bit into her knees and shins as her legs glanced against the rough wood. She hissed in agony, pressing onward.

Ascending to the topmost deck, Liara did what she had promised Krešimir, whispering a spell to enliven a bit of rope and secure her to the ship's frame. Then she cast her hands to the angry skies and did what she did best. Combining magick not meant to go together, knowing the design of individual spellwork, the idea behind its construction, she made use of disparate hexes and conflicting charms.

Untaught, untutored, and untamed, Dvigrad's daughter fought the unseen enemy. Brighter than lightning, her power arced through the air, itself a storm. And the wind fought back. Beating at her, trying the knots at her waist with invisible fingers, the squall tried to force her overboard. The waves did their best to drown her, the icy rain to break her spirit.

Undeterred, Liara kept her gaze on the answering glow at the other end of the vessel. Nagarath's magick. It, too, flickered and danced amongst the towering waves, whipping upward in reddish vortices within the cyclones of wind that buffeted the ship. At times, the effect was almost a conversation. Call and answer.

And then the light went out, drawing a gasp from Liara. Numb hands working the knotted rope at her waist, she fought to free herself, her eyes staring, unblinking, through the storm.

Nagarath. She had to see if he was all right.

A sharp crack rent the air, and to Liara, it seemed that the ship warped. The deck beneath her wearied legs pitched one way while, through the pouring rain, she could see the foremost of the ship's masts lean the other direction. Slowly, slowly it tilted, until Liara realized the truth in an illuminating flash of lightning. Dragging in the water, a broken stump of timber was all that remained of the foremast.

Tears mingling with the rain that streamed across her cheeks, Liara hoped and prayed. And let her anger fuel her efforts. Her mage was fine. He had to be.

Thus, standing tall against the tempest, purple fire sparking at her fingertips, Liara cut through the gale and quieted the lightning. The wind became an ally, filling what storm-tattered sails remained and pushing the ship westward towards the light. The rocking motion of the vessel became a rhythmic bounce in time with the waves as the keel glanced over the sea, a skipping stone intent on the furthest shore.

Anisthe woke with a start as his nose collided with the floor of the ship's cabin with a sickening crunch. Immediately awake, he clutched at his face and drew himself into a miserable ball to swear himself into composure. His fingers confirmed no breaks. But it was tender.

The exploratory prodding ended, he sat up, cursing sea travel. Another violent rocking of the cabin had Anisthe scrambling to his feet.

Domagoj's hammock was empty.

Fingers questing his nose again as he fought the wave-induced vertigo, Anisthe made his way above. He spotted his man almost immediately.

Domagoj stood upon the bowsprit, his arms flung wide and his head thrown back. Lightning lit the air, setting his white teeth to flashing as the half-fey laughed into the howling wind. There was something striking in the way his dark hair whipped about his face, and his muscles corded and bunched while he held his perilous position on the heaving parapet. No sailor dared accost him. The Power arcing around him glared blue-green, visible against the dark skies.

Anisthe smiled at the display. An oriaurant's magick, being half-fey rather than half-mage, appeared slightly different to the trained eye. And, incantate though he was, Anisthe's was a well-trained eye. He would know Domagoj's magick anywhere, even had it not been carried out in the tell-tale brash fashion to which his ward was inclined.

A storm at sea; a changed and fickle *Jugo* wind. Domagoj's specialty and strength. Heritage of his merfolk. And, while Anisthe hated to have been relegated to the role of spectator, Domagoj's was a show worth watching.

"He'll sink us, he will."

Through the gale, Anisthe heard the mutinous words.

"Grab that'n and we'll have our bargaining piece."

Anisthe tensed. The weaker party. Shame warred with fear, and he readied himself for the humiliation. Domagoj would save him, even if they were to cast Anisthe into the foaming waters. And, son of a mermaid siren, Anisthe's apprentice could calm what he had agitated. Though perhaps then he would go so far as to sink the ship . . . out of spite.

"Quiet, fool. Attacking one attacks them both. Best let them at their game. Wizards don't wish to be lost upon a sinking ship, same as you or me." The voice of reason. Anisthe sighed inwardly.

But he did not relax. *What is your game Domagoj? You said that you had scried Nagarath and Liara and that Krešimir had managed passage on their ship. You told me that they'd figured out my objective in Khariton's Mirror.*

"And we are ahead of them by at least a day," Anisthe growled, speaking within the tempest's ear. "There is no need for such."

Picking his way across the deck, Anisthe clung to line and beam, stumbling forward so that he might subdue his vainglorious apprentice.

Domagoj turned at Anisthe's clutch of his sleeve.

"Let it die, Domagoj."

"The captain would not alter our course to Messina. I'm changing it for him," Domagoj shouted. Another bolt lit the heavens, emphasis to his statement.

Anisthe shook his head. "We are in no such hurry. You call too much attention and risk the lives of our pursuers."

This time, Domagoj's laugh challenged not the sky, but his incantate master. "Do you not think I've considered that? What better way to further our ends? Liara—I will make certain she survives. Nagarath . . ." He shrugged, his face growing ugly with its cruelty.

Anisthe let go Domagoj's arm, something inside his chest seizing for a moment. A passing fancy, a blemish upon his emotional landscape. For once it was not jealousy. Not envy over Domagoj's clear Power—limited as it was through the bounds which the Laws imposed on all fey. Nor was it a desire to be the one to finally eradicate his enemy. It was . . . something he dare not entertain. He said instead, "Leave them be, Domagoj. Both of them."

Domagoj's eyes flashed darkly. "Yes, Master."

Another bolt shook the heavens, blue-green lightning and a deafening peal of thunder.

"Land! I see land!" A ragged hurrah ran 'round the crew. The ship's bell rang its triumph.

Nagarath's nostrils clenched, and he pitched forward, gagging. The answer came to him an instant late: smelling salts.

"He's come 'round."

Nagarath turned toward the voice. He had woken to darkness and a searing headache. Working on evening his breath, he gingerly lifted a hand to his face. His fingers brushed the rough ends of a bandage.

"Liara—" he gasped. Memory returned to him in fits and starts. The storm. The magick. Liara's Art glowing through the torrents of rain. And then pain. And nothing after.

"Gone ashore. We couldn't move you, you see—not 'til you'd woken."

With that, Nagarath tore at the cloth which bound his aching head. Daylight returned to stab him in the eyes. He squinted, noting there were three sailors in the forecastle cabin with him. "My stave. Where is it?"

A brief panic seized Nagarath as the men glanced at one another uneasily. If he had lost it in the storm . . .

One man lifted a shaking finger to point at the arcane object. Laid carefully in the corner of the room, the cinnabar stone seemed to wink out at the mage and its surroundings. Nodding, Nagarath reached out, gesturing with a crook of his fingers that it be brought to him.

Another bout of reluctance ran through the room, alongside fierce, silent negotiations. In the end, it was the man nearest the staff who brought it over.

Sighing as the familiar haft was pressed in his palms, Nagarath closed his eyes and called its gift to him. Almost immediately his head stopped its ceaseless thrumming. But his fingers, they would not let go. The words of the Green Language flowed through him, an unceasing torrent—

. . . *hekh'reach avad li. Has'kerah ha n'tiyah* . . .

"Master?"

Nagarath shuddered. The magick fled, clearing his vision. The three men had moved a pace back but remained. He who had spoken—the one brave enough to give the wizard back his stave—repeated his prompt. "Master Mage?"

The hardened men flexed their muscles meaningfully. Nagarath's gaze alighted on the assorted packs and bundles laying in the corner. His and Liara's belongings. An unmistakable message. He and his apprentice had worn out their welcome and would require different passage on their westward journey to Spain.

"Of course. Thank you. For your hospitality and—" He stopped himself. He had no need to apologize. The men had been paid—handsomely—for their services. He and Liara had most likely saved all their lives.

The first of his escort nodded, moving to exit the small space. He left the door wide open behind him. Through it, Nagarath could see that the rain still fell and the wind continued its fitful bursts of anger. The storm had lessened to natural means but was in no way welcoming to someone in Nagarath's state.

Sighing, Nagarath hauled himself back onto tired feet. It was time to buy some silence from their hosts. Shielding his eyes to the change from darkened cabin to clouded day, he flinched as the gray light flooded his aching head. Still he glanced about, wondering where they had ended after being blown so far off course.

Safely set within a thin arcing spiral of land, the port was doubly protected by both man's art and the mountainscape that rose in the distance on both sides—and therefore haven to most any ship in the region after such a storm. The captain approached. "Messina. As requested."

Nagarath blanched at the unspoken accusation but kept his eyes forward.

The hardened sailor continued, "Should be busy. Ought be the right place for you to find passage toward your destination. With a blow like that, no boat will have left here of late. Mayhap you'll get ahead of whomever you're running from, you and that woman of yours." He gave a pointed, sideways glance.

"Her father. He does not approve of our . . . traveling . . . together."

"Powerful man."

"Was. Was a powerful man," Nagarath corrected. "Now?" He shrugged. "I can say for certain that the storm was not his either. I am inclined to believe it of natural import."

"I've traveled far and wide for more years than you've been on this earth, Master Mage. Met a lot of folks and had to be a fast and good judge of countenance. And I do believe that is the first lie you've given me. I do not like seeing that on your otherwise honest face. Now, whatever you and the girl get up to is your business but mine—"

"Will be to say nothing. Leave us be. Let us disappear into the city." Nagarath met the captain's eyes at last. "And, whether the storm was natural or non, in thanks for your having gotten us this far and riding the same perils as we, I would like to leave a protection on the ship against further such troubles."

"One that buys our silence, I daresay," the captain grumbled.

Nagarath smiled.

"Don't suppose we've a choice in the matter. Not an offer so much as it is a warning."

"I'm not that kind of wizard."

"And my men are no gossips. As I said, I can read a face. Your secret—whatever it may be—is safe as I can make it."

"Then we part as friends." Opting not to prod further, Nagarath walked away. He leaned heavily upon his staff, feeling his bones ache. His head began to throb anew.

Steeling himself for the treacherous shuffle down the steep, swaying gangplank and grateful for the solid land which lay beyond, Nagarath stopped short as a hand grasped his elbow.

"As friends then, wizard." The captain's squint-eyed glare had lost some of its guarded aspect.

Nagarath nodded and turned back to the waiting captain and crew. "I had thought to ward the ship against future perils such as we faced together today. The spell would only serve as protection. It will not overtly aid in navigation nor will it dramatically change the weather to suit your needs."

"A bit of luck you're giving us, then." The captain managed a smile.

Nagarath nodded, returning the warmth. "A bit of luck, yes."

Thus gaining permission, he strode past the men to the mast. Placing a hand upon the smooth, rain soaked wood, he closed his eyes and called the magick to him. The power was slow to come, in spite of his having recovered for a bit after his ordeal with the storm. Nagarath found himself struggling to recall the words. Shifting his fingers, he found clarity. "Follow light. Follow fate. Follow luck. *i'shor maa'ome; i'shor goral; i'shor htslah'a.*"

A faint glow emanated from beneath his splayed hand. Pulling away quickly, Nagarath assessed the mark left behind in the wood. Orange-red like a setting sun, the rune glinted before fading. Turning to the gape-mouthed crew of sailors, he announced, "The power, the promise, remains there. Mark its place well with your memory. Should you ever have call to replace that mast, I suggest cutting out and taking that piece with you."

The small assembly parted for Nagarath's passing. No goodbyes, and certainly no thanks, followed the mage off the ship. Gaining solid ground at long last, he felt his knees and ankles protest at the loss of easy motion, though his mind rejoiced. *Liara is probably experiencing much the same. Goodness, the girl is a patient one of late.*

Shielding his eyes as a glint of sun broke through the clouds to bless those who had survived the terrible spring storm—the worst in memory for many in the city—Nagarath looked about for his little magpie. She was nowhere to be seen.

"Liara?" Nagarath turned in a quick circle, fighting a rising panic. "Liara!"

She could not have gone far, not laden as she was with the rest of their belongings.

"You looking for a young woman?"

Nagarath turned to espy a crusty group of men sheltering beneath an awning. Smoke wreathed out around their heads, issued forth from long skinny pipes clutched between sun-weathered fingers. They had an air about them that suggested they knew all, saw all . . . and remembered little.

Cautious—*don't let them see your eagerness, you do not know the game here*—he approached, quietly slipping his hand into the folds of his cloak, readying himself for a hex should the need arise.

"Foreign. Like you'n. Dark hair, dark eyes. Skinny as they come. Went off with a lad about her age. She certainly seemed to know him," one of the men volunteered. He clapped wrinkled lips around his pipe and sucked heartily in emphasis. He continued, bathing his next words in smoke. "You have a fellow on your ship named Krešimir?"

Chapter Eleven

Domagoj would not allow himself to be hurried. He would not let himself be roused, to rush about like some—some insignificant ant.

"A mage does not hasten his movements for anyone, Master Anisthe." Lying with his hands behind his head, Domagoj waited for the lash of the incantate's correction. At the other end of the small room: nothing. He arched his neck, raising his head to espy the former mage brooding by the narrow curtained window. Perhaps Anisthe hadn't heard him, and his insolence would go unremarked.

Domagoj lay back upon the bed taking note of its exquisite comfort after their days traveling aboard that ship. The room was moving, but not. A side effect of finding solid ground instead of a swaying deck? No. Domagoj was trembling. Taught like a lute string, he wanted—nay, he needed—an argument. Somewhere to pour off his passions.

Flecks of magick still floated in Domagoj's vision. Blue-green and sickly, the motes twisted lazily on an invisible breeze, like ash from a fire. He couldn't remember a time when he'd used his Art thus. Under Anisthe's tutelage—under his control—he certainly hadn't found the opportunity. Or the boldness.

Domagoj shifted, turning his burning gaze to Anisthe. "Kerri'tarre made the Laws. Made that which limited the gift of my kind; thrust my people into a hell you—incantate you—can scarce imagine. Tell me again, Master, why he would deign to help us break those Laws?"

The line of Anisthe's jaw tightened.

Domagoj smiled, a battle joined.

"Correction." Anisthe swung his gaze around. Smiling, he caught Domagoj off guard. "A mage commands. Your interpretation of my teachings is far too complacent, Domagoj. We force others into the position of making a choice: react or not. I do not believe we should wait around for Krešimir to find us. If he has managed to separate the girl from that wizard, it would be wise to act."

"Conversely, if we move too quickly, we risk Liara's panic," Domagoj countered, sitting up at last. "She uses magick as easily as you draw breath. Her power will be as exhausted as my own at present. Unguarded spellwork could well draw far too much attention. I do not wish to be hunted again."

He wanted to add "as we were in Vrsar." The words stuck in his throat.

"That was a pretty little storm you conjured. But you forget, what you have, at present, are tricks. Tricks that, if Nagarath were to discover the truth, would make a formidable enemy of both him and my aurenaurae. You are young, Domagoj. And, I am sorry to say, as untutored as Liara—"

"Don't lecture me," Domagoj bit back.

"But there are ways to get what we want without magick," Anisthe rolled over the insolence, his voice low but intense. The walls of the inn were thin. "And that, dear Domagoj, is a lesson in which the praecantator was well versed. Which is why my plan is not to, pretty please, ask

Kerri'tarre for his help. I'll have his power when we have the mirror that houses his soul. He needs me. And then I— we—will do as I long ago promised. The Laws that cripple your fey powers will fall."

"And Liara?" Domagoj spoke through closed eyelids, not bothering to mark Anisthe's reaction. "She is tied to you with the Laws. Her life. Her magick. Does not the altering of the Laws spoil your plans for her?"

He could almost hear Anisthe's smile in his response. "You know me to be a careful man. The aurenaurae's power will always be useful to me—doubly, considering Nagarath wants her so. We must turn her from him. Our new friend Krešimir is the key. He and your powers that Nagarath cannot properly sense."

Domagoj snorted. "And so your plan relies upon a woodcutter's son being duped by your tale of how things truly happened in Dvigrad and my oriaurant's magick that fades with each step I take further from the water's edge."

"If it is rest you require, Domagoj, please say as much," Anisthe's rejoinder came dangerously solicitous. "But do not confuse your Art's weakness with your misgivings of my plan. The woodsman already hated Nagarath—jealousy is an emotion with which I can work quite easily."

"Like with Liara? That worked out especially well, Anisthe." Peevish in spite of having gotten exactly what he had asked for, Domagoj settled back down upon the bed.

Closing his eyes, he felt the power recede from him, a tide pulling away. Even at a distance of several hundred yards from the water's edge, Domagoj felt much as he had in Vrsar. Limited. Sealed. Anisthe's servant once more.

But he'd had his taste. Not only of his own magick, his own potential unlocked by the sea's proximity, but that of Anisthe's precious aurenaurae.

The flavor of Liara's aura. Domagoj remembered it from the night of Anisthe's defeat. Similar to that of the war mage's and Nagarath's but somehow wholly her own. He breathed deep, remembering its smell, its tang on the salt-laden, lightning-charged air of the storm. Like incense. Or perfume.

He wanted more. More of what he was not certain. A battle? A duel? Or something similar to what Anisthe had attempted at Vrsar? As to the latter, Domagoj was certainly closer in age to Liara and more than willing to follow through on such overtures.

Pretty and powerful. Domagoj would have her, and if that meant traipsing across the countryside with Anisthe until he had found the mirror or not, then Domagoj would bow and scrape and "yes, Master" his way to Liara's side.

You see, Anisthe? I am not so unversed in the non-magickal means of getting what I want. Relaxing further into the stillness of the inn's room, Domagoj slept, letting what little power he had come back to him.

One more corner; at least one more alleyway . . .

Go back. Liara's conscience strove to make itself heard over her pounding heart and burning lungs. The voice of reason countered, *But, soldiers!*

Their ship had come under the immediate attention of local authorities. Was this a common practice? Had that been why Krešimir insisted they head ashore before the others? He'd seemed nervous even then; eager to be off.

"Leave him, Liara. Or you're both caught," Krešimir repeated the argument that had set them to running. Hurrying down streets with no aim save to escape, Liara had lost sight of the uniformed men. Her eyes found new focus—checking over her shoulder for Nagarath, darting her gaze to Krešimir's hand in hers.

Krešimir. Alive.

Still, Liara wanted answers before she took another step. She needed to call Nagarath to her. To let him know where she had run off to.

With Krešimir.

Her conscience adopted a new tactic, poking her in the ribs to get at her heart. Or perhaps it was merely a side-ache from running.

It occurred to her then that the wizard had yet to know of Krešimir being alive. When she had gone to check on him after the storm's gentling, he'd been laid up in the fore cabin, unconscious. And then they had gone ashore before she could share the news, assured that her wizard would be quick to follow once he'd woken.

And then soldiers had come. Her mind came back to the sticking place, arresting Liara's feet. Slowing, her hand still firmly caught in Krešimir's, she tried to pull back, heeding her conscience's call at last.

He turned to see what held them back, and Liara found herself bereft of breath as his gaze caught hers. She had almost forgot. And the last time she had beheld such eyes, she had not yet traveled enough to compare their color to that of a sun-washed sea.

Said seas grew stormy. Krešimir tugged her arm—hard, but not enough to hurt. "Come on."

Liara reached for her purse with her free hand. "Just a moment."

Fishing in the small leather pouch, she brushed Anisthe's pendant. She fought the urge to recoil. She had the coin in hand an instant later. Closing her fingers over the cold metal, Liara whispered, "*Atsmi'i.*"

I, Magus. And with those words, a call to Nagarath. Quite honestly, Liara did not know what to expect from it. Curious, she removed the enchanted coin from her purse, noting a faint yellowish glow about it.

Krešimir wrested the coin from her and flung it down the street where it landed out of sight. Liara tried to pull away, eyes on the gutter.

Krešimir held firm to her arm.

"No. Liara." His eyes flashed a warning, and she glanced up in time to see several silhouettes darken the end of the alleyway.

"Hold up there!"

Soldiers. Three. Frowning. Questioning.

Krešimir's hand slipped out of hers, and the distraction centered Liara's mind. She no longer thought in one word bursts of observation. Her lie came easily, an old habit re-adopted: "If you please, we are in a great hurry. Neither of us are from this city. I only now have collected my cousin from port. Our grandfather is very sick and any delay could . . ."

Liara affected tears, hoping the press of a young woman in distress would cover any deficiencies in her having bent her tones to that of the local dialect. It would not do to expose them as Dvigrad's runaways directly to the authorities.

Krešimir looked at Liara like she had grown three heads, and she cringed, hoping he had not given them away.

"My sympathies," one of the men said, his face softening. "Where is it you are trying to go?"

Liara's mind blanked.

Krešimir rescued them. "Tanners," he blurted, then blushed under the weight of his falsehood.

Lowering her gaze, Liara translated, earning herself and Krešimir freedom when the three men moved to the side, pointing and giving rough directions.

Stammering their thanks, Liara grabbed Krešimir's hand while they hurried to make their escape. Heart hammering, she sent a quick word of thanks to whichever powers above watched over the two of them. Had Krešimir not thrown the magicked coin away . . . She dared not entertain thoughts of how that scene would have played. She only hoped that, if Nagarath came to find her, he did so in as least dramatic a fashion as possible.

Krešimir tugged at Liara's hand again. She glanced to him, finding his face closed, dark. "Now you see . . ."

"See what?" She knew what he was about to say, but ire rising, Liara bristled at the threat of the coming scold. Krešimir was but—what? Two years her senior? And yanking her about Messina as he was, she did not find his assumed authority particularly impressive. What had happened to her sweet, playful lad?

"Parentino's wizard brings nothing but trouble—even when he's not here." Krešimir slowed, having at least the sense to look about before lapsing into talk of wizards and magick. Though they'd switched back to their native tongue, his caution was warranted. The word for the Art was markedly similar in most dialects. If someone were to overhear, if one of the soldiers had decided to follow the curious pair of foreigners . . .

"It'll be all right. Liara, please, listen to me." Krešimir rounded on her, catching both her hands in his and lifting them to his lips. Fervent. Ardent. Liara's breath hitched in her chest, and her eyes pricked with tears as she felt his hot breath sweep over her knuckles. Her sweet boy was still there.

Krešimir drew her in. "Hush, Liara. I won't leave you. Not this time; not ever."

Liara leaned into him. Wild thoughts raced through her mind. They could bring Krešimir with them. She could show him how, in spite of all, magick was not bad. Dvigrad . . . that she would have to own to. And sooner rather than later. Closing her eyes, Liara breathed in Krešimir's solid familiarity, and believing his promise with her whole heart, she confessed, "Dvigrad. It was my fault."

She felt him stiffen.

"No."

A thread of ice snaked up Liara's spine, freezing her. Bravely she pursued, "It was for me that they died. He was looking for me, my father—"

This time, Krešimir did pull away. His face stricken, he searched her statement. "No. It cannot be true."

"It is—"

"Liara, we have to run. Nagarath, he'll—"

"Not Nagarath. Anisthe." Shaking her head, Liara stood her ground. "There were two wizards."

"Were?"

Both Liara and Krešimir turned at the sound.

This time it was merely one man who darkened the mouth of the alleyway. Simply clad, he did not look like an incantate wizard. Rather, he appeared quite ordinary. A touch more haggard than when Liara had last seen him, but altogether well.

Anisthe smiled over his little joke, stretching a hand toward his two victims. The curse was invisible, but Liara felt the magick grapple with her own. She fell to her knees, gasping. Out of the corner of her eye she could see Krešimir lurch forward, his face twisted with rage. "You're hurting her!"

"Quiet, fool. Unless you know something of the Art that we mages do not." Anisthe clenched his outstretched fingers, bringing tears to Liara's eyes. She couldn't move; couldn't breathe. "How else am I to free her from that wizard's enchantment, Krešimir?"

Betrayal! And of the worst sort. "Krešimir, what have you done?"

And how does Anisthe have magick? Through gritted teeth, her vision sparking and warping, Liara felt Krešimir step away from her.

"Oh, no." Anisthe arrested Krešimir's steps with a quick snap of his other hand. Liara felt the spell about her weaken with the effort. The incantate's tricks were limited, then.

"I simply told him my side of the truth, Liara. That my wayward daughter-in-magick had taken up with a disreputable mage—something our mutual friend here already knew—and that I required help in bringing her back home to us."

Liara bought time. "Truth doesn't have sides."

"I beg to differ." Anisthe loomed ever closer.

If she could figure out why the magick felt different, then she would know how to combat it. It felt . . . it felt like . . . like a rain-wrapped squall on the sea. Like lightning and thunder gone blue-green with the Art.

"Your storm," Liara accused, feigning weakness by extinguishing what little gift she had instinctively called to fight the mage. It hurt. But, if he looked to it, her enemy would see that her aura had flickered, then faded. "If you're so concerned with my safe return, why send something that could well have killed us all?"

"I would not want you back, my dear, but for how certain I am of your powers in preventing such." Anisthe made a show of helping Liara to her feet. Ever solicitous. Ever cruel. Her stomach turned at his touch, but she did not shy away. She needed enough of her own magick back to escape—with Krešimir.

"You knew I'd fight it. You knew both Nagarath and I would. Leaving us with no magick left afterwards. Clever that, progenaurae." Liara risked a glance at Krešimir, noting vacant eyes and listless limbs. Her fingers itched, ready to curse and punish. Whatever tricks Anisthe employed, it was not his own magick that he burned. And as such, using her Art against him would not imperil herself, so long as she was careful.

"Please, Liara, now that you are free from that swindler spell-caster of Parentino, call me as you ought: your long-lost father." Anisthe's goading set Liara's blood to burning. He was sniffing out the last of her tired Art, one more attempt to rile her, to force an early action on her end. She would not give in.

A part of her reveled in the challenge. Liara scowled. "I don't claim an Artless as my own."

Liara felt more than heard the words of the spell that caused her to duck and wrench her arm out of Anisthe's grasp. A familiar red glow blossomed within a doorway to her left. A cherished voice, deep, with a hint of a rasp, chanted sharp magick.

Dancing sparks on a fiery wind whistled through the narrow alleyway. Anisthe caught the full force of Nagarath's curse. He spun and fell face-first against the stone wall. A shout, a blur of motion seen from the corner of Liara's eye. Krešimir had been freed. He fell to his knees, a marionette with cut strings. But it was to Nagarath that Liara ran.

"I'm sorry—" she began.

The words, the hesitation, were a mistake.

Liara had counted Anisthe incapacitated. She and Nagarath both. But her wizard's eyes told a different story. Widening in fear, they gave Liara little of the warning needed as the mage seized her shoulders and thrust her to the side. She did not note the peril until it was too late.

A knife. It glinted evilly in the blood-red light of Nagarath's fading spell before burying itself in the wizard's heavy cloak. Liara screamed.

Pain. Pain exploded in Liara's side. Her vision sparked red, then black, then every color all at once. Indistinct shouting echoed in her ears—Nagarath, Krešimir. Pure pandemonium. Anisthe, lying upon the cobbles, his face very pale and very still. Black blood pooled on the ground. And through it all, agony. Liara moved without thinking, reaching for Nagarath's staff—

—*goral kala iy'ha ann'f m'ha mot shl' schresch aatz iy'ha dam m'ha nahhar*— The words were in Liara's heart before she knew to call them. The stave screamed its magick in her head.

"*Tra'shuk i'shor levav,*" Liara shouted her encantation, drowning out the words of the stave and setting the alleyway, and Anisthe within it, to blowing away like dust in a gale.

The darkness brightened, coalescing into the blues of sky and sea. Liara caught sight of white stones topped with haggard green brush, noted the soothing warmth of sunny waters lapping about her ankles and calves . . . And pain. The pain continued. It had followed her there.

Dropping Nagarath's staff, Liara clutched her side, as though in doing so she might hold herself together. Lifting her fingers to peek, she saw no blood, no outward sign. *No wound. Magick, then.*

"You fool girl," Nagarath's voice seemed to come at her from a distance. Looking back upward, she saw two figures, each blurred by pain. The tall, thin silhouette of her mentor and the huddled, sandy-haired form of Krešimir. She had managed it, then. She'd saved them both. Staggering forward, Liara saw the flash of a knife, the black of blood on the woodsman's hands.

"Nagarath, watch—" Liara slurred the words, stopping as the mage waved a hand in the air. Krešimir had hardly moved when he winked out of sight, whisked away on the wizard's spell. She only had time to lock her eyes to Nagarath's own ice-gray gaze before tumbling, unconscious, into his arms.

Chapter Twelve

Domagoj raised his hands to incant and then dropped them. His spell remained unspoken. The trio of fugitives escaped without pursuit. He swiftly knelt at Anisthe's side. But nothing could be done. The incantate was dying. His blood stained the alley, rivulets between the cobbles.

Tears sprang into the space the words of magick had vacated, and a tightness seized Domagoj's chest. He cursed through clenched teeth, "Don't you die on me, you useless idiot."

Hopeless at it was, Domagoj's fingers searched Anisthe's side, seeking the edges of the wound. He sounded the depths of his own wavering power. Despair shook him anew. His oriaurant's magick, newly recovered from his expenditure amid-ship, had been squandered to help Anisthe play at having power once again.

"Wasteful display. Fooled or no, the girl will be dead soon per the Third Law," Domagoj hissed. He winced as magefire winked into brightness at his fingertips. It illuminated the gaping wound in Anisthe's side.

Krešimir's errant knife had done extensive damage. It did not much matter that Domagoj could heal a nicked liver or lacerated diaphragm—both having fallen, unluckily, within the knife's slashing path. It was blood loss that would kill the former mage. Time enough for hasty, imperfect goodbyes and little else. Helplessness brought a sour note to the pressure blocking Domagoj's throat.

Tears marked zigzag streaks down his cheeks, horrid mimicry of the blood spilt in the alleyway. Absently, he wondered if the aurenaurae was already dead, or if the Laws would have the courtesy to let his master pass first.

Anisthe's lips trembled, his breathing shallow. His wide, glassy eyes stared up into Domagoj's, holding a mixture of despair and peace. He knew. He knew and had resigned himself to his death. But not without a last word to his servant. "Leave him."

The rasped sentence hung in the air.

Domagoj stared. Like hell he would. There was no place on earth that Nagarath could go to escape his death by the oriaurant's hand.

Anisthe grew agitated, reaching a stained hand upward to grasp Domagoj's collar.

"It ends, Dom—" Flecks of blood reddened his lips, and he ceased to speak.

Domagoj's eyes swam in a sea of hot crimson. Blood. Vitalitas. Einatus.

"Einatus . . ." Domagoj's whisper carried the crazed energy of hope. Wild-eyed, he shook Anisthe hard. "Anisthe. Magus. Do the Laws hold? All of them?"

Anisthe's answering gaze was hard and silent. Unreadable.

"The Laws Eversio," Domagoj hissed. "Tell me." Thinking fast, believing it all a gamble—*no, it is knowledge, it is the alchemy of desire*—the oriaurant rehearsed the Laws, the Hidden Laws, in his mind. Law the

First; Law the Second. Those which governed the sundering spells.

A croaking gasp. Anisthe's eyes had found their spark. But whether he agreed with his servant or chastised him, Domagoj couldn't tell. The incantate showed life. That was all that mattered.

The Three Conditions. They were met so long as Domagoj did not make his demands until after. Closing his eyes, the oriaurant felt the magick leave him. The spells were easy. And infinitely hard. A part of him wondered if Anisthe would ever have been capable of such himself.

No matter. It was done.

He felt the change immediately. Domagoj's well of power had been lessened. Permanently. And Anisthe? He would live. The incantate breathed easier. The blood flowing from his side had lessened to a sluggish oozing.

"Correction, magus rather than incantate." Domagoj sat back on his heels, wiping perspiration from his brow and feeling newly faint with the motion.

Anisthe's eyes—the bright eyes of a living man—were back on him. "You understand what you have done?"

"Yes." Domagoj met the war mage's gaze steadily.

Anisthe sat up on his elbows. Chastising. Grateful. He seemed puzzled and, quite possibly, distrustful. " 'The giving of Power is not directly reversible.' "

"Law The Second of Eversio." Domagoj recognized the quotation and moved past the unspoken challenge. "I understand."

"Why?" Anisthe breathed the word. Domagoj wasn't at all certain the war mage had even spoken aloud.

"You were dying," Domagoj said simply. He shifted his eyes away from his master's piercing gaze. He had shared his Art with Anisthe. A gift given freely, he was not about to take it back. Not that he could. Thus were the consequences of the Forgotten Laws.

But a part of him trembled at his daring. The giving of power was only condoned—would only work—so long as certain conditions were met. Condition the First: Said Power must be given freely and not coerced. Condition the Second: Said Power must have clear and unencumbered provenance. Condition the Third: The purposeful transferring of magick out of a body must be done with the aim of not physically harming said body.

Domagoj had searched his heart, had known the demands of Eversio to be met without question. But the stated requirements of the Laws were incomplete, containing loopholes that he exploited. The soul that had given a portion of his Art to Anisthe held impure motives. For with Anisthe's falling under a simple knife thrust, Domagoj had almost lost that which he'd only recently begun to hope for.

He wanted Liara. And he would demand her of Anisthe. The war mage was in his debt. He owed Domagoj his life and so much more. And, as such a request was surely to fall afoul of the war mage's temper, it helped doubly that Anisthe could not hurt Domagoj . . . not by magick, anyhow. For now—just as it had been with Liara—their signatures were the same.

The Laws Eversio? Defective at their root. There was no such thing as a gift freely given.

~*~

Nagarath struggled to carry Liara from the shallows. The water swirled about his ankles, dragging at his cloak—

much as Krešimir strained at the other end of Nagarath's Art. The young man could not remain in the Void for long. But, Liara . . . oh, Liara. In Nagarath's arms, she was light as driftwood and just as pale. Anisthe lying in a shadowed alleyway; blood on cobblestones—the images swam in Nagarath's vision as he found a spot to lay his little magpie.

He'd go back and save Anisthe. Wasn't there time? There had to be time.

There was no time.

Nagarath knelt and gently stroked Liara's stone-still cheek. If the Laws were exacting their toll here and now, if Anisthe truly was dying in an alleyway of Messina, Nagarath wanted—needed—this last moment alone with her.

A strand of hair lay across Liara's face. He moved to brush it back, then hesitated. No. He hadn't that right. Even in such a moment. His eyes searched her lifeless form, yet wishing for a miracle. Helpless. Hopeful. A hollow vigil.

He felt, more than saw, the change. Liara's last gasp, but one of magick. In the glaring sunlight, it seemed a silvery mist gathered about Liara, then faded. Magick rippled through the air.

And then, the wished-for miracle.

A shimmer. A shudder. Liara's chest rose and fell with one quiet breath. Color returned to her cheeks, faint but unmistakable.

Chest hitching in a sob, Nagarath stretched his Art to sense that of his apprentice. Strong as a heartbeat, her aura pulsed invisibly across her skin. It hummed against his own in soundless duet. Tears blurred Nagarath's vision, and he choked on his own relief. The aborted exclamation echoed against the nearby rocks.

How? Why? Immaterial. Anisthe could be a full war-lock again, for all Nagarath cared; could have somehow, impossibly, found the mirror and revived his Art to save himself from the brink. It didn't matter. Liara lived.

Her breathing resumed its soft cadence. Shallow but regular. But, Liara was yet far from recovered. Nagarath could only guess at how far into the darkness the Laws had taken her spirit. He had time to scry Anisthe. Perhaps Nagarath might do something about that man at long last.

No. Liara first. Nagarath found he couldn't leave her side. Anisthe would have to see to himself for a moment longer. Nagarath now did brush the hair back from Liara's face. The gesture broke him. And brought his magick suspending Krešimir to an end. He appeared just as he had disappeared—had likely never known he was gone.

The shattering of his spell set Nagarath's senses reeling. He only had time to turn and catch the young man with the blow of another hex. Krešimir fell like cut wheat. On his feet in an instant, Nagarath advanced upon Krešimir, wand out and at the ready.

Blinded by anger, Nagarath's world bled to a horrible bleached white. The sound of his wrath deafened the ear. He shouted over it. "You! You could have killed her!" A flick of the wrist. The knife flew away, harmless.

Scrambling to his feet, Krešimir turned terrified eyes to Nagarath. A hand held to his forehead, a trickle of red seeped from beneath his fingers and down to his cheek-bone. The accidental injury made Nagarath pause. With a shudder, he saw how close he was to the killing blow. He could taste the words of the curse on his lips, bitter and bright. This on the heels of sending him to the Void. Of using magick he never, ever, ought to have used—on anyone, much less an Artless.

Finding his opening, Krešimir lunged. Thrown into turmoil by his own capacity for darkness, Nagarath jumped to the side. The blow glanced off his knee and pain stabbed upward through his leg. Falling heavily, Nagarath moved to rise, only to be kicked again, this time in the gut. Winded, dizzy with pain, he tried to shout a spell, make the necessary gesture.

Turn him into steam. Banish him a hundred leagues away. Kill him outright.

But, of course, he could not. The words refused to come. As did that which turned a heart to murder. Liara lived. And he lived for her and would not lessen himself so.

Strong arms—a woodworker's arms—grappled Nagarath. Gasping, he tried to fight his attacker. Krešimir pushed him, face first, into the shallows. Salt water filled his mouth and nose, stung his eyes.

With a rush, down became up. Grateful lungs sucked in air. Krešimir screamed into his ear, "What did you do to her?"

Seawater again, sharp and punishing. Nagarath flailed helplessly.

More daylight. And, again, Krešimir. "If you don't wake her, I'll finish you here and now, then figure it out myself."

Up became down. Water like a thousand stabbing knives. This time, Nagarath managed to get a hold of Krešimir's leg. Panicked, he effected a spell.

The punishing arms fell away. Coughing, Nagarath found purchase and managed to catch his stunned assailant before he himself fell into the foam. Nagarath dragged Krešimir to safety. He shoved the young man next to Liara. "There! See what you've done!"

"You're nothing," Krešimir managed to whisper. "You're nothing but magick."

Collaring Krešimir, Nagarath thrust the boy's face to within inches of Liara's own. "This is you. Your actions."

Separating the bungling youth from his precious charge, he threw Krešimir onto his back. Nagarath grabbed a handful of his cloak, finding the long gash and shaking it under Krešimir's nose. "This. This was as far as you got with me."

"Liar. You . . . you wizard. You deceiver."

"You don't have the faintest idea what's going on! You have no place in this. Anisthe! Liara! Magick and power and Laws and . . ." Nagarath realized he had ceased making sense. He stopped and took a calming breath. "Their lives are tied together—"

"Magick and trickery." Limbs yet deadened by Nagarath's spell, Krešimir managed only a weak protest.

"You! You know nothing of magick. You willfully ignorant, self-important, inconstant dolt."

"Liara—"

". . . is Anisthe's daughter via magick. As such, if *he* dies before she reaches the age of twenty, *she* dies as a consequence of the Laws. An errant knife, wielded by a fool boy who believes himself a man—"

"I was saving her!"

"You were giving her over to the one person she fears more than anything in the world."

"Anisthe—"

"Anisthe is responsible for what happened in Dvigrad! Anisthe would have me dead and Liara in thrall both magickally and physically. He's already tried it once. He would have her body; he would have her soul. You are a tool to him, Krešimir. A weapon. An errand boy. And traitor to Liara and what she wants—what she needs."

Krešimir looked to Liara. "But, how? Will she . . . will she be all right?"

"I need to look to Anisthe to better know that answer. He must have been truly dying for her to fall as she did. I saw the magick bleeding from her. I don't"—anguish gripped Nagarath—"I don't know how far gone she was. But it is beyond my Art to help her."

"Anisthe said—"

Wordlessly, Nagarath locked his gaze to Krešimir's. Krešimir faltered under Nagarath's pain. Reading the man, Nagarath pondered. *He . . . It is possible he actually understands? Or at least wants to. Which is about all I can hope for, really.*

"I love her," Krešimir's fervent declaration rattled Nagarath as much as the attack had.

No. You don't. You think you do but . . . Well, maybe you do, just . . . in a broken sort of way. Wisely, he kept his observation to himself. *Love . . . it listens.*

But do you listen to Liara, Nagarath? His battered conscience turned his own argument against him.

Undeterred, Krešimir continued. "We're all that's left. She's all I have, Nagarath."

Nagarath flinched, feeling as though he'd been kicked in the gut anew. *She's all I have.*

Encouraged by Nagarath's silence, Krešimir began to speak freely and with passion. Adrift within his own heart,

Nagarath only heard discordant syllables. Too busy steeling himself. He checked the strength of his magick.

Could he, dare he, cross the line so blatantly? He'd never bound a man's will. How such a message might be received on the other end of the magick, he shuddered to think. But with such stakes . . . He stared, scarcely seeing Liara's quiet form, taking comfort in the sound of her breath. Nagarath's conscience hammered at him, dragging forth the argument so that he would not have to spend the energy making it himself. Anisthe. Magick itself seemed to be on his side. Over and over. If the war mage should succeed, if Nagarath and Liara should fail, what then?

Decision made, Nagarath unearthed the chained book from Liara's pack and then limped over to where the cinnabar staff had fallen. Touching his stave to the book, Nagarath shut his mind to his actions. The book grew still. He opened to the page depicting Khariton's Mirror. Wincing and with an eye to Liara, he tore free the page. Guilt bloomed in Nagarath's chest.

Nagarath whispered a spell over the limp page and then approached Krešimir. Dvigrad's woodsman still babbled uselessly, draining Nagarath's magick but only slightly with his continued incapacitation. Shame screamed at Nagarath. He moved as if in a dream. As if he, himself, had no choice in the matter. Finger to Krešimir's forehead, he read from the page. It disappeared. As did Krešimir.

Nagarath swayed on his feet. He bent to gather Liara into his arms. Heart eased, he held her close for a moment before they, too, disappeared in a shower of sparks.

Chapter Thirteen

The memory of pain still haunted Liara upon waking. She lay upon a bed, staring up at a ceiling that mostly disappeared into darkness. Not daring to turn her head, fearful that she might well shatter with the effort, she tried to gauge where she was. The sheets itched under her back. The air reeked of stale smoke and sweat. She guessed an inn. If so, it was not a terribly elegant one.

And she was alone.

No, not alone at all. The light in the room shifted as Nagarath crossed in front of the curtained window. He had not yet noticed Liara's having awoken. Sitting heavily at a small table, the muted sunshine played shadows over his otherwise unmoving countenance.

Liara braved the agony of motion to turn her head towards her mage. His stony face was a profusion of despondency. Sorrow. Fear. Anger. Hatred. Each had their turn with the man and all within the space of an instant. Beaten back before her very eyes, he fought an internal war. Nagarath shifted in his chair, passing shaking fingers across his brow and drawing equally unsteady breath.

Liara noticed then the bowl upon the window-side table. The mage waved his hand over the shallow vessel. The motions comforted Liara with their familiarity, though the whispered words of his accompanying spell rang sharp with strangled emotion. He leaned close, his intent gaze upon the scene playing out on the water's surface finally giving animation to his face.

Hooking her fingers around the edges of the soft cloak under which she lay, Liara gasped involuntarily. They were Nagarath's own mage's robes! Her stirring brought the wizard's head swiveling up. His weary eyes locked to hers. The chair crashed to the floor in his wake, her friend nearly upsetting the scrying bowl in his haste to be at her side.

"Do you—do you even—?" He couldn't complete the sentence. Sinking to his knees, Nagarath simply pressed a fist to his lips, trembling. Several minutes ticked past as the mage strove to master himself. At length, he asked, "How are you feeling? Do you hurt anywhere?"

"Not like I did before." Liara let her gaze slip back to the darkened ceiling. "And I still have my magick." Raising her arm, she made a gentle sign with her fingers. The purple-spark trail of her aura lingered in the air before dissipating.

"Magick." Nagarath spat the word. But his anger broke open upon his relief. The wizard moved to rise, assured of her safety. Turning, he dragged the fallen chair over to her bedside, reclaiming it tiredly and shutting his eyes. He said, "You're lucky to be alive. Both of you."

"Both?" It was Liara's turn to give in to a fearful tremor.

"While your condition had me fearing the worst, that the wound Anisthe received would prove mortal—"

"Anisthe!"

"—your progenaurae is mending just fine." Nagarath reached across the bed, lifting the hem of his cloak. A seamed tear jagged across the dark cloth. "He meant to get me, your Krešimir. Anisthe's own attempt to do the same put him into the boy's path. Krešimir's knife sank home—in the wrong target. Anisthe has been ever so furious at his servant these past five days."

Memories of her last conscious moments on the shoreline played through Liara's mind. "Where are we?"

"A traveler's inn at Sassari. No, no Liara, I wouldn't move just yet," Nagarath cautioned. "I truly thought your last act in this world was to get us here to Sardinia. . . ."

Liara's fingers inched towards the long gash that marred the wizard's robes. With that silent occupation, she managed not to ask the question which had next pressed her mind.

But Nagarath knew her all too well.

"Krešimir is safe though," Nagarath said. " 'Twas magick I hope to never again have to employ. You know me. To leave your young man behind in Cagliari was to cross my methods, morals, and self-imposed limitations. But he is safe, and I made certain that he has means. Anisthe will not easily catch him up again."

"Couldn't we—"

"No," Nagarath snapped. "You do not get to make a request today. Today, you rest and recover and consider the events in Messina. Today—"

"But—"

"Today," he spoke over her protest, eyes sparking dangerously, "I find us a way to get from here to the coast. Soon as you are strong enough to travel, we head for Spain. Yes, your little trick saved us a fair deal of traveling. Put us ahead of Anisthe by a week, most likely. And that is all the conversation I would prefer to have upon that subject."

Rising, Nagarath moved over to the scrying bowl. The wizard wouldn't even have to leave the room to learn what he needed. Though with the distance that had grown suddenly between them, it was as though he had. Or worse than.

Gingerly, Liara sat up, holding the mage's cloak close round her shoulders. Her injury did not excuse her behavior. Fate was not pat. "Nagarath."

"Yes, Liara?"

"I'm sorry."

Nagarath pursed his lips and said not a word. He did not even look at her.

The tears which had gathered at the corner of Liara's eyes began to fall. Penitent, she laid back down upon the bed, her sorrow not for herself but for the wrong she had done. Between panic and pride, she'd done a very stupid and dangerous thing. Nagarath had come to her aid. She had known Anisthe had no real power at hand. The truth of it was, seeing Krešimir—hearing his promises—and tasting that curious storm at sea had brought out in her a recklessness, a desire to prove something.

"He tried to take me from you." Mostly to herself, the whispered statement eased Liara's heart. Where once she would have eagerly sought excuse, looked to pin blame elsewhere, there was plain honesty in her confession.

At length, Nagarath spoke, his head bowed. "Anisthe is a convincing person to the unwary. But, yes, I understand the position in which you were placed. If anything, the events in Messina confirm that we are in the right with regards your progenaurae's actions. He can neither be trusted with his own safety nor can we leave him to find the mirror first."

When nothing else followed, Liara concluded that he was either not to be interrupted or he had no interest in lecturing her further.

Nothing would take Nagarath from Liara's side once she had awoken. Inwardly, however, the mage desired escape. From himself. From his feelings and responsibilities and duties and, yes, even magick. As soon as his shaking fingers could manage the spells, he had known his magpie to be safe. Mostly known. Scrying had allowed him to witness Anisthe's incredible return from the brink of oblivion. But the terrible fear had remained. Five days it had taken her to wake; nearly a week of tortured worry and unanswerable anger. He had been forced to fill that time offering veiled explanations to their host, pretending everything was perfectly all right. Their abrupt and nonsensical arrival at the inn had drawn the attention of the ever curious. Nagarath had been too afraid to waste his magick quelling rumor, lest Liara need him.

He wanted to shake her, scream at her over her monumental stupidity in Messina. He needed to sweep her in his arms and hold her close, grateful she had returned to him at last. Liara's magick. Anisthe's magick. In Nagarath's heaving heart it was all very much the same. A topsy-turvy mix of failures and mistakes—much of it his own. Oversights and assumptions. Arrogance and rank underestimation. To petulantly demand the girl's apologies after all that had happened seemed churlish, a mean gesture meant only to humiliate her and satisfy . . . satisfy what, exactly? The answers he sought were not available to him. Scrying could only tell him so much, after all.

"Too much," Nagarath muttered, peering into the bowl of glassy water. Anisthe's recovery worried him. The incantate had magick. Or he did not. The war mage was well and truly on the way to a full recovery and would again rise up in their path as an enemy. Or not. The arguments circled back on themselves in his mind, chasing a dream. To witness Anisthe's small magicks now, to hear him even, was downright maddening. Nagarath needed to feel it, see the aura firsthand, in order to know, to truly know if what he suspected was even possibly true.

"You would not believe it anyhow," he scolded himself. Scowling, Nagarath passed a hand over the bowl, calling the contents to a stillness beyond what one finds in the natural world. Thus separated from the plane of mortality by magick, the surface warped and shimmered before coalescing into the image the wizard sought.

Men dashed about a crowded harbor. Behind them, a forest of masts and rigging reached into a cloudless sky. Sound followed sight an instant late, an echo or afterthought of the spell. The wind was freshening, the merchants of Porto Torres eager.

Another gesture in the air and the scene changed. A different port. Urgency of another flavor. Anisthe would soon be leaving Messina. From his movements, it appeared his injury plagued him but little.

Nagarath drew back from the water-warped tableau to check on Liara. Her regular breathing and closed eyes led him to believe she had fallen back asleep. His heart eased . . . a little. And in its place edged a longing to sit by her side, make his own apologies for his gruff change of mood, confess how deeply fearful he'd felt that—

Motion in the bowl caught Nagarath's eye, and his gaze stole back to the scene still playing out. The servant—the dark-haired fellow with the unnaturally blue eyes—had come into view once again. Settling his chin onto his interlocked fingers, Nagarath used the position to keep his excited breath from disturbing the water.

This is my anomaly. Nagarath kept his thoughts to himself. The two subjects of his scrutiny went about their business: packing their belongings and holding hushed conference. That was part of the trouble. This unknown fellow was always either completely absent or very close by to Anisthe every time Nagarath scried the incantate mage. And, if present, always positioned himself so that his words were both inaudible and unseen to the spell of scrying. It was as if he knew they were being watched.

Which was impossible unless he himself were a mage.

"Correction," Nagarath whispered. "Unless Anisthe is, again, a mage. But why hide the servant and not the master? Talk to me, old friend. Why do you choose to reveal yourself so plainly?"

"I think he wants us to see," Liara's voice called Nagarath's attention away from the scrying bowl though he did not shift his gaze.

"But why?"

Silence. Then, "You said he has a servant with him?"

Again, Nagarath's heart leapt in his chest. Gladness, it would seem, did more for his nerves than did worry. He followed Liara's thread of thought, pleased at her insight. He nodded. "That I did."

"Your workroom in Parentino. Everything with power had its own signature. And every one was different. You saw Anisthe's home. There, too, a myriad of auras. But each was laced with an echo of his own. With everything. Everything, Nagarath. He was proud to show me." Liara choked on the memory. "But this? His home had nothing like how this feels. This aura is wholly different. Strange, even. The storm we faced, it was the same way."

"You believe that it is the servant who has magick."

"Perhaps. But . . ." Liara's answer came wistful.

"But Anisthe lived. When he ought to have died." It was Nagarath's turn to choke on his words.

Liara had sat up, wrapping herself in his cloak. Her eyes peeked out at him, dark within the black folds of cloth. "Zielsor."

Nagarath shuddered. But there was no shaking off the chill which crept into him with that one word. Of course, Liara would know of the high crime of zielsor. She had had one of the world's foremost libraries on magick at her stead. It stood to reason she would have run across the term in one of the volumes while cataloging. Perhaps it was even the volume on—

New pain seized Nagarath. Sorrow, waiting to catch him for five whole days, took the mage for one searing moment. His artifacts. His home. All gone. Even the last of the chained volumes now left with Krešimir.

Plans within plans . . . Nagarath could not have left Krešimir unguarded when he abandoned the young man on the wayside. He only hoped he would understand the hint he had left and act upon it.

Liara persisted. "So whose power did Anisthe take?"

"Zielsor is a high crime. It is a gross violation of the Laws to forcibly steal the Art of another. Few would have the knowledge required, and no mage dare it."

"But Anisthe wants to break the Laws."

"The Laws are unbreakable, Liara. Violation is different."

Liara paused to consider. At length, she ventured, "Please don't take this the wrong way, Nagarath, but . . . I'm not sure how stealing the magick of another wizard would violate any of the Laws."

Nagarath rose and crossed the room to again sit at Liara's side. He was not about to look askance at such a logical question. However, he hoped she would extend him the same courtesy of understanding. He said, "Ah, well, that is because the Laws that govern the giving and taking of power amongst magick users are no longer taught. They are Hidden Laws. Forgotten because of how they were abused. People get an idea that a thing is possible and . . ." He shrugged. "People are people, be they wizards or not."

Liara's shock was delicious. As was her academic excitement that swiftly followed. "Tell me."

Nagarath warmed to the topic at hand, shifting so that he faced Liara for his impromptu lesson. The color was back in the young woman's cheeks, her energy strong. Surprised at how quickly Cromen's lesson rose into his mind, he quoted:

"Law The First of Eversio: Magickal power given to another retains its originating signature. As this typically results in two signatures co-mingling, the larger portion of the Magick held will exert dominance.

"Law The Second of Eversio: The giving of Power is not directly reversible."

Liara leapt upon the wording, as Nagarath had thought she might. "Given versus taken. In the right circumstances . . ."

"Correct. And there are qualifiers. Conditions to discourage abuse amongst the wizarding folk."

"Discourage . . . " Liara smirked, understanding at last. "Hence the violation versus actual crossing of the Laws."

Nagarath smiled. "Precisely. The giving of power is only condoned so long as certain conditions are met: The magick must be given freely. No coercion. Said signature must have clear and unencumbered provenance—this condition meant to prevent passing off stolen magick to an unknowing third party. And, finally, the purposeful transferring of magick out of a body must be done with the aim of not physically harming said body."

"And thus, we get zielsor."

"Correct. And it is a thought not without merit. I considered it, yes. But, too, I dismissed the idea. Such would be too low, even for Anisthe."

Liara rocked from side to side a bit, a ginger experiment in movement. When she next spoke, her voice came out flat. "There's no telling what he's capable of. He must be stopped. Not for me, not for you, not for Dvigrad's memory. But for . . . for everyone."

Nagarath's smile widened. Welcome back, little magpie.

"If he has done it, though . . . per the First Law, dominance of the new aura would be why Anisthe's magick feels so unlike him."

Nagarath nodded. By now, Liara had him half convinced, which was, perhaps, all he'd needed to be certain of his suspicions.

But the girl had more in her. "Again, whose power might Anisthe have stolen?"

"To that question, my magpie, I haven't any clue."

"That's worrisome."

"Yes. It is."

Chapter Fourteen

Liara's seasickness returned. As did her strength following three days of further rest in first Sassari, then Porto Torres. Out at sea once again, this time they went without pretense, no dressing Liara in trousers and cap. Both she and Nagarath were exhausted and—until they landed in Tarragona in Spain and had a lay of the political landscape—abstaining from magick. His staff, Nagarath had carefully wrapped and packed with their things. The chained book that had caused such trouble—lost in Messina. It was not much missed.

One more artifact of magick remained—one that had escaped Nagarath's notice. And this Liara kept upon her person. Her fingers closed around the small oval amber riding in the pocket on her belt. Anisthe's pendant had warmed itself on her body heat and seemed to respond to touch. Standing at the ship's rail, she drew it out into the watery sunshine.

The chain hung dully; the stone withheld its inner light. Liara glanced to the horizon, hesitant. Her fingers trembled, and she clutched Anisthe's pendant close. Her pulse hammered. *Do I dare it?*

Wispy white clouds raced across the skies. The water shone deep and indigo blue. She and Nagarath rode a different sea. Just as a different heart held Anisthe's pendant. Both had grown tempered.

Liara steeled herself before hurling Anisthe's pendant over the starboard rail. Freedom. A declaration of allegiance. Liara turned and hurried to check on Nagarath. Already her conscience felt lighter.

The cry for land rang in her ears. Land. Thank the gods. Even partway down the ladder to the berths, her sickness rose in her chest. Six days was a long time to feel off balance and out of sorts. She hurried to their cramped quarters, sucking air the whole time and wishing the ship would not sway so.

Empty of its wizard and in total disarray, the room set Liara to grumbling as she hurried to ready their packs. Every so often she glanced at the doorway. Nagarath did not return. Annoyed at the mage's absence, Liara clicked her tongue. At least their things were no longer scattered about.

Gaining the deck, Liara found herself hard-pressed to stay out from underfoot. The glare of sunlight off blue-green sea forced a squint. She shielded her eyes to take a good hard look at the foreign shore.

To call it a speck on the horizon would be doing it a disservice. But the espied land was little bigger.

"So eager to be off?" A sailor passed her by, acknowledging her vigil with a laugh. "You'd best wait elsewhere. Deck's about to be a very busy place."

Liara nodded silently, looking around and still not finding Nagarath.

The sailor seemed to sense that she was ill-at-ease for he doubled back. "Your man is aloft."

Sure enough, Nagarath cut a ridiculous figure some twenty feet above her head. And to think she'd been worried after his health! The mage clung to the shrouds of the

AUTHOR MARGINALIA: Fun fact. I love to sail. I refuse to go belowdecks. ★

mizzen, his face to the wind and his eyes closed. It was his "thinking" position, minus the fretful nose-pinching and hemming-hawing.

He's doing magick without me! She'd felt it—thinking to check once she saw the rapt look upon his sun-filled face. Jealousy rose swift and bitter before she could remind herself that they were a team and that his magick was hers.

Ashamed, Liara returned her attention to the espied land. Spain, it would seem, was far more eager to see them than the Republics of Venice and Ragusa had been. The thin line of land had overtaken the horizon, growing into a series of low rolling hills dotted with greenery.

"Behold, the venerable Kingdom of the Visigoths, or so it would have been known in Khariton's time." Nagarath had, apparently, decided to come down from the rigging.

Liara looked him up and down, appraising his health and letting him know that his absurd capers had been noted. He responded to the scrutiny with a small smile.

"Come, Liara, we are about to be in the way, and I have something to show you belowdecks." Laying a hand on Liara's shoulder, Nagarath passed a spell along.

Liara felt the hex in the clearing of her unease and settling of her wave-tossed stomach. While she could not help her surprise from flitting across her face, she tried to let the cure for her seasickness pass unremarked. Her smile was mirrored by a mischievous sparkle in Nagarath's eyes.

She followed him down into the cabin.

The door had scarce closed when Liara rounded on him, her complaint good-natured but well-founded. "You could have helped me all along!"

Raising his hands, Nagarath affected surrender. "I had no way of doing so before now. That was the truth, Liara."

"When? How?" Liara glanced toward the mage's pack, thinking of the few books safely hid within. It was no mystery that Nagarath had spent many days reading by the glow of witchlight—straining his eyes, as she had scolded him. Had he somehow come across the cure in one of his teacher's old books of notes?

"I looked ahead to the land. To see into what sort of situation we are about to step," he explained. "Not scrying, obviously. More along the lines of casting a net and seeing what leaped under its knotty fibers.

"I found much spell working happening upon shore. Nothing large, nothing significant. But the hedge witches are hawking their gifts. The cure for your malady is very much in demand in coastal villages. The housewives are effecting their minor curses and hexes—and apparently without disturbance. It is as it was in Limska Draga before . . . "

Liara helped him past the memory. "Khariton's Visigothic Kingdom holds firm."

"The praecantator would be proud, yes. And perhaps has, in his own way, helped ensure that the tradition of magick remains strong," Nagarath said. "Which gives me hope that the stories of the mirror are true and that Venice's influence will not have reached the ears of the Spanish Empire as I once feared it might. Our path is cleared. And with that—"

Nagarath reached for his pack. He rummaged through it, head half-buried in the flaps of cloth. At length, he surfaced, holding a small wooden box in his hands.

"I feel guilty for having not done this sooner." He hesitated, strangely nervous. "Liara, it is high time you have this."

Shy herself, Liara reached for the case. Almost certain as to what it contained but fearful she might be wrong, she undid the small metal clasp.

Nestled inside on a pillow of deep emerald velvet lay two beautifully wrought objects. One was a wand. Slender and smooth, the golden wood polished to a high luster, it called to her. The other repelled.

Thin and wicked, the knife gleamed at her from within its cocoon of green. *Amésos,* a wizard's last resort for when magick failed. She smiled at the old fashioned gesture, having once read of the ancient tradition in one of the mage's books. The blade would remain untouched. The wand, however—

Liara hesitated. She shook her head, shrinking from both and offering the box back to the mage. "After Messina, I—"

"After Messina, it is clearer to me than ever that, one way or another, your magick will find a way to exert itself. Something, I fear, we had already discovered—if to a different degree—when you were but my librarian." Nagarath sat back, further removing himself from her decision. "I would consider it a very logical and responsible decision to give such power a purpose. Especially if it keeps your hands off the cinnabar staff."

Liara felt giddy as she gently lifted the wand from its case. Flushing with pleasure, she held it aloft and made as if to wave it. She stopped herself just in time.

"Sorry," she apologized. Every novice knew full well the danger of simply whipping a wand around. She surreptitiously switched the wand to her right hand, feeling a fool.

"No need to apologize for your instincts, Liara"—Nagarath smiled at her—"though I am glad you thought better of turning me into a teacup or button. Lessons will start as soon as we can find an out-of-the-way location. Your apprenticeship—your formal apprenticeship—has begun, my magpie."

~*~

"Our route is confirmed. Anisthe has not yet made land. And our story has been established." Nagarath entered their small but comfortable lodgings with a flourish, stretching out upon the second bed and affecting sleep.

Liara narrowed her eyes. "So, what are we now?"

"Distant relations. Your mother is my cousin or some such. The sideways glances may yet continue, but there will always be ignorant folks ready to judge no matter what story or truth they are given. I, for one, am not about to waste my powers on an endless array of disguises. We have better things to do with our Art, especially considering all that I have learned through my careful inquest."

"So we can do magick?" Thus far, Liara counted herself lucky that the wizard had allowed her the luxury of recovering in their room. Arriving on shore, she had quickly discovered that, while Nagarath's training in foreign dialects was fine and good for dealing with books, actually using the living language was another matter entirely. She'd spent her time alone practicing what spells she might employ to cheat having to learn much more than shipboard Spanish.

When Nagarath did not answer, Liara dropped back upon her own bed to stare up at the ceiling. Their situation had improved markedly since arriving in Tarragona. Again, it had her wondering at Nagarath's apparently endless supply of wealth for their travels. But then, his affluence was not all that surprising considering the value and rarity of the books he'd had in his possession in Limska Draga. Her mage had his secrets, sure enough.

"Our cover is that of two non-magick folk traveling." Nagarath's delayed response told Liara of his reluctance to disappoint.

"Wand lessons?"

"I'm sorry, but they'll have to wait a bit longer, I'm afraid. Venice's reach stretches further west than initially suspected."

"So no magick."

"None save for anything unnoticeable to the Artless. Even my subtle inquiries are not something I dare repeat just yet. But scrying and whatnot—those we may continue here so long as we are very careful. Already, I fear we ought to move on to the next town, just to be safe. But first, we rest."

Sleep instead of spell casting. Not the afternoon Liara had in mind. A thought itched at her, one that had risen the moment she had thrust Anisthe's broken pendant from her and that she had not yet voiced. "And then I would like to try scrying Anisthe."

"At the next town, yes, I will teach you how." Nagarath paused before adding, "Thank you, Liara."

~*~

From Terragona southwards along the coast through the Valencia region. Three different inns in three different towns and not a whiff of magick nor hint of trouble. Nagarath insisted they were on the right path. He also relaxed his rules as to using magick. The feared skeptical glances were kept at bay through judicious use of a glamour here, a charm there.

But as there was only so much one could do, Liara and Nagarath had to come to take their meals in the common room and hopefully find gossip where magick failed them. Which meant, more often than not, running into all sorts of folks and entering into all manner of conversation. With the aid of subtle spellwork, Liara found that she could more easily follow conversations and expose her own ignorance far less. Her quick ear improved with each passing day—she made a game of it with herself, dropping her hexes every so often to check her new skills. Even so, Liara could barely keep track of which lie she—or rather, Nagarath—was telling. It seemed to change hourly. Sister; cousin; ward. At Biar. Caravaca. Laen. The only reprieve came in waiting for the carriage's availability. Another forced rest.

And another night of small talk in the commons.

Nagarath's knee collided with Liara's own under the table. "Sorry."

Tall man that he was, everything at that particular wayside inn seemed small by contrast. Not comically so. Just . . . cramped. And as this was the sixth time during the meal that Liara had suffered such bumps and knocks, the mage's apology fell on unforgiving ears.

"Just sit on this side of the table." Liara could hold her own when it came to elbows. And she wouldn't have to eat facing the back cover of a book eight inches from her nose.

"If I do that, I invite someone to use the empty bench, Liara," Nagarath came back at her with a hushed murmur of his own.

Frowning, Liara remembered the last such unwelcome interruption. Two towns back, a young boy—clearly five years her junior but who figured himself Liara's equal had sat uninvited. The youth then proceeded to fill the space with chatter and gossip until the innkeeper himself had to intervene in enforcement of closing hour. It had been all that Liara could do to keep from gumming the lad's mouth closed with a hex.

Not that she would have been so rash and careless. Not like Nagarath, anyway. The mage still brought his reading with him to the table at every public house they had frequented, regardless of rumors of Venice's persecution following them everywhere.

Liara hissed at Nagarath to put the book away.

"It's not as though non-magick folk can even read the title on the covers. They probably think it some foreign script—which, in truth, it is," he argued. "Besides. It is horribly rude to gaze intently at another man's reading."

And so Nagarath read at breakfast and supper while Liara stewed and eavesdropped and tried to appear as forgettable as possible. Not an easy task when one's knees were subject to abuse every five minutes.

"Ow!" This time he'd really jabbed her. Looking up sharply from her bread and stew, Liara found the mage sliding sideways out of his bench, intent on assuming the spot next to her. A gentleman stood patiently by, a beaming smile on his broad face and a clergyman's robes about his equally ample frame.

"*Grazie, grazie,* sir. It is such a full room and I did not want to impose . . ."

"Not at all, Father. Not at all." Nagarath beamed back at the portly priest, seating himself in the space Liara had resentfully cleared. The wizard closed his book and laid it on the table, folding his arms over it. "We are glad to have you. Father—?"

"Rodolfo Adessi. Brother and sister?" The priest's fat finger gestured from mage to apprentice.

Nagarath was quick to cover up Liara's snort. "Daughter of my cousin. Merchant out of Venice taking my Tour."

Father Adessi nodded sagely. "Venice. Good place to hail from. Good culture. But an even better place to be away from at present."

Mentally, Liara had already classified Father Rodolfo as one of Phenlick's cloth: kind, open, and friendly. But now she shrank from the man, fingers itching at her sides and ready for magick. The priest's eyes had flicked meaningfully at the book half-hidden beneath Nagarath's fingers. Thankfully, Liara could feel that Nagarath's guard was also raised, that he now regretted having let this man join them at table.

"Are you staying here?" Rodolfo interrupted their stunned silence. He leaned forward across the narrow table, keeping his voice low. "If so, I suggest you find lodging elsewhere."

"Is that a threat?"

"A warning, friend. And for God's sake, get that book out of sight." Rodolfo sat back, a smile returning to his face. He acted as though he had said nothing untoward but a moment before.

Adessi put in his order. "One of your best and a refill for my new friends here." Approval shone in his eyes as Nagarath quickly hid away the offending book.

"What do you want? We've done no wrong." Nagarath's face darkened further. Under the table, Liara could feel his protective arm move closer, positioning himself between her and whatever threat may come.

"Agreed, sir. Just— Hssst." A small knot of men had entered the inn. Men of the cloth, accompanied by the *corregidor*, they had none of the smiles Father Rodolfo shared so generously. Raising his newly acquired glass, he called out, "Father Chimpioni, Father Tutto, how goes the day?"

A nodding acknowledgment was all they could provide as response across the crowded room.

"Later, my friends. Later, then." With a wave, Adessi dismissed his brethren and turned back to Liara and Nagarath. "There. Now they won't think to look askance at you, being vouched by my reputation"—he gave an illustrative tug to his cowl—"but you'd have had a hard time of it had you continued as you were."

Looking to Nagarath, Liara could see that Father Rodolfo's words and gestures had put him in one of his philosophical moods. She could practically hear him say "fascinating" as he looked over their newfound friend. Behind Nagarath's practiced ease, she could see the flood of questions damming up.

Liara could only hope the scowl she'd felt had been internal to her thoughts and hadn't flitted across her face.

Like Nagarath, it was too soon to play her hand just yet. But she did not like the situation. She did not trust this Father Rodolfo Adessi.

~*~

The Italian priest could tuck away, Nagarath would give him that. Their supper ran long, Father Adessi speaking between bites. Clearly a traveled man, Rodolfo's incisive commentary had Nagarath thanking the powers that his claim of taking his Tour was not too far afield of his own past experiences. And while the exchange had all the earmarks of a test, he was glad for the lively discussion.

But later, when all was quiet, perhaps he could have the answers which flashed in Adessi's sparkling eyes. Both promise and threat. They would get no real information then and there. Not with the common room so crowded and the Fathers Tutto and Chimpioni guarding the door with the local constabulary.

That said, subtlety was clearly not Adessi's instinct. Everything about the man was loud—his laugh, his manner of gesturing with hands and whichever dining implement happened to be within them, and his catching good humor. Everything save for his hushed warning given upon joining them at table.

Yes, best to keep the priest in sight until they had a better measure of him.

At length, the priest leaned back to sigh contentedly, setting his hands to his ample stomach. He fixed an eye to his companions. "A new inn, then?"

Nagarath returned the piercing gaze. A challenge? A warning. "Why? Have you a place to recommend? We have already set arrangements for here. We move on in the morning."

"Ah, yes, your Tour. Far be it from me to turn you from your path." Rodolfo leaned forward, covering the motion by reaching for his mug one more time. "Spell-piercers."

That his cryptic statement garnered no response seemed to surprise him all the more. Rodolfo frowned into his empty glass. "Come. Let us be off. I'll wait for you to gather your things."

"Again, friend, we are not about to be put out at this hour," Nagarath cautioned. He sensed Liara's increased alertness at the exchange. Her spine had grown straight, her fingers clenched and ready for action. He shifted, letting his shoulder come between her and the priest. Protection. And silent request that his apprentice do nothing rash.

"It is that good an inn?" Rodolfo said. "Though with the excellence of their repast, why should I be surprised? And you are correct, the hour is late. If you'll excuse me."

He rose and made his way through the thin crowd of hangers-on, hailing the other two priests.

"Come, Liara," Nagarath said through lips that hardly moved.

They rose, resisting the urge to look behind lest they attract more attention from the trio of clergymen. The corregidor had long gone—either to watch the streets or, more likely, home. They had gained the stairs when a familiar presence harrumphed close on their heels. Father Adessi had caught them up.

"There now," he said. "They've gone. I think we may safely speak of your profession and the danger it poses. Shall we return to the warmth of the hearth? Our host has offered to bend the rules of his house for the likes of me and my new companions. Come."

Liara made their decision for them. "What was it you called us? Spellpiercers?"

"Hsst . . . Not you. Them."

The girl's arch look mirrored Nagarath's thoughts exactly. They joined the priest by the fire, holding their questions until the inn-keep had strayed out of earshot.

"I take from your blank faces that you've never before heard of spellpiercers," Adessi began.

"Never, no," Nagarath said. He could see on Liara's face that she was less certain.

She confirmed his suspicions. "I think I saw the term once. In one of your books, Nagarath. But . . . the reference was skeptical—as unsure of the truth of the claim as you are of fairy stories."

"The skill is rare." Adessi nodded. "Or had been in the past until such folk were sought by us—what do you call us these days? Artless?—us ungifted with magick as a means of sniffing out those of you with the Art. A spellpiercer is, I suppose, an anti-mage, someone who can actually sense magick when it is used while being, themselves, unable to perform it."

"While well intended, your warning is unnecessary. One of the first things an apprentice learns to master is that of concealing their workings from other eyes. It is common practice for any mage doing magick in public to perform their spells blind—concealing their signature, their aura—so as to protect themselves from other magicians. Invisible workings simply cannot be seen—least of all by the Artless. No offense."

"Perhaps you misunderstand. These are individuals who can feel magick—even undetectable spells. They pierce that veil and report the perpetrator to the interested parties. In most cases, that means the local authorities, be it constable or clergy."

Unlike Nagarath, Liara seemed to be giving the claim some credit, although she, too, searched the priest's face for signs that he was being wildly inventive. His eyes gave back earnest concern and little else. So honest as to be un-trustworthy. For already Adessi had proven himself to be well-educated and well-traveled and, therefore, not easily fooled by base chicanery.

Still Nagarath snorted his disbelief.

Rodolfo continued, "Their claims are sometimes hard to prove, of course, but powerful ears have been listening, and it has gone poorly for many a hedge-witch and –wiz-ard."

"Oh, posh." Reclining back, Nagarath removed him-self from the conversation as best he could. His eye to the stairs, he wondered how to end this ridiculous encounter. The priest could cause more trouble by his suspicions than they might find by Nagarath's openly reading a book of spells at the table.

"Well, whether you believe me or not, you'd agree that there's been a frightful stir over magick use. If I were you, I'd be cautious until you can prove these rumors are nothing more than that."

"What you propose is impracticable, implausible, and impossible." Leaning forward, Nagarath jabbed the table in emphasis of each word. Liara's hand on his arm called him back to himself. He took a deep breath, closing his eyes. She was right. There was no need to make a scene just to prove that he was correct.

Liara put forth her own quiet objection. "The Artless are just that: people with no magickal gift whatsoever. To sense invisible workings is to have magick. Perhaps your spellpiercers are mages so desperate to conceal themselves they'd turn on their own."

"I'm only telling you what I've heard." Again, the sincerity in Adessi's eyes weighted his argument.

Nagarath knew better than to continue the debate. And, besides, did it even matter? They had seen how handily Adessi stepped between them and the local authorities, how he ingratiated himself with the inn-keep. Nagarath always encouraged Liara to trust folks. Could he not lead by example? He could always hex the two of them to safety should Father Rodolfo prove a false ally. Especially as Nagarath still considered the rumor of spellpiercers to be simply that: a rumor.

Chapter Fifteen

He could read the Green Language—as he had demon-strated the night of their gaining his acquaintance. That the priest was both well-traveled and well-connected had, too, been established. And he asked intelligent—and, at times, pointedly incisive—questions. Faced with such, Nagarath opted for simple honesty, promising Liara that he could witch them away at the first sign of trouble.

But trouble never came. Instead, Father Rodolfo made their way easy, happily adding his own expertise to their quest. For all that the empire followed Venice's lead in stamping out wizardry where it was found, Andalucía to the south held many legends of the Archmage Kerri'tarre. If there was a right path in seeking Khariton's Mirror, they were on it—his conclusion supported, in part, by their scrying of Anisthe in Nagarath's room in the dark of mid-night.

Nagarath's room. My room. For all the advantages of traveling with a priest—increased safety and less untoward scrutiny—Liara hated that it had prompted Nagarath to procure separate rooms two towns back. The mage insisted they act properly once Father Rodolfo decided to accom-pany them on their journey. "While our paths are so hap-pily aligned," Father Adessi had explained through one of his beaming smiles.

But for all the priest's influence, Nagarath continued to ward their rooms. They kept the secret between themselves lest their companion once more decided to lecture them on the dangers of spellpiercers. And so another day dawned, bright and boring, the only thrill the anticipated knock that reunited Liara with her wizard for all the waking hours.

Expected though it was, Liara jumped at the sound of Nagarath's summoning. "Come, Liara. Oh, and bring your wand."

Liara was thrilled to begin. But fear followed on the heels of her excited shiver. What if they were discovered? Did not they have more pressing things than this?

Liara pocketed her wand and followed Nagarath out into the quiet street. The day grew warm. Most everyone had retreated indoors, away from the glare of the sun. There were few witnesses to their trek into the countryside.

"In broad daylight, Nagarath?" Liara hurried along at the wizard's side, his long strides difficult for her to match.

He slowed—but only just. "There is similar danger in leaving you unskilled in the use of your wand, would you not agree? With Father Adessi pursuing other leads this morning, I thought we might get away with some practice in the wood. Apparently it is quite good for such, being enchanted itself."

"Enchanted?"

Nagarath's response was to quicken his steps.

The forest weaving through Limska Draga valley was old, borderline primordial. Perhaps because Liara had grown up at its edge, the woods of her homeland felt unremarkable. Or perhaps having become deeply acquainted with the wizard who lived at its heart had removed much of the mystery. But, for whatever the reason, Liara had never felt in awe of a wood as much as she did upon entering the forest of Cádiz for the first time.

Green and growing where Limska's was dark and shadowed, the trees grew fat and squat there. And where some might call the trees gnarled and twisted, Liara saw playful shapes and artful design. Labyrinthine paths wove through the low underbrush of ferns so bright they nearly glowed. Butterflies flitted from flower to flower. Birds chattered in the canopy.

The wizards' foray into the wood led them past a small brook. It gurgled cheerily along, a lucky find on so warm a day, even with the broken shade of the trees. Nagarath slowed to a stop, shading his eyes to view the bright sky. Stooping to drink, Liara paused, her palmful of water trickling out as Nagarath cleared his throat.

"What?" she challenged, then, "Oh!" Remembering countless stories she had read, she hurriedly wiped her hands on her shirt. "It's enchanted, too, isn't it?"

"I did not say as such . . ." Nagarath chuckled. "But I agree that it likely is." He crouched down by the stream's edge and ran his fingers through the tumbling water. Scooping some up, he drank, commenting, "It is refreshing, however."

"Nagarath!"

"Not all enchantment is bad, you do realize." Nagarath rose, running wet hands through his hair. "Tell me this does not feel like a most wholesome, vibrant wood . . ."

Liara nodded, warily bending to drink from the stream.

"A pity, this current political state. This wood has long been a home to mages and warlocks. The roots of these trees are steeped in the magicks they worked. Ancient as the age but new as a spring day. A perfect place to begin our lessons."

They had resumed their walk during Nagarath's lecture and came upon a clearing. There, mounds of lavender created a carpet of color. The knee-high shrubs filled the air with a sweet smell, and Liara breathed deep the scent. The butterflies that had dotted the forest flowers gathered in force across the open space, their bright wings catching the warm sunlight.

Taking in the myriad hues, Liara lost track of the wizard. She turned to find him perched on a large rock, book in hand, magick lesson temporarily forgotten. Grinning, she took off at a run, scattering birds and insects as the tall grass whipped at her skirts. Out in the full sunshine, surrounded on all sides by the song of the forest, she flung herself onto her back and stared up at the sky.

"Wand lessons. Sunshine. An enchanted wood. Life is perfect," she mused, closing her eyes with a happy sigh.

Resting against the sun-warmed stone, Nagarath felt the protest fade from his aching limbs. Further inland—away from the sea with its damp, the constant rock of a ship torturing newly knit bones—he had begun to think he might actually heal, after all. *Mayhap we'll find the mirror and then . . . What? And then Anisthe will come for us.*

Discomfited by the thought, Nagarath looked up from his book just in time to see Liara tumble down into the foliage.

Dislike of Father Rodolfo aside, Liara seemed lighter, happier of late. It was as though a burden had lifted from her, the questioning fear which had haunted her had begun to heal. Much as his own injuries were.

It was catching, her enthusiasm. And he was glad for it, glad to have his little magpie returned at last. And while magick was not something to be bartered for, a reward for a job well done, it added to Nagarath's desire to teach her the Art. She was a good soul. Young. Still green in spite of her prodigious talent. *Young. Ha! She's—what—ten, eleven years your junior, Nagarath? You might yet learn something from her, you know.*

Nagarath called to Liara. She needed no second bidding. Wand at the ready, she approached, eager to begin her apprenticeship.

"Remember, Liara, a wand is an extension of the self."

The sun had arced its way across the clearing during the lesson. And, while the late afternoon was still bright, it seemed to Liara that the mage's words came from a place of shadow. Her fire of excitement had been quenched by repeated mistakes of form, of intent, and even—shame of shames—of pronunciation. Things she had known before seemed to flee her poor overtaxed brain. Apparently, no amount of eagerness or natural talent could make her good at using a wand.

Her teacher continued, "Early mages, in fact, used to magick their hands to give their fingers extra length and thinness. A rune drawn by hand"—Nagarath drew an inert figure in the air, leaving behind a glowing outline—"lacks the same definition as one drawn with the aid of a wand."

He drew a complicated rune in the air with his wand. "As magick grew more complex, wizards required more precision. And as magickal theory progressed, the demands of spells grew to a point that it only made sense to imbue wands with a certain amount of power."

"Which means that not all wands are the same, per the Laws of Magick," Liara interjected.

"Correct. Things are no longer as simple as they once were, say two or three hundred years ago. Mages are stingier with their power. And with good reason. The Art has developed enough to be competitive and also dangerous in the hands of the wrong individual. While it can be hard to prevent a wizard from going rogue or using their skills for dastardly purposes, it serves a mage well to protect such a personal item as a wand. Yours, Liara, comes to you with much of that already in place, it having a history of its own."

Liara looked at the wand in her hand, trying to read the worn wood. She examined its gentle taper, tested the comfortable heft.

"Believe me when I tell you, that wand can cast spells. We're just working to connect you to it. It is not a natural thing to learn. I had trouble with it myself when it came into my possession many years back."

Looking up sharply, Liara searched Nagarath's face. Had she deprived him of his own wand? That made no sense. He had a wand.

"Though the gesture is now excessively old-fashioned, it used to be that a master magus would gift his wand to the apprentice for whom he held the most regard, or felt had the most promise." Nagarath seemed to disappear into the past. Though he looked at the wand in Liara's hand, she could tell that he was actually seeing something else, another hand holding the wand in another time. He confirmed it with his next words: "This wand once belonged to Archmage Cromen. And before him, a Master Lumin; Magus Hennypin—contemporary of Hew Draper who, I'm sure, you know; Praecantator Cabal; Master Ryn'ne; Adalgisa Engel . . ."

Nagarath blinked and returned to the present. "Sorry, the official records are somewhere—luckily not in the wreckage of Parentino. Suffice it to say, that wand has been held by many an accomplished wizard and witch, Liara. It might take more work than most to get used to, but I would not have you use any wand less worthy." Nagarath paused and then whipped his wand out. "Again?"

Liara nodded. She then destroyed a nearby tree with her next attempt to follow Nagarath's lead.

Nagarath eyed the tree with chagrin. "Well, I suppose that could be useful. With a little aim."

"It's like it just gets away from me!" Liara covered her face and groaned. "It's as if it's not my wand, as if I shouldn't be using it. Is it possible that I'm all wrong for it?"

"Did I not just say that it might be difficult to adjust to such an artifact, given its provenance?" Nagarath growled the words as he approached. Liara feared she'd found the end of his patience.

He nodded curtly, asking with a mere look that she return to form. Liara did so, feeling oddly exposed as stern eyes raked over her, a flood of lecturing words again damming up under the mage's silence. He gently prodded at her wrist with thumb and forefinger, testing the tension with which she held the wand and making minute adjustments to her grip. The strange intimacy of the moment caused Liara to flush. She shied away, lowering the wand.

Nagarath's eyebrows bunched together. He seemed both hurt and puzzled. "There is something else bothering you, Liara. You can tell me, you know."

"I'm fine. My wrist is just tired," Liara snapped. She turned from him to put the wand back into its box, ending the lesson.

Just as her euphoria had affected Nagarath before their disastrous wand lesson, Liara's sulking had similar repercussions on his mood. He spent the entirety of their walk back into town thinking over her clumsy use of Cromen's wand. She had good form—for a novice. And she always had incredible control over her magick no matter her emotional state. His mind roved back over the memory of their confrontation in Parentino, minutes before the catalogue's explosion. It was almost as if Liara could turn anger into fuel for her sorcery.

There are no less than five trees in the woods outside of Antequera that can attest to that. A brief misgiving shook him. *Unfair, Nagarath. You said you would teach her. Teach her!*

Perhaps Liara's trouble was merely frustration and nothing more. For this he could not fault her. What did it matter that the utilization of artifacts typically came easy for most mages? Indeed many wizards looked no further than the end of their wand and slipped into obscurity due to their limited perspective and skill. Liara had always cut her own path.

"You already knew Father Rodolfo!" Liara broke the silence in a manner most typical of her: unexpectedly.

Nagarath hid his smile and shook his head. "Sorry, no. Happenstance does not fall so thickly in my path. He is merely a fellow intellectual, someone with whom, under different circumstances, I might have been great friends. Much like Father Phenlick."

"Oh."

And with that, the uneasy quiet returned.

Nagarath cursed his thoughtless tongue. Following their encounter with Krešimir, Nagarath had, at last, told Liara all he'd learned scrying in Dvigrad. All. Phenlick's dispatch to Rome; Krešimir had been the messenger to carry it. Waiting for the letter's response had saved his life. In the end, Phenlick's honest plea for advice after Liara's banishment had been what had drawn Venice's attention back to the Limska Draga valley. Liara had received the unwelcome report with a tight-lipped calm that belied her heartache. Phenlick's name had not come up in conversation since.

Nagarath regretted his words, of course. But more than that, he regretted the change in their traveling arrangements. Alone together in the Cádiz forest, he had felt a shadow of former times. Such stolen moments were over all too swiftly. They never had time to talk. And with having to pay for two rooms every night . . . His money would not last forever.

World Tour. Bah. He had already done as much in the years following his aborted apprenticeship. In the dark days following Anisthe's accident—one in which Nagarath himself had been complicit—he had wasted himself, contemplating a turn from magick altogether. But his eternal love for the Art had drawn him back, eventually landing him in quiet Limska Draga.

And it was this difference between him and Liara that preyed upon his mind whenever the girl seemed too eager to give up. To Nagarath, the Art of Magick was life itself, the only way for him to be. To Liara it was a means to an end, much as it had always been to Anisthe.

"I'm sorry to have wasted your afternoon when we could have better spent the time scrying Anisthe. Do you think we can try again with the wands tomorrow?"

Surprised by Liara's query, Nagarath simply nodded. Their time had not been squandered. "If you think that I am not overtaxing you, then yes. For we still have other spells to perform, provided that I can arrange for a quiet moment without Father Rodolfo's interference."

"Oh, I feel quite fine, actually," Liara hurried to reassure him. "I've been thinking about the oddities of Anisthe's signature. It doesn't feel like him. Slippery and sideways, it could be from an artifact, similar to how he put his power into the amber pendant. It's too weak to be the mirror's magick, at least."

Nagarath frowned. Liara had gone from avoiding scrying Anisthe to eagerly keeping watch. And now here she was, inconstant in the matter of learning how to use a wand—magick that she had long begged of him. Mercurial. Worrisome. Much as the changes in Anisthe's aura were proving.

He said, "I would like to scry this time and you watch."

"Oh."

Sighing, Nagarath fixed his eyes upon the road, grateful they were approaching the outskirts of the tiny town. Mercurial. *And I'm not?*

To be honest, the day had been a disaster. Perhaps he should scry the war mage on his own time. Better than entertaining any more of Liara's wild theories. Liara, who couldn't use a wand correctly.

That is uncharitable, Nagarath. His ill temper was getting the better of him.

Anisthe had not moved in days. They could leave him be for one night. And mayhap Nagarath could encourage Father Rodolfo to talk to Liara, to come to some sort of peace.

His apprentice might have control over her Art, but a troubled heart would always interfere with magick. Nagarath wondered what Archmage Cromen would have done in his place. Likely he would have forced his pupil to cast until her fingers bled, or she was so exhausted of magick that they had to leave off.

With that realization, Nagarath concluded he really did not want to be the taskmaster this new arrangement seemed to demand.

Father Rodolfo waited for them in the common room as they entered the inn. His eyes bespoke trouble, and the priest had gathered not only his belongings, but theirs as well.

"What is it?" Nagarath kept his voice low, setting his eyes to the door. Liara trained her attention on that which led to the kitchens.

Adessi begged silence with a finger on his lips. An inclination of his head prompted them to take their things and follow him.

"What is it? What's going on?" Liara did not heed the priest's warning, and Nagarath found himself trembling at the fear in her voice.

"We're leaving," Adessi said simply. "The carriage outside? It waits for us."

"But why—?"

"Because you were seen!" Adessi whirled on them.

The last of the blood drained from Liara's face. "So they know we were doing magick?"

"Inconclusive."

"Doubtful."

Both Nagarath and Rodolfo spoke at once.

Nagarath stepped between the priest and his ward, a belated attempt at shielding Liara from wrath, from guilt.

Adessi noted the movement and gave ground, lowering his voice. "I thought it wise for us to take to the road as soon as possible lest rumor lead to action on the part of our adversaries."

Together they hurried into the street.

Chapter Sixteen

Liara sat herself back against the hard seat of the coach, trying to avoid Father Rodolfo's gaze. If he noted her ire, he made no mention of it, instead focusing on Nagarath with his news. "So, while you have sought the mage—amongst your other magickal pursuits of the day—I have sought the mirror. Nobody was going to second-guess my asking over old folk tales and legends."

A part of Liara wanted to accuse the priest of having forced them on the run. After all, if spellpiercers did not actually exist—as Nagarath firmly maintained—then their none-too-subtle clergyman companion had likely exposed them.

"I believe that I have managed to trace your magicked mirror to a family near Lebrija to the east," said Father Rudolfo.

Nagarath leaned forward, his answering excitement tangible in the small carriage. "How far?"

"Three, maybe four days' ride."

Settling onto the uncomfortable seat as best she could, Liara fell into an uneasy slumber. In it, spells she could not cast and men who could sense her failure filled her dreams.

~*~

Gone was the cheer from their evening meals. Long days riding on rough roads, comfortless carriages, and tense evenings of looking over shoulders made for somber companions. But Father Rodolfo insisted that his information regarding the mirror was a solid lead. His presence made far better cover than Nagarath's stupid stories, often turning the suspicious glowers of strangers into smiles. Where once she might have feared the priest was leading them into some sort of trap, Liara felt a grudging trust building.

It also helped that, unbeknownst to the priest, Liara and Nagarath continued to scry Anisthe when given the chance.

And no spellpiercers have come knocking; no corregidores chased us from their townships, Liara happily noted. Which meant, also, that Nagarath insisted on some degree of wand lessons in the dark of night within the privacy of their rooms.

These proved as torturous as her first attempt in the Cádiz forest, and she quickly found herself siding with Adessi's cautionary ban on magick. It allowed her to avoid her growing fears. She found herself pushed away from Nagarath and closer to Adessi as each sensed the change in her.

Liara felt certain of what was wrong with her. Her heart told her to confess to Nagarath. He'd know what to do.

But then, I already know myself. The argument played in Liara's head over and over. Each bump and twist of the carriage bench beneath her knocked on her conscience. She would have to act. And soon. The guilt would destroy her before long.

And so it was that on the third day of traveling to Lebrija, Father Rodolfo caught Liara with her guard down and drew her confession. The mage had exited the carriage, Adessi making no move to follow. Liara, too, had stayed put.

Nagarath had done this on one other occasion so far. When pressed, he had given a grudging answer that he had needed to see the moneychanger before they secured food and bed for the night. He mumbled something about wanting to protect their monetary circumstances from the prying eyes of innkeepers.

Liara figured he must be using sorcery. Wisely, she chose not to press the issue. She'd rather not think of how Nagarath funded their travels. Willful ignorance was not as carefree as she had expected, however. In the carriage, she frowned her concern, eliciting a comment from the priest.

"He'll be back momentarily, my dear," Father Rodolfo reassured, his guessed reasons at her unease happily far from the mark. It did not matter that she disliked Adessi. She could never confess her suspicions as to Nagarath's activities.

"Liara. May I ask what it is I did to have you dislike me so?"

Father Rodolfo's voice came quietly, carrying no note of reproof or accusation. So why did she feel such guilt over the question? Liara sighed. "I appreciate what you've done for Nagarath and me. And it's not like I don't like you. I just don't want to like you. Because people like you are wonderful and kind and believe yourselves to have your heart in the right place. And then you go and hurt people like me."

" 'People like you.' 'People like me' . . ." Rodolfo paused, seeming to muse over the words. "You refer to George Phenlick."

The name hit Liara like a slap across the face. Nodding mutely, she lowered her gaze, wondering when Nagarath had found the time to tell Adessi about Dvigrad's priest outside of her hearing. Suspicion rose, then fell. 'People like you.' She ought to have realized how incisive, how very like her Father Phenlick, this priest would be.

"For what it's worth, I believe Father Phenlick did not betray you."

Liara did not answer. More lies upon lies. Of course he had betrayed her. The countryside had been crawling with the proof. She let her silence speak for her.

"Did he write to Rome and send word of you and Nagarath? Yes. But did you not experience, first hand, his kindness and understanding when everyone else in your village feared your gift? Why would you think him changed, a false friend, based on the reactions of others to his letter? Did not your fellow townsfolk hear his words, watch his regard for you, and nonetheless come to their own conclusions, one quite opposite his own?"

"If he knew how it would turn out, how he might be misunderstood, why even do it at all?"

"Because, child, from what I know of George Phenlick—from Nagarath's words and others'—he believed in the good in everyone. To him, his letter would be read just as it was intended, an honest plea for assistance and a recount of the wrongs committed by the guard. Such results as it triggered surely never even crossed his mind. Foolish, yes. But not the actions of a false friend."

"But then why write to Rome? It was an idiotic thing to do. He wouldn't have done such a stupid thing if he cared."

Rodolfo raised his eyebrows at her bitter denunciation. "And you've never done a stupid thing because you cared so much for another?"

With a shiver, Liara's old guilt surfaced under the priest's words. She had done the opposite: attack and harm out of a misguided sense of right, her greatest shame. She knew she had carried it most of her life, if she really stopped to think about it. Even under Father Phenlick's care, she'd been a thief and liar, feeding a reckless sense of entitlement until reality had cut her down.

I've a dark heart. It's why I always expect the worst in folk. And why I can't see the world as Phenlick had. Liara wondered anew why anyone had presented her with kindness.

Father Rodolfo misread her silence. "You do understand that by separating 'people like you' from 'people like me,' you are putting up as many barriers as those who persecute those who practice your Art."

Liara shifted uncomfortably on the hard bench. What Adessi said sounded altogether too similar to what Father Phenlick had always preached. Again, she wondered what Father Rodolfo's game was and why Nagarath seemed unbothered by the man.

"When I was a child, I wanted to be a mage." Liara looked up sharply at Adessi's confession, ready to spot the lie, the jest at her expense. He smiled at her surprise and continued. "You think such a youthful ambition incompatible with my calling. Perhaps your experience with Father

Phenlick would have you condemn all those who wear the trappings of a clergyman and my point is lost upon you."

"No. But, isn't witchcraft considered evil?"

"How is it that you perform magick, Liara? By using something within yourself—something you did not put there nor choose. A gift, the mages call it, yes? Can it be used to sin, to hurt others? To cheat or lie? Most certainly." Father Adessi leaned backwards, crossing his hands complacently and shutting his eyes. "But do not all men have the capacity for evil, mage-craft aside? Is not love of comfort, greed, lust, excess equally damning? How is it you use your power, Liara?"

Silence descended upon the carriage.

Uncomfortable, sensing a trap, Liara glanced out the tiny window, praying for Nagarath's return.

Adessi drew her attention back. "My uncle was a mage—or near enough. He was apprenticed in the Art, though he never advanced very far in his studies—at least not as far as I, a child, would have hoped. He could do some spells but nothing flashy or impressive. He had no desire to."

Rodolfo leaned forward now, intent. "I credit his mage-craft with leading me to my calling, young miss. As I grew out of childhood fancies, I learned to respect his attention to life. His philosophy, if you will. He was educated, thoughtful, and loving. Much of his sensitivities came as a direct result of his studies. His personal theology—a desire to improve himself, enrich the world around him with his talents—well aligned to what I found in priesthood. Perhaps, I might not have ever learned it had I not talked with him to great extent."

"Nagarath is a good man—with or without his magick."

"Indeed he is. And intelligent, loving, and thoughtful as my own imperfect wizard ever was. And yours has had to overcome difficult hurdles, has confronted far deeper hurts." Father Rodolfo's voice softened, aware that he was speaking to the purveyor of said pain. "Hurts that in a lesser man might have done ill."

"He shouldn't be teaching me. Magick, I mean. I shouldn't learn it because it's too dangerous." The words burst out of her before Liara could draw them back.

"My dear, if danger stopped us from doing things, nothing would ever be done." Father Rodolfo chuckled. "Even my calling has its moments of peril."

"No. You don't understand. I'm not talking about the magick. I'm talking about me," Liara cried, checking the tiny window of their carriage and, this time, hoping Nagarath was nowhere near. Or perhaps she did want him nearby, coming upon her objections by accident so that she did not have to voice them to his face.

"What about you?" Adessi frowned, alert now. At least he was taking her fears seriously.

"I . . . I can't say." Suddenly shy, faced with having to say her shortcoming aloud, Liara tried to avoid the issue. "But it's bad. I would know; I was Nagarath's librarian before I was his apprentice so I've seen every possible book on my . . . my problem. All I can tell you is that he oughtn't teach me magick. Deep down, I'm not all those things that Nagarath is and that with magick—true power—I might become the sort of magus worth hunting. I'm afraid. I'm . . . lesser."

"Can you tell him?"

"If I could have faced him, I already would have."

"But you can tell me?"

He had a point. Liara? Confessing the secrets of her heart to someone she had, but minutes ago, claimed to dislike and distrust?

"I had to tell someone. And I thought—I thought that if you knew there was a problem, you could try to convince Nagarath to put a halt on our lessons until—"

"Lessons!"

There. Now she had said too much. Liara tried to back out of the confession. "I mean, when he comes 'round to teaching me. Once we're safe again from the . . . spellpiercers."

"The spellpiercers, yes." Father Rodolfo's gaze was keen.

For a moment, Adessi focused his eyes on hidden thoughts, reasoning with some inner voice. Finally, he spoke. "I will do what you ask. Provided you promise me that, in return, you talk to your friend about what really is vexing you."

"I can't . . . yet. But I will. I promise." Liara nodded fervently. She felt hot tears begin to flood her cheeks as Father Rodolfo reached to give her hand a gentle, reassuring squeeze. Guilt? Far from it. Father Rodolfo had just granted her absolution.

~*~

True to his word, the priest found a way, via his usual inquiries, to introduce them to a gentleman who hailed from the Espina family—historically, the family which had inherited Khariton's Mirror, descendants of the line who had inspired Snow White's tale. The ease with which

Adessi found companionship—earning trust from a man he had never met and transferring said trust to two vagabond mages—had Liara wondering, at long last, how many people Father Rodolfo knew in all the wide world. She could guess the number to be well past the population of Dvigrad or even Vrsar.

But Adessi's lead proved to be a dead end.

As it turned out, the Espina family was not the same family spoken of in the ancient story. That line had long died out, its effects sold and scattered far and wide. The mirror was long gone—provided it had even existed.

The gentleman who they met for supper had little practical information to give, not believing in magick himself. The ancient line and the power they had claimed: rumor and myth and nothing more. The trio of travelers returned to the inn of Lebrija, only to find there were but two rooms to be had, meaning that Liara and Nagarath would once more be sharing.

Pulse quickening as she recalled her confession to Adessi from earlier in the day, Liara feared her reckoning had come.

But, first, scrying. At least that did not require the use of a wand.

Since making landfall, Anisthe's movements had generally mirrored theirs, if two to three days delayed. However, that day they learned he had apparently struck out in a direction of his own rather than continue to follow along their path. Intent on the dish, like Nagarath, Liara strained to hear Anisthe's words. She wondered anew at the mysterious servant to whom he spoke.

"Did he say something about a library?" The word had pricked at her ears, and Liara shot a glance to Nagarath, looking away from the shining bowl.

"What about it?" Nagarath was slow to meet her gaze.

"Well, books! They might have more answers. Before finding out about the Espina family, Adessi mentioned a massive archive of records in Madrid. Didn't he? We can go there and sort tale from truth."

"Madrid." Nagarath sighed, looking worn. Waving his hand over the scrying vessel, he ended the spell and moved to make ready for bed. Liara could tell from the stiffness in his movements that his bones were aching again, something he clearly did not want her to know. "Then we go tomorrow."

The snuffing of the wizard's magelight left Liara to her dark thoughts. Over and over, she played out in her mind ways to avoid the awful truth about herself, about what she would have to reveal per her promise to Father Rodolfo.

The promise to me, to magick itself. Closing her eyes to the truth, Liara sought sleep. Perhaps when they reached Madrid . . . Perhaps the next time Nagarath tried to corner her for wand lessons . . .

Predictably, sleep chose to evade her troubled mind. The night had grown long when Liara ventured, "Nagarath?"

No answer. So he slept then . . .

Good, she would wait until morning.

"Mm?" Nagarath turned and yawned.

"Oh. Sorry." Liara felt stupid for having woke him.

"I was not quite asleep, Liara," Nagarath yawned again, teasing, "but I was resting soundly."

Liara slumped back into her pillow.

Now or never. She bolstered her courage.

"The wand. I know what I'm doing wrong." Her voice came out tiny, guilty.

"Yes?"

Taking a shuddering breath, Liara loosed the words, "I think I'm left-handed."

Even in the dark, she could feel the shock that went through Nagarath upon hearing her horrible words. She pictured him recoiling from her and, before he could speak, had buried her face in the covers with a sob.

"Oh, my poor little magpie . . ."

She froze. He was supposed to hate her for this. Well-schooled in magickal theory and history, she knew what stigma this carried. Even if she practiced, tried to go against her natural instincts, the fact would remain underneath it all, stamped on her magickal inclinations. Left-handed. Shadow to the light. An easy explanation for all the terrible misdeeds she had done.

"But you write with your right hand, Liara. I have seen it." Through her tomb of pillows and bedding, she heard him approach. She felt the bed creak from his weight as he sat upon its edge. What comfort could he give? He couldn't very well go ahead with her apprenticeship knowing what he did. That was as good as asking her to go rogue.

"I'm sorry," she whispered, at last daring to look up at him. "I tried and tried but . . . I could tell it just felt backwards. It's somehow different than holding a pen."

At her side, Nagarath nodded sagely. A part of her wanted to scream, supply the anger that, surely, he must feel. How could he be so calm in the face of such a disaster?

No, not calm, unreadable. Trembling, Liara did not move from her buried place in the bed.

"I'm glad you told me. It makes a bit more sense now, the trouble you were having." Nagarath's hand hovered over her a moment, hunting, before gently patting her shoulder. She wondered if he was remembering now the times Liara had approached their lessons, switching the wand over to her right hand before beginning. Had he even noticed?

He paused, an eternity. Taking a deep breath he offered, "You know . . . it might be best if I just teach you regardless. See what happens . . ."

"What?"

"Yes. I'll still teach you. Liara, I know you. This will work out. I promise."

Liara nodded, trying not to fix her eyes on the scar on Nagarath's chin. A scar she inflicted.

This man trusted her, believed in her.

Why?

Chapter Seventeen

Liara woke to a hand covering her mouth. Nagarath's. She locked eyes with the mage. They were not alone in the room. In the muted light of pre-dawn, Liara saw Rodolfo Adessi's worry from six paces off. He said, "Come, we must hurry."

A quick glance about informed Liara that her bag had been packed.

"No time for that," Nagarath read her look. With a wave of his wand, he whisked his own cloak off his shoulders and over Liara's.

Adessi went to the window and attempted to see out without moving the curtain. "I would head into Castilla la Nueva. The region surrounding Madrid, to the north and to the east, tends to keep its own counsel. Venice's influence in matters of magick ought not to have reached there."

"If rumor is to be believed," Nagarath inserted.

"Yes, yes, of course." Adessi waved off the gentle remonstrance, whispering his hurried advice, "And I would hold off on any magick—private or otherwise—until you have set your own ears about the place."

"You're coming with," Liara deftly turned her question into a statement. She would not stand to part company. Too many had been left behind. If she and Nagarath were in trouble, Adessi was equally so.

"Now, my girl—" Adessi started, jumping as angry footfalls rang down the hallway outside.

The cinnabar stone atop Nagarath's staff bathed the room in its eerie red light. Liara shouldered her belongings and clasped the wizard's forearm, steeling herself for the spell. The mage held out a hand to Father Rodolfo, an invitation.

Smiling sadly, the priest shook his head. "There's little they dare do to me. I'll be fine, truly."

The men in the hallway had reached their room. The door shook with the pounding of fists and angry orders. "Open up in the name of the corregidor!"

"Please," Liara gave one more plea to Father Rodolfo.

"Get yourself somewhere safe, if there is such a place for those of your Art. Godspeed."

The door burst open . . . and then disappeared in the sparkling whirlwind of Nagarath's spell.

"Go back. We need to go back." Liara's fists beat upon Nagarath's arm. Her tear-stained face was the first thing he saw upon their arrival . . . where?

"Hush." Nagarath signaled for silence. He peered about them in the darkness of predawn. Thick clouds blackened the sky in that part of the country. Somewhere off in the distance, a barking dog. Brush whispered about the knees.

But nobody came running. No angry shouts reached Nagarath's strained ears.

Safe. Relatively, at the least.

Liara had quieted, leaning into Nagarath's arm. She whispered, "Will he be safe?"

"Of course." Nagarath tightened his jaw to the lie, setting his eyes elsewhere. He knew no such thing. Once he and Liara found themselves new lodgings, he might attempt to learn Adessi's fate, but to scry the priest seemed wrong. They would have to take the continued safety of the priest on faith.

And did not throw us to the wolves as consequence of saving himself, Nagarath noted, doing his best to keep worry from his face. It felt uncharitable to even think such of the pleasant Father Adessi. Uncharitable yet practical.

"I wonder . . ." Nagarath let the half-sentence hang in the air unfinished. He stared ahead of him, unseeing. Whether they had truly then escaped danger or not, whether the spellpiercers were real or rumor, could be answered by a simple question: did Father Rodolfo Adessi tell the truth?

"Can we risk a fire?" Liara shivered in her borrowed wizard's robes.

"Yes, of course." Nagarath smiled. Under his expert hands, a clearing was made upon the hilltop, makeshift seating was procured, and a fire soon crackled into being. Together, he and Liara waited for the dawn. She slumped into an easy sleep before long.

Castilla la Nueva. Having within it some of the last holdings of magickal books and histories. Nagarath scoffed. Trusting to hearsay again. Did they dare question folk? They must. Carefully, for again, such was unfamiliar territory—even for him—and their questions might draw greater scrutiny.

A shiver broke over Nagarath's back. He could harrumph and dismiss Adessi's claims all he wanted. However, something told him that the rumors of spellpiercers were not unfounded. Fear may have inspired doubts of their friend's trustworthiness, but logic prevailed. They had traveled together. They had broken bread and traded in secrets. Rodolfo would have had nothing to gain from treachery. Which meant that the priest, at least, believed spellpiercers to be a real threat, which made for an invisible enemy. Thank the gods that Anisthe had decided to travel northward days before.

The sky lightened in measures. With it, Nagarath could see more of the rolling hills about them. Sparse and shaggy growth dotted the dusty ground. His heart leapt as he saw the thin, ribboning road in the distance. He hadn't deposited them anywhere too remote, then.

Nagarath moved to wake his apprentice, stopping short to watch her sleep a moment longer. Apprentice. You yourself could be branded a rogue for teaching her. Irresponsible. Unrespectable.

He was pretty sure nobody had ever apprenticed a left-handed pupil in all of magick. It simply was Not Done. Which begged the question: was the stigma simply that? If nobody had attempted to teach one of sinistral tendencies, then how were they to know the results? Nagarath, for one, was academically curious if Liara's preference for one hand over the other would produce any interesting side effects.

But, later. They must first find out where they were and how to get to where they needed to be: the archive in Madrid.

~*~

Father Rodolfo had been correct. The prosecution of magick users had not reached that province. The archives

222

of Madrid still recognized the authority of Nagarath's robes of power—surprising in that age. But, likewise archaic, women were not allowed to view the collection.

"I am so sorry, Liara. They simply do not let the fairer sex into the archives."

"You're not serious are you?" Liara spluttered, "But you need me!"

"You think I do not know that?" Sighing, Nagarath spread his hands in hopeless innocence. "What would you like me to do? Steal a book? Not use the archive?"

"Bring me with. You would if I were a boy."

"I cannot." Nagarath echoed her whine, feeling foolish and himself implicated. He served the system that sparked such idiotic rules. Liara was twice the librarian any of these stodgy old men would likely prove to be.

"You know, for an all-powerful wizard . . ." Liara began her old argument.

". . . I have a decided lack of imagination," Nagarath finished with her. "Yes, yes. I know, Liara. I—"

It occurred to him what Liara wasn't saying, and he blushed. "Absolutely not!"

"Why not?" Liara wheedled. "You can do it, right? The Transformation Process—Complete with Illustrations; Transform Yourself, Illusions to Help One Pass as a Member of the Fairer Sex; Change Your Life for the Better and—"

"All right. I need you with me. And . . . precedent is there, as your spotless memory proves." Nagarath gave her a small smile. "But I will be the one laying the ground rules on this endeavor. One: we need to make the change outside the city. Two: I will disguise myself as well to avoid suspicion. Three: we do this as quickly as possible and end the spell. No dallying or roving Madrid as anyone other than ourselves."

He concluded with a simple and rather gruff, "Come on then."

~*~

Liara really wished she had a mirror. Giggling, she skipped along the path, greatly enjoying the freedom of trousers. Shaking her head, Liara felt the unfamiliar short blonde hair brush the nape of her neck and tips of her ears and grinned again.

"I guess I hadn't really thought I'd feel different," Liara marveled, reveling in the deeper timbre of her voice.

Nagarath strode alongside. "If anyone asks—and I am sure they will—you are my apprentice, Michael, son of Nathaniel Clemson of Venezia."

"And who're you?" Liara asked, lips twinging as she again fought a mirthful smile.

"Mordan. Archmage from Florence." Glancing at his smaller, more aged hands, Nagarath hesitated before adding, "My main specialty is alchemy—though, from the look of things, I may claim that as my past specialty."

"That is quite a detailed disguise," Liara observed, raising an eyebrow.

Nagarath frowned. "Come, Liara, you of all people know the secret to a good lie is the addition of a few key details. And don't correct your Master, Michael."

Nagarath indicated his changed appearance. "For example, I need to have a good reason for bringing along an apprentice to such a collection. Appearing as a wizard past my prime, I can bring young Michael along to help in my research."

"Past your prime?" Liara eyed the wizard's shortened and aged form critically. "You haven't changed that much. You're shorter, yes."

"And older!" Nagarath fiddled with the grey edges of his hair.

"Oh, well, you've always been old," she said. She noted Nagarath's crushed look and tried to soften the remark. "I'm sure the biggest change to me is my hair."

The wizard's snort informed her that this might not entirely be the case.

~*~

The archivist completely ignored Michael.

At first his total dismissal of Archmage Mordan's assistant annoyed Liara, but this soon gave way to relief, as she worried she would give up the game with a wrong gesture or slip of the tongue.

It turned out Nagarath was quite a natural at playing the ruse. Yes, he had told any number of white lies around her, but he dove into the persona of another human being with surprising vigor.

In addition to the alteration of height created by his illusionary spell, the man had adopted a different gait—not quite a limp but definitely not the hearty, lively step of the Wizard Nagarath. And though she had dismissed the changes to his face, Liara had found herself taken aback by the transformation, briefly believing that old injuries had returned.

The eyes bothered her most. While Nagarath's eyes were the same steely grey, he'd somehow managed to take the sparkle out of them. He appeared as someone gently approaching the twilight of his life after reading too many books for far too many years.

Likely his own future. Liara again thought of her comment on Nagarath's age. Mentally sidestepping her careless remark, she concentrated on the roles they were playing.

Watching Nagarath try to work, she wondered how much of the frailty was an act and how much was the limitations of the rather decrepit body Nagarath had adopted. Aged hands shook while the wizard turned the pages of a book. For someone as precise as Nagarath, such an infirmity would be frustrating.

She moved to help.

With an impatient shake of his head, he moved the book further out of her reach.

"Boy, you would be of use fetching things for me here," he wheezed. "You remember that artifact I told you about? See what they have on it. I hear they have the most extensive holdings on the Continent for that sort of thing. Came all the way from Pola to enjoy this fine, fine collection, we did. Marvelous. Haven't seen the like in all my days."

Nagarath looked over to the librarian, making sure his compliment had been noted.

Shooed away, Liara almost missed the wink Nagarath tossed her way. His playful sparkle returned for the briefest of moments.

Liara went to discuss their needs with the keeper of the records. Swallowing her trepidation, she gave the story she and Nagarath had concocted along their way back into the city. It seemed she passed the test. The librarian nodded along and then took his leave with a look that bordered on boredom.

Waiting for the librarian's return, Liara watched Nagarath painfully peer at page after page, impatiently switching from one book to another, some of his slovenly habits shining through at last. *Their system does keep items safe from the likes of him.*

Liara smiled as the librarian placed selected items on the table. She hoisted the cover on the first book with a contented sigh. Liara could imagine a happy little lifetime in that one moment. The two of them sitting together within the heavy stone walls, a pile of leather-bound codices by their sides, solving the great magickal mysteries of the ages . . .

Frowning, Liara concentrated on the current problem, Khariton's Mirror. Looking over to the stack of books at her elbow, her frown deepened. *Either they keep an exceptionally clean collection, or these particular books have been recently used.*

Peering at the top edges of the spines more closely, Liara guessed the latter. There were more fingerprints than the librarian's. The pages had been recently rifled.

Liara rose and approached the librarian. "Pardon me, but someone else used these books recently, am I correct?"

"Indeed. The gentleman came in, maybe five days ago. 'Researching an ancient family heirloom' was his story."

"Oh?"

"Family heirloom, bah. Yes, the man spoke with a French accent, but I doubt the mirror was actually his."

"Do you know who he was, then?"

The librarian's face closed. "How should I know! The countryside has been crawling with French swine ever since their king got it into his head that he ought to have the mirror. Until your master spoke, I thought you one of them." The librarian glanced toward the aged mage. "Did you need any other books?"

"No, I think I have what I need." Liara backed away, noting Mordan's disapproving frown.

With a secret smile, she took her seat under Nagarath's stern gaze, cowering meekly as the mage chastised his apprentice for bothering the librarian and for violating the silent sanctity of the library.

He's wondrous good at this. Liara missed Nagarath's cheerful ease.

Nagarath found it excessively difficult to reign in his excitement once Liara returned to him with her news. Trust her to find out what they needed. Nagarath certainly had no luck. Still, he peered ineffectively at the old texts a while longer. There were books to be enjoyed.

Breathing as deep as his aged lungs would allow, Nagarath lost himself in memory, for a moment feeling as old as his magick proclaimed him to be. He had missed it so. Books. Quiet. Might this be his future? Might he be left in silent contemplation of the mysteries of the universe, soaking up the knowledge of the ages, and entering into twilight unmolested by noise and danger and . . .

A sharp jab woke Nagarath, and he blinked his watery eyes to his surroundings.

"You'd dozed off," Liara whispered, looking around anxiously.

The library of Madrid. Nagarath remembered. "Come, I think I've done all that I might today."

Summoning his dignity and gripping his staff, Nagarath rose and, with Liara's aid, tottered from the imposing building on sleep-weakened legs. Thus they went, straight through the city and outward into the country, Nagarath's gait, though still troubled, strengthening as they walked.

Soon it was just the two of them on the dusty road. Well, two wizards and a stray sheep here and there. Distantly, Nagarath wondered how long Mordan's legs would carry him. Liara had been right to call him "old" earlier in the day. *Perhaps, in the name of the ruse, I have overdone things.*

"Maybe we should just let him have it." Despondent, Liara let her enchantment fade to nothing.

"Anisthe or France's monarch?"

Liara shrugged. She knew she annoyed Nagarath through her non-response. The mage valued clarity of thought and expression. He demanded it, even.

However, Nagarath did not chide Liara for her laxness. In fact, he looked rather ill. He leaned heavily on his staff. His face appeared waxen parchment. He had not yet dropped his disguise, and Liara presumed she had been premature on that account.

It had stopped being fun. She found the mage's infirmness alarming. Same as his barked commands, eyebrows that seemed to growl at her, and lips turned permanently downward. Back when she'd been a little girl, wishing for greater things, she had long dreamt of that sort of life: apprenticeship to the mysterious and strict Wizard of the Wood.

Nagarath had played Archmage Mordan so close to her youthful imaginings of what all mages were that Liara wondered if he had somehow pulled the idea of him from her own head. It was uncomfortable. Her longing for Nagarath's return haunted her all the more. It felt as if her idle fantasies had created her path—a path she no longer wished to walk.

She sniffled. "I want to go home."

"Oh, my little magpie." Nagarath stopped in his tracks to regard her.

With the lightning shock of embarrassment, Liara realized she had spoken aloud. She hadn't intended to. It smacked of giving up, the coward's way.

Hanging her head in shame, she tried to explain away her ill-spoken words. "You've traveled hundreds of miles, from one end of the sea to the other. Inns. Carriages. Hilltops. You, who ought have had rest and recovery after what I did to you. It isn't right. It isn't fair. Anisthe is my problem."

"Which makes it mine, Liara. Or have you forgotten Messina?" Nagarath bent to meet her face to face.

Liara almost imagined she could see through the age-wizened face of Mordan to the warm and familiar visage of her own mage.

Voice graveled with age, the counterfeit continued, "I will freely admit to you that I did not wish to go on this adventure. But you already knew that. Wanting to and doing do not always work in concert.

"I did not want to take you in that day last spring when George Phenlick expelled you from Dvigrad. I had happily kept my distance and would have continued to do so, had I any real choice in the matter. I promised—publicly, no less—that I would not apprentice you. And, yet, I have. In spite of all, I have done what was needed. And am extremely lucky and blessed to have found the companionship I was sorely lacking. You even helped me, you know. Got me over some of my indomitable belief that I was always right.

"Doing the right thing does not always work out that way, granted. But the universe does like to protect its own. And so I press forward. Not least because I need you around."

"But that's the problem!" Liara seized upon the argument. "I don't want anything worse to happen to you. If something happened to you and I was— Look at yourself, Nagarath. I'm . . . scared."

"And that, my dear, is precisely why you have me and I you." Answering her last, most pressing fear, with his usual frustrating kindness, Nagarath closed his eyes and let his own spell drop. He was himself once more. Right down to those sparkling gray eyes that now stared into Liara's own. "That mirror must stay buried and forgot, Liara. And you and I are, quite possibly, the only two people who know it and can do something about it."

Shamed, Liara looked away and turned to walk again along the path. She wanted to do what was right. She'd always known the danger.

But the underlying guilt again tormented her. Her actions in Parentino had put Nagarath at a disadvantage. She could see it in his spell-casting, sense it in his voice. It weighed down her soul, a millstone. Liara not only lived with her betrayal, injury, and attempted death of her friend but might yet see him fall from it. On a quest that was hers to take.

So, protect him. Don't allow the consequences to your rash actions be more—cost Nagarath more—than a mere lessening of your friendship.

In that moment, Liara felt a shiver cross through her shoulders and snake down her spine. Nagarath had never told her of what had ended both his friendship and apprenticeship with Anisthe; some instinct whispered that perhaps he understood Liara's current heartache better than she could explain.

Chapter Eighteen

*D*on't *be arrogant and don't get sloppy.* Domagoj voiced the inward reminder as he tailed the female magus leaving the inn. Though sleep would have been nice, he was thankful for the late hour. Domagoj's fey magicks might render him invisible—or near enough—but to work thus taxed his Art. It was more than he was used to.

And he loved it.

Blood singing with the siren's song, Domagoj had to stop himself from humming along to the aimless melody under his breath. Someday he would return to the sea. Someday he would put all these human wizards in their place.

Save for Liara, of course. He imagined the unleashing of her skill once the Laws had changed. A magnanimous part of him allowed Anisthe into the picture, too. And why not? He owed him all. Domagoj's regard was not so small as that.

But the wizard on whose heels he followed? Her he'd gladly kill. Thrice if he could. She served the enemy. Both enemies. Domagoj had seen how she looked at Anisthe during their "accidental encounter." Bravo to Anisthe for sending her off to Nagarath. Those two—they'd go down together, riding the same doomed vessel. Domagoj would see to that.

The urge to hum escaped in a low whistle. It drew the attention of his quarry and forced Domagoj to duck around a building. Careless. He waited, counting his heartbeats, but no shouts of discovery or running feet signaled he had lost the game.

The silence dissolved into a quiet argument. Unguarded words wended Domagoj's way through the early morning gloom.

Two men. Speaking French.

Such a pretty language. And another thing Domagoj owed Anisthe. He could listen out the whole of the exchange without wasting any energy on a translation charm. Most of it, anyhow.

The discussion drifted into his ears, sharp with anger and nearly too fast for him to follow. Annoyed, Domagoj renewed his spell and risked a look around the corner of the building, wondering why the woman did not speak when, after all, it was her rendezvous. Shock nearly took him straight out of his hex.

The witch was gone. There stood the two men he'd heard. And nobody else. Understanding followed an instant later—confirmed by the glitter of the witch's aura to Domagoj's magickal sight.

And so you would disguise yourself even to your own men? Oh, you deceitful thing. Domagoj allowed a grin to cross his face. *This might work out better than even Anisthe hoped.*

He settled back to listen, fascinated by the exchange. Even disguised, the witch was handsome. Gesturing wildly, the false face contorted with her fury. She was smart enough to keep her voice low. But barely.

The man with whom she conversed absorbed the assault with what Domagoj could only call diplomatic blandness. More likely, the Artless fool couldn't understand the wizard's urgency.

"I'm not going to sit around in Almazar for days just because your man could not get his things in order," she argued. "I've better things to do with my time."

"Such as?" The question was left to hang in the air but for a moment before the gentleman continued, riding over any retort he might have sparked. "If you are so busy, I wonder—the king wonders—why you need him to give you the incantation, why you even need his spellpiercers at all. Surely your kind can summon up whatever it is you need."

"If that were the case—" Wisely, the witch bit off the sharp words. She continued, more measured that time, but just as biting, "Would not you rather that 'my kind' turn the mirror directly over to your men? After all, if we are as untrustworthy as you have implied in the past . . ."

The man raised his hands, mocking defeat.

The witch continued, "I found you the town. That's closer than anyone else has gotten in centuries. Remember that. And do remember—this mirror? It wants to be found, to be put to use. It is only through the accident of time that it slumbers as it does. It is . . . It will be the greatest part of the king's collection. Your man will find me in Almazar within the week."

"And how will he find you?"

"I'll be the only one doing magick, you fool. Which makes it your job to keep the Spanish authorities from stopping me getting you your prize."

With a twist of the wrist, the witch had gone, disappeared into thin air.

Leaning back into the building, Domagoj let his own spell drop.

What a woman. It was almost too bad she had to die. Almost.

~*~

Domagoj's master met the news with measured calm. Surprising, considering they had traveled thousands of miles in their quest, and the stakes were beyond measure for Anisthe.

"Almazar," Anisthe repeated, for about the sixth time.

Hiding his impatience, Domagoj smiled his assent. He'd told Anisthe all. He was not about to be forced into recapitulation.

"It's a trap. Clearly. Think of how close we are."

"The fates are on our side."

"Fate," Anisthe spat. "Fate has been nothing but unkind."

"So are you recommending that we ignore the words of your former colleague?"

Silence.

"Anisthe, are you saying we should—?"

"Shh. I'm thinking." Anisthe waved an impatient hand.

For once, Domagoj hoped the best for Amsalla. If she was met with resistance by Nagarath, she would be back to claim Khariton's Mirror before Anisthe made up his mind whether and how to act upon the information he'd just been given.

"She suspects. Has to," Anisthe began, then stopped. More silence filled the room. Finally he turned to Domagoj. "She cannot truly love him, can she?"

Domagoj pursed his lips. "The thought is repugnant, yes?"

That was as far as he dared rub the old jealousy that lay between the two men. A touch, sure. Make Anisthe act. But not so much that it blinded him.

Anisthe smiled, the light from the hearth rendering a cruelty to the expression. "So she lacks the spell to wake the mirror's soul. That I would believe. Only thing that woman ever loved about books was Nagarath."

Domagoj indulged in a chuckle. "So, you'll awaken the mirror, and I'll follow the spellpiercers to where it is hidden?"

"You wish to avoid peril that much, apprentice?" Anisthe's eyes sparked a danger of their own.

Domagoj walked backwards over his words. "I've a better chance of evading detection while I trail the king's magick sniffers. You are far more suited to the role of magus."

Anisthe's narrowed eyes weighed the words and apparently found what he needed to satisfy. "Agreed."

Nagarath and Liara pressed forward towards France. Another inn. Another long evening in the common room. Another book at the table presenting yet another opportunity to glean news of the road ahead.

Liara had to admit to the effectiveness of Nagarath's plan: "Nothing attracts a gossip like the sight of a man quietly reading, Liara." The mage could easily coax strangers to talk without the aid of magick. And Liara? At least one of them bothered to keep an eye on their surroundings while Nagarath read.

His overt rudeness tempted her to complain, but the wizard was right. They often did not have to wait long for Nagarath's book to be put aside in deference to a visitor. That none of them was Rodolfo Adessi proved a constant, tiny disappointment. She wondered if Nagarath harbored similar hopes.

However, Liara knew the mage did not wish to have that evening's reading interrupted. Nagarath's face pressed close to the cramped writing of a journal he endeavored to translate. His eyes shone bright with discovery, and his lips moved silently with the words.

Liara failed to understand why Nagarath had not kept such activity to their room. It did not take long for an interested party to come up beside their table to try to stare the mage into looking up from his work. Instead of attracting an itinerate priest, the owner of a riot of fine colors and endless yards of expensive fabrics stood impatiently by.

"Nagarath?" Liara called the wizard from his reading. The sound of her apprehension startled him from his reverie, and he raised his eyes, first to Liara and then to the newcomer. Nagarath turned white then red as he looked up into the face of the incredibly beautiful woman. She, in turn, regarded him with a bemused smile.

The woman sat on the bench and turned the open journal towards her with a small exclamation of surprise. She managed to make even such a utilitarian noise ring like a bell in her companions' ears.

"Tell me you've advanced beyond all Cromen's dusty idioms in the past . . . oh, how long has it been?" The woman ignored Liara to bat luminous eyes at the mage.

Liara felt a warmth creep into her cheeks: annoyance with this overly familiar stranger and Nagarath's stammering, stunned acceptance of her.

Flustered Nagarath finally remembered Liara. "Liara, this is Amsalla DeBouverelle. She and I studied under Master Cromen." *With Anisthe*, she could hear him silently add. "And this is Liara, my ah . . ." He fumbled for the word.

"—librarian," Liara supplied. She took perverse enjoyment in his discomfort. She could feel him glaring the word "apprentice*"* at her. Regret and embarrassment colored his cheeks anew.

"How charming. Nagarath, I should have known your appetite for books would remain undimmed." The woman exhaled a tinkly little laugh and leaned towards Nagarath ever so slightly.

Nagarath found his composure at last. "You cannot judge if you have yet to crack one yourself. Liara, Amsalla was brilliant under Cromen's tutelage. As a witch—"

"—Wizard, please, Nagarath." Amsalla could keep even her gentle correction coquettish.

". . . wizard in training, she never studied. Never practiced. Natural talent like our Master had never seen."

"Oh, stop." Miss DeBouverelle's blue eyes glittered their thanks at the high praise.

"All true." Nagarath slapped the table in emphasis. "Goodness, how long has it been? Ages and ages since—"

"Ages for you, perhaps." Amsalla flipped her hair impetuously and looked to Liara, "Come now, a lady prefers to keep her age a secret."

Liara had been wondering that very thing. If this Amsalla had been at school with Anisthe and Nagarath . . . Impossible! *If Nagarath is but twenty-nine and began his education earlier than most, could this woman truly be his senior? Then she's using as much magick—or more—on her appearance as Anisthe ever did.*

Liara smirked.

"But it is such a treat running into you after all this time," she gushed. She laid a shapely hand on Nagarath's arm.

"And what, pray tell, do you get up to these days?"

Amsalla shrugged off the question. "Oh, a little of this and a bit of that." Did Liara imagine a catch in her voice as she did so? Liara decided she liked the impossible woman even less and resolved to pay closer attention to her.

Amsalla eyed Liara with equal penetration as she rebounded Nagarath's question. "And what about you?"

"Oh, you know me, Amsalla." Nagarath reached for Cromen's notes, still open on the table. "Never had any ambitions."

"Ambitions?" A sly smile crossed Amsalla's face. "Come now, you didn't give Anisthe a sound thrashing just because—"

"You know about Anisthe then?" Liara's interruption drew a look of displeasure from Amsalla. Nagarath, equally shocked, turned to the woman for an explanation.

"Yes. I had the pleasure of a running-in with old Anisthe a few days back. Poor fool's incantate."

"Did he tell you what happened?" Nagarath fingered his jaw.

"None of the specifics. Knowing that rake, I'm sure he deserved it. But I do find it funny that a man who's lost his Art could so easily predict you'd be shortly traveling the same roads as he . . ." Amsalla let her unspoken question hang in the air. Liara wondered if Nagarath was stupid enough to fall for the batting eyelashes and sweet smile.

"Hmm. Curious indeed. I, for one, think Spain is lovely at this time of year. As someone who has lived abroad, I thought it good for Liara's education to see something of the world." Nagarath smiled back at Amsalla.

"How thoughtful of you." Amsalla gave his unhelpful response an arch look. "Putting aside your own studies to run all over the world with your little bookminder. So, you're staying here?" She gestured to their tawdry surroundings.

"Yes." Liara found her tongue. "Nagarath takes the spirit of adventure quite seriously."

Nagarath solemnly affirmed her jest with a curt nod. But then he made it worse. Much worse. "In fact, Amsalla, if your own travels may be detained longer, perhaps you would care to join us for dinner?"

Nagarath had shut and pocketed Cromen's journal. Signal for them to depart. Liara's only consolation at the impromptu invite? The uncomfortable glance Amsalla gave the room. Clearly, the elegant, sumptuously dressed woman felt such surroundings beneath her.

The witch's smile withered, and she agreed to return in the evening to reminisce over a meal. A spiteful thought sprang unbidden to Liara's mind: whatever would the woman wear? However, her mirth was short-lived as the small party rose to go their separate ways, and the wizard outstretched her hand for a parting bow. Liara scowled as Amsalla's fine-boned hand lingered in Nagarath's own strong capable one.

And with that, Magus Amsalla DeBouverelle left. And in her wake: a fuming Liara and thunderstruck Nagarath. Long moments ticked by. Neither of them moved.

"Well!" Nagarath exclaimed at last, the word a mixture of effrontery and awe. "That was a bit of a surprise."

Liara dismally pondered the excited change that had come over her mentor. His face held too many emotions for her to sort through. Again, she considered the heaps of praise given Amsalla by a man usually cautious with his accolades. Liara roused herself to follow Nagarath out.

"Whatever possessed you to invite her to dinner?" she pounced as soon as they were clear of the inn's dining room. "You know she's after information."

"I am not a complete sot." Nagarath's answer made Liara blush. She hadn't been aware of how obvious her feelings were. "But so far she has revealed more than we have. As I seriously doubt you would give her even a peep, how could I pass up the opportunity to glean more tidbits from that historically transparent woman?" He smiled down at Liara, comfortably like his old self.

Trepidation marked Liara's afternoon. Empty, restless minutes brought her ever closer to seeing the astounding Amsalla DeBouverelle once more. And so Liara had set about going through each of the spells that might be safely performed in their room. Much to Nagarath's annoyance.

Twice he went so far as to reprimand her, lest she set the curtains afire. Liara's retort rang petulant. As his librarian—correction, apprentice—practice of her Art was necessary. He had his vices, and she had hers. Simple as that.

Thus, the sun ran lower in the sky, and Liara ran low on magick. The clock wound down at long last. Liara moved to replace her wand in its carrying case. Nagarath stopped her with a minute shake of his head. "I'd suggest that you get in the habit of carrying it on your person, Liara."

"Oh!" She flushed with pleasure.

Having bought Liara's goodwill with his quiet suggestion, Nagarath then came 'round to the topic she had wished to avoid. "You do not like her very much, do you?"

Even his ostensibly direct question had taken him the better part of the afternoon to voice. Liara's private anger redoubled, then quelled.

She really had no good reason to dislike Amsalla—not one that she dare explain to Nagarath. Liara opened her mouth to explain and then closed it. She did not have the words.

"She was never in thick with Anisthe, if that's what you're worried about," Nagarath missed the point. Oblivious as always. For once Liara was thankful for it.

"Though she came between us in her studies, neither of us could hold a candle to the wizardry of which she was capable."

Again, Nagarath adopted that annoying far off look. "I suppose that is how I managed to lose track of her."

"And now she's back."

"Yes. And I am guessing that, once she found Anisthe and saw that he was incantate, Amsalla planned on tailing him, curious to see what he's up to. Until she discovered us, the bigger prize."

"What you're suggesting is luck. Extraordinary luck, at that. And for all her cooing and batting of eyes, she certainly did not seem overly surprised to see us. Yes, us. She hardly looked at me. Not the reaction I would have otherwise expected," Liara reasoned. "Which means he told her everything."

"That I would doubt." Nagarath paused, then at Liara's blank face, explained, "If he had, she would have been even more interested in seeing his game. Me? I am"—he waved a hand—"I am consistently uninteresting to her. And besides, I think it was my scrying of Anisthe that tipped her off."

"You exposed our whereabouts to Amsalla?"

"Where we were was guesswork on her part. But yes, she knew I—we—were interested in Anisthe's actions. She must still recognize my magickal signature after all this time. Regardless, I ought to have been more circumspect in my spying."

"But we might have encountered her in any event. Amsalla would have already been in the vicinity."

"Near Anisthe, yes."

"So she's working with him."

"Knowing him? No." Nagarath shook his head. "Again, that she has not, until now, come calling is telling. She likely just ran into him and got curious when she realized that I was nearby keeping an eye on him."

"So how will dinner with her help us?" Liara challenged. "She knows nothing, yes? Then the only information spilt will be our own."

"Oh, I sincerely doubt she knows so little as she let us believe. Anisthe tends to give out the most interesting lies, and Amsalla is a notable collector of the same. She's a sly one, that is for certain. But there's no real harm in her," he hastened to add.

"So . . . we're doing this—?"

"For the intellectual stimulation." Nagarath winked. "And blatant curiosity. If you wish, I could have some supper sent up to the room, if you would rather not go down."

Liara shook her head. "No. I'd like to hear firsthand anything she lets slip."

"Excellent!" Nagarath was visibly relieved. He offered his arm to her. "Shall we?"

Liara raised her eyebrows at the unusually gallant gesture. She smoothed the front of her best frock and linked her arm through the mage's. They descended the stairs to the common dining room where Liara's sharp eyes spotted Miss DeBouverelle. The mage sat by herself with her attention turned inward. Radiant. An island of calm elegance in a sea of noise and semi-organized chaos. Liara again remembered Nagarath's courtly bow over the wizard's hand, and the image of herself in that place flashed through her mind.

Goodness, girl. You nearly killed the man at the start of the year, and now your head's taking a romantic turn? Liara risked a quick glance to Nagarath, half-certain that her brief desire had been written on her face for all to see. But the man smiled broadly at Miss DeBouverelle as they approached and didn't even look at Liara.

Amsalla half-rose to greet them. The plainness of her dress surprised Liara, and she cast a quick glimmer. The witch was all over magicked—spells masking her signature as well as her sumptuous, rich dress. She certainly fit in better with their surroundings than earlier that day.

Unique way to dress down.

Enacting a hex of her own design, Liara masked her own workings before she attempted to see past Amsalla's defenses. The magick was risky in that she would have to work without seeing her own spells to guide her. The combination of enchantments that would negate most spells of warding in Liara's eyes and her eyes alone. Luck was on her side, and after a couple of misfires, she pierced Amsalla's spells and could see the wizard's aura.

How interesting.

With a quick glance to Amsalla's face, Liara ascertained that the woman was either unaware of her prodding or chose not to acknowledge it. The wizard, in fact, seemed unaware of anything in the room outside of the mage. Animated and chatty, she captivated Nagarath. From the one-sided conversation Liara rapidly gleaned such basic details as Amsalla's having traveled extensively in Italy and Spain for the past decade, though she lived primarily in France.

What else have you been up to? Liara wondered. The woman's magickal signature was a puzzle. It differed significantly from Anisthe's and Nagarath's despite Amsalla having also studied under Archmage Cromen. Clearly her studies hadn't been extensive enough to alter her aura to match that of the Archmage, as Nagarath and Anisthe's had. That or she had been a very busy mage once her apprenticeship ended all those years ago.

Auras. Signatures. Apprenticeships and parentage. Under her mage's tutelage, Liara had already come to spot the subtle differences between Nagarath's aura and her own. Vrsar's war mage had been quick to take advantage of her haphazard education and her pride. Liara's fingers twitched. They still remembered the spells that had so violently stripped away Nagarath's defenses. She would not believe Anisthe's lies again.

Which led Liara to consider the changes in her progenaurae's aura. Sparkly blue and wild. Small. Whatever the source, the magick for the wizard was limited. He was a shade of his former self.

And he had made Amsalla believe him incantate. In some ways, the lie was more interesting than the truth. What reasons might he have for deceiving the witch in such a manner? Could it be that Liara and Anisthe actually lived on the same side of an issue?

Amsalla DeBouverelle. Liara looked at the decorative puff of a woman and scowled. Perhaps Nagarath was closer to the wizard than he cared to admit.

"So I am to understand the pupil has become the teacher at last?" Amsalla turned judgmental eyes on Liara.

"I made him teach me once I started caring for his books." Liara's daring elicited well-bred shock from Amsalla and a half-hidden smile from Nagarath.

"It is true." Nagarath gave a helpless shrug. "But to my credit, I could not have her waste such a gift, so it was not all that hard to convince me in the end."

"So the Limska Draga valley is just bursting with wizardly talent?" Amsalla's lip curled slightly.

Liara's cheeks grew hot, and she opened her mouth to defend her home.

Nagarath rescued her from the rash words sure to spill out by inserting, "She's Anisthe's."

Now that got Amsalla's attention.

"Anisthe has a daughter?" Amsalla looked at Liara with renewed interest—less like a bug to be squashed and more like an exotic curiosity to be studied. Liara wasn't sure she enjoyed the change.

"Daughter only in magick," Nagarath managed to pull the attention back to himself. And good thing, too. Shamed tears sprang unbidden to Liara's eyes at Amsalla's next words.

"I always knew one of Anisthe's hexes would get away on him." The witch sat back with an amused smile, tapping an elegant finger on her cheek. "And that you'd be nearby to clean up his messes."

Her own hurt put aside, Liara looked up sharply. She caught the mage swallowing a hasty and angry retort.

Don't. She wants to rile us. She had realized too late what the tricky Amsalla was up to and worried that this line of conversation would lead one of them to give away more than intended.

"My finding you here now makes much more sense—as does Anisthe's incantate state." Amsalla leaned forward to address Liara. "Very clever. Now you just need to make sure he lives until you reach the ripe age of twenty and gain magickal autonomy."

Amsalla winked. Clearly, she chose to view Liara as a charity case and not a rival. Relief swept through Liara, and she snatched up the idea. "Yes, so it's imperative that we didn't let him just whisk off to goodness-knows-where and why our motives for following him were less than forthcoming."

She paused the barest of moments before daring, "But he's . . . He seemed fine when you saw him?"

Liara beamed her warmest disarming smile. Said smile on her girlish face had deceived Father Phenlick many a time in Dvigrad. It seemed to work now. She could practically hear Amsalla weighing the option of playing her cards and ingratiating herself with Nagarath.

He didn't even have to ask. Amsalla volunteered.

"Anisthe never gives up. You know he'll find a way to regain his Art. For that man, it's not a matter of 'if' but of 'when'." Raising her eyebrows meaningfully to the mage and his pupil, Amsalla let her dramatic words settle in the air.

"Oh!" Liara was rapt. "Wait. Is that good or bad for me if—when—he does?"

Amsalla rolled her eyes at the question. Liara crowed. *That's right; believe I can't see past my own nose. Go ahead. Enlighten us.*

"For you? Goodness! You, of all people, should be hoping the best for him. Until he has it back, you're as good as dead at any point within the next two years."

Liara recoiled, tears smarting.

"It's a tricky business, regaining your Art—dangerous. With very few shortcuts. If Anisthe were anything but a fool, you wouldn't have to worry a minute longer. Had he asked me, he would have Art enough to last a thousand years, not just the measly two you require to reach your magickal autonomy. But then, you'd have to have my connections to even get your hands on such a prize. Poor fool doesn't even know how close he has stumbled to Power, true Power. But then, if he hadn't told me of your being nearby, I might have thought my having scried your signature but wishful thinking, so perhaps I owe him . . ." Amsalla flashed one of her coy smiles to Nagarath.

Even disgusted by the witch, Liara struggled to keep her triumphant smile off her face. She could feel Nagarath endeavoring to do the same. Amsalla did not seem to note it. She almost certainly knew about Khariton's Mirror.

Jealousy gone in the minor victory, Liara sat the remainder of the meal in silence. *Yes, enjoy your fawning glances, Amsalla. The mage is mine on the morrow.*

Chapter Nineteen

"Good morning!" Amsalla spotted Liara and Nagarath the moment they entered the common room. That Anisthe had omitted to mention his aurenaurae at all still infuriated Amsalla.

Even from across the crowded space, she could see the girl—Nagarath's pet—stiffen. Liara, in fact, looked as though she might dart into any dark corner at a moment's notice. Still suspicious, then. Poor dear. The smiles that greeted Amsalla? Equally wooden. Quite a contrast to her own dazzling expression of warmth and morning sunshine.

However, Amsalla's mind strayed elsewhere as the two approached her table to bid her good day. She still tried to figure out if wizard and apprentice traveled under a cover story. Rumor had it that the two had not procured separate lodgings. But beyond that, there was little more to say. For Amsalla, that could mean only one thing. She tried to turn her mind from such a possibility, aware of a rare twinge of jealousy.

Perhaps it was Liara's tender age, though—Amsalla guessed she was but eighteen—that kept the two travelers so close together. Nagarath had always been the chivalrous one and more than a little bit protective. This second conclusion satisfied Amsalla's possessive streak.

"Good morning, Nagarath." She let her arm drape over the air. Pitiful poor surroundings though they may be, there was no reason to skimp on formalities. Especially as they seemed to make Liara so deliciously uncomfortable.

"I hadn't known you lodged here, Amsalla. I was under the impression that you were going out of your way to stay as long as dinner last night." Nagarath ignored her waiting fingers.

"For all that it's a shabby, common little place, they do offer a decent night's rest," Amsalla said. She moved over on the heavy wooden bench to make room for Nagarath. "And you two look positively radiant. I suppose I'll have to learn your secrets so that I'm able to keep up."

Nagarath accepted the news with coolness. She could feel him steeling himself, vowing to not get ruffled.

Liara took Nagarath's lead with less seamless grace. The girl hid her scowl by giving the woodwork of their table a close examination.

Oh, the two of them were most decidedly up to something. But what?

Amsalla had decided to make it her business to find out. She doubted that it would be difficult to change her own plans for the immediate future. Staying alongside Nagarath would . . . he better suited Amsalla's needs at present, provided Anisthe's daughter hadn't too big a hold on the man. She raked the girl a penetrating gaze. "How could one pass up the opportunity to observe first-hand what is left of Anisthe's talents? And besides, traveling with another woman will offer our little party the respectability you currently lack. Fewer prying eyes may turn your way should I join you as the girl's chaperone."

"Yes, and you want to spy on whatever it is I am up to with my apprentice."

"Oh, you have me all wrong, dear. You did already tell me that you're following Anisthe for his health—and the health of his, ahem, surrogate powers." Amsalla made sure to preserve the sweet lilt in her voice despite her growing aggravation. "I simply thought it would be great fun to stay on with you and share a bit of my worldly wisdom with Liara, here. I can only imagine how she is pining for a woman's companionship."

At least, Liara had the sense to keep her mouth shut for the remainder of breakfast. And Nagarath appeared to assess and then to take Amsalla's second denial at face value. Small victories. Gambit made, the rest of the meal carried less accusation and ambition. There would be time later for Amsalla to move forward with her hastily hatched plan.

The big question for her: how much could she tell Nagarath? What she ought to tell him being significantly larger than what she might. She would have to proceed with care. Again, he'd likely go running to Liara with whatever information she divulged. Separating them was out of the question—for now. Such things took time.

And so Amsalla would wait and watch for her opportunity—provided Nagarath did not separate from her sooner than she intended. The wizard's naked suspicion yet rang in her mind as they quietly chatted over breakfast. Though still annoyed at the mage's directness, Amsalla congratulated herself for it. *So Nagarath is not a complete fool, after all. Even better.*

This was going to be fun.

~*~

"I can't handle her," Liara fumed. She stormed uselessly about their tiny room while Nagarath packed their few belongings. "I won't. I'm already at my wit's end, sick of all this bouncing about with nothing to show for it. I won't. She has to go, Nagarath."

"Liara. Listen—"

"No! No, you listen. She's mean, and she's all kinds of wrong, and she's so pretty . . ." Liara sat down at last, feeling miserable. She also felt stupid.

Certainly there was a risk in keeping the nosy woman about. A huge risk.

Granted, Liara had never been readily forthcoming, and Nagarath was notoriously cautious—enough to drive anyone mad. But the real reason Amsalla bothered Liara so much was how the wizardess looked at Nagarath—her Nagarath. And how the wizard basked in the attention.

"Can't we magick her away somehow?" At Nagarath's raised eyebrows she added, "I'm kidding, you know."

"Duly noted." Nagarath had taken her outburst with measured calm. "And you do realize she doesn't much like you either."

He turned back to his packing, adding, "I'll wager it's your presence here that's caused her to stay. She wants to keep an eye on you, figure out what makes you tick and what is so special about you that would merit my attention."

"So you're saying it's my fault we're stuck with her?" Liara was incredulous.

Nagarath smiled wickedly. "Yes, it is, so no complaining, little magpie. I'm counting on you to steal her secrets while I distract her by, well, being me."

The door to Nagarath's room whispered open and shut. He sighed and looked up from his reading, chastisement ready on his lips. Nervously licking the admonishment away, he saw that his visitor was Amsalla. Amsalla, with longing in her eyes and a secretive smile.

"No." Nagarath put his book aside. In rejecting her, he also rejected his secret wild hope that Liara might, instead, have been his late-night visitor.

"No magick?" Amsalla slid into a chair and leaned towards Nagarath, casually letting her wand catch the light of the room's sole lamp. It glinted, the polished wood golden like her hair but all the more tempting. "I've secrets to impart. A way to scry our mutual friend without tipping our hand to any spellpiercers."

"Spell—!" Nagarath nearly forgot himself in his surprise and only barely remembered to lower his voice. "The spellpiercers are not real, Amsalla. It's all a lie. They will make any number of lies to keep us in line beyond the reach of their soldiers, their ecclesiastic censorship, and so-called superiority of soul. I have made it my life's work to know every little thing about the history of our Art. There is no such thing as an Artless who can sense—"

"Such protestation and pride, Nagarath. I've seen them torture those whom they suspect have the power. Spells cast until the poor wretches scream in agony. The tests for a spellpiercer are brutal. And worse for the mage whose hand they force. Were it me, I'd choose death as the kinder sentence. And they say that we are the monsters."

All softness from Amsalla's aspect fled. Cold conviction stood in its place, and a chill slivered into Nagarath's heart. He might not trust the notions of an Artless priest. But Amsalla was learned—almost as much as Nagarath. And scared. He did not like seeing it in her face. He hadn't realized he had half-risen from his chair to comfort her until he saw the light shift in her eyes.

Playing the fool again, magus. Nagarath settled back into his chair and left the wizardess to her disappointment.

Amsalla pouted prettily and moved to sit on the rug before the hearth. She reclined so that her skirts fanned beautifully about her. Her ankles crossed demurely one over the other, she leaned upon an arm while reaching with the other to stir the low-burning fire with a charm. The spell was unknown to Nagarath, though he recognized the one-syllable word which had sparked it. His curiosity roused, their sparring returned to safer grounds. But the menace of her words remained. It made the air close around them.

"The trick is to employ the natural Art within the world, sparing your own," Amsalla explained. She stared into the flames. "A nudge, a request put forth in the Green Language—or any other you might prefer—and you will have your scene, thus."

Nagarath watched as two figures rolled together in the flames, tight in one another's arms. He blushed and looked away, recalled to the intimacy of their own current situation. Amsalla smiled. "My employer. He is a lusty sort."

"Scrying without use of your own magick . . ." Nagarath fingered his jaw thoughtfully. "Fire would be suitable for such. Clever, if unorthodox and potentially volatile. Yes, the theory is sound, even if your reasoning is suspect."

He repeated the spell, improving upon Amsalla's by using not a word, but a quick gesture. A figure slept alone in a pallet bed, peacefully unaware of her watcher. Nagarath was unsurprised as to where his thoughts, again, had led him. He turned back to Amsalla and asked, "But why tell me?"

Fear returned to poison the air. Nagarath almost regretted having reintroduced it, save for that he needed Amsalla to speak plainly to him. If the witch were capable of such.

She, too, seemed to be debating whether she had within her the capacity for unadorned honesty. Amsalla shifted closer, moving between him and the fire. Backed by the blaze, her hair became molten sunlight, her eyes dark and luminous. Her lips trembled as she confessed, "I need your help."

"My help?"

"Someone's. Anisthe's. Yours." Amsalla waved her hand, dismissive of the details.

But Nagarath needed such details. "You went to Anisthe first—"

"Found Anisthe first. To be honest, I thought it you in my scrying. Your signature still retains much of Cromen. You can imagine my surprise at finding the incantate instead." Amsalla laughed, her face finally losing its edge of dark worry. With the change, she was beautiful again. With the change, Nagarath remembered how he had missed her—at times fiercely—over the last decade and more since the ending of their apprenticeship. She too seemed to sense the closing of the space, the dangerous blending of past and present. She moved away, if but slightly. She said, "Remember the night we bespelled the stars? And how furious the archmage was? To have such times again. The zeal of youth."

"The beggaring of judgment," Nagarath cut in. "Anisthe—"

"You really don't get it, do you? That man meant nothing to me save for how he goaded you so." Amsalla lifted her face to his. "It made you ever so much more interesting for me to know—to know as a woman knows—that you cared for, wanted me, and couldn't stand the idea of him having me."

"Tricks. Games." Nagarath found that his voice had become thick.

"You love it." Amsalla smiled, closing her eyes and giving a minute shake of her curls. "You love the game, the competition. Oh, Nagarath, such a mage's response: 'My spell beats yours'; the ambition of discovery and compulsion to win. You revel in it. You. And me . . . And magick."

Nagarath entered the past. He entered a world of elicit nighttime encounters, sharp jealousies, and sharper urges. Zeal of youth, indeed. He had lost that somewhere in the rush and danger of Anisthe's apprenticeship-ending mistake. All their lives had changed that night. There had been no goodbyes. Only shame and regret.

Nagarath had told himself that he had merely been young and stupid, so often and for so long that he had grown to believe it, forgetting even wherein the lie had found origin.

But his heart remembered. Seeing Amsalla rekindled the youthful fire that had so consumed both him and Anisthe. Nagarath shifted from his chair to claim the space at her side, the hearth-warmed spot heating his passions.

Every part of him wanted her. She was every wish come true. Or near enough. Even wizards could not have every desire of the heart—and often far less. Magick was too dangerous to hope for any other fate.

And Amsalla . . . she embodied that as well. Danger. He wanted to burn from her flame. Already did. And there was no hiding it from her.

Nagarath wanted her to know it. She deserved to know how absolutely, utterly beautiful he found her. Enchanting. Yes, he would fall under her spell without protest. Who wouldn't?

Together they would never be more than magick. He knew this. Even choosing him, wanting him back, Amsalla needed the Art more than anything. He would be second. A safe second. For if she did not want every part of him, he did not have to give all.

And none of that mattered, either, for she was there and in Nagarath's arms. Sixteen years later and his hand stroked that golden hair, his thumb caressed the line of Amsalla's jaw, tantalizing him with thoughts of how her lips might feel against his own.

Amsalla was right. He had finally won. With thoughts of his victory over his rival and former friend, Nagarath's eyes involuntarily lit upon the hearth. Liara still slept peacefully under the watch of the spell he'd left burning. With a pang, he extinguished the magicks. But it was too late. Nagarath was back in the present. The dark present with all its pressing concerns, fears, needs.

"Anisthe." Nagarath breathed the name.

Amsalla gently turned Nagarath's face back to hers. "Leave him be."

And Nagarath might have. Once. The intervening decade and a half had changed him. What he had almost had with Amsalla—it was another lie, one he had never before considered. But his realization broke the spell the night had made. And angered him.

Nagarath wanted to live this new lie, his old truth. Would that not be simpler? And fairer?

Amsalla waited, willing and lovely and available. Nagarath had changed without meaning to. And yet . . . He had meant to. And that was very much his own fault.

"I cannot," he choked, cursing the ruined moment. But even that resentment was short lived. Nagarath rose and attempted to help Amsalla to her feet.

She pulled against him, her face rife with disappointment and anger.

"Please, Amsalla."

"No?"

"Not never. Just not . . . not now. You have no idea how hard it is for me to say that. After hoping for . . . From the moment I saw you, I—"

"Don't." She'd risen and placed a finger to his lips. A finger Nagarath wanted to kiss as much as he wanted to take back his words.

Nagarath closed his eyes, wanting to be someone else in another time, for things to be other than they were. Perhaps . . . Perhaps Amsalla's greatest power was in making a person lie to himself. In every conceivable way and in every possible moment.

When he opened his eyes a moment later, Amsalla had already gone.

Chapter Twenty

Warmth, revelry, and song. Those three heralds of cheer passed Domagoj by as he sulked within the deeper shadows of nighttime Almazar. What he wouldn't give to have been inside the inn. A damp fog had settled in, making misery of his vigil. But in spite of his misgivings and discomfort of heart, Domagoj agreed with Anisthe. Traps set about the same forest glade caught but one rabbit and generally missed all.

Lips loosened by cheer in the common room often dropped the most delicious crumbs of information. However, at present Domagoj listened not for secrets but for French.

The disparate tidbits that Amsalla dropped had been instrumental in confirming Anisthe and Domagoj's next move. A bit of luck had secured the rest. Luck coupled with the most basic of humanity's weaknesses: love.

Amsalla couldn't stay away from Nagarath.

Oh, she would be back. She had her rendezvous to keep with a man in the employ of France's monarch. But such plans would keep while she scared up her old paramour.

Domagoj's smile widened as he pictured Amsalla's likely reaction when she found Nagarath not alone. Again, a purposeful omission. Anisthe could be quite the artist when painting with emotion. A touch of this, a dab of that; in the right light, jealousy and anger would shine through.

And provide the window for Anisthe and Domagoj to slip in and steal away with Khariton's Mirror—the praecantator's very Art and soul.

Domagoj wondered if they might use Amsalla. She reeked of desperation and fear. Stronger than Anisthe, for sure. He had lost his edge somewhere along the way. Perhaps she would succeed in separating Nagarath from Liara where Krešimir had failed. Twice they had tried to entice Liara from her wizard's side. Perhaps it was time to work on the mage, rather than the apprentice.

Soft sounds of French reached Domagoj's ears. The king's spellpiercers. He whispered a short charm, signaling Anisthe, and hoped his master's surmise was true: that spellpiercer abilities were limited when it came to oriaurant magick. If all went as planned, on the other end of his hex, Anisthe would have begun to work his own spell.

And I shall miss all. Domagoj let his mood match the dark of the night around him. He had so desperately wanted to witness Anisthe's awakening of the mirror. Instead, he contented himself by imagining the scene, his lips moving along with the words.

Power that within thee lies, With my command, awake . . .

A cry of triumph and men rushed past Domagoj and into the inn where Anisthe waited. Domagoj tensed. That was not how they'd meant things to go. A possibility, perhaps; fears that the man with whom they were to meet might betray the informant mage. In his hesitation, Domagoj lost the chance to barge through the door of the inn and rescue his master.

The men returned a moment later, dragging the limp form of Anisthe between them. Again, Domagoj moved to exit the shadows, this time his heart giving a painful twist. Compassion coupled with fear. A jeering crowd followed the spectacle outside. This Domagoj joined, managing to stay close until the wizard was imprisoned in a jail—little more than a reformed cellar.

The crowd dispersed when it appeared no one was about to hang. Domagoj did not have to wait long to approach the low window. But the cellar had iron bars. They rebuffed fey magick and sent ice into Domagoj's half-mer heart. Pulling back with a hiss, he peered into the deeper darkness, seeing that Anisthe had yet to stir.

Domagoj pondered his dilemma. Everything had been set against them. His fey Art: useless against the iron of Anisthe's prison. The freeing of his master would have to come through non-magick means. And while spellpiercers might not have the ability to properly sense Domagoj's Art, their touch could similarly deaden all magicks within their reach. He would have to both draw off the men who blocked his Art and—somehow—rescue Anisthe in the short moments before anyone came 'round to check on the prisoner. Not too tall an order, save for the fact that lives hung in the balance—Liara's included.

Fretting, Domagoj almost considered following the thread of his magick to where he had last scried Nagarath and Liara. Lodging—ironically enough—in the next town over, they might be roused to aid Anisthe. But then they would have to believe him first and choose the war mage's safety over the chance to get at the mirror themselves.

The mirror. *Mayhap I could—*

Movement in the cell at his feet set Domagoj to crouching in the mud and dirt outside.

"Anisthe!" he hissed.

"Domagoj?" Anisthe's response came stronger than he had a right to expect. Relief swept through Domagoj, and he reached out a hand to aid his master.

"The metal rebuffs my hexes."

"Same. And I haven't the strength of Art, in any case. Not on my own," Anisthe countered. "But I've been reassured that the man with the authority to see me freed is coming shortly. I was caught by the wrong set of spell-piercers."

"Betrayal?"

"No. Zeal."

Domagoj considered his words before speaking, knowing that Anisthe could misinterpret them. Still, he asked, "And the spell? Did you manage it?"

"Half." Anisthe snorted. "Hence my arrest. I don't yet know if it was enough for them to discover the mirror's whereabouts. The king's man will need me yet, I presume. Him and his Artless hounds. Stay close. I may have need of—"

The rest of Anisthe's words were lost in Domagoj's mad scramble to get away from the jail window. Someone approached. He'd best stick to the shadows until things grew quiet. There would be no actions taken before morning. And if there were? He'd rescue Anisthe the moment he was removed from his cell. In the meantime, he would lie in wait for the king's man.

~*~

Much like Nagarath was positive he did not snore, Liara had long insisted she did not grind her molars during her sleep. But the first morning of waking in Amsalla's direct company was more than enough to set Liara's teeth on edge.

Liara had never been a morning person.

On the other hand, Amsalla apparently was.

Liara eyed the witch from the safety of her pillow and moaned her complaint over having been awoken. If Amsalla heard her, she did not acknowledge it. Liara furthered her protest by burrowing deeper down into the woolen blanket. She would gladly play the staller-up and steal a few more minutes of peace for herself. The only way Liara would allow herself to be forced out of bed was by magick.

Or danger.

Liara bolted upright in bed as she discovered what the wizard was about. Amsalla was packing her bags, and hurriedly.

"What's wrong?" Liara slithered out from under the covers, eyes on the still-dark window. Amsalla froze.

"Come, Liara. A lady mage does not lie abed all day. Get dressed." Amsalla's tone had Liara second-guessing the guilt she thought she had seen. The woman was tense, certainly. But she seemed upset rather than alarmed. This woke Liara more thoroughly, and she moved to obey. She distantly wondered if—how—she ought to comfort the older woman.

Amsalla spoke again, addressing the door. "Don't bother knocking, Nagarath. Enter. We're decent."

"Come. We must be away. Quickly." Nagarath crossed the room to help Liara whisk her things into her bag, his quick eyes missing nothing. Sparing an empty smile for his former school-mate, he added, "But then you already knew that, Amsalla. Let me guess. You'll be able to tell me near everything I did this morning."

"But of course, dear Nagarath. Every single thing."

"Including my scrying?"

Amsalla hesitated and did not answer straight away. She dampened the fire in the grate and thrust her arms into the waiting sleeves of her traveling cloak which had risen to hover behind her. "Of course. Which is why we are awake and why I bothered to pack early."

Again, Liara wondered at the catch in Amsalla's voice. The flirtation felt hollow, forced.

"Then you would have done well to warn my apprentice to also pack her bags."

Don't yell at her, Nagarath. Can't you see she's already upset? Liara kept her defense of Amsalla to herself. Some warning sounded inside, some realization that the two wizards were holding a silent conversation before her eyes, and she hadn't the faintest idea of what it all meant.

"I'll go on ahead and secure us a carriage." Nagarath left with Liara's bag as quickly as he'd come.

"Come, girl." Having mastered herself but clearly angry at Nagarath's chiding, Amsalla swept from the room, leaving Liara to follow in her wake. The elegant woman's skirts swished anxiously around her ankles as she practically flew down the hallway and out into the street.

Nagarath was already waiting in the faint pre-dawn light. A hard-looking man stood at his side.

The conveyance the wizard had hired was less than what they were accustomed to. Shabby and long in the tooth, the horse was in only slightly better shape than the rickety wagon which stood awaiting its passengers.

The driver gave Liara the shivers as he took them in. Distrustful, disgusted but still quite eager to take their coin, though he gave Nagarath a piercing look for it. Without comment or explanation, Nagarath handed first Amsalla and then Liara up into the wagon.

Liara cast a quick glimmer out of curiosity. The three of them were all-over magicked. Even more interesting—it appeared that Nagarath was the one who'd done it.

Paupers. Vagabonds.

"Anisthe." Nagarath bent close and whispered the one word of explanation she'd be offered this morning in their harried flight.

Liara felt her heart do a queasy turn. Anisthe. Nagarath gave her hand a reassuring squeeze. In spite of her fear, Liara's heart thrilled. She was still living and breathing. Whatever had befallen the former war mage could not be all that serious. Could it?

"Stop here," Nagarath called out. He rapped the side of the wagon in emphasis. He had run through possible scenarios during their short and comfortless ride. A tiny village—and hardly that, even—Nagarath had witnessed Anisthe's capture via the scrying spell Amsalla had taught him the night before.

And why had she done so?

Guilt flourished in Nagarath's cheeks. He could not read the frustrating woman.

She had a game. She always did. *But if she is playing us for fools, why provide me with an enhancement on my magick that allows me to see Anisthe's movement with greater clarity?* That clarity now had them running through the cold hills of early day to rescue the mage from local authorities.

Blush deepening, Nagarath recalled Amsalla's visit to his room but a few hours back, comparing what he had felt from her to what he had heard—and carefully ignoring what he felt. The wizard seemed burdened by something. Torn. And deeply afraid.

She had done something to get herself in trouble. That much was clear. The consequences had grown beyond the means of her Art, and she had sought out any wizard who might help her. Any wizard.

She had first approached Anisthe. She might claim she had sensed Nagarath, but it was to Anisthe she had spoken.

Unkind, Nagarath. But I can't help her if she doesn't tell me what the problem is. Nagarath grimaced, cross as he gathered both his and Liara's belongings and turned to help the ladies disembark.

"We have everything. Thank you. And thanks, also, for accepting such humble . . ." Nagarath found he addressed the backside of a retreating wagon and horse.

"Probably didn't want to hear thanks from the likes of us." Amsalla sidled up to Nagarath in the half-light, making him jump. "Shall we?"

"A moment." Nagarath whisked his wand over to their bags. A brief answering green-gray glow emanated from the untidy pile, and he nodded in satisfaction.

"Don't bother with mine. I already secured them." Amsalla eyed their surroundings with poorly concealed contempt. "I dare say we'll have the element of surprise. Did you have a plan?"

Nagarath eyed the wizard with mistrust. Her tone rang too bright, too familiar. He could see that Liara was just about done with being dragged this way and that with nary a word of explanation. And Amsalla was enjoying it. Nagarath retracted some of his generous thoughts toward her, moving to comfort the girl. "Liara, Anisthe was captured late last night. Charge of witchcraft."

"But—"

"Yes, he's incantate. Though I fear the authorities here may care little about that, as he has done more than enough in his past to merit a hanging, should his former activities come to light."

"But—"

"Connected to the Habsburgs or not, Anisthe's actions in Dvigrad and elsewhere often went far beyond the bounds of decency. As you well know."

"But how?" Liara got her objection through at last.

Nagarath hesitated. But he could not lie to Liara. He could read her suspicions in her dark eyes. Dissembling would only make her conclusions worse. "Amsalla snuck from your room to mine last night. We talked at length about spell work, and she shared with me a clever advancement in scrying techniques—"

"They allow you to sense, not just see, pet," Amsalla cut in.

"And so, I managed to witness Anisthe's arrest," Nagarath completed. "Now if we're all satisfied here, can we move on, please?"

Liara led the way. Her gait stiff, her head erect, she let such silent signs speak further of her ire with Nagarath and Amsalla. The depth of her anger was telling in that this freed Nagarath to walk alongside the wizard.

And it is unfair, Nagarath conceded. *She's last to know but would be the most affected by Anisthe's fate.* He moved to catch up, unsure how he could have done anything else in the circumstances, but wanting to make amends.

Amsalla stopped him, her hand on his arm. "A plan, dear? After marooning us in this wilderness, you did have one, yes?"

~*~

Liara hated Nagarath's plan.

But, for the moment, Nagarath did not care. The day was arriving faster than they could want. He and Amsalla had gained access to the jail where Anisthe was being held. The two of them were disguised—*Father Phenlick, forgive my indiscretion*—as priests, representatives of the Doge of Venezia. Liara stood watch outside. Amsalla clicked her tongue as she walked at Nagarath's side. "I don't think Liara was too happy with you."

"I don't recall Liara having much of a choice in the matter." Nagarath refused to let Amsalla rattle him further. She'd done enough damage in the last half day.

"I would have stayed to watch, you know."

"I don't quite trust you enough for that, Amsalla. Surely you know that by now?"

Amsalla pouted. "How can you say I'm untrustworthy if you never give me a chance to prove myself?"

"Fine." Nagarath stopped in his tracks. "Here is your chance. Tell me why you were packing your bags this morning and not Liara's. Tell me what has you so scared. Explain to me why you're here—why you're really here."

Silence. Amsalla cast her eyes down and to the side. Anywhere but his face.

"This morning. The past two days . . . Last night. Any number of those moments were open to you. You are still not forthcoming. Not even now. I don't know about what, but it is painfully clear you are hiding something. And in light of last night, that makes it even worse."

"Is that why I, too, am wearing a charm? So that you can keep track of me?" Amsalla held up her wrist in illustration.

Nagarath opened his mouth and closed it. The witch knew full well why all three of them had the charm about their wrists. A quick turn, thrice about, and the alert would be sounded for the other two. That Amsalla now questioned it just to goad him spoke of her desire to get him angry. When he was angry, he made mistakes—mistakes such as trusting when he ought not.

Amsalla turned from Nagarath. Her magelight illuminated the tiny, dark jail.

And now we shall find out whether Amsalla's account of meeting Anisthe was anywhere near the truth. Nagarath wondered if the wizardess had similar thoughts. If she had lied about the encounter, it would out very soon.

Anisthe huddled against the back wall of his cell. He looked well, considering the circumstances. He grimaced when he saw the arrivals. "Rome persecutes those who would use magick but employs it herself? How hypocritical."

Nagarath let drop his disguise for but an instant. Amsalla did so as well, eliciting a gasp from the prisoner.

"Not who I was expecting," Anisthe stammered.

"Expecting?" Nagarath stood back, amused. "You're hardly in a position to expect anyone, save the hangman."

"Is this a . . . ?"

"A rescue. Yes." Nagarath smirked. The lesser part of himself enjoyed watching Anisthe squirm.

"Then be gone with you. You're ruining my plans."

Anisthe's pronouncement startled Nagarath's smile from his face. They were ruining his plan? His grand plan was getting arrested. Interesting.

Anisthe continued, unasked. "But you wouldn't understand that, you with your magick. The rest of us Artless must use other means to get what we want—"

"Like . . . being arrested." Fine. If Anisthe was going to be ridiculous, he'd call him on it.

Anisthe narrowed his eyes. They glittered in the glow of Amsalla's witchlight. "If this is a rescue, you are wasting precious time. Especially as you'll find yourself with a most uncooperative prisoner." He craned his neck to look out the narrow window in the wall behind him. "The sky has lightened considerably while you stood and mocked me. And besides, your disguises won't hold up long. Not with what my jailers seem to know."

"We dispatched them." Amsalla enjoyed the encounter even more than Nagarath.

"Not them. The ones who can sense even the slightest slip of magick," Anisthe hissed. Real fear shone on his face. "Where's Liara?"

"Hush." Nagarath bent to inspect the lock on the door. "She's outside."

"I'll move on ahead and see our way clear." With those words, Amsalla was off.

Nagarath nodded, still caught up in the lock. If he was not mistaken, there was a power signature on it. Or rather, a signature of non-magick, a blankness which sucked the magick from his fingers when he touched it. He jerked his hand back. Anisthe's fear was catching.

"Hsst—" the incantate mage hissed for Nagarath's attention. A shadow fell across the window on the outside wall. Ducking, Nagarath moved to the side, out of view of the newcomer.

"Well then. The rumors were true. The King's pet mage got himself caught. By superstitious Spaniards, no less. Their spellpiercers are, shall we say, not attuned to our plan. But their skills, while rudimentary, are serviceable. I dare say they'll be ever so disappointed when they find you gone."

Aristocratic, learned, the voice seemed to Nagarath both clean and dirty, light and dark. Something in the stranger's tone set him to shivering. This man would have walked right by Liara as she stood watch outside. Spellpiercers. Did they truly exist, as this man had claimed? As Father Rodolfo—*as Amsalla*—had warned?

"Yes. Well, I thought it prudent not to argue. And it gave you an easy rendezvous point. And the artifact? It is safe?"

"It is on its way to the King as we speak. You have done well, mage."

Quiet assent. Nagarath could almost picture Anisthe's simpering smile. *Mage, bah.* Questions abounded: Who was this unseen stranger outside the wall? How did he know Anisthe? Why would Anisthe have sent the mirror onward to France's king when he might have used it himself?

"Well, are you going to let me out or aren't you?"

Nagarath smiled in the darkness. Anisthe's ally had left him to hang, the prize won.

The air shifted invisibly, and Nagarath gasped. He knew without knowing that that which held the lock had been loosened. The cultured voice called out quietly in the dark, "You'd best get yourself back to the king. He doesn't like to be long parted from what is his."

And with that, the scuffling footsteps retreated.

"Nagarath?"

Gliding back into view, Nagarath eyed the prisoner. "You know I heard every word. And that I don't believe, not for a second, that you're with whom the king's man meant to meet."

Anisthe slumped back down, defeated. "And the witch?"

"I'm breaking you out." Nagarath ignored the question, steeling his nerves as he reached out again to touch the heavy lock. His fingertips met cold metal and nothing more. No magick-stealing mysteries bit at his art. "Stand back."

"No thank you, Nagarath. I'm to wait here until the proper rescue arrives," Anisthe scoffed.

"I think he has already deemed you not worth rescuing." Red sparks arced through the air. Nagarath felt his spell rebound back at him, stinging his hand.

"I warned you, friend. I'm to remain here, the mage under King Louis' pay, until—"

"You're not the mage." Annoyed that he wasn't certain what spell to employ against the iron lock, Nagarath's snapped words echoed louder than intended. "You're bait. That message was meant for someone else."

Anisthe did not answer. Confirmation enough of Nagarath's theory. Suddenly it all made sense. Which meant . . . unless there were another mage in the game—

"Sorry about this, *friend*." With a twist of his wrist, Nagarath reached through the bars, simultaneously activating the charm he wore and transporting himself and Anisthe out of the jail in one quick move.

~*~

Liara really hated Nagarath's plan.

I'm a boy again. Glancing down at her worn trousers and wrinkled shirt sleeves, she scowled. At least her magick was good. Liara had changed little of her disguise. Nagarath and Amsalla might be playing the proper authorities to gain Anisthe's freedom, but Liara was perfectly suited for blending in as a street urchin.

Lounging on the street corner, first leaning back on a building—until a disapproving glare from a member of the local *hermandad* roused her—and then rocking back on her heels, Liara waited. And waited. The quiet slap of booted feet echoed once more in the still air. The guard's return.

Liara made a sign in the air. She breathed a sigh of relief. Invisible as a gust of wind but still at her post. What need had she to be seen? Besides, if all went well, she wouldn't be needed. And, so far, it appeared that all was well. *It would have been nice to at least teach me those enchantments that sharpen scrying.*

She was dying to see, firsthand, the rescue. Of course, now she knew it possible, Liara had her own ideas on how Amsalla's scrying without water might be accomplished. *Maybe just one more quick spell—*

Movement at the end of the street drew Liara's attention. Three men . . .

. . . and Amsalla.

Fear poked angry fingers at Liara's spine. The plan hadn't worked. Was Anisthe in trouble? Was Nagarath? Logic cut in and reminded Liara's eyes of the pertinent details: Amsalla looked like herself.

Amsalla had dropped her disguise.

Liara moved to follow. She smiled as the witch now nervously darted her eyes over the corner where Liara ought to be waiting for Nagarath's signal. *Seems none of us here have stuck to the original plan, Amsalla. Is it not terrible when that happens?*

Amsalla was in heated conversation with the three men, and Liara could catch snatches of their words. Soft and colorful, the sounds which reached her ears were not the rounded notes of Spanish.

French. Hurrying, lest she miss more of this clandestine meeting, Liara had the misfortune of kicking a small stone. The tiny clatter was enough to spook her quarry.

Four heads now looked around in alarm. All speech halted. Quickly, Liara rehearsed what shielding spells she knew, not that she would likely be any match for Amsalla, should the mage find her. Palms sweating, Liara waited, unmoving, as Amsalla and the three Frenchmen looked through her one last time.

A tickle at Liara's wrist. Nagarath's signal. Torn, she hesitated before turning back to the summons. Amsalla wore the same charm. Surely she would come at the mage's call, taking leave of whatever else in which she had become enmeshed.

Rounding the corner, Liara let her invisibility drop. She quickly peeked back around the building. Amsalla was gone, as were the three men with whom she'd been talking.

Liara let out a screech as a hand fell on her shoulder.

"Shhhh!" Nagarath angrily silenced her. "We only barely got away!"

Anisthe was in tow, his face unreadable.

"We just saved you from hanging. You're welcome." Liara raised her eyebrows in arch judgment.

"There was no danger, as I told Nagarath," Anisthe hissed. "It's good to see you, my dear. Nagarath tells me that you're officially apprenticed at long last."

Anisthe's plan was to get captured? Truly? Liara looked to Nagarath, unswayed by Anisthe's claim.

"Come. Amsalla is missing. Who knows what her game is. She could be working with him for all we know." Nagarath tugged on Anisthe's restraints.

"Frenchmen. Three. She went to meet them. They were talking across the street a moment ago." Liara pointed. "Your charm itched me before I could follow her or signal you."

"You've lost her? Why does this not surprise me," Anisthe said.

"Shut it," both Nagarath and Liara spoke at once, silencing the incantate mage.

"French. Then we must go. Quickly," Nagarath said.

The three of them hurried to the edge of the street. Anisthe stumbled and strained against Nagarath's magickal hold on his bonds.

"We're not taking him with us, are we?" The very idea turned Liara's stomach.

"If you do not release me, I'll—"

"We're releasing you. We're releasing you!" Nagarath roughly shoved Anisthe from him. "And we're going after the mirror. Understood?"

Laughing, Anisthe shrugged, the gesture lessened by the bonds on his hands. "A race, then? Oh, I do like a good challenge."

"YOU would do well to stay out of trouble. We've already followed you halfway across the continent—"

"Out of concern for poor Liara here, yes. My health, of course, being something you would otherwise be unconcerned with after what you did to me—"

"What we did to you?" Liara's wand was out and at Anisthe's throat. "How DARE you. You whom I trusted. You whom Nagarath once called friend. You should count yourself lucky. If I was older and my life not tied to yours, you'd be dead. Do you understand?"

"Liara. Liara, please." Nagarath gently reached for his ward's shaking shoulders, drawing her off. Fixing Anisthe with a stern glance, he warned, "Again, I caution you to be careful, lest we have to interfere again in your affairs."

"Why wouldn't I keep myself safe? What's in it for me if I die?" Anisthe sneered. His eyes darted to Liara.

Still shaking, Liara lowered her wand. Her voice came out thin as she asked, "What will we do with him?"

"Good question. Not a thing. Especially as we both know, now, where the mirror has gone. *Tra'shuk.*" Nagarath made a sign in the air as he spoke. Anisthe's bonds fell to the ground in a heap, their captive having vanished into thin air. "Come, Liara. We'll talk on the way."

"Where did you send him?"

"Somewhere else."

"And what about Amsalla?"

"Hang Amsalla!" Nagarath swore. His long strides did their best to take them both far from uncomfortable thoughts of the missing wizardess.

Returned from the blackness to which he had briefly been banished, Anisthe turned this way and that, trying to gauge where Nagarath had whisked them.

Not them. Him.

He was alone.

"Nagarath? Liara? Amsalla?" Anisthe whispered into the brush and dust of the barren countryside. He tried to bury the unease rising in his breast. "Nagarath, you black-hearted wizard. This is low, even for you."

It felt better to curse the absent mage. But it did not solve the problem.

Where am I? Anisthe took a few aimless steps forward then doubled back on his path to try for a better vantage point. Not that it would likely be of any use. Nagarath would have made certain to deposit him somewhere out of the way. Anything for him and Liara to gain the advantage, now that he knew of the mirror's whereabouts.

Oh, the mirror! To have missed it by a matter of moments! To have been stuck in a cell, instead. Useless. Powerless.

"When I get my hands on that Domagoj . . ." Anisthe struck out for the nearest hilltop. He thought through his dilemma. Nagarath's range couldn't be all that great—a half dozen leagues, at most. The logic provided little comfort. Anisthe continued to curse his absent companion in his frustration. "Idiotic plan. We should have risked Domagoj instead. I could have freed him as easily as he would me, once the mirror had been intercepted."

The last was an overreach. He could not have. Not with iron bars and a half-fey's magick. A chill struck his heart. *Without Nagarath's help . . .*

And the mirror! Khariton's Mirror, lost to the greedy hands of France's king. Or had it? A new tremor shook Anisthe's soul.

Where was Domagoj in all this? Anisthe had been betrayed. Outsmarted! His servant had set him up to take the fall and run for the mirror himself.

"I played right into Domagoj's hands. And even worse, Nagarath now knows as much about the mirror as you do. Fine mess you've made, Anisthe." He gained the summit of the hill at last. Precious time had been wasted. The horizon was reddening with the advent of the day. And here he was, stuck gods-knew-where.

"That aurenaurae of yours is a fiery little thing, isn't she?"

Anisthe whirled around. "You!"

Domagoj raised his hands. "Hold. I'm not the one who transported you a good fifteen miles from Almazar."

"Where were you when Nagarath and the witch came to ruin that plan of yours?"

"Staying out of sight. You know that I couldn't risk the spellpiercers sensing me. Outwitting them is a tricky business. I'd hoped that one of your captors might still be around to apprehend Nagarath and Amsalla, taking them out of the game for us."

"I don't want Liara hurt."

"Neither do I."

"Your past actions beg to differ."

Domagoj waved off the accusation. "Past, Anisthe. All in the past. You have my loyalty. Have you forgotten that?"

The words were a test. Anisthe wondered how much of his cursing Domagoj had heard.

Anisthe's servant did not wait for an answer. Staring into the rising sun, he offered, "So. Nagarath knows of the mirror's whereabouts."

"He was there. Attempting the rescue of yours truly when Amsalla's informant showed up with the message meant for her. It was only through an extraordinary turn of luck that she wasn't there herself."

"Not luck, Anisthe." Eyes still on the rising sun, Domagoj let slip a small smile. "The situation is not as out of control as you would fear. You taught me well, after all."

"You drew her away."

"Merely aroused her senses. Played to her own insecurities over Nagarath. My touch was light. She never knew I was there." Domagoj shrugged and turned his full attention to Anisthe. "Amsalla is a threat. She's in league with the other side."

"She's in league with all the sides."

"True. But the spellpiercers—"

"We need her."

Domagoj snorted. "Bah."

"We do. The king has the mirror now."

"Because of her!"

"And so the only way to get at it is through his court. The witch has connections . . . with the king—with Louis himself. And I know that woman. She needs something, some sort of help, else she would not have bothered scaring up both me and Nagarath. If we work with her, I promise you that I can get her back under my thumb. The witch has a weakness."

Silence.

"Unless you have courtly connections of which I'm unaware," Anisthe sneered.

"Fine," Domagoj crumbled. "But I don't trust her. Whatever your history with her, I don't trust her. And if we're going to rely upon her help, if you're going to play this game the dangerous way, then I would ask for something for myself."

Anisthe regarded his servant warily.

Domagoj noted the look, once more raising his arms in a gesture of innocence. "Remember I owe you my life and freedom. Never mind that your promise to restore me to my proper birthright only holds if you can regain your Art—your own art—and continue your work towards our mutual goal."

"But?" Anisthe could tell there was more. There always was. The slow smile growing on Domagoj's face mirrored his own. Understanding between the two men.

"But, in return, I want Liara."

Chapter Twenty-one

A dizzying pile of cloth lay on the bed, its bright richness contrasting oddly with the drabness of the room. Liara stared at the garments, already worried about touching them, never mind wearing them.

"So, when we leave, you're going to magick us so we look like we do now?" Liara checked again with Nagarath. From gypsy to gentry in an eye blink. How could anyone not notice?

"Yes, so as not to arouse suspicion. Just like I did when we first purchased the garments and needed to blend in—only in reversal of fortune, of course." Nagarath compared two shirts side by side, expertly eyeing their individual merit. He eventually chose the less loud of the two and disappeared behind the wardrobe screen.

Liara shyly picked at the array of dresses before her and lamented, "So why can't you do that the whole time and save us this rigmarole?"

"You know I cannot do that, Liara. The constant effort, vigilance . . . and you know no illusion is perfect. They are designed to be temporary. Quick fixes."

"Amsalla did it," Liara grumbled sullenly. She meant it as a test, to see how Nagarath would react. At mention of the woman's name: a heavy silence. So he wasn't as at ease with Amsalla's abrupt disappearance as he claimed.

Nagarath came out from behind the screen and turned in place for her approval. He had donned coat, shirt cuffs, and dress shoes in addition to the breeches he already wore. "How do I look?"

"Like a gentleman." Liara giggled and bowed, striving to hide her true feelings. She sensed the distance between them more keenly than ever. Now he looked a stranger in addition to feeling like one.

Nagarath turned to reach for his staff and became himself once more. The chasm between them closed at the sight of the familiar object in her friend's possession. Though she thrilled to see Nagarath looking wizardly in spite of his finery, Liara knew better than to expect that the mage would walk around the court of King Louis XIV with a staff of power so obviously in his possession.

Nagarath addressed the staff. "That will not do. Not one bit. But what to do with you?"

Frowning, the mage stood with arm outstretched, eyes roving the length of the worn wood, the twinkle in his eye matching the spark from the staff's jewel. Mischief. He wore it as well as his new silken cravat and ruffled overcoat.

Liara moved half a pace backwards. Her legs collided with the bed and folded unexpectedly. She sat.

"Indeed." Nagarath gave Liara a quick glance and then set the staff against the tall screen before coming to sit beside her on the edge of the bed. He regarded the magicked artifact with dark intensity. Neither of them moved for one long moment.

Liara broke the strange silence. "What are you going to do with it?"

"I'm doing it." Nagarath's response came tight with carefully restrained emotion. Liara noted the bright beads of sweat which dotted his forehead and marred his jawline. That he hadn't barked at her for interrupting his strange, silent concentration surprised her greatly.

Understanding without understanding at all, Liara slid her hands under her and fixed her gaze back onto the wizard's staff. Her whole body tightened in involuntary mimicry of the mage.

Nagarath seemed to waver in the corner of Liara's vision as he worked his silent spell. The effect much the same as that of intense heat warping the view of objects at a distance, Liara looked to the wizard, tearing her eyes from the staff.

Giving vent to a heavy exhalation, Nagarath closed his eyes and shuddered. At his side, his fingers clenched and unclenched. Once. Twice. His whole skin looked sickly. Liara suspected he would be clammy to the touch.

And touch him she did, unable to stop herself. Her heartstrings wrenched at Nagarath's changed appearance. Liara felt the heat of his magick through her fingers. The sudden surge of power drove out the chill and brought color back into the mage's aspect.

"I'm fine. Thank you, magpie." Nagarath's words buzzed in Liara's ears. She could barely hear him over her realization that he had placed his hand atop hers, clasping it gently. Sudden shyness forced Liara to turn away. Her eyes sought escape in his staff and whatever spell Nagarath had been attempting.

No, not attempting. His spell worked. That or someone had come in and replaced Nagarath's staff with a walking cane in the brief span of time Liara had looked away.

"Oh!" Openmouthed, Liara could do little more than stare. An artifact of such power—a will of its own, even—was as unchangeable as a mountain. And yet, here it was, become something new.

New-ish. The familiar cinnabar stone decorated the head. The wood of the shaft evoked the same twisting design that its predecessor had.

"It is inert, Liara."

Liara jumped. She hadn't realized she had risen and approached the object of her scrutiny. Clasping her hands behind her back as though to deny that she would have dared touch the mage's staff-turned-walking-stick, Liara felt her face flush with embarrassment.

"Bring it here." Nagarath reached out a hand. It left Liara little choice but to do as he asked. He turned it over in his hands. "The question will be, of course, whether or not I can safely reverse the transformation. So as to not draw any attention from the spellpiercers, I have locked away the staff's signature."

"But that's a good thing, right?" Liara interjected. "After all, if its power is locked away, it's not dangerous."

"Nothing this dangerous is ever rendered safe. But the ability to tap its magick—and therefore fall prey to its designs—is limited, yes." At Liara's worried frown, Nagarath hastened to add, "But the key to unleashing the power within the stone is no nearer to being discovered than when the cinnabar was buried in my staff. So we are really talking mere appearances here. Which is all I required.

"And now for you, Liara."

"Me!" Liara had all but forgotten the part she would be asked to play. The shapeless heap of taffeta—Liara's traveling gown—still lay upon the bed, a garish peach promise that she would shortly look and feel very little like herself.

"As for you, dressing yourself is out of the question. And obviously I cannot do it." The wizard paused and unearthed the watch chain from under his jabot, wincing as he noted the time. "Your lady's maid shall be here shortly."

"My what?" Liara's answer dripped incredulity. She looked intently at the man. No, he was not joking. "Too far, Nagarath. You're taking this way too far."

"Just wait until you see the coach and horses," Nagarath muttered. He plucked at a ruffle on his sleeve. "How else did you expect to be let into court? As a chamber maid?"

He took her hands, the act drawing a sharp breath from Liara. She felt the heat of a blush rise in her cheeks and cast her eyes downward. Nagarath just didn't look like himself.

"There is a waiting list to work in the residence of the King. And even if we could secure a position—and mind you, the access would be well worth it—there is no way of knowing where he secrets that mirror."

"If he even has it . . ." Liara wished she could extract her hands from those of the dapper gentleman before her. She felt plain, drab, and—again—terribly shy. Her thoughts returned to Amsalla, memories of ill-expressed jealousy springing into her head. Seeing Nagarath now, Liara knew exactly how to express it. Her blush deepened.

"Oh, assuredly the king has Khariton's Mirror. But so far, it appears we might be ahead of Anisthe. Neither of us have scried him in days, and we would do well to maintain that lead." Nagarath waited for Liara's reluctant nod of assent. "And besides, courtiers are common as dust and come and go all the time. Three days in those gowns and you will feel invisible to most eyes. Remember, they are all there because they too want something of dear King Louis. We will likely be ignored within five minutes of our arrival."

They forwarded the story that Liara was Nagarath's cousin's daughter; that somehow her father had gotten it into his head that his precious little girl ought to see something of French court; and that Nagarath—a gentleman with courtly aspirations of his own—would do well to introduce her, having studied in the south of France long ago.

Sophie, Liara's lady's maid, companion, and chaperone, seemed completely unfazed by their story. The young thing—she couldn't be much more than Liara's age—was as plain as they came. Quiet to the point of unnerving. But kind and patient with her lady's many eccentricities—such as not knowing the faintest thing about how to dress for the station for which Mademoiselle Liara was aiming.

Again, Liara found herself cursing the gaping holes in her education. Books had given her a working command of any number of languages and scripts, but they had not taught her anything practical of the societies in which they had been born.

She did know the right questions to ask, though these she kept to herself.

Where was this girl's family? Were they actually willing to send her off with these two unknown people to run halfway across the country? Were she and Nagarath paying her? Was it enough? How could he afford it after the clothing and the coach and everything that had preceded that leg of their journey?

Perhaps she's been witched away with us.

Liara had half a mind to accuse Nagarath of magicking the poor girl, save for the fact that they had not yet had a moment alone together. Sophie took her duties as chaperone quite seriously. But it was in her heart to ask at the first opportunity.

And if opportunity was not going to find them, then Liara would find opportunity.

By the time they had gained the border to France, Liara had become very adept at losing things—hats, gloves, and the like. She sent off Sophie to ask after one such item that Liara had just then remembered having left behind at their midday rest. A shawl, Mademoiselle wanted it back in the worst way and would not leave town until it had been returned. Nagarath and Liara sat alone together in the carriage, a good quarter mile from the scene of Liara's most recent absentmindedness.

"There is no shawl, is there?" Nagarath shook his head at his apprentice's ingenuity.

Liara's answering smile was enigmatic.

"Hmm, perhaps this will work, so long as you keep up with all of that."

"All of what?" Liara tried on her best imitation of courtly coquettishness.

"Well. That, actually. The mystery and flirtatious coolness. The rest of the time your attitude is just so . . .

drab. Not only would I never send my young daughter to Louis' court to expose her to all of loathsome society . . . you are not the daughter I would choose to send."

Liara made a face, perversely as ugly as she could make herself with a look.

"She would be plump, blonde and rosy, sunshiny, flirtatious . . . the sort of young thing who thrives in the circus of court life. In fact, she would be someone who did not make faces and would remember to sit more ladylike in a dress."

Sighing, Liara readjusted how she sat in her corner of the carriage.

"So the shawl . . . ?"

"Yes, I sent her away on purpose. It actually worked, for once."

"And are we to be talking secrets in her absence?" Nagarath prodded.

"Do you actually believe His Majesty managed to get ahold of Khariton's Mirror? Amsalla did make her disappearance rather fast, after all. Perhaps this was all some elaborate plot to throw us off the scent."

"She was not there when Anisthe received the notice from the king's own. Her hand was not in that. And besides, we have the evidence found in Madrid. In the archives. What the Sun King wants, he usually gets."

Nagarath felt, more than saw, Liara's flicker of emotion. The look recalled Sophie's pointed absence. It stirred a corresponding note within himself that he needed to sound. He leaned forward, hoping to draw out his magpie.

But no, whatever else she had wanted to say, and then hadn't, remained behind the closed doors of her dark eyes.

Unsatisfied, he settled back against the cushioned walls of the carriage. "And there is Khariton himself to think of."

"He, too, tends to get what he wants," Liara completed the thought. "Which is why Anisthe is both dangerous and in danger. I know. So, getting the mirror . . . ?"

"Will not be easy, no. But it also means that our enemy cannot have already danced in there and stolen it away. Yet. Sit up straight, Liara."

A hard day's ride into France with nary a sign of Anisthe and then . . . disaster. Their coachman had run off in the night. Stranded in Pau, Nagarath busied himself with hiring a replacement and left the women to find their own amusement. Which left Liara forced into the one thing that seemed to ease her maid's mind. They went shopping.

It took two days to find a driver—just about the absolute limit of Liara's patience with feigning interest over every ribbon, trim, and accessory the town had to offer.

And so there they stood, in the dusty streets of provincial Pau, Nagarath arguing with their new driver while Liara and Sophie waited off to the side, mortified at the gentleman's ability to make a scene.

Standing in the street, Liara felt her skin prickle, the strange and subtle realignment of energy felt when the object of invisible scrutiny. She glanced quickly to Nagarath—the gesture as much a check that it wasn't his gaze she felt as it was a question: *Did he feel it, too?*

The mage and coachman still engaged in fierce negotiations. Nagarath ignored Liara entirely. And it seemed his attention would be thus engaged until the question of transport was solved. And Sophie seemed completely engrossed in the effort it took to appear both politely uninterested in her employer's business, yet ready should she be suddenly needed.

Sighing, Liara carefully focused her eyes on the lively street in front of her, feigning boredom while she set her attention on the quieter scene beyond. Who watched them?

Knots of people chatted on corners. A woman and child ducked into a shop front. None of these looked her way.

An old man gave vent to a phlegmatic exhalation, spitting onto the dirt a moment later. That Liara did not react one iota spoke of her long history with spying and skulking. Unfazed, she let her eyes dance over the backs of the snorting, stamping horses, watching with apparent interest as a stable boy strode forward to calm the animals. Struggling with the steeds, the youth cast a sharp look at the arguing men. Liara couldn't blame him and, at this, allowed a smile to cross her face.

Travel at night. Liara rolled her eyes. She had heard just enough to set her to agreement with the driver. *Bah! Use magick, Nagarath, and we'd not have this problem.* The request—nay, demand—was odd. And embarrassing. More than once, she had caught the driver looking her and Sophie up and down. It seemed he drew his own—likely colorful—conclusions as to the nature of their situation, reading their urgency in his own common way.

Perhaps his scrutiny is what I sense. She felt stupid for her paranoia. She raised her eyebrows at a still-exasperated Nagarath and decided to join the conversation . . .

after a fashion. A little nudge with a spell and their reluctant coachman would be much more amenable to their odd request.

Hiding her efforts with a guileless smile, Liara reached for the well of her power. She could feel more than hear the spell reverberate in her mind—more will than words. Within the space of an eye blink, the hapless driver had thrown his hands in the air. Defeat. His pesky employers had won this round.

Nagarath's eyes did flick to her now, ice gray and forbidding. Steeling herself, Liara defended her actions. The voice in her head grew as strong as that which had enchanted the driver. The prickly feeling had not lessened, and something was screaming at her: Run! Get away from that place and its invisible eyes.

Liara carefully kept her face neutral and her motions unhurried. *Who is out there? What do they want?*

Handed up into the carriage, Liara's ducking of her head became an alarmed hunch as a loud crack rent the air. Even Sophie blanched. Every head whipped around—Liara's included. The tension quickly dispelled as guffaws and unhelpful jests assaulted a laborer who had just broken the wheel on his cart.

Cabbages rolled in the street. Liara's willful eyes followed one. She darted her gaze up to find herself staring directly into the forceful eyes of a stranger.

But not a stranger. Not exactly.

Him! Every prowling instinct in Liara labeled the man as the one who had put her on edge with his covert surveillance.

Deeply tanned skin and a dark mop of hair framed stunning azure eyes. He seemed as surprised to note her returned gaze. Surprise turned to blazing earnestness. Liara's heart leapt in her chest.

"Liara?" At her back, Nagarath's query spoke of both impatience and concern.

Even having fled to the safety of the carriage's dark interior, she could still feel those piercing blue eyes.

Liara found herself wishing Sophie would have accompanied them inside the carriage, rather than perching up top with the driver. An unnamable instinct suddenly spurred her desire for a woman's quiet company.

Nagarath pounded his signal to the driver and then swung deftly onto his own bench. The carriage jolted into motion. It caught Liara off-balance and threw her so that she nearly collided with Nagarath. She recovered by pretending she had meant to move forward for a last glance out the narrow window.

The last was true. Mostly. Liara could not have said why she needed another view of the familiar-yet-not face in the crowd. He had given her the shivers, most certainly. But there had been something compelling in the way he had regarded her with those penetrating eyes of his.

But the man had gone. And in his place? A strange unease. "Frightened" was too strong a word for how she felt, but Liara found she couldn't settle easily back into her seat as the carriage rocked and lurched its way out of town.

Haunted. That was it. As if the man's face had been etched into her memory even before she had laid eyes upon him. Rediscovery rather than discovery. But how? Until recently, the only faces with which Liara had been intimately familiar were those of Dvigrad, long dead neighbors and victims of Anisthe's cruel magick. And her tiny village did not produce eyes such as that: exquisite and challenging.

Quickly, Liara cast her memory over the faces from the ships that had brought them across the sea. The man sported an extraordinary suntan. And yet . . .

"Am I to presume that your sudden silence is remorse over what I sensed with regard to our driver, Liara?"

Nagarath's soft words kindled a heat in Liara's cheeks.

"You were making a scene," she explained. In her mind, she could still see the blue-eyed man staring at her with terrifying intensity. Looking up into Nagarath's own warm gaze, she felt her fear subside. Alone with her mage at last.

He sat back, putting a comfortable distance between them. "My request for immediate departure was most unseemly, I will agree. Thank you for recalling me to myself and our station. Losing our lead on Anisthe is no excuse for endangering the cover that will get us into the court of the King."

Chapter Twenty-two

"Your aurenaurae has left town." Domagoj entered the tiny rented room with a flourish. When his thunderclap of news provoked no response from Anisthe, he moodily claimed the pallet bed, cursing anew that they had yet to attain a station as high as their quarry's. Days from Paris and they were little better than they had been since leaving home—and perhaps worse.

"Do you know how many butterflies I had in Vrsar, pinned under glass or dissected for my Art?"

"I'm sorry?" Domagoj voiced his confusion, certain he had only half heard Anisthe's strange statement.

"Butterflies. I've been watching this one for the last ten minutes." Anisthe motioned for Domagoj to join him at the window. He pointed to the bright object of his scrutiny. "I don't think I remember a time in my life where I simply observed one for the sake of seeing. Although I've the Art to stop it, to change its course or steal its innate power . . . I haven't the desire. Strange, yes?"

"Yes, sir." Domagoj slid him a sideways glance, looking for the trick, the lesson in his mage's words. Pensive and philosophical, Anisthe had been like that for days. Ever since Almazar. Nostalgic. Thoughtful. Ineffective. It made Domagoj sick to see it. It made their inevitable parting all the easier.

For Anisthe will never love you, Domagoj. The reali- zation stung. And because it hurt, Domagoj repeated it of- ten, growing hardened under its lash.

"I have been nothing but a wizard for as long as I can remember. Even as a child untutored, I used what Art I could to manage without cold, without hunger. I survived. Life hurt. To hurt like that again . . ." Anisthe shivered. "I need Khariton's Mirror and the Art it promises. I do. But—"

"But you have lost the desire to exact your revenge." Domagoj's lip curled as he finished Anisthe's sentence for him. "A pretty butterfly having effected a change of heart in the great war mage of the Habsburg monarchy."

Angrily, Anisthe rounded on him, ready to strike. Wrath. The fire rekindled. "Amsalla is as much a mere pretty face as Liara is a mere dabbler in the Art. And, I need not remind you of my aurenaurae's besting you."

"Twice." Smiling crookedly, Domagoj called his magick to him. Faint sparkles—blue, like the Adriatic— flitted about the air, angry on his behalf. But it was not the insult of Anisthe's words which rankled but his repeated questioning of Domagoj's loyalty. Did he not know that Domagoj understood what it meant to suffer? Did the mage not yet see how his fate so clearly matched that of Domagoj and his kith?

On his own, Domagoj hadn't a chance of breaking the Laws which bound his Art—not limited as he was. He would just as soon wait for lightning to start a hearth fire as for the arbitrary conditions to restore the Art of his mer- folk.

No. Anisthe had come into his life for a purpose. And not just to save him from a life of slavery amongst men who saw him as lesser. The war mage's goals aligned with

Domagoj's own. What's more, he had the knowledge and drive to get things done.

And if Anisthe did not, there was always Liara. The aurenaurae would serve where the progenaurae would not. Especially after Domagoj's own spellwork had faltered just then in the streets of Pau.

His harmless hexing of Liara and Nagarath's coachman had met with resistance. Liara. Domagoj smiled to think of the silent shove of his power against hers, her blissful ignorance that she had an enemy other than obstinance. For Domagoj had, at Anisthe's urging, begun to make a habit of masking his hexes to all eyes. No sense in alerting Nagarath and Liara to how close the chase had become.

And then a stumble, a snapping of Domagoj's magick. How? A fault in the spell? Simple error on his part?

"Did you note where they were heading?"

"Paris. *La cour du Roi Soleil.*" Domagoj waved off Anisthe's question. He didn't know such specifics of their path. His mind still lingered on Liara. And on her mentor. That man had no subtlety or grace—the pairing was an insult to Domagoj's senses. Oh, to tear her from Nagarath and have her for himself. He'd watched Nagarath make his scene, the man holding to his own ridiculous choice not to use magick on a person in his employ. And then Liara. For Liara to have noticed Domagoj, to have looked directly at him . . . the memory prompted another shiver.

Fierce, beautiful, magickal Liara. Domagoj felt certain Liara would see it his way in the end. She had her ambitions. That much had been made clear to him from the very beginning. It was only too bad he'd read her wrong, allying himself with Anisthe without question. Perhaps if he had acted sooner, it would be him to whom she clung, rather than Nagarath.

Mages past their prime. Bound by books. Anisthe and Nagarath? They could have each other, so far as Domagoj was concerned.

Anisthe rose and drew the curtain over the window. "The mirror will be ours, and we will bend the Laws to our will. Beyond that I don't much care. Insects, all of them."

Liara and Nagarath rode in silence until the last of the light had faded from the sky. Bumping along in the dark, jostled this way and that, Nagarath regretted his earlier insistence that they leave at once. His bones were tired. The road was bad, and a fast-driven carriage was only so comfortable. And Liara was right. He had made a scene.

Nagarath had forgotten much of living in genteel society. Too caught up in his magick, he simply had no time for niceties. He did not concern himself with politics, or even money. His only interest in the news of the day was if said news came with rumor of a book or artifact of magick. And romance? He had shown how terrible he was at that game—and to a woman such as Amsalla for whom courtship came as easy as breath.

There Nagarath's conscience rebounded, congratulating his tendency to overthink. Courtship. Love. For Amsalla they were the same: they meant nothing. He knew she felt such, and it had stopped him from being untrue to his heart. He had known as much, and yet he had let Amsalla entice him into taking her in his arms. Nagarath's inner voice prodded him again, forcing honesty. Thinking things through meant nothing if he couldn't act on his principles.

But Liara was off limits. Firmly and nonnegotiable. Therein courtship and love most certainly did not intersect. Which was, ironically, exactly what was expected of the society in which he and his charge were about to step. Court was cruel, romance a weapon—or at least a means to an end.

That was the dance, was it not? Same as politics, money, and all the rest. Was he a fool to wish otherwise? Mayhap. Or maybe he was, somehow, less cynical, less hemmed in by everyone else's rules.

But then, he had never fit in with proper folk. Liara was lucky he had finally stopped reading over meals. Always the dreamer; always the mage. He had been like that his whole life, always dashing this way and that, his head caught up in the sort of oddities a true gentleman never worried about. His family would not be all that surprised with how Nagarath had turned out, had they lived long enough to witness it.

Slumped in sleep, Liara stole a few moments of peace. Watching her, Nagarath considered his own costume. Even if he did not sulk and slouch as Liara did, he fit the finery no better than did his magpie. Nagarath moodily fixed his eyes on the bouncing roof of the coach, trying to escape his conscience.

But, dash it all, none of it matters. These prissy, dressed-up, puffed-up people, they are ignorant—willfully ignorant—of how an entire subset of their world works. It rankled. It bothered Nagarath that they thought him, thought Liara, their 'kind,' a problem. All Nagarath wanted to do was stretch his legs out in a comfortable chair, settle down in front of a cozy fire, and work at his Art. And here he was spending the last of his family's money on some hare-brained scheme to save people who would rather he not.

Hang the rest of them.

He was honest with himself at last. *Hang Amsalla. Hang Anisthe! This is for Liara and Liara alone. Never mind that it is the right thing to do.*

Eyes back on Liara, Nagarath let himself fall into the gentle ebb and flow of her breath as she slept. He shut his eyes and allowed the wave of tenderness to engulf him. The space between them closed.

Hyper-aware of Liara's physicality, Nagarath drowned in the idea of her. He imagined what it might be like to have Liara's head rest in the crook of his arm, her hand on his chest, safeguarding him even as Nagarath sought to protect her. Her warm vibrancy, hard and angular, setting his skin to tingling. She shifted in her sleep, the small movement sending lightning through to his heart.

He loved her. Loved her like magick. Fierce. Fervent.

Wild promises flitted through his mind. Hastily rehearsed confessions, ardent hopes. He burned from it.

Eyes snapping open, Nagarath ripped himself from the reverie. No. For all that he desired to be connected to her, longed to simply bask in the light of her einatus, he mustn't. He was her protector and her mentor. To force the truth of his feelings upon her . . . unthinkable.

Angry with himself at having indulged in such intimate thoughts, Nagarath fiddled with the window, not daring to look at his apprentice any longer. The moon was rising, a broken disk which peeked tentatively over the distant hills. He watched it gain the sky, soothed by its cold cleanness.

The coach shook as a wheel made contact with a rut in the road, jostling Nagarath from his vigil. Liara sat up in her seat, yawning and rolling her shoulders to shake out the stiffness. Strands of her long, black hair had tumbled down out of her coiffure. Soft. Beautiful. Liara's face, pale in the light of the newly risen moon, looked at him with an intense scrutiny.

"What?" Liara's query, consisting of that solitary word, still managed to arc electricity through Nagarath's veins.

Impulsive, he found himself reaching into one of his hidden pockets. Even if he could not tell her . . . Even if he could not risk thinking of it himself . . . Nagarath fumbled over the words, "I've— Liara, I would like you to— But only if you want it—"

He held out the small silver charm to her. Dangling on a delicately wrought chain, it winked in the moonlight that streamed through the newly opened window. "It is a charm to keep you safe. To keep you connected to me and I to you, should we have need of one another. I should have done this before but—"

If she heard the husky tone to his voice, she did not note it. If she wondered at the tremor in Nagarath's hands as he delved for the matching charm at his own neck, concealed beneath his shirt collar, she did not comment. "Yes. Please."

"By wearing it, you can find me—even if I am beyond the reach of normal scrying . . . I will teach you its use. But—"

"Nagarath. I know you will." Liara's hand lay gently within his own, her eyes unreadable. But the grace with which she accepted his gift spoke to his hidden hopes. No challenge, no antagonistic quip about jeweled finery or the doling out of magick.

"It's beautiful. Help me?" Turning in her seat, she raised her arms to lift her fallen hair to aid him in putting on the pendant.

Nagarath watched his fingers undo the clasp. His eyes followed the bright thread of the chain as it fell over Liara's smooth skin. Murmuring the words of the spell, he felt his breath catch as the magick took hold.

Liara, too, gasped, her eyes brightened with excitement as she turned back to him.

A particularly large jostle swayed the carriage once more, breaking the moment.

Grateful for the interruption, Nagarath looked back to the window, thinking not of Liara's closeness or of the magick he could now feel burning around his neck. Rather he wondered over her poise, her seamless understanding of what he had been asking and acceptance of it. Without hesitation.

Trust, rebuilt. Magick, pledged.

The moon was laughing at him. A moon that had long seen Nagarath's heartache, his ruin, and his vows that he would never again give so much of himself to another. But then, the moon was, herself, changeful.

'I want to visit it. Tell me there's enough magick in the world for us to visit it someday, Nagarath.'

Words from another time, a world apart.

'If there is magick enough in the world to get us there safely, Liara, I promise that you are who I would take.'

Another jolt and the carriage came to an abrupt halt. Nagarath darted his arm across the small space, shielding Liara as he drew his wand. He could feel her trembling at his back, and he cursed himself soundly for his foolish insistence that they travel under cover of darkness. Together they listened for the danger.

A gentle rocking shook the carriage as the driver jumped down.

"You're going to have to take her in. Girl's acting all funny-like. Dizzy or sommat and I can't have her falling off." The driver moved to hand Sophie down after him.

"I'm fine. Just a passing weakness. That's all. Truly. I think it was the movement of the coach up top."

"That's why passengers should always sit within the carriage and not up top takin' fresh air and such nonsense." Their driver steered the white-faced Sophie to them.

Sophie's embarrassment deepened as Nagarath exited the coach and bent to peer intently into her eyes. His face level with hers, his steadying hands on her shoulders, he couldn't see much wrong with the young woman and so could not charm up a cure.

Nagarath thanked their driver and ushered her inside. Settling into his seat once more, he endeavored to get some rest. He instead found his attention drawn to Liara, charming and solicitous as she asked after the health of her maid. Watching Sophie's own reaction, he considered her near accident and peevishly decided that he could have used some fresh air himself. His fingers strayed to the silver chain about his own neck, believing that, perhaps, he'd discovered a new danger in traveling a nighttime road.

Chapter Twenty-three

"And there it is, Liara. Paris." Nagarath smiled out the window of the carriage, leaning back a moment later so that Liara might have an unimpeded view.

The traffic on the road had increased with their growing proximity to the great city—center of art, culture, and power. Their going had slowed to an abysmal pace over the previous two days. It tested Liara's patience, perhaps beyond endurance. There was, as yet, not much to see.

Paris, a cluster of spires and rooftops in the far distance, appeared little different from any other place, save for its evident size. That, and for the fact that every person in the known world seemed in a hurry to get there.

Liara sat back in her seat, lest she fall to unladylike gawking. There would be time enough to see the sights once they were closer and there was anything to see. She understood Amsalla DeBouverelle's overly sumptuous taste in clothing. Even that far from the city's edge, large estates loomed. Fashionable eyes seemed everywhere. Already Liara could see where her own toilette failed the high fashion of the metropolis.

"Have you been?" Turning to Sophie, Liara's question startled the maid. Not the effect she had meant to have.

Rushing over Sophie's sudden shyness, Liara tried to be a little more of the young woman whom Nagarath had said was welcome at court. Outgoing. Vibrant. "The closest thing I've seen to a city of this size is Ragusa. But that has the sea and the massive walls."

"And they speak your language."

"Yes. There's that." Liara laughed.

Since Sanzay, through careful effort, Liara had drawn Sophie out, answering a good many of her questions. Coming from a good family, Liara's maid had three older siblings but few prospects in a place so small and far from opportunity—her parents were deceased. She welcomed the change Nagarath's offer had afforded, glad to take on the challenge of making an innocent ready for the court of the Sun King.

In many ways, Liara had come to enjoy Sophie's company. When the mage was not around, the young woman was pleasant, loquacious without lapsing into shameful gossip. And she was endlessly patient with Liara's sometimes flawed adoption of her tongue. She rarely asked that Liara repeat herself and was gentle in her correction. If only Liara might somehow help Sophie overcome her timidity with regard to Nagarath. Such had begun the night the poor woman had nearly fallen from the coachman's perch in her exhaustion.

Perhaps time will thaw that coolness. After all, she has managed to get me—reticent me!—to talk to her. Liara mused. A somber thought cut in. Whatever would they do with Sophie when this was all through? Would Nagarath return her to her village? Would Sophie be given a reference to work for some young courtier's family? Liara would inevitably have to say goodbye. The thought pained her.

"Look!" While Liara might have to reign herself in, Sophie indulged in enough excitement for both of them. As trees and brush gave way to the brick and stone of buildings, she even overcame her reserved manner in Nagarath's presence.

Liara couldn't help it then. She stared at every sight her eyes could touch.

She had seen Messina, Ragusa, Porto Torres, massive exotic ports which made Vrsar small by comparison. She had witnessed the variety of cities and towns their journey inland had given them. Liara was over the shock of finding how many people could live in one place at the same time. Commerce at every turn, the needless complication of life—the shops alone—had lost their exotic surprise.

But the press of buildings—block after block after endless block—still astonished her. The slow crush of people, in endless variety of both finery and frippery, seemed frantic and aimless. Liara was unsure how it all worked.

Then she saw a warehouse here, a hotel there. Houses. Banks. Government buildings. Liara craned her neck, trying to glimpse the palace. It remained hidden amongst the press of commerce. Even the shabby buildings were impressive. Matched brickwork and rows of windows stretched the length of the street only to meet another building, equally grand. It was as though the buildings were courtiers, too, each trying to outmatch its neighbor with its perfect proportions or grand entrances of arch after arch.

Everything seemed so delicate, breakable. The exact opposite of what Liara had grown up knowing: solid, simple, rustic, and serviceable. In Paris, everything seemed designed to look like something else. Gloves looked like curtains, pruned trees resembled statues. Every available surface had been carved, patterned, and decorated. It was dizzying to look at.

Like stepping inside a jewel. Liara trembled. How could she even leave the carriage? She was sure to be found out as soon as she opened her mouth. Sophie's well-intended joke about language suddenly seemed an impossible obstacle. Liara's new worries set her to remembering her first encounter with the fine clothing she had become accustomed to wearing, the silks and satins and Nagarath's ease with it all.

He has been here before. Eyes narrowing with the realization, Liara looked slyly to the mage. Perhaps aware of her scrutiny, her silent accusation, Nagarath's eyes met hers. Covering the heat in her cheeks, Liara looked away. She had forgotten that Madame DeBouverelle was of France. Of course Nagarath had been there before.

As if in confirmation of that very thought, Nagarath rapped on the carriage roof. They slowed to a stop, moving out of the sluggish traffic for the gentleman to disembark. Liara moved to follow, surprised at how quickly they might have arrived at their destination.

Whichever it is. Again thoughts of Amsalla flitted through Liara's head, and she barely managed to hide her displeasure. There had been almost no mention of the witch since her apparent betrayal during their rescue of Anisthe. Surely Nagarath would not take up with the enemy?

The mage motioned Liara back, smiling thinly at her before turning his eyes up to their driver. "If you could wait here, I have just got to call in a few favors."

Half-in, half-out of the carriage door, Nagarath seemed distracted. No, uneasy.

Liara fought the rising panic that threatened to choke her. Was he really going to leave them here? Amongst all these people? In this big place?

"On second thought, I may be a bit long. Perhaps a turn about the Gardens?"

The carriage walls and din of the street outside muffled the rest of Nagarath's instructions.

Her mage peered back into the depths of the carriage, although he continued his instructions to the driver-turned-guard. "Deliver them safely and without incident to wherever it is I later direct you. They are not to be left one moment out of your sight, do you understand? Not in this city."

Liara turned her worry towards Sophie, seeking commiseration and finding the maid's eyes politely downturned. So far, half the people she had seen from the carriage window had appeared aristocrats and the other cutpurses. She muted the shiver that danced across her spine.

"Liara, I—" Nagarath gave Liara a long look. But, like Liara's panic, whatever he had to say to her seemed to stick before it could find its way out, and he instead simply backed away, his eyes still locked to hers. He substituted, "Sophie will see to it that you have what you need for the duration of our stay here. I will see you later."

The carriage jolted into motion, carrying Liara and Sophie away from Nagarath as their capable and long-suffering driver—Jean was his name, but Liara knew precious little more than that—took his instructions and led the horses towards the center of town.

Liara again buried her apprehension, smiling in response to Sophie's shy return from her quiet retreat. Commercial buildings slid past in an unending array as the carriage crawled through the throng of people clogging every street and thoroughfare.

At least the money seems real enough, Liara mused as Sophie uttered occasional compliments at dressmaker's shops and other such destinations which passed by their small window to the wider world.

Liara, too, found herself eying the signs for various shops with unexpected anticipation. From the safety of their carriage window came the reminder of how provincial she looked. Even her small instinct was piqued at the sight of the elegant, bright young ladies wearing considerably more luxurious things than her own ornate and expensive, yet practical, traveling garb. She could feel Sophie's anticipation beside her, wound tight like a spring, ready and eager to get Mademoiselle Liara into one of those shops.

Remembering their heavily laden state, Liara wondered where they would even put a new purchase. Delivery was clearly out of the question and, hired or not, the coach was only so big. Would they be staying at one of those large, splendid hotels she had spotted from the window?

As she pondered this new dilemma and tried to imagine where Nagarath had gone off to, Liara felt the carriage slow to a stop for what felt like the thousandth time. And this time it stayed immobile, their driver clambering down from his seat. Liara espied an oasis of greenery amidst the noise and stink of the metropolis. Feeling as if in a dream, she let Jean hand her down from the carriage, Sophie shortly behind her.

Beaming, Liara stepped out onto the manicured paths of the public gardens of Paris, the wizard temporarily forgotten in the hustle and bustle, the throngs of beautiful people striving to see and be seen. "Miss Sophie. Welcome to Paris."

Giggling, they set off to conquer the city.

Setting off down the street at a leisurely pace, Nagarath debated his best course of action. Clearly they would need inroads with the local nobility, someone who could introduce them at court. But were his connections still viable? Would he be remembered by what few people he dare call upon?

Looking down a once familiar street and finding most everything changed, he worried that the contacts he had in the city were tenuous indeed. If his own cursory knowledge of Paris was twelve years outdated, he could guess that old acquaintances' memories were at least as stale.

Still, he had to try. Approaching the ornate and imposing door of a former friend, he assumed a carefree, foppish smile.

Hopefully, he's at home. Nagarath fretted in the brief moments before the door opened to an imperious doorman.

Not a familiar face. Nagarath fixed the servant with a dazzling smile and overdone greeting. The doorman sniffed and silently waved him in.

In the silence of the drawing room, Nagarath fiddled with his buttons, at once afraid he had gotten the fashion wrong, his knowledge built on hearsay and country tailors.

A muted exclamation brought his attention back to the present just in time to hear an undignified clatter of footfalls on the stairs.

Well, it seems I am remembered after all! A man as lanky and tall as himself burst into the room.

"It is you! Good gracious, man, when Georges here told me who was at my door, I told him it couldn't be. Where the devil have you been all this time?" Chevalier Talaffe Sauvageau enthusiastically bypassed all niceties, nearly toppling Nagarath with a sharp pat on the back. "You haven't turned old and stodgy on me, have you?"

Cracking a smile, Nagarath chuckled. "Not unless you have, Tally. Been traveling, seeing the world." He gestured half-heartedly as if to say he had seen it all and been extraordinarily bored by the sights.

Talaffe laughed all the more. "Ever the unimpressed, eh?"

Nagarath shrugged and sat without invitation. "And what, pray tell, have you done with yourself?"

"I haven't improved nor refined myself, if that's what you're after." The gentleman grinned and settled in the opposite chair. He snapped his fingers for claret. "You remember Matty and JJ, of course?"

"Of course. Was hoping we might have a reunion of sorts." Nagarath nodded. He raised the beverage that had been whisked to the table at his side.

"Well!" Telaffe drew the word out in a stage whisper, as if engaging in the deepest sort of gossip, "JJ's settled. There's no counting on him. And Matty's been dutifully playing the fool at ol' King Louis' court."

"But that's brilliant! We can save them both in one deft maneuver."

Talaffe saluted Nagarath with his glass. "Any prior engagements tonight?"

Nagarath shrugged. "Just got in a bit ago. Still need to look for lodgings, in fact—"

"Nonsense," Talaffe waved him off. "You'll stay here, of course."

"I'm not alone," Nagarath cautioned. He smiled inwardly at Talaffe's animated reaction.

"Oh?"

"Not that kind of not alone," Nagarath clarified. Rolling his eyes, he took a generous sip of wine. "I've been saddled with my cousin's daughter. He'd hoped I could show her a bit of the world now that she's just come of age. They live in Venice—"

"Pretty?" Talaffe perked up.

Nagarath pictured Liara's likely reaction to the Parisian dandy and snorted. "Very—but you're not her type."

Throwing his head back in an exaggerated laugh, Telaffe winked. "We'll just have to set you up with JJ, then. He's respectable, at least, now that he's gotten himself a wife and children." He paused and added slyly, "Suppose we'll have to get him drunk first before he'll think to offer. How much time did you say you have?"

It was just past luncheon.

Nagarath sighed inwardly. How had he ever found such a crowd amusing? Fixing his carefree smile back on his face, he said, "Well, Liara and her lady's maid have been set loose on Paris with a full purse. You do the calculations."

Grinning, Telaffe rose. "Well, we'd best hurry then. Let's go scare up Matty and JJ."

~*~

Liara spotted the smart-looking runner as he entered the café.

Really, Nagarath? She cast a doubtful eye over the maître d' as he accepted the runner's message and turned to approach their table. As Sophie fished for the appropriate coin, Liara read the message with angry eyes. It appeared that Nagarath would not be meeting them until later, though it seemed he had at least secured lodgings for them.

Setting aside the note, Liara endeavored to have herself a pleasant meal but found her mind wandering. *Clearly Nagarath knows people in town—well enough that he was able to call upon them and receive an open invitation to both him and his traveling companion.*

His absence and subsequent note put her ill at ease over the whole plan, however. Even if his connections did get them to court with relative ease, Liara did not relish the idea of solitary dining while Nagarath was off with goodness-knows-who doing goodness-knows-what. In a court full of strangers, she could imagine her discomfort magnifying tenfold.

Sophie—good, solid, dependable Sophie—seemed to be taking it all in stride. While Liara hadn't disclosed the contents of the message, she knew the maid was sharp and had a more or less accurate appraisal of the situation formed in her head. Unperturbed and non-judgmental, she sat with an attentive eye to Liara while doing her level best to cover her mistress's melancholy turn of mind.

"Begging your pardon, Mademoiselle. But I take it the message was about our lodgings for the evening?" she inquired. She eyed the sun's passage across the afternoon sky as the source of her reasoning, rather than Liara's vexation at Nagarath's absence.

"Yes, Sophie. It seems we've been invited to stay with an old friend of Nagarath's. He'll be meeting us there later, it would seem. I've been provided an address."

Sophie nodded. "Well, that helps matters some; we'll know where to send your new things."

Smiling, Liara marveled at Sophie's seamless ability to say the right thing at the right time. Closing her eyes, she pictured again the beautiful golden wonder of a dress she had ordered not two hours before. With any luck, it would be ready in time for her to use it for their introduction to court.

That would get Nagarath to stick around a bit. Liara smirked, thinking of how striking the cloth had looked when draped against her pale, even skin. Yes, Sophie was a perfect companion.

Opening her eyes, Liara smiled devilishly. "Well, it seems we are to make our own entertainment before we find Seigneur Julien Jeffers' residence."

Two hours later found the girls in the carriage on their way to their host's residence, lemon ices in hand, Sophie joyously clutching a new hat to her head.

Nagarath met them there.

And he was not at all himself.

Flanked by two gentlemen, he peeled himself off from where he lounged against the gates of the large estate and approached the carriage. One of the men—the shorter and stouter of the two—followed. The other remained in his indolent stance, toying with the cuff of his glove.

Liara darted her gaze from the two strangers back to Nagarath. She decided then that perhaps he wasn't all that altered by his afternoon away. For a moment, she had thought his bearing, his very gait, somehow different. But all that disappeared as he locked eyes with her. Visible relief. And a bit of pride when Nagarath's sharp eyes noted the evidence of how the girls had spent their free time.

Liara barely noticed being handed down from the carriage. She hardly saw the manicured street nor Nagarath's second companion as he made up his mind to approach at last, aloof and cool, his own man on his own schedule.

Nagarath made the introductions. In exquisite French, Liara's name rolled off his tongue to bump gently against that of the two Parisian gentlemen. She attempted a wobbly curtsy, lowering her gaze to hide the heat creeping into her cheeks. Monsieur Jeffers: their host. Monsieur Sauvageau: the rake. And who was, effectively, sizing her up in a most ungentlemanly manner.

It occurred to Liara, then, the real difference in Nagarath. He was showing off. Why? Confusion cleared her budding blush and gave Liara back her wits. With a flashing bite of directness, she met M. Sauvageau's audacity with some of her own. She read approval in his eyes and almost laughed aloud.

Taking leave of their small party, M. Sauvageau flashed a quick smile meant for Liara alone. He then proceeded down the street, as leisurely and sure of himself as before. Liara resisted the urge to beam her triumph at Nagarath. Not the young woman he'd choose to show at court? She would see about that.

Chapter Twenty-four

The next morning, Liara concluded that, this time, Nagarath was most definitely not himself.

Late-night, post-dinner revels amongst the men had taken Liara away from her mage's side. And while polite society simply did not allude to their decrepit state, the bleary-eyed dishevelment of both JJ and Nagarath was noted at the breakfast table, with Sophie trying not to glare at the men and failing miserably.

Liara pretended not to notice, breaking her fast in quiet affability. And she took refuge in Sophie. In addition to being apt distraction from her wizard's plight, the woman's trepidation helped Liara force herself past her own. For all of his inattention concerning his own presence, Nagarath had considered the troubles of leaving shy Liara without a proper companion in the days ahead and—via a second note the day before—promoted Sophie from lady's maid to traveling companion before their arrival at the Jeffers' residence.

Liara soon became doubly grateful for the change. As the table was cleared and its diners scattered, it became obvious that she would again be without her wizard. Mouth set in a straight line, eyes hard, shoulders high and tight, Liara waited until they were safely back in their rooms before she let her mask slide. Then, and only then, did she round on Sophie, frightening the poor woman with her outburst. "What is wrong with that man?"

Sophie flinched. "Some men, when faced with the temptations that a city such as Paris has—"

"He's not 'some man,' Sophie. He's not." Liara stopped herself before she said more.

"Come, let's make you ready for the day. Madame Jeffers appeared rather eager for a chance to show you about town."

Liara's grimace deepened. "Probably looking for an excuse to leave her husband to his suffering. But if our absence gives Monsieur JJ another chance at ruining Nagarath, I'd rather claim a headache myself."

Sophie clicked her tongue in dismay. Settling by Liara's wardrobe, she beckoned. "Come, we'll get you all set for the day and see about some of your other options before we set out for the shops. That should fill our time neatly before heading to court tomorrow."

"Tomorrow?"

Sophie rushed to explain. "Yes. I'm sorry, miss. I overheard some of the gentlemen's talk late last night. Add that to the card sent by Monsieur Poulin. And Master Nagarath's attempts to gain your eye over the table. Perhaps I am wrong. It could be the day after."

"I won't be ready in time!" Panic overtook Liara's senses. Suddenly, the wardrobe of dresses seemed inadequate. Her manners, awkward. Her head, stuffed full of French, emptied. The threatened headache began to look all the more tempting. Might she beg one for a whole week?

"Ah, but then they will not expect too much of you as of yet, begging your pardon. You might benefit from your accent and your manner of dress."

I am more than fully aware of my deficiencies, thank you. Liara eyed the assembled finery, seeing only Nagarath in his foreign frippery, the man looking and feeling a stranger to her. Clearing her head, she bowed to Sophie's expertise in picking out a dress for the day. Liara was to don something a touch more fashionable—so as to not entice Madame Jeffers into too many dressmaker shops. Such would also strategically leave her more provincial ones for the first few days at court, to further secure Liara the safety of her "accent and manner of dress."

Liara cast a critical gaze over Sophie's own ensemble. "And what about you?"

"Oh, Miss, I—" Blushing, she dropped her voice to an embarrassed whisper. "It's just not right to pretend to . . . to presume myself at such a level as—"

"You're presuming nothing. Nagarath's orders, yes?" Back in territory with which she was much more familiar, Liara's tone came brusque. "And my request. As a frie— I need your companionship. And besides, this whole arrangement is as awkward for me as it is you. Changing clothes for every social situation. Having to have someone dress me as though I were some doll. Me! Who've dressed myself my whole life." Liara stopped short, her hands leaping to her mouth, her ears burning in embarrassment.

The damage was done.

Sophie gave too long a pause. It gave Liara time to quickly recount her candid confession. *'He's not "some man," Sophie.'* Twice since breakfast she had spoken too close to the truth of her and the mage. She recalled the maid's eyes flashing with some unreadable emotion as Liara complained over Nagarath's conduct. She had then deftly changed the conversation. It pained Liara to ponder what Sophie might truly think of them.

But worse than that, Liara's thoughts had reversed back to the mage. There they stuck. Nagarath. Whom she'd ceased to feel comfortable around. She wanted to be near him. She wanted to be far, far from him. Unhappy and unsettled, Liara peevishly concluded that it was all stupid. The whole plan was stupid. The mage was stupid. Her hair was stupid.

Liara hardly realized she'd sat and allowed the maid to begin her tedious work of looping and twisting her luxurious dark hair into a sweeping updo. She glimpsed in the mirror to find Sophie's eyes still on her. The woman wanted to say something, Liara was certain of it. "Sophie, I . . ."

"Madamoiselle?"

"Nothing." Carefully rearranging her face, Liara moved past her unspoken thought. Instead, she confronted her own reflection, wondering anew if Nagarath felt the same for her as she did him.

Sophie continued her work, lifting here, tucking there.

Liara mastered herself at last, and she flicked her eyes to Sophie's. "Don't you wish we could just cut it all off?"

"Oh!" Sophie looked up in surprise, a protest ready on her lips.

"No, no. I'm kidding." Liara's smile became impish. "Mostly."

"Ah." Sophie let her face fall, nodding wisely before responding with a sly smile of her own. "But then we could have shopped today . . . for hats!"

Together, they laughed at the poorly crafted joke, not employer and maid, not companion and lady, but true and proper friends.

~*~

Nagarath lay dying upon his bed.

Well, perhaps not dying, but wishing he were.

The morning so far had been a near disaster, the only consolation being that JJ seemed as bad off as he. And far beyond the physical maladies to which Nagarath was victim: the embarrassment. Oh, the embarrassment! Sophie glaring at him over her breakfast plate; Liara doing her best not to see his haggard, sickish appearance.

I could magick myself well. Nagarath groaned, hiding from the light. *I always did in younger days.* His old friends had noticed the difference, too. He'd taken no end of mockery for his loss in fortitude. The jibes had come that they had to get him back into shape if he were to keep up with them.

Keep up with them? He wanted to have nothing to do with the Messieurs Matty, JJ, and Tally. Miscreants. Inebriates. *As were you, Nagarath. Take the high road all you want now, but you were just like them a dozen odd years back.*

And that kept Nagarath from magicking his way out of his predicament. He'd grown beyond such abuses of power.

"But it would seem that Liara has not." Roused at last to action, Nagarath absently reached for the pendant about his neck. The sensation had been subtle—Liara likely trying to work her spells so that he would not notice. Crossing the room to splash water on his fevered cheeks, he could feel that she was somewhere out in the city, not all that distant. But not around the corner, either. He would have to have a talk with her when she returned. If he found opportunity.

Nagarath turned to find solace in his bed once more.

A knock sounded on the door to his room, the sound knifing through his skull and setting his teeth to rattling. Hunting about for his dressing gown, Nagarath wheezed through his excuses, hoping to stem another summons.

The knocking repeated itself.

Don't be rude. Don't be rude. Don't be—

"Go away."

He had opened the door only to immediately shut it. Directly in the face of Julien.

"Oh, surely it's not as bad as all that?" JJ's harassment came muffled through the door.

"Have you no respect for the deceased?" Nagarath called back, enjoying the game in spite of himself.

"None whatsoever."

Nagarath could almost hear the man grinning. For a moment, he hated JJ. Hated that he was on his feet and squarely in the land of the living.

But he hated himself more, for, short minutes later, Nagarath was as right and well as his friend. His guilt doubled to think that Liara had felt the twinge of his magick on her end.

"This heat, Mademoiselle, it is unseasonable."

Liara stood outside on the street, waiting by the carriage and trying to make idle conversation with Jean who seemed discomfited by her sudden interest. And so they spoke of the weather, together suffering through the delays of Sophie and Madame Jeffers' shopping detour.

"I rather like it," Liara defended her obstinate refusal to wait in the carriage. Shaded or not, she found it stuffy. Though she was not going to admit that to Jean.

Her swarthy driver nodded. "You are from the seaside. I had forgot. The sun seems to burn brighter there. Or so the rumors say."

Liara's answering smile cracked as a spark shot through her magick. The pendant at her neck tingled—the change invisible to any observer save for herself and the soul of her Art. Guilt brought a new heat into her cheeks.

Nagarath was performing magick. Perhaps in answer to the jinxes she herself had used but a moment before. A gentle reminder that he, too, was aware of her use of power.

As she had waited for her companions, Liara had endeavored to combat the oppressive heat by jinxing to life a slight breeze. The tiny spell had benefited Jean, too, providing her the personal justification she had needed. And she'd been careful, Nagarath having been adamant against her using any magick in Paris until they'd better determined the state of things in the city.

A shout pulled Liara's attention back out of thoughts of her mage.

Jean ran forward to assist Madame Jeffers. Sophie looked pale and shaken as she leaned heavily upon a fence rail.

"What is it? What happened?" Jean found his tongue before Liara could.

"She nearly had a faint," Madame Jeffers explained.

Liara tried to offer the maid an arm for support. Sophie, fully in possession of her faculties, protested through the assistance. "I tripped. I merely caught my foot on something as we left the shop."

However, Sophie did have a gloved hand pressed delicately to her forehead, her face terribly pale.

Jean offered his critique of the weather once more, "It is so unseasonable. I don't doubt that it is causing all manner of mischief."

"I'm fine. Truly," Sophie assured, her eyes locking with Liara's, pleading.

"She's fine. Let's get away from the prying eyes." Liara fixed the passersby a most unladylike glare. To her, stares of the assorted men and women idling nearby seemed more interested in judging than caring. Whispers and raised eyebrows followed them into the safety of the carriage.

Poor Sophie.

Again, Sophie's gentle protests cut through Madame Jeffers' assurances that they would return home for an afternoon of quiet diversions. She had merely lost her footing. Everyone had overreacted.

Her words swayed Liara, now seeing Sophie's apparent weakness as mere embarrassment. She bit her lip, wanting to shout at the onlookers still waiting for the carriage to move, their curious glances turned at the carriage windows.

"It's these horrid little shoes." Sophie leaned back with a sigh. "Tripping me up, making me believe that up and down had inexplicably changed places . . ."

"Oh, but they are so very pretty," Madame Jeffers interjected, as kind as she was elegant. "With them, I daresay you managed to make your brief upset look quite fashionable." With the words—and Sophie's own answering smile—Liara felt a stab of jealousy. The woman was a credit to Nagarath's friend, Julien. A creature from another world, the noblewoman reminded Liara of things she wanted and could not have.

The mood lightened as the city rolled past. The slight accident forgotten, the two women chattered away in their musical language, leaving Liara to follow along as best she could. She was, of course, wholeheartedly included, the Frenchwomen often slowing or rephrasing things so that she might better understand. But, in laughing along, Liara felt false. And it stung, the reminder that she would never quite be the bright and carefree twittering bird of a woman that the courtiers so admired.

Stealing a glance out the carriage window to the grand buildings and elegant pedestrians, Nagarath's words filled Liara's mind, his lament that she was no sunshine-bright flirt. *The sort that even Nagarath clearly admires.*

A wave of homesickness shook her. Dvigrad. Parentino. Simple. And gone. Father Phenlick, who had wanted the best from her but had never asked her to be someone she was not. Krešimir, who had liked her for who she was. An unfair yet uncomplicated world. And a world where Nagarath did not carouse and wear preposterous finery.

Liara wondered if she might see the wizard later in the day. She felt wobbly herself and—preposterous finery or not—Liara needed the mage's reassuring manner to set her heart at ease.

She would be found out. She'd be found out and would have to leave the court before they found the mirror.

And Nagarath would be exposed as a fraud to his friends. And Anisthe would get exactly what he wanted. And then he'd come after her. Liara. Who couldn't smile and laugh like Sophie and Madame. Liara, who had none of Amsalla DeBouverelle's poise.

Jealousy rose again, hot and bitter. But this time, instead of shrinking away, Liara could feel the challenge. She was left-handed in more ways than wand-work. Awkward. Counter to expectations, always. The sort you did not bring into good society.

Here you are, Liara, a lying, sneaking orphan. A thief, kicked out of your own village. A witch who defeated one of Europe's most dangerous and renowned war mages. And they believe you're the daughter of a merchant and that Nagarath is merely your chaperone. Truly, how hard can it be to nod along with their jokes and gossip? It is a role, no different than an innocent smile delivered while concealing a stolen trinket. Slight of hand.

Surrounded by the comforts of station and connection, Liara tried her best to emulate her bright-eyed, lady-like companions for the rest of the afternoon. The hours passed slowly, but at least time moved forward.

Liara congratulated herself on her progress as she returned to their rooms to change for the evening's meal. Nagarath—were she ever to see him again!—would be pleased. But it was such hard work. She feared she had no more words left in her, no more smiles. She fingered the pendant at her neck and wondered if there was any sort of spell, anything at all, that might transform her into the courtier she needed to become.

Feeling Sophie's eyes on her, Liara stopped her fidgeting.

"Madame Jeffers is quite kind," Liara said.

Sophie nodded, turning to fetch Liara's gown for dinner.

"She talks so much. I'm not used to that." Liara paused, waiting to see if Sophie would respond. Something in the maid's silence unnerved her. Some instinct roused.

Liara waited further, attempting to hear what her conscience was trying to say.

Watching Sophie's efficient assemblage of her toilette before turning to her own, Liara saw the disparity, remembered her words from but early that morning, her own admission that she was no noble. "Here, let me help."

"No, Mademoiselle. Please."

"Oh, pooh." Liara waved off the protest, lifting her dress and turning it this way and that, mystified. Bothered as she had been by the embarrassment of having near strangers helping her into clothes—and measure her for more—these past days, Liara had simply not troubled herself to note the complicated way in which she was gotten into said clothing.

"Come." Sophie would have none of Liara's nonsense. "It is fine. Truly. I am aware that you are more than you appear to be."

More than. Not less. Liara blushed, feeling doubly foolish. She allowed Sophie to change her from one dress to the next, her apology still ready on her lips. Their eyes met and Liara flushed, all words escaping her. Pausing, the maid stepped back, admiring Liara's costume before approaching to make some small adjustment.

"Tell me— Tell me about Nagarath." Sophie's eyes had darted to Liara's pendant as she made her bold request.

The maid's cheeks reddened; her hands trembled slightly with her daring.

Smiling, Liara sat on the edge of the bed. "What is it you want to know?"

"Is he . . . ? Have you ever . . . ? There's something about him that, when you look at the man, makes the world go all topsy-turvy. He's also something . . . other. Isn't he?"

"That he is." Laughing, for dangerous as it was to speak close to the truth, it felt good to talk of something other than fashion and art. Liara volunteered, darkly, "Nagarath reads at dinner tables."

"Truly?"

"And is forgetful. And plain. And stubborn. But never truly improper."

"And kind." Sophie's eyes grew soft.

"Very much so," Liara agreed.

"Like his niece."

From the way she said the word, the gleam in her eyes as she stared pointedly at the pendant around her lady's neck, Liara could tell Sophie didn't believe their cover one bit. Staring down her challenger, Liara silently dared her to outright call her and Nagarath into question. It would be a relief to confide in Sophie. She'd already done near enough with her hints and miscues.

And she could trust her. Of this Liara was certain. A wave of homesickness rose again in her chest, a need for a friend who knew her secrets, who could trust her in return.

The awkward pause continued. Liara begged for Sophie to gather her courage.

"Liara, have you ever felt as though—?"

A knock on the door jolted Sophie from her question. She hurried across the room to answer.

It was time for dinner.

Leaving for the well-mannered torture that was mealtime in a nobleman's house, Liara wondered if she would ever get to hear what Sophie had been hoping to ask.

Such questions fled as Liara found herself confronted with the promise of yet further discomfort. Nagarath and M. Jeffers stayed in for the evening, inviting two other gentlemen to stop by—one of whom was none other than Monsieur Talaffe Sauvageau.

Of course, Liara had to be seated by him and not Nagarath. And, of course, Monsieur Talaffe appeared eager to continue his game begun in the street outside of the Jeffers' home. The question was, did Liara dare play along? Was she supposed to?

Monsieur Talaffe—Tally, to use Nagarath's nickname for him—began by using Italian on Liara. "And are we well this evening?"

Interesting. Eyebrows raised, she answered in Croatian, testing him right back. "Fine, save for yesterday's rain."

The result? Nagarath sputtered into his wine glass. The shock on his face reminded Liara that she hadn't used her own language openly since their fleeing Limska Draga. Tally merely half-hid his smile and leaned in to give Liara his response in exquisite French. Liara felt heat rise within her cheeks. She'd meant to speak of the weather, and he had deftly turned the conversation to her: some nonsense about sunshine and her smile.

"Ah, so she knows the practical side of our language." Leaning towards her, Tally gave a pointed glance to Nagarath and so, for politeness' sake, she could not. Liara's blush burned all the hotter. "Either you've a very quick tongue or an astute tutor—one who's made a point of arming you properly. You'll make your way tomorrow without much help from him or your companion. It is a shame, for I had hoped to offer myself as your translator."

Panicking, for Liara was fully out of her depth, she quickly muttered a word of the Green Language under her breath, coyly reaching to brush her finger along the chain that held her magicked pendant. *Help.*

Talaffe apparently thought her muttered spell a word meant for his ears, and he leaned closer still.

Flustered, Liara blurted out, "I am simply well read, Monsieur."

The sparkle that had rendered him attractive but the day before returned to Tally's eyes. That time, Liara felt his assessment of her went deeper than dress, hair, and form. With an electric shock, she could tell Nagarath's interest was piqued by the exchange. His eyes flitted her way. A studied disinterest, she knew the look well, having often worn it herself.

Talaffe inserted himself between the silent pointed non-exchange, smiling warmly. "Illuminate me, Mademoiselle."

Twenty titles—completely inappropriate to the situation—flitted through Liara's brain. Again, her hand strayed to the pendant. This time she believed she felt a spark of magick rebuff hers. Or maybe it was just guilt. In any event, it helped bring the clarity she sought. Smiling, Liara replied, "Why, everything from *Commentaria in octo libros Physicorum Aristotelis* to Nikole Zrinskog's *Adrianskoga mora sirena.*"

"And all that falls in between, I daresay." Nagarath's attentions were roused at last.

Triumph! Liara tried to meet her wizard's gaze, but he had again turned away. Talaffe loomed in between. He actually looked quite interested.

Surprise looks good on you, Monsieur Sauvageau. Liara rewarded his attentions with another smile.

"Aquinas. Interesting. Your house must have quite the library." He steepled his fingers and became an eager pupil. "Any of Chamier? Beza? Someone not French, then, say, Agrippa?"

"*Declamation on the Nobility and Preeminence of the Female Sex.*" Liara laughed as Tally's wide-eyed response came as she had anticipated.

"What about *Of Magical Ceremonies*?"

"Falsely attributed to him." Liara quickly called back her dearth of knowledge. "Or . . . or so I've heard."

Again it became clear to Liara that Nagarath listened in on her conversation with Tally. His jaw tightened, and he—if it were even possible—ignored Liara all the more.

"Bound in books. Perhaps the diversions of our city bore you then, Mademoiselle?"

"Oh, no." Liara hadn't realized her gaze had fallen on Nagarath and stayed there until Tally roused her from her thoughts. "I just know so little—"

"—But have read so much."

"Exactly." Liara sighed in relief. For a moment, Tally had helped her feel like herself.

He drew close to conspire, whispering so that Nagarath would not hear, "Well, there are a number of things you cannot learn from books. Tell me, are you fond of dancing?"

For one wild moment, Liara had thought the gentleman might be so uncouth as to openly refer to courtship. But dancing? She felt the blood drain from her face nonetheless.

Talaffe had the sense to politely direct his gaze elsewhere. To his credit, he seemed flustered for having distressed her so. Having let her recover herself, he gave his apology and returned their conversation to safer grounds.

Liara retained her composure for the rest of the evening. But inwardly she remained shaken. None least because Tally had inadvertently shown her where her disguise was weak. No, the thought most preying upon her mind? Under Talaffe's attentions, Liara finally realized what Sophie might have been driving at with her questions earlier that afternoon.

How many times had Liara, eager to have a moment alone with the wizard, sent Sophie away on ridiculous errands? How many shawls, hats, gloves, and the like, had she left behind for the maid to fetch? *What Sophie must think of us!*

We have to set the record straight.

But Sophie begged off early, claiming a headache. This left Liara in the clutches of Madame Jeffers after dinner. Safer conversation, to be sure. But dull.

When at last the men rejoined them, the chosen diversion for the evening was cards. For Liara, this meant a divided attention while she attempted to learn the game. In the Royal Game of War, she soon learnt that the suits did not matter—only the rank of the cards.

Nagarath found himself out before he even got to play, having been dealt the Death card twice at the start of the first two games. Liara feared she had done more damage than intended with her lively dinnertime conversation with Tally, for her mage spent his afterlife haunting his friend Matty, rather than coming to her aid as she fumbled hand after hand. By the time Liara had the knack of it—even winning one or two rounds herself—the night had ended and all retired to their rooms.

The hour was late when the knock sounded upon his door. Nagarath had known Liara to be up and about, the charm around his neck alerting him to her use of magick. He had already guessed she would be around shortly.

Raising one chastising eyebrow as she slipped into the room, Nagarath did not stir from his bedside chair nor did he lower his book. "Acting a lady doesn't necessarily start tomorrow when we enter court, Liara."

He looked up and saw she had donned one of her dresses from home. The sight of her in homespun familiarity hit Nagarath's heart. For it seemed, to him, to indicate where hers lay. He sighed and marked his page, Liara—ever his librarian—wincing involuntarily as he crisply folded the corner over, slamming shut the cover on the damage.

"I trust you took precautions?"

"One simple glimmer, passing as a servant girl"—Liara nodded—"and pillows in the bed, just in case."

"Well, at least you can sneak properly." Nagarath chuckled and moved to rise. "If you please? Even with your precautions, I, too, should be properly attired in the event you are discovered here."

Liara looked away as Nagarath disappeared behind the room's screen. Changing into something akin to presentable, he considered his position. Though Tally's attentions to the young woman over dinner had irked him, he had taken pains to put a wall around his emotions. He rebuilt the barrier as quickly as he changed shirts. Nagarath would see her protected—she would never be so far out of his ken as to jeopardize that. But his previous lapse in judgment during their nighttime ride from Pau would not be repeated.

"Now what is it that could not possibly wait until morning?" He returned to find Liara fiddling with the hem of her sleeve and looking at his recently vacated chair, clearly debating whether or not she should sit. Changing her mind, she abruptly turned to pace the room, either finding too much intimacy in the choice of perch or requiring the motion to better express her flustered mood.

"I can't sleep." Liara kept her outburst quiet, still mindful of the late hour. It would do no good to sneak about under a cheap but effective illusion only to give oneself away through excessive noise. "I know we can't delay. Yes, out of the question. Especially if Anisthe is ahead of us. Though hearing nothing, I'm guessing he isn't."

Nagarath waited patiently, letting Liara's one-sided conversation wind down. At last, she turned to him with a heavy sigh and hope in her eyes.

Of course she was scared. Truth to tell, Nagarath was not without apprehension himself. But they had the perfect opening available to them with Monsieur Poulin, one that could easily have taken months of work to build. Anisthe would never even enter into the equation if their luck held. "And what, pray tell, would you like me to do?"

"I don't know." Liara slumped down into the chair at last, defeated. "I just . . . I need more practice. I'm not sure I can do this."

"Liara. You can. You're clever and determined, yet you love to dissemble." Nagarath grinned. "If that is not a lady of the court, I don't know what is. Besides, they will expect you to be a bit foreign and unpracticed. And your command of languages will win them over when empty-headed flirting will not. I fear that France will find Liara of Dvigrad a force to be reckoned with."

Liara, you are more of a graceful, alluring woman that you realize. Nagarath suddenly grew restless and wondered if he ought to pace the room. Anything to dispel the sudden tension.

"I'm not ready. I'll beg a headache, something. I'm just not ready."

"Liara, in what way could you possibly not be ready? If anything goes wrong, fall back on the story. If anything goes terribly wrong, you have still got your wand and an arsenal of knowledge. Beyond that—there are the charms." Nagarath unconsciously brushed his as he spoke.

She jumped to her feet. "Witchcraft and wizardry, Nagarath! I don't know how to dance!"

Liara's pronouncement, combined with the late hour and the young woman's very aggravated expression, proved too much for Nagarath. Succumbing to helpless laughter in the face of Liara's concern, he saw how poor of a gentleman he made. To think he had been so concerned with defensive spells and wand maneuvers that he

had forgotten his apprentice would have to actually function at court. Yes, Liara had every right to be concerned.

Feeling sheepish for such an omission to her courtly
education, and reckless from how much she looked like
herself, Nagarath's carefully rebuilt barrier came crashing
down. Propriety be damned. She was going to know how
to dance when she entered the court of the King of France.

Nagarath made a neat half-bow and waited. He
prompted, "Liara. You're learning to dance."

"Now?"

Nagarath simply waited for Liara's answering curtsy.

"But . . ." Liara hesitated, and seeing how Nagarath
was going to keep waiting for her, she clumsily curtsied
and then stood awkwardly.

"We shall start with something simple, the *Menuet*,
before we attempt a *Gavotte*." Nagarath hurried to add,
"And this will make much more sense to you when there
are more partners and better music." With a grin and flourish of his wand, Nagarath set into motion the music box
which sat on his mantle, the tinkling melody repeating itself in perpetuity through the lesson.

"And one, two, three . . ."

Chapter Twenty-five

The house of Seigneur Jeffers was in an uproar. Or so it seemed to Liara.

Trunks assembled in the front hall contained no end of coats and hats, shoes and hose. Julien Jeffers was not a man who packed light. Their belongings—Nagarath's, Sophie's, and her own—would soon join the pile.

While she had come to terms with the idea that they would be spending days in the company of the king's courtiers—the inner circle of nobility and anyone else connected enough to gain entry into Palais des Tuileries—Liara had not realized they would actually be staying on in the palace for the duration of their visit.

Liara remembered how she once could bundle all her worldly possessions under one arm. She laughed at the incredible array of colors and materials which met her eyes as she surveyed her wardrobe, still waiting to be packed away. Spread about her rooms, draped over nearly every available surface, the dresses were not to be touched. Sophie's orders.

Oh, she still hated the endless yards of finery—Liara detested looking like some strange bird alongside Nagarath's easy nobility. And though she had early mastered the gliding gait that made such dresses move well around her lithe form, she sometimes wondered if it was worth the effort. It wasn't as if she was looking to impress after all. She merely needed to blend in.

Blend in. Bah. More than once Liara had wickedly considered hitching up her skirts and going at it at a run. Imagine the looks she'd get! Instead, she had to content herself with magick on the sly and silent, private mockery of the Messieurs and Mesdames who thought her *of* them but not quite *one* of them.

Liara nearly ran down Sophie on three separate occasions in the pacing of her room. At length, she sank anxiously into a chair to watch the proceedings in restless silence. Eyes following Sophie's crossing and recrossing of the room, Liara found herself keeping time, likening the maid's movement to that of a dance.

Accompanied in her head by the light tinkling of notes—reminiscent of a music box in the quiet of nighttime—Liara counted her way through *Menuet, Sarabande, Bourrée,* and *Gavotte.* She treated her new knowledge as though it were a spell. The pronunciation by her feet must be perfect, lest she falter and bring disaster upon herself. A hand held just so, the eyes lowered bashfully, her role must be complete so as to gain access to as many wagging tongues and secret places the palace might hold.

The mirror was within their reach at long last. Kerri'tarre, archmage of old. Khariton, sorcerer who managed to seal away his einatus—his very soul—into an artifact that had lasted over a thousand years.

Liara wondered if they might keep what they had found, a first piece of their rebuilding. Would they then return home to Parentino? With the mirror, she and Nagarath might even stand against the Doge and his men. Perhaps she and her mage might stand against the whole of the modern world.

No. Liara blinked, startled out of her daydream, surprised at how easily such visions sprang to mind. The warnings from hastily learned history had been clear: beware the mirror's promises.

More dangerous than Anisthe; more dangerous than sneaking into Nagarath's rooms in the middle of the night. Khariton's Mirror was not to be trifled with. It would be buried away. Buried and forgot.

Already Nagarath, too, had cautioned her.

The whole of the Palace was likely subject to its influence, depending on where it was ensconced. Even without Anisthe's presence, they were to expect treachery and meanness of heart. Liara was to stay close to Nagarath's side at all times, lest the more favored courtiers pick them to pieces. She might dance—indeed it was to be expected—but she would dance with no one save him.

The thought thrilled her. Nagarath was to be hers. They would be close once more. Secrets and magick. The illicit nighttime dance lesson had proven to her the mage was indeed much on the mend, his elegance and control over the intricate footwork far different from the tired limp that had taken so long to fade from his gait. He seemed young, vibrant, ready to forget the dark past.

Forget. Forget and forgive. Fervent like a prayer, Liara let her eyes un-focus, the colors of her endless dresses bleeding into a sparkling magickal aura, the cadence in her head of the previous night's lessons louder than the haunting roar of Anisthe's Power fading into nothingness.

"Mademoiselle Liara? It is time."

~*~

As Nagarath handed her down from the carriage, all thoughts of dancing fled Liara's mind, and she concentrated on not tripping over her wobbly feet. Briefly, wildly, she wondered if it was all real. Her, in far-away Paris and entering the court of the king! Liara felt a twinge of understanding for when her wizard declared something in magick "impossible," even when the evidence of it lay right in front of him. Tuileries Palace, already seen from the window as they had approached along the river, filled her vision. Imposing, it seemed to frown down at her. Surely it, too, viewed the scene in disbelief, seeing past the sumptuous gown to the unworthy orphan beneath. Liara of Dvigrad, low as any beggar, sulking in the shadow of the Sun King's home.

At her side, Nagarath gently touched Liara's elbow, a reminder that she should be but lightly resting her hand atop his arm. M. Jeffers waited several feet off, his carriage having arrived at much the same time. Liara breathed deeply—as deeply as she could in her restrictive gown—and buried her fears in her excitement.

Liara made peace with her uncomfortable and overly ornate dress as she saw the other ladies of court. Confident now, she strode forward boldly, lost in the awe of Louis XIV's court.

How is this man not a wizard? She nearly gawked in wonder at the rich sights around her. The floors were as bright as the glittering chandeliers. Liara found herself wishing she could fly upwards and inspect, up close, the domed ceilings with their intricately painted and carved scenes. *How are we to admire them properly from such a distance?*

It was as if all that was beautiful and powerful had converged in this one place, transporting Liara and her companions to a higher plane of existence. Sun King, indeed. And he lived amongst the clouds of heaven itself. Gold-leafed columns and door panels glittered amongst the shifting crowd of courtiers, the very walls as fine as any gown.

"Where's the King?" Liara whispered as they espied Nagarath's other acquaintances in the throng. Mathieu—Matty—Poulin and Talaffe Sauvageau embraced their friends with warm smiles and greetings, immediately introducing them to those with whom they had been conversing. Names and titles flew in and out of Liara's ears. She smiled and nodded, trying not to appear overwhelmed under the scrutiny of half a dozen well-dressed gentlemen.

"His Majesty, *Monsieur le Roi Soleil*, is likely spending his day elsewhere in political maneuverings with some of the more fortunate," Nagarath whispered back. "Being of the lower echelon of courtiers, we will likely see a glimpse of him later in the week, if we are lucky."

"Oh." Liara's cheeks warmed. A misstep from the first, she would look a fool for having entertained hopes—expectations, even—that she would soon be seeing the Sun King himself. She endeavored to cover her error by asking over the desire next close to her heart, "So . . . there'll be no dancing today then?"

Tally broke in with a hearty chuckle and smiled kindly at her. "Goodness me, my dear Nath, I can see why her father thought she'd do well at France's court. Not here ten minutes and she plays the game without playing it at all."

Liara felt her face go white with mortification as no less than six pairs of eyes turned to look her over. Nagarath waved off M. Talaffe's remark, trying to draw attention back on himself and save Liara the scrutiny. "If I recall, your idea of game play used to revolve around attaching yourself to the nearest pretty face and creating as much intrigue as one might."

"I do believe the prettiest face here is already amongst our number. But, by all means, let us go find some refreshment and splendidly youthful company whilst we await the pleasure of His Majesty." M. Talaffe's wink had fire returning to Liara's neck and ears—each exposed all the more for her ridiculous décolletage and coiffure.

Alarmed, she had the pleasure of seeing Nagarath grow red himself, a rumble of warning rising in his throat.

But rescue came by way of Sophie.

"Your fan, Mademoiselle. You looked flushed from the heat and must have chanced upon a pocket of stale air," Sophie dove in from the fringes of their little knot of courtiers. The practiced ease with which she gave her excuse caught Liara off guard. Through her actions, Sophie had drawn attention from Nagarath's unguarded response and onto herself. Tally, it would seem, was used to causing a stir, and no one blinked an eye at him. Liara breathed a sigh of relief as the gentlemen fell into step behind the ladies, the initial scrutiny over and done.

She would have to thank Sophie later for her quick thinking. As it was, she felt a new kinship with the woman whom Liara realized they had greatly underestimated thus far.

Court, Liara found, was far more about the seeing than the doing. And there was much to see. Their sumptuous surroundings stretched for miles. Room after room, each resplendent as the last, drew the eye this way and that. Women and men milled about, gathered in knots, flirted, dressed in the most astonishing combinations of finery. It was distracting.

And boring.

Liara simply did not know anyone and so felt as though she had been reduced to something as unremarkable as a wall or chair—of which there were but few. Liara had quickly discovered that His Majesty secured the chairs for himself and his most favored courtiers. Far cry from the comfort of Parentino, with its well-loved winged chairs crowding the corners of every room.

Sophie, too, had stepped back, blending into the shadows once more, a few cruel comments and pointed gazes putting the maid back into her place.

Liara felt invisible. And not in a good way. For all that she had desired such upon entering the palace, she soon realized that her status as "beneath notice" left her out of the conversations which might further her and Nagarath's quest.

Tired of standing, smiling, nodding where appropriate and looking confused where . . . well, where her limited French failed her, Liara decided to take matters into her own immaculately gloved hands. She drifted to the edge of their small grouping until she was separated from the mage. Separated enough to try her daring plan, anyway.

First putting up the requisite shields so as to protect her magick from prying eyes, Liara worked the necessary spells without word and nary a gesture. It made for difficult work, bespelling with just her will, but it kept all present unaware of her magick. Save for Nagarath, of course, who would feel it through the pendant he wore hidden beneath coat and cravat.

Grateful for the brief period of tutoring Amsalla had bestowed upon her, Liara let her gaze drift over the grand men and women who had little idea of the witchcraft happening in their midst. Enhancing her perceptions, Liara could better hear and pick out individual conversations within the large, ornate hall. She worked a hex to translate for her, finding the rapid, garbled French too much for her senses. Slowly the tangle of noise unknotted itself for her listening pleasure.

Ugh. They are as bad as the folk I grew up around. Liara's illicit listening exposed her to gossip, bawdy jokes, catty remarks, and deep suspicions. Everyone was watching everyone else. Even her!

Provincial. Simple. Ill-educated.

Strumpet.

Ending her spells with a start, Liara felt a new blush rise into her cheeks.

How dare they! How dare they say so, think so! Her honor aside, the blemish to Nagarath's, the bold implication, had her seeking the wizard's eye.

His gaze already fell upon her, wrathful, forbidding. She wilted under the glare, shrinking from his anger even though no less than eight people stood between them and calling her out on her use of magick there and then posed no danger.

"I'm sorry." She mouthed the words, seeking clemency.

Nagarath answered by frowning, his eyes suddenly darting up and over her shoulder to something behind her, alarm animating him. A commotion behind her, shuffling feet and muted exclamations. Liara turned. Uniformed men were coming straight for her.

Fear shot prickles of ice up along her neck and arms, into her scalp and freezing her in place. A gentle hand tugged at her elbow.

Father Rodolfo Adessi.

Father Rodolfo Adessi!

The priest smiled at Liara's wide-eyed recognition. "Step back, my dear. The king approaches."

Oh! Liara stumbled backwards, forgetting in her shock that she ought to be elegant and unruffled. In attempting to keep her eye on Adessi and the open doorway where all other eyes had turned, she bumped into another gentleman. Her apology stuck in her throat, and Liara worked her mouth emptily. *For we haven't been introduced!*

As Liara pondered the proper course through the silly rules of etiquette, it was Father Rodolfo who again rescued her, saying in a low voice, "Mademoiselle Liara; Monsieur le Chevalier Vincent." Liara swore that she saw a hint of a good-humored smile playing about his lips. However, his eyes stayed on the door where the king would shortly enter.

"My apologies." M. Vincent, gallant and handsome, further stemmed Liara's unease. "I am far more mobile than you are in that stunning gown, Mademoiselle. It is I who ought to have watched my feet."

The energy in the room changed, and the most beautiful man Liara had ever seen stepped into their midst.

The king was not handsome—likely not by any definition. But he was magnetic. Commanding, yet clearly desirous of the acquaintance of all present in his palace,

Louis XIV seemed taller, younger, older, larger, than he likely was. But, just as when looking at the sun itself, it was almost impossible to see him directly. The majesty about him was too great.

Liara found that she had to admire him in pieces. His hair, soft and almost understated in its styling, fell down about his shoulders in ebony ringlets. His chin and hands, delicate and yet somehow iron-hard, had Liara lamenting that the man had not himself been born a mage. What spells those capable hands might have worked. His legs—a dancer's legs—explained better than rumor and tale why it was the king forbade anyone leave an evening's entertainment before he had retired. And his eyes? Liara did not know, for she could not look there.

The moment passed. The assembly seemed to sigh with relief in the wake of the king as he moved to another part of the palace. Lifting her head back up, Liara found she had bowed along with the rest, the gentle bend in her knees coming naturally, in spite of all the tremendous work she had put into getting the motion just so.

Father Adessi now turned to her fully. "What a fortuitous meeting, Mademoiselle Liara. I'd have hoped to introduce you to Monsieur Vincent, considering your cousin's desire that you should see something of court life. Monsieur Vincent is quite fond of dancing and studied in Italy in his youth. I thought it prudent that you should meet."

"You're . . . here." Liara was still finding it hard to squeeze any words past the confusion lodged in her throat. She wanted to smile—tried valiantly—but couldn't. Father Adessi. Here. In Paris. Alive and well.

"Come, let us remove ourselves from this pressing crowd." Adessi seemed to at last note the danger that Liara might actually faint from the shock of it all. His warm eyes flicked to M. Vincent, and together they made their way towards the edges of the room.

The air was still hot, if less stuffy. Liara arced her head, looking for Nagarath. He needed to know that Father Rodolfo had arrived. Would he be excited? Suspicious? At her side, M. Vincent rattled off polite inquiries to her health in halting school-boy Italian. That centered her, and Liara managed her smile at long last. "It's all right. My French is not all bad. Not as bad as my balance, at least."

Raised eyebrows met her joke—mild approval. "Perhaps I may help test your balance in the future? The king's unexpected presence has me believing we'll hear summons to one of his grand happenings before the day is through. I would like to further our friendship with a dance."

"Oh!" Flustered, Liara looked to Father Adessi and discovered Matty had come into view. Which meant that Nagarath was likely nearby. Her heart fluttered anxiously. How had she managed so easily to get in such a mess of people?

"Come now, Liara, court is all about meeting people, being seen and seeing," Father Rodolfo leaned close to whisper his words of encouragement. "I'll find Nagarath and bring him here."

Liara nodded numbly, her eyes still on the knot of people wherein she could espy M. Matty's backside, as Adessi left her alone with her new acquaintance.

Sophie rescued her from further mortification. Materializing deftly, almost as though she had sensed Liara's despair, the woman shrank from Monsieur Vincent's scrutiny as she came to check on Mademoiselle. But, unlike the painted ladies of court from whom her magick had allowed Liara to learn of silent cruelties, the gentleman with them seemed to hold none of the reserved judgment associated with courtiers. His smile for Sophie was as generous as it had been for Liara. "Perhaps on another occasion. My apologies for my presumption as to your desire for a dancing partner."

His response helped Liara find her tongue at last. "I've only just learned," she said. "You might find that I tread upon you again if we were to dance."

"That is a risk I am willing to take." M. Vincent's smile bedazzled. "Tell me, how is it you know—?"

"I've found the rest of your party, Mademoiselle." Father Rodolfo returned to them, as had his typical gregarious manner. He moved to indicate a path through the crowd, stopping to eye Sophie. Oddly enough, under his scrutiny, the young woman wilted.

Liara quickly made introductions. Through it all, Sophie's apparent discomfort grew. But the strange moment passed swiftly. Nagarath and his friends had, too, followed the wave of the priest's arm and soon caught them up. M. Vincent made an easy addition to the Mssrs. Matty, Tally, and JJ. Nagarath was shortly engrossed in a deep and animated philosophical debate with Father Adessi. Which left Liara and Sophie a moment of reprieve to simply stand and be admired.

And feel a little less alone, Liara concluded. She eyed her disparate collection of friends with a quiet sort of joy.

~*~

Just as the custom at the Jeffers' residence, everyone retired to their rooms to change for dinner. The transformation of the maid came immediately, and Liara found herself taken aback by Sophie's delighted caper about their rooms.

"Oh, isn't it just rapture!" Sophie gushed her excitement the moment the door had closed behind them. Liara had not thought that the maid enjoyed herself at all. She had been more or less placed in the background—even more than Liara herself.

And then there had been that odd moment with Father Rodolfo—one that had felt like an argument though no words had passed between them. Liara made a note to ask about it later, for just then, Sophie was not to be contained. "And that young gentleman to whom you were introduced, aren't we just the luckiest young ladies in the world?"

"But you—"

Sophie waved aside Liara's concerns before she could even voice them. "Pooh. I am glad because you are glad. I saw that pretty little blush you put on for that young man. And the king. We've been in the presence of the king. We are staying on in the palace with the finest people in the land. It's like a fairy tale, Mademoiselle Liara, all magick and romance."

You have no idea how much. Liara grinned at the woman, older than herself by three years and yet somehow more youthful. She found herself wishing they could switch places.

'Like a fairy tale . . .' Perhaps I could tell—

A knock on the door to their suite startled Liara out of her impulsive and wild idea. Sophie hurried to answer.

Nagarath stood in the doorway. "I'm sorry, Sophie, but I need a moment alone with Liara, please."

With a quiet curtsy, Sophie moved aside to usher in the gentleman, turning to repair to the attached inner room.

"Alone alone, please." Nagarath cast a meaningful glance to the hallway. "Again, my apologies. It is important, else I would not ask it of you."

Pursing her lips, Sophie shot Liara an unreadable look, removing herself from the room with haste.

Chapter Twenty-six

Nagarath stood awkwardly in the middle of the room, his eyes darting to the evening's attire already laid out upon the bed. He seemed to be debating something within himself. Fiercely.

"Well?" More annoyed than curious, for now Liara would have to make up some unbelieved excuse for Sophie when she returned, she challenged the mage. "What could possibly be so important and secretive that you would break the rules of etiquette so brashly?"

Nagarath darted magefire into the corner of the rooms. The act clearly weighed on his conscience. "Magick."

"Yes, I know what magick is." She knew that was not what Nagarath meant. But if he was going to make her admit her error, he'd find he had to wait until supper was put away and the court long abed.

"Don't do that, Liara. I am serious. I was serious before, and I am deadly serious now. You were performing magick right under the nose of the king and his men. In the presence of—"

You're doing it now. Liara bit back the retort. She knew Nagarath's magick necessary to their sharing such secrets so close to prying ears and eyes. Likely he had produced quiet talk of goodness-knows-what softly emanating through the door. Blushing, Liara figured that she knew what excuse the mage had come here on. After all, hadn't one day at court assured her that such was all people ever considered? Tiresome.

The wizard continued, his temper reined. "In the presence of men who might see it for what it is. Sorcery. Illicit and un-condoned. Father Rodolfo Adessi—"

"Why is he here?"

Nagarath smiled, putting a hand to his hair before re-thinking the gesture. He settled instead for his other lecture pose, tapping the bridge of his nose in thought before offering, "He wants to help, I think."

"You hope."

"Hope is good." Nagarath heavily claimed one of the chairs. "In the current circumstances, yes. I'll take hope."

For a moment, Liara began to think that was all he was going to say. Glancing meaningfully to the door, she tried to remind him with a look: Sophie would be back any minute. Had Nagarath really come by just to sulk and stammer and fret at her over doing magick? She had said she was sorry. *Or near enough.*

At length, the mage spoke. "Father Rodolfo Adessi understands both sides of this fight. Magick and non. He knows the perils of attempting to stamp out wizardry. Our Art, its history and artifacts, are out there in the world. Some forgotten; some working their mischief."

"Werewolves." Liara's breathed interjection brought a smile to Nagarath's tired face.

"And Kerri'tarre's Mirror. Yes, Liara." Nagarath rose to pace the room. "Father Adessi agrees that, if you stop us mages from practicing our Art, you loose all sorts of miseries upon the world. Would you know that the king has taken it upon himself to seek out the truth behind each and every fairytale he can set his ears on? He has a woman hired whose sole purpose is to tell him such stories. Louis collects magick. Or at least the stories of it. It is why Adessi is here. He believes. Believes in all of it. And the king, he knows nothing about what he has brought into his palaces. The dangers. He thinks he has made himself safe with his spellpiercers."

"So you believe they exist?"

"Adessi does." Nagarath stopped his pacing to look at Liara. "And so I . . . I don't rightly know. Which . . . He has the mirror, Liara! The king has the mirror. We must be careful. We must. At least until we can get to the truth of the matter."

Liara's mind stuck on something Nagarath had said. About the spellpiercers. But the mage spoke again before she could put the thought into words.

"Where Venice would stomp out magick, France would cage it."

Stunned, Liara looked to the glittering corners of the room where Nagarath's spell still burned.

"Yes. I ought not be doing even that. But I had to take the risk so that I could speak to you in private. To tell you, most earnestly, to please refrain from magick until we better know the situation."

"And the pendants?"

"Inert magick and therefore not likely to give us away should the rumor of the spellpiercers be truth. But, yes, I think that I would put them away for now." The thought seemed to give Nagarath some pain.

Standing before the mage, Liara felt the newly rote manners as fully as ever. She could see the wizard and his black robes under the shining silks and embroidery. Could he still see his Liara? Plain, uncourtly, magpie Liara? She wanted to touch his hand. She wanted to whisper her apology and assurances that it would be fine. It would be fine, and they would soon be able to return home, triumphant. Things would be as they were.

As they were. Home. They had left behind pain and betrayal. They had run from persecution and the wreckage of Liara's anger and distrust. Neither of them desired going back. Where did they move forward to?

She knew where she wanted to move to. Memories of dancing, a tinkling music box on the mantle; a cold winter's night and a large bespelled telescope . . . She wanted more of that. Even if it was mere companionship. She wanted more of him.

The door opened. Liara jumped backwards, adding space between the two of them even though there had already been several feet. Looking in alarm at Sophie, Liara saw that Nagarath's spell had ended. No more sparkling aura filled the corners. And the mage himself was already halfway to the door.

Nagarath left without a word. And Liara found herself without any as Sophie took up her place at the dressing table.

"I found the, um . . . You had wanted some fresh water. They'll fetch it but it will arrive while we are gone for the evening, Mademoiselle," came Sophie's halting explanation.

Liara found it endearing. She sat down, still silent.

Supper. She could not possibly eat anything. Not with her stomach jumping about so. It was as though an entire family of birds had taken up residence inside her chest, and she was half-afraid that she would chirp as soon as she opened her mouth.

"Oh, Mademoiselle, if I had hair like yours, I'd never tire of dressing it up." Sophie moved past Liara's silence, unpinning her dark tresses and brushing out the snarls so that the hair fell in one soft, black waterfall.

"Really?" Liara frowned into the mirror. "It just seems like so much work for a few hours, only to do it all over again. It's just hair."

"But so worth it, miss." Sophie chuckled. She took a quick breath, daring at last, "I can see what he sees in you."

Liara looked up sharply, jolting a pin out of the maid's hand. "Monsieur Vincent? But we only just met. It would be unseemly. Nagarath even came to counsel me against too much familiarity with the man." She thought it high time that she at least supply some sort of explanation for Nagarath's unusual visit.

"No, not Vincent. Why, I mean the gentleman Nagarath, of course." Sophie blushed, chastised but unwavering under Liara's glare. "Don't you worry, miss. I won't tell a soul. I swear it."

"Oh, but we couldn't—"

"He's not your uncle or cousin or whatnot. That much has been clear to me since the second day I was in your employ. Don't paint me a fool, miss."

"But we're not . . . we're not together romantically. Or anything like that."

"But you'd like to be," Sophie pressed, catching on to Liara's wavering frown.

"Goodness, no. We're just . . . traveling together. Friends."

"Well, deny it if you will. I've seen how he looks at you." Sophie proceeded to loop and tighten, pin and pull

Liara's hair into submission. "And if a man like him looked at me like that . . . if I were you, I'd—"

A knock sounded on the door, startling them both into a guilty silence. Sophie rushed to answer, blushing as the object of their conversation stood uncomprehending at the door.

Liara listened from her place at the dressing table in the adjoining room as Sophie promised that Mademoiselle Liara would be ready in *"un moment, s'il vous plait."* And, in spite of herself, Liara felt a slight thrill at the sound of Nagarath's voice responding with a polite nothing of a compliment.

Blast you, Sophie. It was one thing for her mind to wander over such possibilities. It was quite another experience to have someone else confirm her deepest wishes.

"Goodness, he only left us but minutes ago. How long do men think this takes?" Sophie returned to the dressing table, clicking her tongue in annoyance. A pin fell to the floor under the maid's trembling fingers. Another followed the first.

"It's fine, Sophie. Look—" Liara shook her head gently "—it stays."

Pressing her lips together, Sophie appraised the hasty updo. With a curt nod, she helped Liara from her day dress in silence. A smart if bold design, the dress for the evening—all rich maroons and grays—required a bit of fussing to secure Liara within its bounds. As such, she was only able to hold to her own wordless scrutiny of the maid's sudden moodiness, wishing she had in her the means to comfort her for having been so outspoken. No, not comfort: correct.

"Ow." Liara's complaint gushed out of her. Not the tension dispelling she'd hoped for, but it sufficed.

"Sorry, Mademoiselle." Sophie worked her fingers in to loosen the lacing on Liara's copious sleeves.

"No, don't do that. It's fine. But, all the same, ouch." Liara pulled away, turning to find that tears marred the corners of Sophie's eyes.

Her heart went out to the woman. Liara's hands reached out to capture Sophie's. "Nagarath is a fine gentleman. That's the truth of it. And he and I? We couldn't be more than companions after all we've been through. He's a good man, truly. And . . . and he deserves someone who doesn't—who isn't—who's not me."

Sophie opened her mouth and stopped short.

A polite knock sounded at their door once again. This time Liara hurried to answer it, leaving Sophie to pull herself together. The maid was right, how long did men think this took?

Nagarath had known the moment Liara had removed her necklace. With the pendant moved so far from her heart, the magick which connected the two of them had faltered and died. But the sight of her in the doorway, the now-familiar object gone from around her neck, still brought his breath hitching in his throat. Never mind that she looked . . . stunning.

Liara's shy blush gave way to the bright flash of a smile. "Oh! Matty, you're here, too."

Monsieur Poulin's manners rescued Nagarath. The gentleman offered his own answering smile and fixed his eyes to Sophie. "Mademoiselle? We are heading out to dine with some friends, and as I am without a partner this evening, if I could be so bold as to presume . . . ?"

The joy with which Matty's offer was met had Nagarath second-guessing whether he had imagined the troubled look on the maid's face when the door had opened. But then, he could not blame her for being anxious. Sophie had hired on as a mere lady's maid, had been forced into companionship with historically taciturn Liara, and here she was attending court functions on the arm of one of France's more powerful men.

And a good-hearted man, at that. Nagarath remained equal parts surprised and grateful over Matty's kind gesture. But then, in the old days, Poulin had been the best of them. Small wonder he had found a way to become successful without losing himself in the process. Nagarath felt the pinch of his own conscience. How many other stray dogs and foundlings had the good Monsieur le Vicomte adopted into court these past years?

Please, gods above, let the result of our actions here with regards to the mirror not fall on Matty and the rest. But what was done was done. They were here. They were to dine and dance in the company of the court, to listen and to seek rumor of that which had so obsessed the monarch.

And Liara played her part admirably. Nervous as Sophie, perhaps—Nagarath could feel the quiver in her light touch upon his arm—but brave and, at last, obedient to his prohibition on magick.

Which leaves me terribly in the dark. Again, Nagarath felt the dismal lack of magick as keenly as, he presumed, Liara did. Inert as the pendants' power was, he had come to rely upon the hum of her aura mingling with his own via the magick that connected them. He had known her expenditure of Power, yes; could check in on her whereabouts if need be. He had also been able to gauge her mood. He had become used to her magick signature leaping and wavering much like a candle flame within his consciousness.

Through his own good judgment, Nagarath had been cut adrift. And it was horrible. Especially as it occurred to him that Liara had been keeping her eyes anywhere but on him as they walked towards the gathering. Was she angry? Upset? Or was her avoidance a mere side-effect of her attention being called elsewhere? His fingers fairly itched with the temptation to witch his way to an answer. But no. There were other ways to go about it.

Again, Nagarath wondered at the look which crossed Sophie's face as the door to their rooms had opened. It was almost as if he and Monsieur Poulin had stumbled upon an argument. There certainly had been something awkward in the maid's answering of the door, long moments prior to the ladies' eventual appearance. Something that went beyond mere nerves.

The night had grown comfortable enough that they might walk. Nagarath slowed his pace so that they hung back behind Matty and Sophie. He leaned in. "Liara, I do believe most gentlemen of this court—men who traffic in words—would find themselves lacking an adequate way to express how lovely you look in that gown tonight."

"And you?" Liara looked up into Nagarath's face. Her eyes and lips twinkled their mirth. Coquettish. Beguiling. The illusion complete at last.

He smiled crookedly. "It suits you."

And now he had disappointed her. Liara's gaze fell away once more, the distance between them a howling hole Nagarath did not have the energy to fill.

Bright greetings interrupted further thought. They had arrived at a restaurant more flexible in its patronage than the palace. There were a few familiar faces amongst the throng, but not many. Nagarath maneuvered for introductions and place-taking at the dining table. He and Liara were but a small portion of the gathering, and he once more marveled at Matty's apparently endless connections.

Matty, who was on the receiving end of one of Liara's rare and dazzling smiles.

Jealousy slid into the silent space still hanging between Nagarath and Liara. What did she want of him? Some empty compliment, dressed up in flowery language? This life to which they were pretending: it was all a disguise. Liara knew that. She had rebelled against it. Or she had until arrival at court.

His Liara was changing, opening up. Take Sophie, for example. She and Liara seemed, to Nagarath, as though they were becoming fast friends. He darted a glance to the maid, discovered her hastily looking away but not without a coy glance at Liara. Liara answered with the barest shake of her head. Her dark curls quivered with the minute motion.

Nagarath frowned. Something was amiss. Some play between Sophie and Liara.

It felt, in some ways, like when he had to deal with Amsalla. Amsalla DeBouverelle with her secrets and that frustrating, unnavigable female language whose translation was hid from men.

The comparison was unfavorable. For it brought closer to mind memories of a ride through the dark countryside, a moment of weakness which Nagarath dare not indulge. He could feel such things about Amsalla. Indeed, he had done so on and off through the years. But Liara was . . .

Liara is alluring, smart, talented, everything you could ever hope for, and completely unavailable to you in any romantic sense. Nagarath lost himself in his private misery. He fixed back into place his disguise of good cheer and proper mealtime small talk. He could sense both Liara and Sophie peering at him from time to time, their unknown game still playing out. Whatever those two spatted about was their problem. His was to keep his feelings to himself and his eyes and ears open to any whisper, any rumor, about the king's magick mirror.

Deprived of magick and finding supper too exotic for her simple tastes, Liara fought the urge to hunch miserably in her chair. Nagarath had complicated everything. Him with his carefully reined compliments and "let's not use any magick, Liara" sentiments. He had said they needed to blend in. At least he could have complimented her on the effort.

Effort. Hah! Liara scolded herself, settling further into her bad mood. *Your only contribution was to sit still long enough for Sophie to make you up nicely.*

Worst of all, Liara had come to rely upon the steady pulse of Nagarath's magick in the pendant he had given her. To have it gone, to no longer sense through spellwork what Sophie had espied through observation? Liara felt naked despite her finery. She felt exposed and bereft of all connection.

Quite simply, had she the bravery to risk it, Liara could have likely used the pendant to confirm whether Sophie surmised the truth.

But then, Nagarath would have to be wearing his.

And the bravery Liara would require went far beyond that of merely confronting the wizard's wrath over yet more unsanctioned magick. In considering Sophie's insinuation that Nagarath might harbor for Liara feelings which eclipsed simple friendship, Liara realized she was not entirely ready to confront her own. Unknowing, she could deny what she felt for the man. If she were to learn that he did not feel the same for her? Liara could not entertain such a heartsick possibility.

"Your wish for dancing is to be granted, my dear." Nagarath bent close, startling Liara from her reverie. Turning quickly, she could see the warm tones with which he'd spoken did not quite reach his eyes. Liara could read warning there and wondered at it. Nagarath explained further, having had the information passed on to him from down the table.

Monsieur Vincent's prophecy had proven true. The king had come through Paris as he returned to another of his palaces and had invited all of his friends—every courtier in France, it would seem—to a grand party. The theme? Magick.

Chapter Twenty-seven

"Up, Mademoiselle Liara. Up, up, up!" Sophie mercilessly threw wide the drapery and exposed Liara's sleep-shocked eyes to the brightness of morning.

Liara moaned her protest and tried to bury herself farther into her bedding. To rise would be to face the day. And to face the day would be to face the task given them. And the task before them? Herculean.

Not to mention terrifying.

The king was throwing a party, and Liara hadn't a thing to wear. But then, likely, nobody had just the right thing lying about, copious as most courtiers' wardrobes seemed to be. The party was not until the following evening, at least. Still, they would all have to get decidedly creative before setting off for the king's other palace of Versailles.

Truly, all these people do is shuffle around from place to place and change clothes at every opportunity.

It was all rather tiresome. Especially if the mirror was hidden somewhere within Tuileries.

Or Fontainebleau or Vincennes or any other of the king's sometime-homes. It's a pity we have to follow him around at all.

Technically, Liara did have magnificently appropriate effects amongst her belongings. She and Nagarath both did. But such accoutrements were to stay well hidden.

Which left a dilemma. What did a wizard wear to a mag-ick-themed party that looked good but not suspicious-good?

Sophie had ideas, apparently.

Liara winced as a heap of mismatched, jumbled finery thumped down onto the bed, left by the maid for her lady's perusal. Warm morning sunlight streamed through the window. It lingered over bright fabrics and exotic patterns, sighed through airy feathers, and glinted off metallic bau-bles, setting sparkles to dance over the walls and ceiling.

Sophie gave vent to a dramatic sigh, one that seemed dragged up from her toes, and fell to sulking on the nearby divan. "And to think I wasted the dress from last evening on something so trivial as supper. 'Twould have been no work at all to make you up into a sorceress with those pen-sive grays and reds."

The complaint had its desired effect. Liara felt the cor-ners of her mouth twitch with humor in spite of her own despondency. Sophie would rescue her from her troubles. The maid's idea of "magick" was sure to be commonplace and ridiculous, as would be expected. Before the morning was through, they would have to secure a moment with Nagarath so that his aesthetic might match their horribly inaccurate one.

That or, perhaps, set Sophie on him directly. Picturing Nagarath, his courtly attire adorned in flashy runes, a peaked hat atop his head, further encouraged Liara's spir-its. She had lain awake until the wee hours, worrying about the reasons behind the party's chosen theme. In the end, logic prevailed. After all, if she and Nagarath had been found out as wizards, they would be heading to jail instead of Versailles. They were safe. Liara wondered what Father

Adessi might think, wondered if he would even be there for the grand event.

Liara moved to sort through the mound of habiliment. She added a sigh of her own as she encountered hammered tin medallions with crudely drawn runes—complete gibberish, of course—absolutely preposterous robes, and a fanciful, frowning mask that seemed determined to evoke the concept of a wolf-person. Safe or not, it disheartened her to be reminded of what the layman thought of magick.

Where had Sophie gotten such . . . utter nonsense?

"Monsieur Jeffers and Monsieur Poulin sent some of their cast-offs here, understanding that we, as travelers new to court, might be without the resources necessary to create our own ensemble on such short notice." It seemed Sophie could read Liara's mind.

Hopefully she cannot read all. Liara tried hard not to frown at the mishmash of erroneous arcana. She, quite honestly, hadn't the faintest idea of where to begin. Her wealth of knowledge kept crowding out potential costume ideas. A little voice inside tut-tutted over inaccuracies here and wrong assumptions there. It was like having her own personal Nagarath lecturing inside her head.

"Oh, yes, Mademoiselle. Paired with the right dress, I'm certain I could make you up to look like one of the fair folk." Sophie gave a little clap of ill-contained enthusiasm.

Liara put down the circlet of silk flowers, biting her tongue and looking for something more . . . more authentic. Goodness, the garland even had a tiny stuffed bird and diminutive nest tucked amongst its petals. Her eyes roved the pile, not ready to make herself such a spectacle. There had to be a mask within its depths. Hang the rest of her attire! She needed a way to hide from Nagarath and the stirrings of emotion she still felt for the man following yesterday evening's conversation with the maid.

But Sophie pressed on. "And there are any number of feathers here. With the majority of the morning and the beginning of the afternoon at our disposal, we might—"

"No, Sophie. Please." Liara remembered, belatedly, to soften her tone.

"Well, then to the wardrobe I go."

Liara did not bother to look up. She had found her mask. Silvery-white, it luminesced in the morning sun. Under the luster of palace chandeliers, it was sure to beguile. And safe within, she could observe all. Perhaps this fakery had a power all its own she could use.

A knock at the door had Liara starting to her feet. Nagarath. Her heart thumped in her chest as she turned wild eyes to the far end of the room. Hope, fear, and excitement jumbled together.

Sophie did not move from where she stood by the dressing table. Why didn't the woman answer the summons? Liara's scolding promptly died on her lips as she realized her mistake.

"Sorry, miss." Sophie reddened and gestured to the contents of the table in illustration. It had been her knocking about that had Liara thinking someone was at the door.

Vexed anew, Liara sank back down to the bed, trying to quiet her hammering heart. If she started at every little thing, she was sure to give herself away, twisted in knots as she was.

It had all seemed so easy, once upon a time. Dreams of magick, apprenticeship to the wizard of the wood. Even the task of tracking down the wayward mirror, with its promise of closer companionship with the man she'd hurt so deeply . . . she hadn't bargained on what that closeness would give rise to.

Sneaking, tricky, thieving Liara was sick of secrets.

The hands that held the mask began to shake.

"Liara?"

Liara heard Sophie's soft footfalls, felt the maid sit down upon the edge of the bed.

"Nagarath—" Liara choked on the name.

"Liara, if you are you angry with me for speaking out of turn as I did, you have every right. I thought it right you should know what I could see happening. Before anyone else did. My only aim was to help. I can keep a secret, Mademoiselle. I can. I have from the moment I suspected that you were sending me off on one of your silly errands so that you might have a moment in private."

The dam burst. "I'm a mage, Sophie. Nagarath and I both. That's the truth of us."

Relief flooded through Liara's veins, warming her. The tears she'd been holding back now loosed upon Sophie who leaned close. That alone stunned Liara. Sophie was not running, not screaming. She did not call her names, throw stones. Instead she sat alongside Liara, ready to throw a comforting arm about her mistress' quaking shoulders if need be.

"And I'm afraid."

"Oh, now, Mademoiselle Liara . . ."

"Myself and Nagarath. We are in danger. There are people in the king's employ. Bad people who can sense our Art if we dare use it."

Sophie turned white, her comforting arm went rigid. "Why do you tell me of such things?"

"The theme of King Louis' grand event. It scares me, for I feel the noose tightening even without your having pointed out the potential flaws in our disguise." Liara turned to Sophie, wiping her tears and clasping hands with the maid. "If you could sense that all was not as it seems between he and I, then what else might be noticed? Even if we don't perform any spells. You were right about—at least, I hope you were right . . ." She blushed and found herself unable to continue. Some things were simply too personal to say aloud.

"Is this your secret to tell, Liara?"

Liara shook her head. "No. Yes. No. In any event, you needed to know. If we are walking into a trap, I wanted you to have the knowledge to keep yourself safe. You've the freedom to leave, to not follow us into danger, knowing what's really going on."

Silence.

"I'd show you, but . . . again, the king's spellpiercers could be anywhere." Liara lowered her voice, afraid that even her confession might well be overheard. Relieving as it was to confide in Sophie, Nagarath's caution rang in her ears. The maid's face had retained its pale shock.

How could Liara have been so impulsive? When had she become so trusting?

"Then I must tell you something as well." Sophie cast her eyes downward. The maid's hands fidgeted with the lacework on one of the costumes. No further words came, and for a moment, Liara wondered if she'd imagined that as well. When the maid looked up, a shadow seemed to cross through her eyes, a hastily thrown veil between the two of them.

Liara suddenly felt that perhaps she ought apologize anew. "Our story was never meant to cover something so personal as you suspected. Rather, we meant only to protect—to explain—our being here."

"To the others." There was no mistaking the emphasis.

Liara flinched. "Yes. To those painted, puffed-up people outside those doors. And even then . . ."

"They do not believe you, either."

Liara's heart resumed its frantic hammering, and she searched the maid's face.

Sophie moved to undo some of the damage. "Not the magick, Mademoiselle. That secret no one would guess at. But your feelings—your and Monsieur Nagarath's . . . well, gossip, though not entirely baseless, is merely that. People like to talk of such things, especially when jealous. One must be close to truly suspect what I spoke of last evening."

"Monsieur Poulin . . . Monsieur Jeffers and Monsieur Sauvageau—"

"Monsieur Nagarath's friends do not seem aware of the lie. I've seen the respect they give you, give him."

"Why do you suppose—?"

Sophie laughed. "Nagarath has good friends who believe what he has told them about you. They would not entertain such wild notions easily, even with rumor to support it."

"And you, Sophie?"

"We were not always friends, no? I made my conclusions long before."

This last drew a laugh from Liara. Relief.

The long-dreaded knock on their door sounded. It was followed by Nagarath's unannounced entrance into the rooms. He looked ridiculous.

"What are you supposed to be?"

"And doesn't a knock most often herald a patient wait by the door?"

Both Liara and Sophie spoke at once, giggling anew—aftermath of their conversation and in observation of the strange sight the wizard cut. Red. Crimson. Auburn. Black. Charcoal. Pale yellows, pinks, and blues. Flame and shimmer, sparkle and glint. Nagarath had somehow managed to encircle it all with his long arms, feathers and finery, satin and shine all spilling outward from within his grasp. He was enveloped in long, flowing robes of midnight.

"Rag man. That's magickal, is it not?" Nagarath huffed. He dumped the pile on the other end of Liara's bed and eyed the lot skeptically.

Sophie rummaged carefully through the finery, sorting out an outrageous amount of red feathers.

"A phoenix, Nagarath?" Liara cocked an eyebrow of her own.

"And drake scales"—he held up an ornate helm in illustration—"painted black just this morning by yours truly. I thought that Sophie might enjoy playing at being one of the *fata*, that is, one of the fair folk. I have the makings of some fantastical wings, if we wanted to be so bold."

Liara stared open-mouthed at the mound of make-believe, scandalized anew. She thought quickly. "I claim the dragon, then."

"Not so fast, little magpie. I am the only one tall enough to wear and not trip all over the black robe that completes the ensemble. Not sure where JJ found such a thing. I do believe you would look quite resplendent as a phoenix, Liara."

"Oh, Mademoiselle, and it would complement your new gold dress perfectly." Sophie clapped her hands, giddy with delight.

They arrived to find the palace buzzing with activity. Impressive even at a distance, the Palace of Versailles commanded the surrounding countryside and bedecked itself in finery of its own. Magnificent gardens abounded. They, like many parts of the building, were off limits—though for different reasons. The Palace itself was in a continuous state of construction. A rumor had already circulated that the gardens were reserved for the following night's fête.

All guests were free to amuse themselves as they saw fit until that time. Liara's entertainment came from readying her exotic plumage and worrying. By the next afternoon, she also confirmed their party of friends had all made it to Versailles without incident. Still no whisper of the mirror; and still no confirmation nor denial on the issue of Nagarath's feelings for her.

And still no Anisthe, thank the gods. Liara considered the last observation the most important.

In the end, Liara could not help but be excited as she donned her phoenix feathers. Fiery and fantastical, she whirled for Sophie's approval. When Nagarath's knock came upon the door, she did not jump. She finally, truly, felt a part of the story being played out around her.

Sophie hurried to the door. With every movement, her fairy wings glinted in the light. Liara smiled, pleased with the effect. She had worked alongside the woman to fashion them in their limited time.

A dragon stood in the hallway just outside. Unlike Sophie, Nagarath had fashioned his wings to lay close against the long black robe he had claimed for his use. They glittered darkly, a subtle but effective promise of power. His helm he held under his arm. Liara was glad of it. She had feared she might not see his face and gain the reassurances she needed in spite of her excitement.

And then Liara regretted the wish. Her heart lurched as their eyes met, and she realized at last how little she needed Nagarath's compliments to know how he saw her. Hardly thinking, hardly tearing her eyes from him, she gently laid her fingers on his forearm and allowed herself to be escorted out into the gardens.

Together they strode past wizards and witches, ladies and gentleman bedecked in outlandish finery. Courtiers greeted one another with festive enthusiasm, resplendent in the trappings of all manner of mythical creatures, some recognizable, others ridiculous.

Sophie leaned close, touching a hand to her modest headpiece. "I'm glad that you fashioned these wings and forced me to wear this absurdly dazzling circlet."

"I do believe they did not expect Titania herself to come calling this evening." Nagarath smiled warmly, giving life to his otherwise dark aspect. Upon entering the gardens, he had donned his dragon scale helm—Liara couldn't begin to guess at what purpose it had served before the mage had altered it so. It surrounded his face in shadow and functioned in much the same way as a mask . . . perhaps better. He looked both menacing and delicious.

Liara let her eyes dance over the dark scales, still glinting beneath the black paint the wizard had applied to the bright metal over the course of the morning. She would not have been the least bit surprised if he had have come up with a way to breathe fire given more time.

Liara tore her gaze away, lest her cheeks redden to match her plumage. She again looked over the assemblage. She wondered what Vincent would be wearing for the evening. No matter his handsomeness, he couldn't be the dragon Nagarath was. Liara forced her thoughts away from the mage and onto Father Rodolfo who, unexpectedly, she really did wish to see that evening.

Rounding the building's corner, Liara glimpsed large trees, a green lawn, and many fantastically dressed folk. Accurate or not—from her vantage point, she saw no less than five creatures Nagarath had once pointedly told her "did not exist." It was magickal.

Liara's extravagant plumage trembled. How in the world would they find a familiar face in that masked and costumed crowd? The answer came quicker than could be expected.

"A phoenix and a dragon! My, my, Mademoiselle Sophie, you are playing with fire associating with these two." Matty. Liara smiled in spite of her nerves. Any fears they had overplayed their role melted away at the sight of the gentleman's attire. Some sort of sea god, Matty was head-to-toe sea-foam and wispy elegance. Bare arms sported gold bracers, and his ringed and jeweled fingers held a magnificent trident. He had even whited his beard. Luminous and larger than life, the effect rendered him handsome.

This last observation had Liara scolding herself soundly. *What is wrong with you? Since when did you become a romantic, a dreamer?*

Even so, it did not stop her from peering at every courtier over her glass as food was passed to the company. If she did not find M. Vincent before night fell, she was sure to miss him once the rest of the evening's entertainment commenced. Already it was becoming harder to see the outer edges of the party, even with the lights which had twinkled into existence over the past several minutes. The king's outdoor ballroom was ringed by a long set of curved stairs, giving the space the appearance of a sunken bowl. It hastened the sun's joining with the distant horizon and made the shadows long.

People had begun to gather in excited clusters. Spirits brightened by food and drink and anticipation, everything seemed to glow. Liara found the fantastical finery almost convincing. She soaked in the spectacle, momentarily not caring whether she found Vincent after all. There were diversions aplenty. And soon the king would arrive. The whisper lived on every lip. Remembering her first glimpse of the man, Liara could hardly suppress a tremor of excitement.

It had her second-guessing their presence at the palace. They were stealing from a good man. Would not the mirror be safer in his hands? Louis was so controlling, so exacting. Anisthe had no chance of gaining the mirror for himself. Perhaps the mirror was in the king's own bedchambers.

Maybe what they had really needed was to come all this way and see that the mirror was safe. Maybe she and Nagarath had required the common goal, something to draw them together again while they healed. And maybe Sophie was right and Nagarath was jealous, and he cared for her more than as his ward, his apprentice. Maybe . . .

All was blackness. A hundred lights extinguished in a heartbeat.

Liara gasped and felt Nagarath's hand reach for her own in the dark.

A whistling hiss erupted on all sides. Arcing upward into the night sky, streamers of sparks burst into brightness. A combination of lightning and embers, the massive explosions above their heads had Liara ducking instinctively into Nagarath's arm.

"Fireworks." He bent close to whisper the explanation, his eyes still upturned to the sky, reflecting the thousand sparkles which danced in the air. Liara nodded. She wasn't scared. It simply overwhelmed, in addition to being a shocking surprise.

A new brightness drew attention back from the heavens. Atop the crest of the bowl that formed the ballroom's border stood a figure arrayed in gold and silver robes. Fountains of sparks sprang up from the ground on all sides of the man, the king. He, like Nagarath, wore a fantastical helmet. But unlike Nagarath, the king's seemed designed to show off the wearer.

Blinding bright in the light of the fireworks, the helm was fashioned after an eagle's head. A lion's tail and mane filled out the rest of the costume, along with golden wings and taloned boots. He stepped forward, entering the space as new illumination flickered to life on all sides. Countless beautiful chandeliers had been moved out beneath the stars. Crystals winked rainbows over the assemblage. At one end of the amphitheater, musicians took up their craft. The air filled with their sweet, plaintive notes. It truly was otherworldly.

Liara turned to Sophie. "The griffin was said to pull the Sun God's chariot through the sky, bringing light to the world."

"I believe it." Sophie gaped at the sights around them. She was not alone in her wonder.

But, magick or not, the topsy-turvy kingdom of fey or not, etiquette and order were rote. Courtiers moved to the edges of the open space to make room for their monarch. With the king's dance, the ball would officially begin.

Liara could only hope that, by the time the favored dances had been completed and the floor was opened to the lesser nobles, she might find M. Vincent. Again, her eyes strayed over the crowd, listening for rumor and looking for her new friend.

"Well, it would seem that the king and his favorite pet have gotten over their little spat," one of the gentlemen in their group—Liara had forgotten his name—commented with a sly look around at his companions.

"How do you know it was a quarrel? Maybe she had been sent on one of her diplomatic missions?" Madame Ellisa cut in. Her name Liara remembered. Wealthy beyond measure, she had her eyes set on JJ—despite the man being married. Not the prettiest thing, she more than made up for it in elegance. And gossip.

Liara had made it her goal to stick close to the woman whenever possible, no matter how detestable she might be. She had dressed as a wizard for the affair. The uninspiring move further eroded Liara's opinion of her. "You know that the king's teller of tales is gone for weeks on end, and when she returns, Louis always requests so very many hours in her company. Alone."

M. Talaffe cut in, "Of course alone. If I had a woman like her at my behest, I'd not send her running over hill and dale. And if I must, I'd welcome her back all the more. Fairy stories. I'll say there's a happy ever after happening in the king's rooms." He raised his eyebrows suggestively and elicited an ill-mannered chuckle from the group.

Raising herself on her tiptoes, Liara tried to catch sight of the object of their attention. The woman in question had ascended the bottom steps to speak with one of the king's men on the other side of the arena. Liara only achieved a good view of the woman's shapely backside. Clad in ice-blue, the lady had ducked demurely behind her large feathered fan, leaving nothing for Liara to gaze upon but a coif of brilliant blonde hair.

Not that it mattered to Liara what the woman looked like. Anyone who had the ear of the king was so far out of reach to Liara that she might as well have been standing on the moon. She needed to discover the circles in which the storyteller moved. Though, with Tally's insensitive remark, the woman clearly had few friends—ones who she might trust, at least.

Liara inclined her ear back to Madame Ellisa, font of so much information. In doing so, she caught sight of Nagarath's face. His white, shocked, enraged face. And something else. Pain. He mastered himself a fraction of a second later, his mask of polite vacuousness back in place. Only Liara had seen it slip.

What is it, Nagarath? What have you seen? Sensed?
Liara tried to catch his eye, quickly running through several possibilities. Could Anisthe have arrived, a valet, usher, or footman?

Their little knot of companions loosened and crumbled, leaving Liara and her mage standing alone together in the crowd. Liara stiffened as Nagarath bent close. He kept his voice low as he eyed the king's man and his artful companion. "Amsalla DeBouverelle."

Chapter Twenty-eight

"**D**oes she have it?"

Liara's harsh whisper would not leave Nagarath alone. Following his sighting of Amsalla by the king's side, he had forced Liara to take a turn with him about the gardens, Sophie in tow. He wondered if Amsalla would find him or if she would make him wait until far later in the evening, a cat with a mouse.

"Does she?" Liara put the question to him again. Anger had risen in her voice, and while Nagarath heard her, he just couldn't seem to get his jaw working on a response. Staring unseeing at the fanciful hedges and manicured paths, he tried to master his crush of emotions. They threatened to bury him whole. Amsalla DeBouverelle. Here.

"I would assume as much." The words came out dry. His angst became tangible.

"And Anisthe?"

"She would not work with him. She would have no need if she has already gotten what she wants."

"The mirror."

The mirror. Yes, Liara. Believe it is only the mirror that DeBouverelle wants. Nagarath did not trust himself to look into Liara's concerned eyes. *Oh, Amsalla, what game are you playing at? What are you not telling me?*

"Are we going to speak to her? Question her? Or are we going to play along, polite and untroubled, courtiers to the last?"

Closing his eyes, Nagarath slowed to a halt. Outwardly calm, his insides quaked. He did not know how to make Liara see, how to make her understand. She hated Amsalla. Distrusted her.

As should you. He opened his eyes to face Liara. "If you saw Krešimir—a guest, a footman, an usher on the other side of a door—would not your heart be troubled? Would you not desire to speak to him, to beg explanation?"

Liara sucked in a sharp breath and turned from him. Put to the disadvantage, he crossed back in front of her. He confronted a face he had crushed with his honesty. Still, she met his searching gaze. And Nagarath saw how she struggled against impulsive, wounded words. They flickered behind her eyes even in that moment.

Nagarath longed to take Liara's hands in his, to plead with her. Etiquette forbade it. "Tell me you understand what I mean."

Liara's eyes glinted. And then she tucked her unspoken thought away. Her response came measured. Calm. "You will not expose her for the fraud she is."

"We are frauds, Liara," he reminded her. "And yes, I will not. I owe her that. I owe her the benefit of the doubt. She is in trouble. I could tell from the first. The hesitation. The need to be near us but not telling us all. Her cut and run in Spain. If I can just get her to speak to me . . ."

His apprentice stepped closer, inclining her chin. Stubborn, angry, the familiar spark that made her his Liara blazed brighter than the silks and satins which had made her a courtier. "Then I will dance and flirt and do what it takes to stay out of her way and out of her suspicions—and out of your immediate protection. Do you understand?"

She was going to make him choose. Liara's jealousy—no, her logic—came through where his fears and yearnings would not force his hand.

"Understood." He paused, debating saying more, some reassurance that he would always, always choose Liara over Amsalla should it come to that. Instead he said, "Then, keep Sophie close. Please."

Liara embraced her newfound freedom. She became the fluff-headed, bright-eyed flirt who Nagarath had once lamented she was not. And to spite the mage, M. Vincent would be the first of her conquests. The evening found Liara surrounded by any number of young ladies and gentlemen. Her own circle ever expanded as the evening wore on. She grew certain that, once it came time, Nagarath would find her dancing until her slippers wore through.

And she learned ever so much more of court. Its intrigues, its politics. History of Versailles; the monarchy. In embracing the courtier-version of Liara of Dvigrad, she found she made friends easily. Or at least made acquaintances freely.

And then, a friend. Father Rodolfo materialized at Liara's side as easily as he had her first day at court.

"Have you seen Nagarath?" Liara blurted the words before she could call them back.

"Yes," Rodolfo chuckled. "And he did not appreciate my joke."

Liara put together the clues of blackened armor, the red-on-white Saint George's Cross upon the priest's shield, and arched her eyebrows.

"Well, what else is someone of my set to dress as amongst all you heathens? I thought it appropriate," Adessi sniffed. He gave a grand wink to Sophie who trailed behind. "Though, in light of you two, I'm beginning to think I greatly undershot my mark. Bravo." He gave a funny little bow, and Liara could not help but laugh. The man certainly was enjoying himself. Even Sophie managed a smile, though she still looked like a cornered cat, all wide-eyed and ready to flee.

Vincent entered their midst a moment later, invisibly called by Adessi. Liara eyed his ensemble with approval. He had dressed as a satyr, somehow managing to make such a shabby idea into something splendid. The gentleman was clearly relieved to chat idly with Mademoiselle out from under the stern watchfulness of her dragon and quickly found the means to extricate the two of them from the larger group. He had friends of his own he wanted her to meet. Liara was only too happy to oblige.

Let Nagarath chase down after the tricky and untrustworthy Amsalla. Liara would pursue other leads. She was finding hidden corners and trysting places in the labyrinthine gardens. As a "pretty, young thing," those who might otherwise limit her exploration overlooked her. With few connections and thus no threat, people used unguarded tongues around her.

Especially as Liara was so halting in her understanding of French. She could listen and nod along, giggling and playing the fool with her informant none the wiser. For example, M. Vincent was especially interested in comparing what languages he had mastered. He never suspected that his assumed superiority rapidly became his downfall.

Parading Liara about the gardens, he spoke to his friends in rapid French, introducing her to his fellows. She caught the words "charming," "shy," and "graceful."

We'll see about 'graceful' . . . Blushing, Liara smiled back and allowed herself to be led to the dance floor.

To be taught dancing by a close friend and mentor is one thing. To be held by a stranger and guided breathlessly about the floor under the eyes of all is quite another thing entirely. Three songs and three partners later, Liara realized: she liked dancing.

And she missed Nagarath.

Liara's companion had been left alone with the Italian priest, the one bold enough to make himself up as Saint George. This left Domagoj with both dilemma and opportunity. Jealousy told him he ought to follow Anisthe's aurenaurae. But to shadow Liara when she so clearly desired to be unchaperoned with M. Vincent? There was only so much he would learn from that exchange. No, he'd best use his vantage point to learn what he might from the two interlopers.

Obscuring his presence with a quick hex, Domagoj pressed as close as he dared.

"Don't worry, my lady, your secret is safe with me as well." The priest kept his eyes, his beaming smile, outward towards the party.

"Secret?" The maid did not seem to know what to make of the priest's cryptic statement.

A sideways look from Father Rodolfo set the young woman to quivering. From his hidden vantage point, Domagoj almost gave up his own game. Silently swallowing a gasp, he quickly worked to mask his spellworkings. The priest! The priest was a magick user.

Sophie looked ready to run. A cornered rabbit, a frantic fox. Jaw tight with discovery, Domagoj redoubled his enchantments, grateful he'd learned enough to work wordlessly. If the maid was a mage as well . . .

"I could do it again, if you'd like. Or we can talk like civilized people." The priest turned. Domagoj could see that his eyes burned with the fading spark of magick. "Would you know that I have not used my gift—small as it is—in over twenty years? Such is my regard for my calling and for the safety of our mutual friends. And so, if you please, could I not get such avoidance from you again?"

Father Adessi offered his arm. Sophie hesitated still, and he sighed. "Come, I'm not trying to court you, lady. But your touch upon my sleeve will neutralize my Art, giving you whatever semblance of trust you think you need from me."

Domagoj's hands balled into fists. Anger, incredulity fought for the freedom to direct his Art. The maid. A spellpiercer! A chill broke over him, naked comprehension that he'd been saved because his oriaurant powers were not visible the way a normal wizard's Art was.

Granted, from the way Sophie blinked with confusion at the priest, she likely did not understand her powers. Her dissembling to him had been borne of ignorance rather than treachery. Domagoj let relief take him.

The priest continued. "You honestly don't know how it works do you? I mean, I suspected as much but . . . What does Liara say of it?"

Sophie lowered her gaze. It earned her more of Adessi's incredulity. And Domagoj's. Impossible odds. How dare she not know? How dare she travel with Liara—a threat, a danger—and not know of it herself!

"Liara doesn't know, does she?"

Sophie shook her head, meeting the priest's eyes reluctantly. "I only just found out myself. There's . . ." Alarm brightened her features, and she whirled her gaze around, staring at—staring through—Domagoj. She whispered, fearful, "There's someone here besides the two of us."

"Come." Adessi, too, looked past where Domagoj stood not daring to move, not daring to think save to maintain his illusions. The priest beckoned. "I'm not going to hurt you, girl. But, please, we oughtn't have this discussion here."

Domagoj waited until the odd pairing, priest and servant, mage and spellpiercer, had gone from sight. Quickly dropping his invisibility, he hurried to find his master. A part of him wondered if he might be better telling Liara first of the maid's betrayal. But no, there was the chance that the aurenaurae already knew of Sophie's gift. Best to stick with Anisthe until he had a better chance with Liara. Until his own shock had worn off.

A spellpiercer! With such hidden within the mages' midst, Domagoj's particular flavor of magick had just become indispensable. He grinned into the darkness as he wound his way back towards the ballroom.

~*~

Begging a need for refreshment, Liara allowed herself a brief respite to locate the mage. Craning her neck to see past coiffed hair, hats, and feathers, she caught no sign of her mentor. Pouting, she took one more quick glance around.

I hadn't meant that I wouldn't see him for the rest of the night. She wondered where Nagarath had gone off to.

Another courtier appeared at her elbow, friend of Vincent, a Monsieur Tremblay. He smiled his invitation to dance. His eyes lingered over the gold tones of Liara's rich dress, her fiery feathers. His own ensemble impeccable and expensive—*another mage, how original.*

Goodness, I'm becoming adept at this! Liara confidently rested the tips of her fingers on his arm. She looked at the other fine ladies of the ball through eyes that shone and felt as if she'd become an equal to their rank through the magick that was the Menuet.

Between the whirling and champagne, the changing partners and constant flirting, Liara never felt the evening slip away. Monsieur Vincent was still her favorite, him being her first. She found herself entertaining the idea that perhaps she need not return to the humble beginnings from whence she had come. Perhaps this was the life she was meant to lead. Perhaps she could present herself, her services, to the king himself. Not as a war mage, as Anisthe had done for the Habsburgs, but as advisor. Researcher and librarian of magickal history for the Sun King.

Caught up in the headiness of her ambitions, Liara was slow to leave the floor at the song's conclusion. Her smile for M. Favager was automatic, dazzling but empty.

"May I have the next?" The voice spoke crisp but lightly accented French. Both Liara and her partner turned. The young and lively Favager politely took his leave.

Oh, how Liara wished he would have stayed. Her knees turned to water beneath her massive, flowing skirts, and she felt certain all the blood had drained from her face. From the corner of her eye, she had but seen a mage, dark and mysterious in robes that were as authentic as Liara had yet observed, and he had offered her his arm. But she could not tear her eyes from his face.

"You."

"Come, come. I asked for a dance." Anisthe smiled, his arm still held out. Impeccable. So very French. The corner of his eye twitched, evidence that he wanted oh-so-terribly to wink at her. Wicked. Triumphant.

Quickly, Liara resumed her own charade, successfully suppressing the urge to scowl at him. Automatically, she assessed his clothing, his form, placing him in the hierarchy of the court. "When did you arrive?"

"Just this evening."

Breathless, Liara could only interrogate her progenaurae in short bursts. Not only from the shock to her senses but because the dance's movements kept bringing her close and then far from the mage.

"And you are here . . . ?"

Anisthe explained in his smooth, honey-toned voice, "I came at the invitation of an old friend. Clearly I am here to enjoy the same diversions as you."

Liara's confidence returned in a rush. She had the upper hand, provided she continued the game. She smiled warmly. "The king's court holds interest to you?"

"It does indeed," Anisthe laughed. "Do recall that I am from the south of France."

"Perhaps then, before we leave, I should do to your home what you did mine?" Liara managed her cutting remark a moment before the dance took her from her partner. Craning her neck as she circled away and back, she could tell she had angered him. Good.

Liara reveled in Anisthe's dark silence as the line of the dance reassembled, and she faced the wizard once more. "Come, Anisthe, a gentleman should smile at a lady whilst he dances."

His eyes flickered to hers, then down. Still he did not speak. He seemed . . . disturbed, the fire from their sparring quenched. But Liara knew no other game with him and still had her own hurts to address. With Nagarath nearby, she would likely never get another chance to confront her progenaurae. "Silence, Anisthe? How unlike you."

"And cruelty is unbecoming of you, Liara. Dvigrad was an accident. Unintended."

Frowning, Liara tried to pass off the claim as yet another of Anisthe's lies. Nothing he said could be trusted. But the earnestness in his eyes as his gaze met hers caused her to suppress a shiver. "How dare you? I remember your words, not least amongst your cruelties."

"Amongst everything I have done, that transgression is not mine. Please, Liara." Anisthe turned to face her. "I'll leave you be. I'll leave Nagarath be. I just want—"

"You're unforgivable, Anisthe," Liara interjected quickly. The two lines of their set separated once more. The music continued, guiding her steps and carrying her away from Anisthe. And then back, echoing her own fascination with the man, her father-in-magick, her progenaurae.

"Unforgivable. And you? Has all been forgot between you and Nagarath?" Anisthe had mastered himself during the brief reprieve. "Come, Liara, a lady should smile at a gentleman with whom she dances."

"I try, Monsieur. But I am still rather new to dancing." Liara snatched at the threads of her unraveling bravado.

"You, my dear, are quite an accomplished dancer."

A return to safer ground gave her back her tongue. Frowning coquettishly, Liara retorted, "I thank you, sir. You too are quite smooth with your boots."

Chuckling, Anisthe nodded his receipt of the barbed insult. "A double compliment, that. For your tongue and wit are of me."

"And very little else." The final notes of the dance sounded. She found Sophie's eyes through the crowd. Her scarcely proper leave-taking of Anisthe did not weigh on her mind too heavily. He was not worth the grace.

Nagarath had just returned to the festivities when Liara regained the dance floor. He felt a small pang of regret that he was not out there with her.

But she was right. If they were to find Khariton's Mirror and wrest it from Amsalla's grasp—a task mightier than taking it from the king himself—then they needed to divide their efforts.

But his efforts had been mainly in vain. Madame De-Bouverelle had proven singularly difficult to find after her short appearance at the king's side. Nagarath began to wonder if he was wrong in his assessment of the witch. If she flitted about so freely, who was he to assume she was in trouble, trapped in some way?

But, as the ball had waned into the late hours, he had learned more amongst a circle of Italian noblemen who had evaded the dancing by situating themselves in the grove just outside the amphitheater. Though they knew little of the king's storyteller, they found the night's theme interesting, knowing as they did that His Majesty's interest in magick had impacted Venice's designs at quashing the Art.

Therefore, finding the mirror was as important as ever, if only to return things to status quo.

Nagarath wondered if Liara had had a fruitful evening. She certainly looked happy. Whirling about the dance floor, her face glowed as it did when mastering a difficult spell.

Perhaps when the music ends. Maneuvering to the edge of the floor, he positioned himself to ask for the next dance. But another gentleman was at her side before the final notes had died away, his arm outstretched in greeting.

Why am I surprised she's proving popular? Nagarath refused to give in to disappointment. He contented himself with looking at some of the pretty but empty-headed ladies hovering about the perimeter, mentally comparing the elegant courtiers to his little magpie.

The music began anew, and the dancers turned. White-faced and close-lipped, Liara looked as though she had seen a ghost. An instant later, Nagarath saw why.

Starting forward without thinking, Nagarath only barely managed to get a grip on himself before he made a scene. He watched from the side as Liara—his Liara—

smiled and laughed in the arms of his enemy, his past transgressions apparently forgotten. Nagarath berated himself for his visceral reaction at the sight of their dancing . . . his primary feeling not fear, a concern for Liara's safety, but jealousy.

And why not? His eyes followed the graceful couple over the floor. *She's witty and beautiful, talented, and tempestuous. You know perfectly well you'd have given voice to your feelings long ago had she not entrusted herself to your care.*

But Anisthe. Not only was his presence here proof that they must hurry in their discovery of the mirror's whereabouts, but it meant that Nagarath's earlier premonition—a memory, a warning deep inside that history could repeat itself—might indeed come true.

Chapter Twenty-nine

"Liara."

The use of her name set Liara shuddering, and Sophie maneuvered herself to cut in front of Nagarath, lest he upset her further. "Not now, sir. I'll see to her."

Nagarath brushed past as he attempted to come face to face with Liara and frustrated the maid in the process. "Not tonight, you will not."

"It's fine, Sophie. He and I need to discuss something." Still stunned, Liara allowed herself to be led to the edge of the amphitheater. Sophie forgot. Monsieur Vincent forgot. Adessi. Talaffe. JJ. The world narrowed itself to Liara and Nagarath . . . and Anisthe. She whispered, "It was him. He's here."

She needn't say more. Nagarath shooed the maid off with his usual carelessness and escorted Liara away from the sound and light of the dance floor. Away from the spectacle—away from Anisthe. Liara's feet made their own path.

Liara's hands still trembled when she got to her rooms. Nagarath had simply followed her, a hand gently laid on the small space between her shoulders.

Liara scolded herself for her stupidity. Of course, they had expected Anisthe might gain access to the king's court. They had planned for that very possibility. She had erred but in her sparring—her eager sparring—with the man.

Some dark little corner of her soul had welcomed him in, rose to the promise of action and drama.

Perhaps there is some war mage in me after all, alongside the scholar. Liara wondered what Anisthe thought—what Nagarath thought!—for the former war mage had, too, left the ball around the time she had to "take some air."

Liara noticed that her shaking hands had ravaged her coiffure. She'd simply begun pulling at pins and curls when she had sat down before the mirror. Nagarath stood beside her, patiently waiting to say something.

"I'm not going back there." Liara made the dark promise to her ruined reflection. Hair half up, half down. Only Sophie could right the mess now.

Still the mage did not speak. Instead he lifted a hand and drew an intricate sign in the air. The glowing rune vanished in a glitter of sparks. Liara's ruined curls lifted and tidied themselves once more, pins inserted themselves into place. "You are going back, Liara. We both are. Leaving before the king has retired would excite comment."

"You said no more magick," she muttered mutinously. She looked him over. A part of her wondered just how he had come to learn how to do a lady's hair with magick. Blanching, she realized she really did not quite want to know that. "And besides, what does my reputation matter? You can simply rely upon your connection with Amsalla. Oh. That's right. Anisthe was quick to tell me. He's here at her invitation."

Liara was rewarded with Nagarath's shock.

"Anisthe is a liar. Always has been. Or had you forgotten how easy it is to be taken in by him?"

Liara opened her mouth then shut it, stunned at Nagarath's cutting remark.

"Liara—"

Rising and rushing from him as rapidly as her horrid little shoes and ridiculously over-feathered dress would allow, Liara did not wait for the mage's apology. What? *What* had made him say that?

Nagarath followed. Of course. "Liara. I—Wait."

Angry past the point of tears, Liara quickened her steps. Nothing he could say right then would have been enough. Better he not even try at all. She herself could not be trusted with words in that moment and so punished him with her silence.

Nagarath quickened his steps to match hers, overtaking her with his long strides. From the corner of her eye she could see he had taken off his dragon helm. His eyes were wild, frantic, upset. Liara's heart ached, thinking back on their earlier conversation. He caused this! He had put her aside—

No, I put myself aside. And said as much. Guilt, an echo of her unease over Anisthe, darted through her consciousness. How was Nagarath to know her mind? *But he ought to know my heart.*

Liara pasted a careful calmness on her face as they approached the footman at the door. Distantly she noted Nagarath do the same. A hitching sigh wracked Liara's chest as she gained the nighttime air.

Nagarath donned the blackened dragon helm and, again, caught her up. "Liara, I didn't mean it that way."

"No? And in what way did you mean it?" Liara refused to slow her steps. A part of her screamed at her to stop. Part of her screamed at Nagarath. But mostly it was just screaming. Loud, angry, hurt, jealous, disappointing and despairing discordance. She dared a glance, darting her eyes to the wizard and arching her eyebrows over his nonresponse. "Nagarath, in what way?"

Goaded, his face dark within its mask, he said, "You did not even want to go inside Anisthe's empty house while we were fleeing for our lives. You would not stand to hear his name spoken. But tonight? I look, only to find you smiling and dancing in his arms? How am I supposed to feel about that?"

"And you've all but called Amsalla untrustworthy at every turn and yet also keep saying you owe her the benefit of the doubt." The sounds of the king's grand party drifted towards them. The time in which she and Nagarath could speak freely was fast fleeing.

"She is likely our best—our only—chance of getting to the mirror before Anisthe. Unless one of your silly suitors has privileged information, of course. That was the purpose of all your dancing and flirting the night away, was it not?"

"Well, that was the idea until Amsalla showed up. I suppose, to you, I would seem fixated on Anisthe. As you've been conscious of nothing but Amsalla's smiles."

Liara managed the last word, edging it in before they gained the circle of light and had to pretend once more.

Pretending everything's fine. That's all I ever do now.

It was a pity how good she had gotten at it. It made it harder to be honest with herself.

Liara found Sophie where she and Nagarath had abandoned her.

"Is everything all right, Mademoiselle?" Sophie's eyes never strayed from her face, and Liara knew without looking that she had lost her wizard somewhere at the edge of the crowd.

Liara fought the sudden tightness in her throat. She looked around, feeling adrift.

Sophie somehow understood Liara's need to put distance between herself and whatever had just happened back in the palace and rapidly explained as they walked, "Monsieur Vincent has been asking after you. I did my best to try to make the proper excuses in light of my not accompanying you back to your rooms but—"

"Mademoiselle, are you well? You look pale."

Sophie had led Liara to the gentleman himself. M. Vincent smiled broadly, though his brow was furrowed in concern.

"Too many people sometimes overwhelm me. There are more people here in this one space than in the entirety of where I grew up." The false smile that had begun to fade renewed itself under Vincent's warm solicitation. It helped, the game of poise and posturing, if only to provide a place for Liara to pour her passions.

"Then we do not need to dance. We can merely catch our breath and watch from the shadows." M. Vincent shot an anxious glance to Sophie. "Provided that is proper, of course."

Sophie suddenly found the night sky of particular interest. Together Liara and M. Vincent made off for one of the more out-of-the-way corners of the gardens. With their escape, Liara found the peace she had sought. Until Vincent spoke.

"Your chaperone is a stern sort."

"Who? Sophie?" Alarmed, Liara looked around, thinking the maid had decided to follow them after all.

Laughing, Vincent shook his head. "No, that tall fellow. The man who calls himself your uncle for the sake of staying on as your guardian. The dragon. He's a jealous one, is he not? I saw him nearly start out after that gentleman who danced with you following Monsieur Favagar."

"Jealous? Nagarath? Hardly." Liara found that her voice took a funny upturn. "Protective, yes. But not only is Nagarath not jealous, he has nothing to be jealous of in that other gentleman."

"Oh, it's jealousy. A man knows these things, you know."

"Is that so?" Liara suddenly found it very hard to breathe, to even think.

Vincent leaned in, close but not oppressively so. "Have I anything to be jealous of from him, then?"

Did he? Liara was no longer certain. Most especially not after the words she and Nagarath had just had.

"I see." Vincent stepped back.

No, don't do that. Liara stepped forward, trying to fix whatever she had inadvertently just ruined. "See what?"

"You really are an innocent, Mademoiselle." Vincent smiled crookedly. "He has come into the clearing twice to glare at me these past several minutes. I have seen you look around anxiously half a dozen times since we came out here. But it is fine. You are with me at the moment, and you've been kind enough to send most of your smiles in my direction. Perhaps I might change your mind. A man can hope, yes?"

"And a lady can dance, no?" Liara did not believe—not for one instant—the claim that Nagarath could be jealous. For that, she would have to want Vincent. *And Nagarath not desire Amsalla.* No, the jealousy between them was one-sided, Liara intimately familiar with which side she stood. But then . . . there was Vincent, more than willing to even the odds. At least, he was available and did not say stupid, cruel things.

Liara inclined her chin, trying to center her attention on the gentleman before her. She put behind her all thoughts of the wizard who had so hurt her feelings with the truth.

"If you go in again, you'll only make yourself angrier that she's dancing with that boy."

"Amsalla DeBouverelle." Nagarath turned toward the lit threshold of the amphitheater. He recognized the voice if not the silhouette. In their overwrought finery, all women looked much the same.

"Come to get away from the stuffiness of my set?" Amsalla approached. Her slippered feet made nary a whisper on the gravel.

Nagarath gave the night sky his full attention. He needed no more tricks. No tests. He was clearly in a mood to make mistakes without Amsalla's provocation. He did not need her information, either. He knew Liara was with that Monsieur Vincent. He said, "We both know dancing is not quite to my liking."

The moon had waned until it was little more than a crescent, a sliver of light in an otherwise dark sky. But even there, Nagarath could see Liara whirling amongst the stars. Both his mind's eye and conscience conspired to remind Nagarath what a fool he was.

"And yet you cannot stomach Liara enjoying it." Amsalla sighed. "Least not when her partner is her pro-genaurae, Anisthe."

Amsalla's eyes truly were everywhere, then. Nagarath turned to her at last. The wizard had positioned herself so the light from the palace would illuminate her graceful form. Temptress. He tried to move past the observation, the sting of Liara's words—and his own wounded heart—reminding him that he had a role to play. If he could but do so carefully. "Funny how you, me, Anisthe all turn up at the same place at the same time after all these years."

"Indeed. I, for one, could have done without an incantate here spoiling my plans with his ambition." Amsalla frowned. "But, then Anisthe always had his uses."

"So you did invite him."

"Is that what the Artless fool is saying?"

Liara's claim, from Amsalla's mouth. It hit Nagarath harder than expected. He lowered his gaze, half turning from the woman. Angrily he looked to the dragon helm in his hand, wishing he had kept it on. Anything to keep Amsalla from seeing how his jaw tensed with the effort to contain brash words.

Unlike with Liara, he was successful in reining in his frustrations. And with a woman who would have more readily forgiven him, no less.

Amsalla laughed throatily, leaning in. "Oh but he does have a way with your apprentice, does he not?"

He could still go in there. Force a next dance with his apprentice. Liara played her part admirably—too well—and could not refuse him. Hopeless. Foolish.

At Nagarath's nonresponse, Amsalla continued, "No, after Anisthe got in my way in Almazar, I lost all interest in him, save for hopes that he would stay far from my plans. Digging him up was a mistake I would not repeat again. Not when I might have help elsewhere."

"Help!" Nagarath turned the blaze of his anger towards Amsalla. "You abandoned us, may I remind you. And alerted your men to our presence." With his last shred of control, Nagarath managed to turn his outburst towards untried theory. To accuse her thus was a gamble, but he wanted to goad Amsalla into speaking, even if it were further denial. What Amsalla didn't say was often of greater importance than what she did. *Like every woman. Ever.*

"I saved you! I saved me! If the—" Amsalla lowered her voice. "Precious few know of my Art. Precious few. The king himself does not know. I've taken pains to disguise my other persona. Case in point: the contact whom Anisthe intercepted did not seem at all surprised that the mage he was to meet was a man instead of a woman, yes?

"I hurried back to stop you and your . . . apprentice . . . from doing anything rash. The king is mad. Mad with power. He's being set up for a fall. The mirror is but a part of that. Politics on a grand scale. But then, you had never troubled yourself with all of that, did you, dear Nagarath?

"Magick is as forbidden, as persecuted here as anywhere else. But I—we—have a plan."

"We." Nagarath folded his arms, skeptical.

"Take a turn with me, dear."

Amsalla's fingers were light on his arm. They trembled. Amsalla, who was never frightened. Obedient, Nagarath led the witch around the gardens. His eyes watched for any signs of treachery.

"Come. I would not have brought you to court simply to have you arrested. You are yet part of my plan, Nagarath." Amsalla leaned in, her tinkling laugh lighting up the dark night.

In an instant, Nagarath's mind was back in Malagon, learning spells from Amsalla in front of the fire. Riddles and hints. This time, he would not break the moment before he had what he needed of her. After all, with Liara's unacceptance of his apology, what objections could there be? He, too, leaned close, whispering huskily, "And that plan?"

"To restore magick to its rightful place once more."

"That is ambitious."

Amsalla turned from Nagarath, drawing him further down the torchlit path where they might speak more intimately. In silence, they walked amongst the tall, glistening trees of Versailles' gardens. It would have been romantic had Amsalla not been so clearly tormented. She turned to him, her eyes luminous. Heavy with the promise of unspilt tears, they sparkled in the light of the nearest flickering light. "We owe the Art, Nagarath. Tell me that you understand, that you love it as I do. Tell me that we still have that and that you'll help me."

'Help me.' The words detached themselves from the rest of the witch's plea, rattling around Nagarath's ribcage, piercing his heart. A riot of blonde curls, a smile borne of an unfettered independent spirit, flashed before his mind's eye, a memory of what this woman had once been. Strong. Capable. Unflinching and untamable. Anisthe had loved her.

Had I? Or was that mere boyish fancy, misplaced infatuation for someone who became my friend when I had none? Looking at Amsalla, Nagarath had his answer. The reason he could never simply walk away from Amsalla. He had to tear himself from her.

Help her? How?

The Art was everything. She knew he felt that way. And she played to that, the lifelong commitment all mages made. He could not turn her away when she put it thus. But, more than that, her underlying fear still cried out to him, resonating with the part of him that still adored her whether he wanted to or not.

And from there the pain came in. That she would not outright tell him what had her terrified, what had her running, saddened Nagarath. Amsalla could blame the king for his power and control, but Nagarath sensed she feared someone else far more. Far more.

At the risk of making her run once again, he had to confront that fear. "There is no question I love magick. To see it persecuted, going underground—away, even—breaks my heart. But I am still not certain what role you want me to play. You are making me a puppet, a player, when I do not know the lines. It rankles, Amsalla."

"If I told you what I planned, what I have set to do . . ." Again, tears threatened. "I tried to do right, you know. You know me. He has me. And my life has not been my own since. The mirror? It is the key which will free me from this prison. And start us on the path to greatness again. The awesome ambitions we once held when we were but children playing with magefire could come true.

"But I don't know how. And I cannot tell you. He'll see. He'll see and he won't—"

Amsalla burst into ugly sobs, looking away from Nagarath at long last. The spell between them broke. He could move again. He made use of that freedom by folding her in his arms.

"Hush." Over Amsalla's heaving shoulders, Nagarath looked to make certain her collapse went unobserved.

"My name is in the ledger, Nagarath. One pen stroke, one wave of his wand, and I'm finished." Amsalla looked up at him.

As their eyes met, Nagarath fell to the scent of her, the softness of her hair, her skin. No longer safely at arms' length, Amsalla's hard physicality crushed against his own. His hand slipped around her side, clutching gently at her waist, and thrilling even in the smooth folds of her dress. He could feel the heat of her through it.

Nagarath emerged from his thoughts to draw a shaky breath. He searched her face and saw no treachery there. He saw the girl who had brought him back to magick when he had failed his first test under Archmage Cromen. He saw the young woman who had pitted his adolescent passion against Anisthe's own. He saw a lady mage the like the world had never seen. And she needed him.

"Tell me, Amsalla. There is nobody about. Tell me, and I can help you. I promise I will help you. What ledger? Who wields such power over you and why?"

Mutely, Amsalla extricated herself from his embrace. Together they walked further from the palace, deeper into the darkness of the gardens.

The king had gone to bed at long last. Liara's ordeal was over. At present, she could not have said which hurt more: her feelings or her feet. She felt certain Sophie thought her a determined flirt—and perhaps she was. Vincent's kindness, the promise in his smile and hope in his eyes, had taken some of the sting from Nagarath's words. But, in the end, Liara had discovered that no amount of dancing could carry her away from the guilt which the mage had laid upon her.

'You're unforgivable, Anisthe.' Liara's words to her progenaurae returned to haunt. Unforgivable. Was she? Unforgiven, surely. What else could have sparked such senseless words from her mage? Nagarath had said he trusted her. He had taught her magick when, by every tradition of the Art, she ought to have been banned from it. They'd traveled together in any number of ridiculous circumstances—a party at Versailles with the king of France included. But forgiveness? Nagarath had never said as much. He had never voiced the words. Liara had thought it implicit.

And to have him bring it up then and there. With every worst fear she had coming true around her, right down to Anisthe showing up at Versailles.

And Liara meeting him eagerly.

'Oh, it's jealousy. A man knows these things, you know.' Liara's heart still thrilled over Vincent's words. His observation was, perhaps, nearer the mark.

But not with regards romance, no. There Vincent, Sophie—both were wrong. Nagarath's love was books. He had no passion save for magick. His jealousy, his fear, was for Anisthe and how his victory could affect all their lives. It had been Liara's mistake that had her briefly believing she meant more to him.

Jealousies and passions. Perhaps the mirror was hid closer than they thought.

Through the haze of utter exhaustion, Liara wondered what Nagarath had gotten up to, if he'd managed to find and question Amsalla. Turning the corner provided the answer.

Liara stopped. Heart; breath; eyes and ears—for a moment, she simply ceased to be.

Motion returned to her in the trembling of the feathers on her ridiculous costume. Time hurried to catch up. Its rush past her face buried Liara in a deluge of sound and light.

From a hallway alcove spilled a collection of silk and beribboned finery. She recognized that ballgown; recognized the wearer of it.

Liara backed away on silent feet. She needn't have bothered with the caution. With their attention so lost upon each other, neither Amsalla or Nagarath would have likely noticed her had she screamed and shouted and threw hexes at each of them.

But she had no screams. No shouts. No magick. Only tears.

Turning, Liara brushed past Sophie and fled for the sanctuary of her rooms.

Chapter Thirty

L iara had strength enough to see herself safely hid
within her room.

And then? Utter collapse. She practically crawled to
the bed, making Sophie skitter around her helplessly.

Endless tears. They came welling up out of secret corners of herself. Sorrow flooded out from beneath doors in
her mind she had kept locked for years. The shock of its
intensity nearly brought Liara back to herself.

Certainly, she had faced heartache—Liara and the
wizard both. And fear and danger and tragedy. But nothing
broke her like the sight of Nagarath and Amsalla together.
It was a new kind of loss; a different sort of betrayal. And
one she had no idea how to confront. Save to cry and cry
so as to mourn it all—all of their shared experiences and
all at once.

Liara found her tears did have an ending point. Turning onto her back, she noted that Sophie had sat herself at
the foot of the bed. The maid gave the gentlest of nods and
beckoned. "Come, Mademoiselle. Let's get you readied
for sleep."

She did not allude to any of the events of the evening.
Nor did she coo and fuss over Liara's tears. It helped. A
little.

Liara rose and went over to the dressing table. Sophie
followed.

Liara flicked her eyes over her reflection as she sat in front of the mirror. Everything was puffy and red from crying. And she had a crease across her chin from where she'd lain upon a fold in the bed covers. Flushed cheeks; trembling lips. She looked as though she had been in a battle or only barely escaped drowning. In a way, both were true enough.

Sophie's fingers darted tentatively over Liara's hair. The maid seemed quite mystified and Liara recalled Nagarath's magicking of the mess. She pictured him standing there, could almost see the glowing rune and feel his spellwork. She imagined a different ending.

Sophie began the tedious unpinning of Liara's coiffure, sighing her confusion, only to jump as a knock sounded upon the door to their rooms. Her eyes met Liara's in the mirror.

More a shiver than a nod, Liara gave silent permission to the maid to answer the summons. Liara regretted her decision the second Sophie made for the door. She didn't want to see him. She hoped it was him. The shiver became a tremble became all out quaking. The desire to punish, to hurt—to save her own heart—renewed itself. But ignoring Nagarath only mattered if he cared for her at all. Which he didn't.

She held her breath and listened as Sophie quietly made Liara's excuses for her, wonderful woman that she was. "Mademoiselle has a headache, Monsieur. She can see you in the morning."

"Sophie, please. I would not ask—"

Liara could practically hear Sophie's eyebrows arching in judgment. "Then do not ask, Monsieur. And I do not have to refuse."

"Please." Even whispered, Nagarath's plea broke upon Liara's waiting ears like a thunderclap.

"In the morning, Monsieur."

In the morning. Liara had until morning to sort herself out. But it was already morning—after a fashion. But then, she figured she might hurt forever. What difference would a few short hours make?

In Sophie's brief absence, the tears had returned. They served to clear her fevered cheeks and empty more of her heart. Pain crowded into the vacated space. Liara watched, dispassionate, as Sophie made short work of her hair. Though her touch came gently, Liara could tell from the black look on the maid's face that she, too, had needed something to destroy after her brief conversation with Nagarath.

With the stripping down of Liara's costume and effects came new relief. Exhaustion stole from righteous anger. The ocean of tears had made her eyes heavy. Liara slipped into bed barely aware of Sophie's own quiet well-wishes.

"Sleep, Mademoiselle. In the morning, rest assured I will perform my duties as companion as you would have me do. You are within your right to have me hold that man at bay as long as is practical. We can even fall back on Monsieur Poulin or Monsieur Jeffers if you would rather return to Paris. We'll think of something. I will not let his disgrace become yours."

Liara simply turned over into her pillow to hide away from everything, wishing with all her might that she might someday, somehow feel different than she did just then. *I wish, oh I wish, to just be me again.*

And not the me who loved you.

~*~

Liara's short rest was further shortened as, scarcely an hour later, she woke to find that a dry-eyed heartache was as terrible as a tear-filled one. A steadying pain had built in her chest along with a throbbing pressure between her temples. She paced her rooms in the darkness, hoping she could burn away the maddening energy of her restless mind.

Over and over she replayed the events of the night. Nagarath's dalliance with Amsalla? That had been bound to happen. The witch was everything that man admired. Liara? She . . . well, she was just a fool for hoping otherwise.

Nagarath's careless words hurt the most. But even then, earlier in the night in Vincent's company, even as she worked diligently to rile the jealousy the mage supposedly had harbored, Liara had wavered. She had wanted to forgive Nagarath as much as she had wanted to punish him.

And punish him she would! She would find the mirror on her own. She would save herself from her ties to Anisthe and thwart Amsalla and Nagarath all in one deft maneuver. She—

In the dark, Liara's foot caught on the edge of the rug and she fell heavily against the bed. "Get back to bed, fool. Lest you trip yourself up so bad that you sprain something and aren't able to go out amongst the court and smile and pretend everything is just fine."

With the hissed warning came an idea. A wicked idea.

Oh, but I couldn't. Liara eyed the rug. Oh, but she could.

She listened for any sign her upset had woken Sophie and then hurried across the room. Liara dug in the wardrobe for her wand. *We'll see about no magick.*

She rose and turned to find the rumpled edge of the rug, then stopped short to turn back and don her dressing gown. A lie was only as good as its details, after all. Throat tightening as she returned to where The Incident was to take place, Liara looked to her wand and wondered if she had the nerve.

But to have to face all of those people the next day? In a choice between half-heard whispers and, at most, two days laid up and in control of whom she might and might not see? Liara would take the sprain. Gladly.

A swish of the wand and it was done. Liara fell heavily. Her ankle screamed. Breath catching and her vision sparking, she briefly wondered if she had done more damage than intended. Her panic called the maid to her.

Sophie's face was white with fright behind the flickering candle in her hand.

"Oh! Mademoiselle Liara!"

Liara understood only those three words within the maid's concerns. The rest of Sophie's worried outburst came at her ears too fast to discern, and she had to wave the woman back. "I'm fine. I'm fine. I just tripped, is all."

Liara tried to rise and found she could not put any weight whatsoever on the ankle. Hissing in agony, she dared a glance. Swelling rapidly, the injury was telling. And with it, Liara believed she had just learned the French for "sprain."

Clicking her tongue and—worse—blaming herself for having allowed Liara to fall prey to such an accident, Sophie helped her patient back onto the bed and set about doing all she could to cocoon the injury in softness. For all that her actions had been both cowardly and wrong, Liara had to admit that it felt nice to be petted. In punishment, her ankle throbbed most horribly—a match to her aching head. She had effectively ruined whatever rest she might have managed until morning and so waited in misery for the sky to lighten.

The day dawned at last, and Liara had managed a small miracle. She had slept the remaining hour of the night. She opened her eyes to find that Sophie had returned to Liara's room to sleep as best she could in the chair by the window. The act provided much needed balm for Liara's aching heart.

Liara moved to sit up and had to grit her teeth against her ankle's sharp complaint. She looked and found it appeared less swollen, less angry, than she had feared. And thank the gods for that. An idea born of misery and sleep-deprivation, her self-imposed infirmity seemed utterly idiotic in the light of day. *What now, Liara? Refuse all comers and draw even more attention to yourself?*

That was exactly the plan! She could imagine Nagarath pacing futilely in the hallway, Sophie guarding the door with a frown. Liara smiled, cruelly thinking for a moment that she might even let Amsalla come calling. And why not? After her conquering of Nagarath, the witch would surely crow about her victory to Liara, un-guarding her pretty tongue around the fool girl who was no longer any threat whatsoever.

Liara shifted the covers aside. Sophie was on her feet in an instant, ready to help. "Thank you, Sophie. For—for watching out for me."

"Yes, Mademoiselle."

The guilt had gone from Sophie's tone. In its place had edged a curious shyness. She seemed to be peering at Liara, unspoken questions hanging in the air between them. Though, of course, she did so without being so bold as that. Liara's impression was merely a vague instinct. Or maybe her uneasiness came from hurting, quite literally, from head to toe.

And everywhere in between. Taking a deep breath, Liara said, "I suppose I ought to try getting dressed."

Sophie smiled broadly. Her eyes darted to Liara's ankle.

"Oh, yes, it's still utter agony." Liara laughed. What else could she do?

The maid pursed her lips. "We'll get you dressed and seated by the window. Then I'll see about discreetly having some food brought here."

Liara welcomed the assistance and had almost begun to feel everything might actually be all right in the end by the time Sophie left to fetch some breakfast. She returned and began to rearrange the pillows and bedding. "Monsieur Vincent will lament your absence, I fear."

"I take full responsibility for my accident, Sophie."

Again, Liara found herself confronted with the maid's odd disquiet. A knock at the door broke the moment before she could challenge it further.

The door opened before Sophie could get to it.

Nagarath.

He stood in the doorway. In his hands he held a breakfast tray. In his face? So much misery.

Sophie didn't even try to stop him—likely couldn't have and wisely knew as much.

Liara only had time to give the mage an arch look before he'd divested himself of the tray and gained the chair opposite hers.

"Servant in the hall. Timing was quite accidental. I took the liberty of—" Nagarath waved to the breakfast he had brought, his sentence unfinished. His eyes lit on the table and stayed there.

Liara had suspected Sophie to be nervous. But Nagarath she knew to be so. His energy, frayed and snapping in the air around her, evoked a storm. She found it hard to think within its roar. It was almost like having him back.

"You've likely just now made my accident the talk of every courtier in Versailles, Nagarath," Liara chided.

His eyes snapped to hers. The softness in his gaze shocked Liara. It held her as he said, "My apologies."

Blinking, Liara couldn't trust herself to words. She broke the connection first, centering her attention on the breakfast tray and rebuilding the careful distance she had placed between herself and Nagarath.

"Ah. I almost forgot. The girl said she'd forgotten the jam. If you'd like any . . ." Nagarath looked to Sophie.

She didn't move.

Bless her. Liara smiled her thanks to the woman. "Jam would be nice. Thank you, Sophie."

Within two heartbeats the maid had left the room.

"How—?"

"Middle of the night. I tripped on the edge of the rug." Liara made certain to speak with no catch in her voice. And she certainly could not look back into Nagarath's eyes. Alone in her lofty perch of disdain, she ignored the mage at her peril. For he swiftly knelt and made his own examination of her injured ankle.

Surprise stole Liara's protest away.

"Merely sprained. You're lucky for it."

"Lucky." The hitch in Liara's throat caught her up at last and shaped her exclamation into something bitter.

It drew Nagarath's gaze up to hers. "Liara, I—"

Yes?

"No. No magick." He rose and settled back into the chair opposite hers. "Blast it all. Why did you have to go and—"

Liara's hopes hadn't even had time to take hold. She hit back. "Why did you—!"

"I tried to apologize, but you would not hear it." Again, the broken anguish in Nagarath's face met hers.

But Liara no longer punished him for his foolish words. She was not, in fact, even holding his actions with Amsalla against him. She had numbed to the pain of both during Nagarath's protests and apologies. Liara closed her eyes and asked, "Did she say where the mirror is?"

"Not as of yet. No."

She waited, curious if he would say more. When he did not, Liara found she hadn't the indecency to inform him that his actions with the witch had been seen. If anything, his unawareness served to help maintain the wall she had built around her heartache.

"And your evening? Anything learned?"

Liara shook her head.

"And I . . . I ought to go, yes?"

Liara gave a wordless nod.

"Please, Liara." He paused. "Be careful these next couple of days. Even with our cover story being what it is, I cannot easily come here without further gossip being raised."

Liara opened her eyes to give the mage a brittle smile. "Oh, I'm sure I've had my fill of your intrigue."

This time she did not have to steal it. He let her have the last word, and with a quiet, formal bow, he left. By the time the lump had cleared in her throat, Liara found the tea on her breakfast tray had grown bitter.

Chapter Thirty-one

Nagarath found Anisthe in the hallway outside of Liara's rooms. The former war mage turned away, feigning to merely pass by.

"Don't you dare. I don't want you passing two minutes alone in her company," Nagarath growled. He laid a hand on the incantate's shoulder so that he was forced to face him.

"Why, Nagarath—"

"Not a word. Or I'll do to you what I did in Almazar. And this time I will drop you somewhere from where you cannot hope to bother us again. Safe but secure. Liara will be able to achieve her autonomy of you without interference."

"Tsk tsk, an empty threat." Leaning close, Anisthe warned, "A hex would be noticed in a heartbeat. From how I understand the state of things here in King Louis' court, I say 'mage,' and you're as good as dead."

"And in doing that, you imperil Liara. Your threat is as empty as mine." Nagarath separated himself from the former war mage.

"I am so glad we understand one another, then. Truly," Anisthe laughed.

"I am serious. Do not talk to Liara any more."

"I'm not certain how you have any call to prevent who she does and does not see while laid up with her unfortunate . . . accident." Anisthe raised his eyebrows. "Very clever. Your trick or hers? Will she now be sneaking off to parts unknown then while you, ahem . . . distract . . . Amsalla DeBouverelle?"

Acting before thought could interfere, Nagarath had Anisthe's cravat in his fist, his free hand raised to break the man's nose.

"And here we are again, old friend. Ready to come to blows and that woman between us," Anisthe hissed, his eyes alight. "She is not to be trusted."

"And this from the mouth of the prince of lies himself." Breathing heavily, shocked at how nearly he had forgotten himself, Nagarath loosed his hold on Anisthe. He darted his eyes down the hall to check if his indiscretion had been seen.

Anisthe took advantage of his hesitation. "I would not lie on this. Not when the outcome would affect Liara. Please listen; just this once. Amsalla needs a pawn."

"I am aware of her plans," Nagarath snapped.

"Are you? Then you know why she needs the mirror? Why she sought first me, then you?" Anisthe's eyes darted over Nagarath's face. Another test; another challenge Nagarath could not meet. "Yes. She came to me first. Remember that. Remember that when you ask yourself how dirty she's willing to get her hands to save herself."

Nagarath knew that he was worn, tired beyond measure. What he hadn't realized was that, in addition to being exhausted, he was transparent. To Anisthe. To Amsalla. To Liara . . .

Forcibly separating his thoughts from Liara, lest he be driven to do something altogether ruinous, Nagarath instead gave himself to the jealousy Anisthe briefly roused in him. "Did she tell you then? Amsalla thought you worth her time?"

"I've lost my magick, Nagarath. Not my wits. I can put two and two together. Amsalla wants it for the reasons I do: Khariton's soul—"

Nagarath snorted. "She does not want the archmage's soul. She wants a spy within the king's court. Don't conflate her ambitions with yours."

"Oh, what delicious lies. Even if I had not suspected the truth of her plans, your face just now confirms it. You wear your guilt well, old friend."

"And with your secret knowledge—your *guesswork*—of Amsalla's plans you planned to do what, exactly?"

"I was going to tell Liara." Soft spoken, the sentiment challenged Nagarath's embattled conscience.

Nagarath scowled and, again, leaned on his convenient jealousy. "Tell her and not me? Considering that I am the one Amsalla has her eye on, that would have been a courtesy."

"I did not anticipate that I would find you receptive to anything I had to say."

"You would, instead, leave your words to drive a wedge between me and Liara."

"If it kept her from further harm, yes! But I would rather we work together. Why on earth would you pick a time like this to—? You were always like this. Always. Proud and obstinate to a fault."

Nagarath felt his own breath hitch. It was Anisthe's turn to be transparent. He cared what happened to Liara. And not merely for how it impacted his designs. This from the man who would stop at nothing to get what he wanted?

Anisthe pressed further, darting anxious eyes down the hallway. "I've studied these histories, Nagarath. Once freed, the vessel for Khariton's einatus has to be a mage. I had my pawn, an expendable. Ask yourself who Amsalla's is. Think of the Laws, the magick, and promise her nothing. Nothing. She lies."

Anisthe's searching gaze held Nagarath's for one long moment.

"As least consider my words." Anisthe turned from Nagarath, his mask back in place. Uncomfortable for having entertained the possibility of the incantate's truthfulness, Nagarath turned to acknowledge the approaching servant.

"Monsieur Anisthe." The man darted anxious eyes to the floor, avoiding Nagarath's gaze.

"What is it?" Anisthe moved farther down the hall, ushering his valet away from Liara's door and away from Nagarath.

"Madame DeBouverelle has asked . . ." Lowering his voice, the message from Anisthe's man was lost in the feminine clearing of a throat.

Whirling around, Nagarath found himself face to face with Sophie. Staring at one another over the discarded breakfast tray, he wondered how much she had heard. From the look on her face, quite a lot.

"Am I to understand that Liara is not to entertain well-wishers, Monsieur?" Sophie inclined her head, a challenge that dared him to question what she knew.

"No, Sophie." Nagarath rubbed a hand ruefully through his hair, leaving it to stand on end. "Mademoiselle can see anyone she wants."

Awkward, he took his leave, distracted by his splintered thoughts and wishing fervently that he had any move open to him which would not end in his utterly hating himself. If it was not already too late for that.

"Promise her nothing," Nagarath growled. "And yet you bow to her summons."

Far better to confront an absent Anisthe than his own conscience. For then he would not have to see how his feelings for Amsalla had swayed his better judgment. He would not have to consider how ignoring his regard for Liara had been a blatant and hurtful error. Both for himself and his magpie. But lastly—and possibly the most cutting—he might pretend that his arrogance on all matters relating to magick had not let him down. Again.

A knock sounded on the door, reminding Liara anew of her helpless state. Not that it would have been proper for her to answer under normal circumstances. But "ought to" and "able" were far different things. She changed her glower to a wry smile as Sophie entered.

"Nagarath said you are to receive visitors," the maid said.

"I'm not letting him back in here."

"And Anisthe?" Sophie sat on the edge of the bed, her hands occupied with smoothing the covers. She elaborated, "He was arguing with Nagarath in the hallway."

"Fine. Nagarath can come back, if he must. But not Anisthe." Liara crossed her arms. "Not today, anyhow."

"Just Nagarath?"

The query was a test.

It caused Liara's heart to renew its hammering. She sought distraction from it. M. Vincent was out of the question. As were Matty, Tally, and JJ. She added, "And Rodolfo."

Sophie flinched, growing still.

Ah-hah. Liara had wondered if mention of the priest's name might draw a reaction. She hadn't been so caught up in herself the night previously that she hadn't noticed Adessi trying to draw out the maid.

Wordlessly, Sophie rose and left the room, exiting through the door which separated her quarters from that of her lady's. She returned a moment later, a handkerchief laid out across her palms and worry in her eyes. Liara struggled to sit up and found that her hands sank uselessly into the endless pillows at her back. *Oh, for goodness' sake.*

Sophie reclaimed her bedside seat, shifting her grip on the object in her hands so that she might offer it to Liara. A familiar haft of maple peeked out from the snowy whiteness.

"My wand! Where did—?" No suspicion colored her question, but Liara could not help but peer intently at Sophie.

"It was on the carpet, next to where you had taken your fall. I"—Sophie blushed—"I thought it prudent that it not be left lying about but did not know where it was you kept such a treasure."

Liara reached for her wand, stopping as Sophie gently pulled back. Tears dotted the woman's face, and she whispered, "There's more . . ."

More? Liara hesitated, curious and fearful. The wand was wrapped in a handkerchief. Perhaps it had been damaged. Perhaps, in her carelessness, Liara had broken the delicate object. After all, she had forgotten it in her agony.

Sophie gestured for Liara to take hold of the end, sucking in her breath as the handkerchief fell away.

And then . . . nothing.

Liara frowned. The wand was empty. Magickless. The sensation was so odd that, for an instant, she forgot to be worried. And then the wand was wholly back in her possession, and she could feel its living Art once more. Same as it had always felt. An invisible glow; an aura all its own.

"If I may?" Sophie reached out a trembling fingertip. She did not wait for permission, and the wand went dead at her touch. Gasping, this time Liara felt the deadness reach up past the wand into her fingertips. She let go, snatching her hand to her chest and shrinking from Sophie.

"I'm one of them." Sophie's confession left no room for uncertainty. Liara knew which "them" the woman meant. It became as clear as the tears streaking down her face.

"You pierce spells." Liara looked from wand to maid.

Sophie nodded. "Father Rodolfo knew. He felt the intrusion from the moment of our very first meeting. He knew even when I didn't. Seems he's met quite a lot of my kind in his travels. Just as he has met many a mage."

Impossible. Liara mouthed the word, feeling trapped. She darted her eyes to the door.

Reading the look, Sophie raised her hands and moved to rise. "No, Mademoiselle. I don't mean you or Nagarath any harm. Honest. It was just that . . . I didn't know what to say. Things kept happening and then I was scared and it was so clear that you hated and feared spellpiercers. And I was only, myself, just finding out."

"And Nagarath doesn't even believe in them," Liara interjected.

"He doesn't— Really?" This brought Sophie back from the edges of her fear. She settled back down upon the bed. "I'm sorry I didn't tell you sooner. I'm sorry it took Father Adessi to force my hand at confessing it all."

Liara tried to quiet the rushing roar that overtook her senses. Rodolfo had felt Sophie's touch from the first. Did that mean . . . "Father Adessi is a mage?"

Sophie smiled. "According to him, no. Apparently there are degrees to the Art and his is—as he called it— manageable."

"Manageable," Liara repeated, eyebrows raised.

"Not a mage. Doesn't interfere with the rest of his life. More a character flaw or weakness." Sophie winced. "Again, his words, not mine."

This time, Sophie's eyes darted to the door. "So, what do we do?"

"Do?"

"Do we—do you—tell Nagarath?"

"No." Liara's vehemence surprised even her. "Not as of yet. I mean, it's good you told me but . . . No, I think we don't bother him with all of this yet. I'd like to . . . Do you know, exactly, how it all works?"

Sophie shook her head.

"Would you care to find out—? Oh!"

"Mademoiselle, what is it?" Alarm colored Sophie's features.

"Your upset in Paris at the shops. The carriage ride. Does it— It doesn't hurt to do what you do, does it?"

Sophie smiled warmly. "Oh, no, Mademoiselle. Most of my discomfort has, I believe, come from my ignorance. Though I suspect truly large spells might overwhelm me. I think . . . I think I need to practice more to be sure. So, yes. Yes, I would have you teach me about magick, Magus Liara."

Magus Liara. And with an apprenticeship, apparently, cut short by a disinterested Nagarath. Her heart ached to think of the absent wizard and the strange opportunity thrust her way. But then, she needed such to keep her from glancing to the door every other minute in wild, frustrating hope.

Perhaps they could use this unexpected problem. After all, it meant quite a lot that Sophie had come forward with her news rather than keeping it to herself or, worse, betraying them. Mayhap this was the advantage over Anisthe, over Amsalla, she had been seeking.

Nagarath might believe Liara open to visitors at present, but for that day, at least, she would shut out all comers. Save for Nagarath, of course, whom she couldn't keep away if she tried.

Sophie. Spellpiercer. It all made a mad sort of sense. Which took care of one of Liara's two days of self-imposed hermitage.

Domagoj made yet another discreet pass through the hallway outside Liara's rooms. Luckily, the day had turned fine, and so he had but few interruptions of his vigil. Most in the palace chose to amuse themselves with diversions outdoors. Anisthe was off with Amsalla. Nagarath turned to his friends for solace. And Liara? Rumor had it she had twisted an ankle dancing.

Paired with another rumor—that of Nagarath and Mademoiselle DeBouverelle's sudden romance—some residents of Versailles had their own ideas as to Liara's reasons for staying sequestered. Domagoj considered such speculation vulgar and so had taken up his watch.

There was little to see.

And nothing to feel.

Worried from the first over his discovery of the maid's spellpiercing abilities, Domagoj's fears grew as the afternoon waned. Exploratory hexes met a fog, the curious blankness of a spellpiercer's touch that only told him the maid was in and exercising her powers apurpose.

A brazen and foolhardy display considering the other spellpiercers. Domagoj adopted, then dropped his concern. Spellpiercing, he gathered, was not like spellwork. It was averse. Opposing. Water thrown on a fire. Only the other mages in Versailles would notice through their own use of magick. And they were avoiding its use. He stood as the only one with this knowledge—himself and Liara.

But if not by nighttime . . . Domagoj began his promise to himself, only to fall off it quickly. The rescue of Liara from the clutches of the spellpiercer; he had considered and dismissed the idea with a regularity to match his measured hallway pacing.

Liara in need of rescue. Nonsense. Even the fool Nagarath would not leave her in such peril. And how could she not know of Sophie's skills? Anisthe gone soft and sentimental for old friendships; Nagarath and Amsalla renewing their own attachment; and the aurenaurae's all-too-convenient accident and subsequent disappearance. It stood to reason they were working together. Liars and cheats.

"Liara included." Domagoj returned to his other theory and glowered at the blank and unhelpful walls. "She's slipped off into the night, and Sophie's been made to cover for her absence because Anisthe has caught on to you, Domagoj."

No. That was not right. Could not be. Panic and distrust took turns with him.

Sophie. Spellpiercer. Jailor? Confidante?

Domagoj's ire built alongside his distrust and panic. They tumbled together like flotsam in the shallows after a storm.

What he needed, what he really needed, was to talk to Liara. Sense her truthfulness eye to eye. Domagoj feared disappointment. Could taste it.

He would wait all night and the next day if he must. He would talk to Liara. He would be there for her where Nagarath had failed. Perhaps, by then, Amsalla would have convinced the mage to finish the spell Anisthe had begun in Almazar. Khariton's einatus, with his newly freed but long-disused magicks, would be no match for an aurenaurae and oriaurant's combined power. Not housed in the skinny, book-bound scholar Amsalla had chosen for her dupe.

The power was theirs for the taking so long as everyone acted as Domagoj knew they would. Fears allayed, he threw his half-mer hexes into the void of the spellpiercer's reach and looked to go see to the troublesome and untrustworthy trio of Nagarath, Amsalla, and Anisthe.

~*~

Nagarath raised his hand to knock on Liara's door. Tension gripped him. It robbed him of the ability to carry through with his intent, and he lowered his hand and turned to leave.

He hadn't seen Liara since the morning following her accident. Amsalla he had managed to avoid until that evening. In the intervening day, he had hid from both, attempting to learn of the mirror's whereabouts through less dramatic means. But the king's teller of tales had ears and allies everywhere. Nagarath was tired of pointed glances, closed mouths. Guilt a constant companion made worse by his cowardice, he had found he had trouble thinking through the demands Amsalla had made upon their last meeting.

In the end, logic saved him. Logic and learnedness. Anisthe was right. He could not go along with Amsalla's plans. He would tell her as much. Hopefully, he might convince her to abandon her plan altogether. And save himself in the process.

A laugh echoing down the empty hallway startled Nagarath from his reverie, and he felt his face flush with embarrassment. In searching for Amsalla so that he might give his answer, he had been directed to Liara's rooms. The cruel gossip would only redouble if he were found standing thus.

He knocked and was bidden enter.

"Oh. I must be of some use after all." Liara answered the door herself with her usual brashness—alongside a cautious limp.

Nagarath's surprise got away from him. "Oh, Liara! You're up and about!"

Sophie was nowhere to be seen. From the window-side table, Amsalla's arch look wilted him.

Well, how was I supposed to know the maid was out? He wanted to growl it at the perpetually proper Mademoiselle DeBouverelle. But that would be giving her exactly what she wanted.

As if he hadn't already.

"What? Did you believe a small injury would put me out forever?" Liara's cutting remark had him setting an accusatory glance to Amsalla. Witch. Small wonder the archaic word for wizard was synonymous with "poisoner."

Nagarath felt a fool. Worse than. And both women knew it.

He prayed Liara would not long hold his mistake against him. And Amsalla? He would soon be out from under her thumb. Both he and Liara would be.

Under Amsalla's burning gaze Nagarath barely trusted himself to look back to Liara, but he must. "I need to borrow Amsalla, if I may. If you could please—" He stopped to clear his throat. His paltry request of her came out a near whisper. "Please wait for me here, magpie?"

Liara darted her attention away towards the window. Nagarath was left to imagine what look had passed over her face at his pet name for her. All he knew of it was rejection. This in the set of Liara's shoulders and Amsalla's smirking smile as she approached him. Only later would he know if forgiveness were possible. His heart wrenched to consider the worst.

Amsalla joined Nagarath in the hall, her sly smile brightening. "Miss me?"

"I managed over ten years without your company. One day is hardly enough to bring me to my knees." Removal from Liara's company had given Nagarath back his ire.

"Then I shall have to stick close for the foreseeable future, whether or not you are willing to see me."

Together they walked through the king's palace, nodding politely at the few passersby the halls held. Most were out of doors, enjoying the weather which had turned fine with the arrival of a cleansing breeze. Nagarath could guess they were headed in that direction as well. Far easier to talk secrets that way.

Hand resting atop his arm, Amsalla claimed Nagarath as hers. A lie. And one he would have to correct as soon as they were out of reach of any potential eavesdroppers. Nagarath welcomed the stay of execution. To volunteer his thoughts would take some effort.

Give up all to the mirror's will? Madness. But Nagarath could never speak so plainly. Not to Amsalla. As much as she was, herself, in danger, Amsalla could still be for him a very potent threat.

"You're not going to help me, in spite of your promise."

Nagarath had worried she would see it as such. He stopped so that he could face her as he spoke. "Please understand that any offer I had made was to help you. Not forward your plan come what may. Not blindly obey your every whim."

Anger and disappointment warred in Amsalla's face. The disparate emotions clearly wanted each to have their turn with him. "Khariton would serve us. You would not be subject to anyone's so-called whim, save your own."

"There are the Laws, Amsalla. Please do not pretend I am ignorant of them. No matter their reputation, the Laws of sundering still hold—"

"Exactly my—"

"Which is why I am only open to helping, as you asked, under conditions that I set." *There. A compromise.* Nagarath's conscience refused his call. It had all but given up on him by that point.

"Conditions."

"I would speak to Khariton before entering into any arrangement. Any arrangement we make would be temporary. And for such a conversation Liara is present. Anisthe is not. You are not. And there are no tricks."

"You ask the impossible, Nagarath." Amsalla had mastered herself once more, a smile decorating her features anew. To look at her would be to be completely unaware of the crushing defeat the woman felt. Nagarath only knew of it because of how he knew her.

"In which case, you leave me no choice but to leave you to your fate." Nagarath closed his face off to the witch. "I will collect Liara. Unfair as it is, I will force Anisthe to come with us. And you, I shall wish the very best."

"I'll expose you."

"To whom? You're as complicit as I—even more so. Your finger prints are all over Khariton's Mirror. Admit it, Amsalla—"

"Laws can be bent, Nagarath. Laws can be—"

"Damn it, woman. Did you truly learn nothing of Cromen, of years of study under the archmage? Did Anisthe's mistake teach you nothing?" Nagarath raised his voice, enjoying the discomfort it caused the wizard.

Eyes flashing, Amsalla's response was cut short by the arrival of one of the king's closest courtiers. "Madame DeBouverelle? The king has need of you."

Leaning close, Amsalla's parting words to Nagarath were as quiet as his had been loud, "Khariton has taught me more about those Laws than has been passed on to us modern wizards. You know but the tiniest fraction of all the magick there is in this world, Nagarath. And it will be your downfall. This I promise."

"Then we both have promises to break." It took every scrap of his strength to reign in his fury at the witch's challenge. She was protected by her position. If he was anything but polite, word of their spat would be the next scandal on everyone's lips.

Nagarath stood, unmoving, as Amsalla walked away from him and back into intrigue. He willed his heart to break. Something. Anything to show him that his time with her had not been mere conceit. But he only felt relief.

Not a clean break, no. It was the sort of relief that twisted his guts and kicked him in the stomach. He still had to talk to Liara. Nagarath still had to find Anisthe and determine if what he claimed was true. Separate more lies from truths.

Safety would be short lived. They might well have to give up the mirror. But Liara . . . gods help him if he had ruined what he had with her.

He would fix it. He would make amends. He would tell her right then; tell her all. Even the parts of his regard for her that he had thought he could never voice. Why not? He had promised her honesty at the gates of Dvigrad, only then to have done what he always had. His silence was the very thing which hurt her most—and more so. For he knew—he hoped!—he knew!—that the spark within him was also answered within her. And he'd been too cowardly, too fearful and academically detached to see it.

More fear sliced through him. If she did not forgive him? If he'd hurt her too deeply?

Then he would live with that. But he would not live broken and divided.

The thought—the sweeping surge of hope—set Nagarath to chuckling. The few courtiers he passed turned from his maniacal smile, thoroughly scandalized.

Nagarath gained the salon. More knots of people, more hushed whispers and averted glances. Tension crackled in the perfumed air.

The guard had removed The King's Person to a place of safety. Tragedy. Danger. The nobility were planning their exit, Versailles giving one massive exhalation and expelling them all.

Matty. A familiar face threaded his way through the tight clusters of courtiers. Tally followed on his heels.

Nagarath started forward, gasping as his chest clenched uncomfortably. They had spotted him, and he had seen their faces. Something was deeply wrong, something that belied words or description, something that hearts instinctively knew and minds only grasped at.

"What is it?" Nagarath's exclamation had a life of its own, forcing itself from his throat, shrill and broken.

"Dear God, he hasn't heard." Matty's face turned parchment white.

"Mademoiselle Liara," Talaffe said. "I'm so sorry, Nath. Truly."

"The palace guard have been looking for you, Nagarath. A young woman was found dead—"

No.

"—in the wing where Liara was staying. Her rooms. We've been looking for you."

No!

Tally clamped a hand on Nagarath's shoulder, steadying him.

It was no use. Nagarath was falling. The world was falling. He could not breathe. He could not stand. Everything turned white, all the colors of light all at once. It was blinding. It stopped his thoughts.

"God, no." Nagarath heard his words. His mind struggled to process the idea of Liara dead. Liara. Dead. Impossible. It was as if it was happpening to someone else.

Maybe it was.

"It cannot be." Nagarath lurched forward, shaking off Matty and Tally's supporting embrace.

"Wait. Nath!"

He ran from them. He ran from their words, their terrible, impossible news. He had to see for himself. Perhaps it was a mistake . . . perhaps there was still time.

He gained the hall outside of Liara's rooms. Several of the king's guard milled about, carrying in their faces the strange, knowing guilt of being privy to an accident and yet powerless to prevent it.

"Liara!" The name was ripped from Nagarath's throat.

"She's inside, Monsieur."

"No. God, no." Nagarath rushed into Liara's rooms. His eyes fell to the still form that lay prone at its center.

Chapter Thirty-two

It was a strange thing, complaining about a sprained ankle that she herself had caused. But Liara played her role expertly, laughing at Vincent's jokes as needed, leaning more fully upon his offered arm when necessity dictated.

Not that it was that difficult a task. Two days of taking things slow had done far more for Liara than she had ever dreamed. Vincent hung upon her every word. He had chased his friends away deciding, at last, that she was wholly his.

Liara did not mind in the least.

They both knew her ankle hardly troubled her now. The swelling had all but gone away, and at that point, Liara leaned upon Vincent's arm in mere flirtation. Together, they strolled Versailles' intricate gardens, publicly playing their little game. Liara turned her face gratefully to the warm sun and simply enjoyed the quiet moment.

Being outside felt nearly as good as resting her hand upon the wiry strength of Monsieur Vincent's arm. With a contented sigh, Liara offered, "If you're careful with me, I might be able to risk dancing again when the king has his next party."

"And share the sight of you with all those people, Liara? You ask so much of me!" Vincent teased. "I thought perhaps I might, instead, whisk you off in secret." He pointed. "That up there? Overlooking the gardens? That used to be a terrace. It is now closed to everyone. But I know what the king plans for it."

He leaned close. "Late night garden revelries offer many opportunities for one to move about unnoticed. I should very much like to steal you away and twirl with you alone before his Hall of Mirrors."

"Mirrors?" Liara's heart hammered. She tried to be casual with her question, certain she was about to be found out.

Vincent misread her trepidation. "Do not worry yourself, Mademoiselle. You haven't a side that would not be worth reflecting a hundredfold. And it is an idle threat. Your watchdog wouldn't let me make off with you, especially to a section of the palace so prohibited."

"Hence the deliciousness of the idea." Liara thought fast. If it was true, that Monsieur Vincent might have knowledge hid from the majority of court, could she, perhaps, singlehandedly secure the mirror for herself? *Thank you, Father Rodolfo, for the introduction.*

Her thoughts were interrupted as the man himself approached. He came accompanied by a liveried gentleman. Quickly, guiltily, Liara removed her hand from Vincent's arm, distancing him from her colorful notions. The two men did not appear to notice, however. The palace servant outstripped the portly priest to gesticulate at Liara and her escort. Wild-faced and out of sorts, he spoke his rapid French as Adessi hurried to catch him up.

Bewildered, for the man continued his verbal assault, Liara waved her hands to beg a reprieve from the flood of words. She was drowning in French—could he not slow down for her sake? She looked to Adessi. Her heart hitched at the sorrow written across his face. Frowning, Vincent clearly understood little more than she, and he barked a command.

The servant jumped and gestured for Liara to follow, still talking. This time, she caught some of what he said. Nagarath needed her, apparently. Urgently. The reason had not been given, but he was to bring her to him.

Rodolfo still had not spoken. He took a place by her side and broke all manner of courtly rules to capture her hand and give it a reassuring squeeze. Again, the illness in his face was such that she began to think the kind gesture for himself rather than her. At last he managed, "He's fine but . . . Sophie."

The white gravel of the path crunched under Liara's slippers as she hurried after the servant. Rodolfo and Vincent fell a step behind.

Liara blinked the sunlight from her eyes as they entered Versailles. The palace had grown dim and dull; the people they passed seemed muted.

A foreboding rose in Liara's throat, a menace she could not name and guided by some invisible instinct. They turned the corner, gaining speed. At that rate, they would be running by the time they reached her rooms. She could walk this path in her sleep—and almost had after a long night of dancing.

Nagarath. She saw him as they turned the corner. His tall frame put him half a head above the king's guard who stood idly by. He ducked into her rooms, not waiting for her.

"No. God, no." Nagarath's broken exclamation drifted out through the open door, cutting through the tension in the hallway.

Sophie! Liara ran, passing the servant at last and causing several of the king's guard to retreat from her in surprise. She was in the room before anyone could think to stop her.

It had only just happened. Someone had draped a cloak over the body, but Liara could still see the hem of Sophie's dress, the tips of her shoes.

Nagarath turned at the sound of her entrance. Liara tore her eyes away from the still form on the ground to meet his gaze. Time stopped. Frozen in place, they looked at one another, unmoving and unbelieving.

A shadow passed through the wizard's face, and he emitted a strangled sob.

The heart-rending sound broke the spell, freeing Liara's tears as comprehension dawned. Everything blurred. Nagarath. The king's men. Rodolfo and Vincent. The still form that lay on the floor of her room. All bled one into the other, a ruined watercolor of hurt and horror.

"She isn't. No. Sophie. Don't—" Screaming, Liara bent to pull back the cloak, struggling as Nagarath's arms folded around her.

"Mademoiselle—"

"Get her out, please, Seigneur. It is too—"

Words, half-heard phrases flitted through Liara's fractured consciousness.

Nagarath, warm and familiar, his face hidden against hers. Tender fingers touched Liara's curls, her cheek, caressed her forehead. She could feel his breath on her shoulder. Sounds, spoken by her wizard, coalesced into words, "I thought it you. Dear God, I thought it you."

Clinging to Nagarath, Liara gave in to grief. It was not her, no. It was Sophie. But why? How?

"Please, Seigneur."

"Give us a moment." Nagarath's sharp answer brought Liara back to herself.

"What happened?" Liara barely managed the question. Lifting her eyes from where she'd buried herself in Nagarath's chest, her gaze swept past the cloak-covered body. Seeing it anew set the room to spinning again.

"A most unfortunate accident, Madame. We do not know how the girl met her death. It's as though she was burnt from the inside. Shriveled."

Hard as iron, Nagarath's arm grasped Liara about the waist, and she sagged into the support. Kind as the king's guardsman was, he looked away from their close embrace.

Improper. Alarms rang in Liara's head.

Propriety. Had the two of them not needed it, Sophie would be alive and well, back with her family and far from the tragedy here.

"It's our fault, Nagarath," Liara sobbed her realization into his shoulder, drinking in the reassuring warmth.

He was still Nagarath.

Liara and Nagarath. Nagarath and Liara. How many sorrows had their friendship seen? How many senseless deaths? In the midst of her tears, Liara realized that Nagarath hadn't protested, had not corrected, her words.

'It's our fault . . .'

Liara swallowed the guilt. "She was found like this . . . alone?"

"She was found by the maid who came to air the rooms shortly before Seigneur and yourself arrived."

"Come, Liara. Let us let these men—"

Liara shook her head. "May I take a few of my things?"

"We will send them to you. Monsieur?"

Nagarath nodded, his face dark. "Come, Liara."

Steeling herself and giving Sophie's prone form one last look, Liara allowed herself to be led from the room. Nagarath cut through the handful of the king's guard who still hovered in the hall. "I shall see to it that Mademoiselle Liara is fine."

Turning, they made for the wizard's suite of rooms. Proper distance developed between Liara and her mage once more. With the return to etiquette came a sense of normalcy. Normalcy that was interrupted by a riot of satin and tears the moment they turned the corner.

Amsalla DeBouverelle. "He'll kill me. It's all gone wrong. Magick, done right under the noses of our spell-piercers. I'm doomed."

"Hush. Who'll kill you?" Nagarath's tone wavered, but his eyes flashed their warning.

Amsalla inserted herself between Liara and Nagarath, crying and carrying on.

Liara simply stopped in place, feeling cool pressure building behind her eyes. With Nagarath's stunned acceptance of the witch's maneuver, he had abandoned Liara. Again.

She said nothing, only waited, nervously looking around. Surely Nagarath would notice. Surely his regard for her rang louder than Amsalla's frantic blubbering. But he did need to make that woman be quiet. Liara's shattered nerves began to quake under the onslaught of wailing.

"He'll kill us both, Nagarath. I'll be found out, and he'll know what I've been doing here." All of Amsalla's usual poise had gone. "And then he'll come for you, for everyone I've ever aligned—"

"Hush, Amsalla." Fear replaced the annoyance in Nagarath's face. He drew Amsalla close to him. It muffled the remainder of the frantic woman's words. "Yes, yes. I'll—Come with me. No more talk until we are out of sight of prying eyes. You're fine, Amsalla. Everything's just fine. Hush."

That does it. I'm getting my wand. Disgusted, Liara turned and hurried back towards her rooms. Neither Nagarath or Amsalla noticed her about-face.

Rodolfo had remained behind, and with his gentle intervention, Liara gained access to the scene of the crime unhindered. He left to placate the guards.

The wasted body lay on the floor just inside the doorway. The sight, this time confronted without Nagarath's strong arms to lean on, nearly brought Liara to her knees. *But Nagarath is comforting Amsalla.* Heartache chased heartache. Steeling herself, Liara crossed the anteroom to the maid's quarters.

It was strange, being in Sophie's rooms. Or at least that's to what Liara assigned the prickly sensation. She looked over her shoulder twice as she rummaged at the bottom of the maid's wardrobe. They had hidden Liara's wand and pendant amongst Sophie's things to better protect them. *I will find out who did this to you, Sophie.*

Liara breathed a sigh of relief as her eyes fell upon the wooden box. She felt whole for, perhaps, the first time in weeks. The relief was such that she nearly missed the quiet click of the door swinging shut behind her.

She whipped around in fear. Perhaps whoever had followed her would conclude she had required her jewelry box, nothing more. The obvious conclusion for non-magick folk.

But the man facing her from across the room most certainly did not fit into that designation. Magick slithered sideways through Liara's senses, questing, almost flirting with her own untapped well of power.

Magus! Exotic, wild, and yet also carefully controlled. She knew his aura, had puzzled over it for weeks before eventually putting it out of her mind as another of Anisthe's tricks. But this was no trick. Blues and greens, the man's magickal signature smelled of the sea and tasted like lightning. Could he have been the one who had killed Sophie? Why? How?

He wasn't masking his power. But neither could she see it properly with her own Art—Liara, who had become intimately familiar with the reading of a magickal signature after her own hard lessons on the topic. Notes of spellwork flitted in and out of focus, bright fireflies in a dark night.

And that is how he dares use his Art so brazenly in the midst of the king's spellpiercers.

From his darting eyes, she knew the stranger recognized her wand case for what it was. If he were the one responsible for Sophie's death, she was in great danger herself.

"Your storm."

The man did not deny Liara's accusation. Instead, he merely leaned back upon the door he had shut. He made no other move against her. She found herself transfixed by his bright gaze. An unnatural cerulean blue, his eyes bored into her with a strange intensity. Liara shivered and wondered why he did not speak. He seemed rather stunned, in fact.

She tried again, falling back on politeness. It came out cracked from a mouth gone dry with fear. "I do not believe we've been introduced."

"Domagoj. My name is Domagoj." He stepped forward, his hands raised and his magick extinguished. "Please, Liara. I mean you no harm."

'I mean you no harm.' Then why was Sophie dead in the next room? Him with magick which could have prevented it. She took a half-step back, tensing and wishing the other door were not so far away. "You're with Anisthe."

"No longer."

"You're how he's had magick."

"Yes."

The man's simple, open response took Liara by surprise. As did the renewing of his questing magicks. She fumbled to open her wand case.

"Shh-hh." He held up a finger for quiet. "You'll call them in here if you use that."

Them. Spellpiercers. Sophie. She paused, transfixed again by those eyes. "And how is it you're—?"

"Oriaurant. Half-mer, from my mother. Anisthe is—was—my adopted father. After a fashion." He smiled crookedly.

Oriaurant. The term was distantly familiar. Something Liara had read somewhere. A lifetime ago. In Nagarath's library.

"Anisthe. Why would you break with him after coming all this way? This close to the mirror?"

"Come with me." Under Domagoj's piercing gaze, Liara was not all that certain he even spoke. It seemed to her that his impulsive, fervent words had struck her mind. "Please. I mean you no harm."

Liara shrank from his outstretched hand, from his repeated false assurances. Her eyes darted to the door at his back. She again considered the wand in her possession. She tried to weigh with her dazed mind the dangers of simply calling the king's men to them and giving up the game altogether. For some stupid reason, the spell to test the magickal soundness of an object kept repeating itself in her mind. Useless little hex. A distraction. Finger on the clasp of the wand case, she dared his wrath. "Did you do it? Did you kill Sophie?"

"I was saving you."

"Saving me?" There was no question in Liara's mind that this Domagoj had killed Sophie with his magick, but to have him confirm it set her mind to reeling. Dizzy, she challenged, "What happened?"

This man—this unaccountably strange mage. He will kill. Liara considered the other door and took a tentative step backwards.

"No, no no no. You're going to listen to me, Liara."

Domagoj's spells snapped around Liara. An invisible curse, same as in Messina. And, as then, she found she could not move nor scarcely breathe. Domagoj turned from her, burning energy in his steps as he paced in front of the door. "Sophie. Your pet spellpiercer. Amsalla De-Bouverelle placed her in your path. Amsalla who approached Anisthe first to try to use him for her plans to free Khariton's soul from the mirror. But she needed a mage."

"According to you, he—"

"Hssst. Listen! Don't. Don't talk," Domagoj rounded on her, his eyes sparking dangerously. "Anisthe has kept secret my giving of power to him. Nobody knows. How many weeks did you and Nagarath follow my—our—signature and not suspect?"

Liara opened her mouth only to be interrupted again.

"An idea, perhaps. A curiosity. But you did not know." He approached. Liara cringed.

"Giving of power," Liara whispered.

Domagoj smiled his approval. "The Laws Eversio."

"Why?"

"Anisthe, he . . . he touched the gates of death in Messina. There was no choice left for me if I were to save him—to save you!" Domagoj grew troubled once more. His lips trembled and his hands shook. The spells holding Liara wavered. If she could keep him unbalanced, she might break through. She might gain the hallway where enough of the guard still lingered, and she might be safe. And all without doing any magick herself.

Domagoj continued, "And with it, I protected myself from him. You see? I've known he would betray me. All along."

"His signature is yours now. Your magick being the same, cannot hurt the other."

"Precisely. And doubly important now that he's in league with her. Along with your own champion."

"Not Nagarath."

"And where is he?" Domagoj reached for the door handle, as if in anticipation of another's eminent arrival. He stopped short, fixing Liara yet another meaningful glance. "Not here. Not even within earshot. I believe I heard Madame DeBouverelle carrying on and clinging to your champion's arm as they left."

He let his words do their work. "You see? Nobody would see us run, and our magick could ensure our freedom."

It was terrifying. Not just that Domagoj's words assaulted her in a manner almost physical. But that what he said resonated, played to her most secret fears.

As if sensing Liara's slow thaw, Domagoj approached, a strange light in his eyes. Those same, remarkable azure eyes that let her see his very heart as he closed the distance between them. If he lied, he believed his lies.

"Sophie." He still had not answered her question.

At this Domagoj's face closed. The sparkle in his eyes extinguished. It seemed to Liara that a chill entered the space between them. She wished she hadn't allowed Domagoj to step so close.

"I could not reason with her. She, instead, tried to stop me." Domagoj's voice grew flat and strangely strained. His magick flickered and then died. When he looked at Liara again, his hungry earnestness had returned. "She could have told us where the mirror is! I know the words to call the archmage's einatus from his prison. And we could have had it for ourselves."

"No."

"That she would not help me proves she was working for Amsalla, you book-bound fool."

Impossible. Sophie? Honest, kind, utterly delightful Sophie? *My friend?*

"Spellpiercers are rare—nearly impossible to identify. The woman was placed in your path a'purpose. She held you safe should Nagarath fail the witch once you arrived at Versailles. You were an unknowing hostage. But Amsalla did not—could not have—counted on me."

Bitter fear rose in Liara's throat. Nagarath was with Amsalla.

"Forget them. Run with me. Leave that wizard to his fate. Perhaps it will even work in our favor." Domagoj loomed ever closer.

"Nagarath." *'His fate.'* What did Domagoj mean?

"As I said, Khariton's einatus needs a mage."

No! That was all the argument Liara needed. Heart pounding a frenetic dance in her ears, she fumbled with the clasp on her wand case, stopping as searing brightness ripped through her magick.

Liara gasped and fell to her knees.

"You would turn me in to the king with your magick? I spent my childhood as a slave. I won't go back. I won't." Domagoj stepped towards her, his head cocked to the side. No gestures. No words. No indication of how he did the magick that immobilized her so.

It was pain without pain. Robbing Liara of the ability to move, she bled magick.

"Their loyalty is to one another. They are lost, Liara; old friends who've forgotten us bastards save for when our powers are convenient to them. See the truth of it. Say you'll come with me."

"I won't."

A part of her was weeping, a part of her dying. Dying alone and in darkness. It was theft of breath, of blood, of heart. He stole The core of her was being stolen away. It was rape. It was murder. She fell to her knees, cringing as Domagoj knelt to continue his torturous theft of her soul.

"Oh, you will. You're coming with me whether you like it or not." Domagoj's face twisted with jealousy. His humanity lost itself to his rage. "Or, at least, your Art is. And with it, my need for protection from Anisthe is over."

"Zielsor," Liara shot her accusatory whisper. To whom? Him? The Laws of Magick themselves?

Domagoj blinked slowly. Confirmation? Denial? It did not much matter. Liara's fingers met the wooden case which held her wand, and she tried to locate her thinning aura for one more spell. Something to stop the agony, to stop this evil man.

The words of the Green Language heaved and swelled in Liara's mind, refusing to settle, turning to ash and whirling away from her before she could grasp at it. The magick refused to come, refused to make sense in spite of her knowledge.

This is what she had done to Anisthe. Incantate.

Her fingers sought the long, narrow item nestled within its velvet wrappings. The mage's last resort.

His eyes on hers, Domagoj did not see Liara whip the long, thin knife upward and into his chest. Crimson stained his waistcoat, his face going equally red then pale. The attack on her aura fizzled and died.

Liara watched in horror as Domagoj slumped forward. His fingers grasped futilely at thin air. His mouth moved, yet produced no words save a surprised gurgle.

"I . . . I didn't—" Liara felt paralyzed. What had she done? She quickly removed the weapon.

The fading light in Domagoj's beautiful azure eyes seemed to ask that same question. His silent lips gave voice to nothing save a thin trickle of blood.

Run, fool. Unable to tear her gaze from Domagoj, Liara felt her own heart turn to glass. It shattered as it again began to beat.

She had to check, repugnant as it was: wand and knife, safely cased. And her magick? It was there, bright and beautiful, returned deep within herself. She was whole and well while her victim lay dying on the ornate floor. Shards of pain lanced through her veins—guilt and terror over what she had done.

Liara hurried from the room via the servant's door. She would rip Nagarath from the king's witch by any means necessary.

For a moment, Liara thought she might make it all the way to Nagarath's rooms without confrontation. With that fervent wish of her heart and her vision swimming in the red of the oriaurant's blood, she turned the corner, and ran headlong into an all-too-familiar face.

Anisthe.

"Liara, what—"

"Don't you come near me!" Liara screamed at the man. His stunned surprise allowed her to rush past him. She ran and left her father-in-magick standing open-mouthed in the empty hallway.

Tears blurred Liara's vision as she rounded the corner and nearly collided with Nagarath coming out of his room.

"What is it?" Alarmed, he steadied her and sent his gaze over her shoulder. Distantly Liara noted that he wore one of his long mage cloaks, and his wand was out. He looked utterly frayed.

"It's nothing. I know where the mirror is," she whispered. "Come on."

Blinking away her distress, Liara grabbed her wizard's hand and led the way, but not without a fearful glance behind.

Chapter Thirty-three

The door to Liara's quarters was guarded. But then, that came as no surprise to Anisthe. The whole castle buzzed with the murder of Liara's servant, and he had come as quickly as he could. However, Liara had shouted angrily at him in the hallway. She was likely more than fine.

But the shiver he had felt in his own Art concerned him. He was certain it emanated from there. And there were the guards, enough of a presence that Anisthe would be hard pressed to find a proper excuse to enter.

With a deft flick of his wrist, he felt the magick return to flood his veins. Domagoj's magick rather than his. Grateful beyond measure, Anisthe whispered the words of a spell, smirking when the tell-tale flash and boom of his hex sounded in the other direction. Booted feet and shouts of alarm sounded, then retreated.

The hallway was clear.

Anisthe entered Liara's rooms. Stepping over the body which lay sprawled beneath its cloak in the anteroom of the suite, Anisthe gave his surroundings a quick scan.

The door to the adjacent servant's quarters stood ajar. Anisthe's heart stopped. An outstretched arm, lying prone upon the ground.

Two victims. Not one.

Ansithe ran, falling to his knees by Domagoj's side. "No. No, no, no."

Domagoj did not respond. Turning him over, Anisthe saw the dark stain of blood on the oriaurant's waistcoat. He felt for a pulse and placed the back of his hand in front of Domagoj's mouth. He had both breath and heartbeat. Both faint.

"Anisthe?" The back of Anisthe's hand tickled with Domagoj's weak exhalation.

"Save your breath." Anisthe's Art tested the wound. It went deep. The oriaurant bled from the inside.

"No, wait. Liara—"

"I said save your breath," Anisthe growled, risking a glance at Domagoj's face. Ashen. He had little hope of saving him.

"Liara, she . . . I wanted to make it right . . . I told her every—" Weaker than his last, Domagoj's words died of their own accord. He closed his eyes. His energy slackened.

"Domagoj, no!" Angry now that he might lose this fight, Anisthe tried to calm himself, to find the magick which might save Domagoj. Spellpiercers be damned. He would fight his way out of the palace. They both would.

"I have him, Anisthe. Go. Finish what you came here to do."

Anisthe looked up in surprise. Amsalla's arrival would be about the only thing in the world capable of tearing his gaze from Domagoj.

She knelt swiftly at his side, shouldering him out of the way. She inspected the wound as best she could. "It's too late for him."

"No—"

"Go find Liara. It's too late for your man."

"He's an oriaurant, Amsalla. He's all the magick I have left." Anisthe heaved the words at her. "And I owe him everything. In spite of all."

This seemed to give Amsalla pause. Costly hesitation during what precious moments Domagoj had left. Anisthe wanted to scream at her, hurl lightning bolts into her face.

"The mirror. It is in the king's Hall of Mirrors."

Anisthe's heart clenched. The mirror. Power of his own. "Why are you telling me this?"

"Because we need to leave. An oriaurant's magick is the only thing a spellpiercer cannot quell—besides that of a pure fey. Get the mirror. I can save Domagoj with my magick. We will find you."

"Hall of Mirrors—"

"It's not yet ready for public eyes. It—" Amsalla sighed, exasperated. "I forgot. You cannot hope to get there on your own. Here—"

An explosion of light hit Anisthe's face, and he raised his hands on instinct.

Liara and Nagarath stood in the doorway of the imposing hall. The late afternoon sunlight threw the long room into golden splendor. The day was setting on the Sun King's monument to his own glory. The Hall of Mirrors stood before them, silent and gilt with the trappings of the king's wealth. And somewhere in this architectural crown lay the priceless jewel of Khariton's Mirror.

"Well? Which one is it?" Nagarath's whisper echoed eerily in the large space, the sound reflecting as neatly as an image might.

"How should I know?" Liara shot back, her own whisper harsh against the gilded harmony of the room. Seventeen arches. Each with twenty-one mirrors. They had a one-in-over-300 chance of picking the correct mirror, unless they could somehow sense its magick. And if it were that easy, it would not have lain forgotten for nigh on a thousand years.

Liara let Nagarath think. She watched as he absently rubbed the scar along his chin. Stepping forward, he examined the first archway, craning his neck upwards. "It would have to be in reach. Somewhere for the king to easily see it when he passed. A reminder for him to gloat over. Khariton's einatus would have seen to it that the mirror is placed prominently, some place it could work on whomever gazed upon it."

Liara approached, doubly cautious of the mirror's influence. She knew full well what she was capable of when her pride was incensed. "Well?"

They stared in abject defeat at the bright mirrors, moving quietly through the room until they had reached its center. There was no telling which was Khariton's Mirror. Despair gripped Liara. Alongside an overwhelming sense of victory. They had found the mirror before Anisthe. The power was theirs to take.

A familiar mocking laugh cut through the tense golden air.

"Mirror, mirror on the wall . . . reveal yourself to one and all." Anisthe made a courtly bow from his place in the doorway. He raised his hands, innocent. Unarmed. "Hold. I'm not here to imperil your great plans. In fact, I'm here to help."

"Help . . . yourself? Because that would be very much like you," Nagarath growled. He moved in front of Liara. "Very in keeping with how you tend to view the concept of help. The mirror is ours. And you haven't the Art to take it from us."

A tremor shook Liara. Realization. The mirror was working on Nagarath. Just as it was working on her. Khariton's einatus, inserting whispering doubts as cleanly as it encouraged foolish words of pride and greed. Divisive. Controlling. Manipulative. She placed her hand on Nagarath's arm. "Stop. Let him talk."

"Thank you, Liara." Anisthe paused and cocked his head. "I am surprised at you, Nagarath. You don't typically threaten without provocation."

A sneer curled the corner of his lip, and he moved quietly forward, his eyes darting from side to side. Paranoia. Fear.

Subtle and seductive, the mirror had him too.

"You said you were through with the mirror," Liara ventured. She moved in front of Nagarath so that she stood between the two men. "Anisthe? You said you were through with it."

Anisthe came to a halt, locking his gaze to hers. For a moment, no one moved or spoke.

A shadow passed over Anisthe's eyes. For a moment, he was almost himself. Whatever that might be. "I did. I did say that, yes. But you have no interest in it, either. Unless your champion's morals have changed since last we spoke."

"That's about all I—"

"Stop it. Both of you." Arms outstretched in a feeble belief that she might actually separate the two men, Liara shrieked as Anisthe and Nagarath barreled past her, throwing themselves at one another. "Stop it!"

Liara watched in horror as the two mages crumpled to the ground, fists flying and all sense of decorum forgotten. The sounds of the melee would call the guards. Didn't they see? She looked to the empty doorway. How long would it be until streams of uniformed men poured through into the room?

"Who are you to speak to me of morality? You liar and—"

"Me a liar? You're the one in league with the queen of deceit herself."

"You leave her out of this. She—"

"She's the architect of it all. But then you enjoy playing into her hands, no doubt—"

"Liara!" For one brief moment, Nagarath managed to gain the upper hand. His eyes connected with Liara's, radiating surprise. It was as if he hadn't even realized what he was doing. He looked to Anisthe, bloodied and locked in Nagarath's frenzied embrace.

"Did you tell Liara what that woman asked of you?" Anisthe gasped the words, locking his own gaze to Liara's.

Nagarath loosed his hold, moving to rise. "She—"

"Did you tell her?" Anisthe twisted, pulling Nagarath down and bloodying the beautiful polished floor. "Not so strong now without your staff or wand."

"No. I didn't. Because I was never going to do what Amsalla asked."

Amsalla. Liara felt her own anger rise at the witch's name. Fury and hatred. *No. Stop. It's the mirror.*

"The mirror . . ." Murmured half to herself, Liara was not conscious she even had a plan until Nagarath's cinnabar walking stick was in her hand

Rolling as they kicked and punched, neither of the men saw her actions.

The first mirror shattered under the impact of her blow. The shards sparkled like a magickal aura as they fell to the ground.

"—such a liar, Nagarath."

"I was protecting her."

A second mirror fell to Liara's furor. A third.

"Like you did in Parentino? Dvigrad? She's not yours to protect."

"And you're capable of it?"

Liara moved on to the next alcove, destroying every mirror within her reach.

"You knew I wanted her. I've changed."

Another alcove. Another set of mirrors. Another violent shattering.

Liara. Liara, what is it you want?

The cane slipped in Liara's anxious grip, her arms aching. She risked a quick glance to the two men who battled on.

What is it I want? Liara looked down dumbly at the stick in her hands. The cinnabar stone seemed to wink at her in the fading light of the sun. There was an odd buzzing in the back of her mind, like a crowd of voices muttering to themselves.

Liara. Dear child, come to me . . . Look at those men, grappling and struggling for power. Power that you have. Just as I once did.

"Stop it." Liara's command came strong, but her arms would not obey. The cane clattered to the floor from her useless fingers.

Look at him, Liara. Look at Nagarath. He was going to betray you. He would have chosen her. In turn, she would have betrayed him. Look at your teacher. Look at his former friend. They split with one another over that same Amsalla DeBouverelle. And now they fight because of a mutual regard for you.

In magick, you can never have friends. Only rivals. It all comes down to power. It always has. Look to the Laws if you do not believe me. Designed to stop the madness, the violent betrayals of power-hungry mages, the Laws are but a shade of the perfection I had planned. Come, fair one, and let me show you a better way.

Again, Liara looked back at the two wizards, hesitating, then looked up into the mirror. Understanding blossomed. Shadows of a thousand years flitted within the mirror's dark surface. A millennium of magick danced before her eyes, crises averted and rogue wizards thwarted by Khariton's work. Miracles worked through the Art. Khariton, dying before his time and sealing his einatus in the mirror for the future saving of wizard-kind. Soldiers burning witches upon pyres, torturing mages in dark dungeons.

You have deaths to avenge, have you not?

And Liara knew she had found what everyone had sought. Something that would be terrible to destroy. Something that could give them anything they wanted. Some of the most wondrous magick the world had ever known had been worked by the man who stared back at her from inside the mirror. The fleeting shadow of the once powerful Kerri'tarre whispered its promises to her.

Mesmerized, Liara spoke, the words drawn into her mind's eye pale and spidery, as if from a time long ago in a far-away land:

"Power that within Thee lies,
With my Command: Awake!
As Fairest, I demand and take . . .
Unto my Soul, your Spirit flies."

Chapter Thirty-four

"LIARA!"

She hardly heard Nagarath's warning cry, entranced as she was by the mirror. Dreamlike, the world was bathed in shadow. The last rays of the sun illuminated but the upper reaches of the room. Everything moved slowly. Even the motion of her own arm, reaching out to touch the mirror's shadowed face, was slowed as though against a rushing tide of water. Whatever Nagarath had to say could wait. Did he not hear that Kerri'tarre was speaking?

She opened her mouth to chide Nagarath, the words stolen from her as something big and heavy slammed into her, knocking her to the ground. Anisthe.

"Quickly." Leaping back up, he and Nagarath half-lifted, half-dragged Liara to her feet. Loud reports rang through the room, violent incursions which seemed to make the gold leaf and marble accents quiver in fear.

"But the mirror—" Liara's protest was cut off by a rifle-ball pinging off the column next to her. Wildly, she looked up into the alcove where Khariton's Mirror hung.

Cracks radiated across the surface of the mirror from a small hole in the upper left corner. They had killed it. They had killed the mirror.

Liara scrambled her retreat and looked back to the end of the hall. Soldiers swarmed the doorway. Already the foremost ducked to reload while those behind readied their shots. Sparkling shards of glass littered the floor.

'Deaths to avenge . . .'

Liara called no spell and gave no utterance. She splayed her fingers and let fly her Art. Lightning and thunder crackled through the long hall. Rain, sharp and ruthless as stone, loosed upon the soldiers. Pandemonium broke out, and Liara ran toward Anisthe and Nagarath. "Go."

"This way." Anisthe beckoned to a doorway, disguised to blend in with the mirrored panels. The first grand room gave way to another, and they slowed to a halt. Anisthe looked from Liara to Nagarath. "Can you get us out of here?"

"Not at present." Nagarath winced. He had his arm pressed tight to his side. A growing stain of red showed the reason why. "One of those fellows had good aim. I'll be all right but my magick is a bit tied up at present. Liara?"

"I, um—"

A crash on the door behind them made them jump.

"This way." Anisthe ran for the next door. It opened on a room much like the first. He offered his explanation, "One of the king's apartments, if I am not much mistaken."

"You know a surprising amount about—"

"Hsst. Not that one."

Too late. Nagarath opened the door.

The room in which they stood was, indeed, one of the king's. For next to it: the guards' room.

Liara raised her hands. The door slammed itself shut in the faces of the surprised soldiers. Turning toward the window, Liara pressed her open palm against it and closed her eyes. A shimmering copy of the trio appeared in the courtyard outside, running in the opposite direction.

"Did I know you could do that?" Nagarath eyed Liara in surprise.

She shook her head. "I'm not sure I knew I could do that."

"This way." Anisthe motioned for them to follow. He led them into yet another sumptuous yet silent room. The sounds of their pursuers momentarily grew louder, then faded. "Amsalla's magick did not deposit me where she intended. I ended up next to the Hall, rather than in it."

"Amsalla sent you!" Liara hissed angrily. They had come upon a small room, no bigger than a closet. It led to yet another, and another, before finally depositing them in a bedchamber. "Then you are not to be trusted, in spite of what you—"

Anisthe rounded on her. "She called the guard. She set me up to take the fall. Do you understand that? Whereas Nagarath—"

"I parted with Amsalla. We were coming to get you." Nagarath gently separated them.

"Was that before or after you decided to come all the way here for the mirror?" Anisthe spat the words at Nagarath, then turned to cross the room to the next door.

"Enough. Escape first. Argue later." Liara brushed past the two men and eyed the door. "We haven't much time. I think my diversion is about to run itself out. Where does this one lead?"

"If I'm not much mistaken, this way leads back to the Hall."

Nagarath peered out of the large archway windows to their left. "Which would make this the gardens and our best chance of escape."

"Soldiers," Anisthe warned. "Not ones likely to have been led astray by Liara's illusion. That way is untenable. Liara, if Nagarath cannot whisk us away from here, perhaps you—?"

Liara snorted. "I'm a bit busy keeping up that illusion that sent the guards the other way. I don't see you helping much other than to lead us round and round—"

"Look out!"

Nagarath's warning came a fraction of an instant before the door burst open, bristling with bayonets and angry men. To their right, the other door opened, cutting off escape. A shot rang out, deafening within the small room and filling the air with the fetor of black powder.

The gardens it is. Liara raised her hands and blasted away the furthest floor length window. She cried out as one of the guards' rifle-balls caught in her skirts.

"Go!" They did not need Anisthe's shouted command. Liara and Nagarath tumbled through the gaping opening and into the night. Another shot rang out. This one flew wide, almost on ricochet, though it hit little more than air. Another. This, too did not land.

Anisthe still stood within the palace proper, his back to the window, his hands outstretched before him.

"Come on!" Nagarath moved to grab Anisthe. Liara stopped him as she saw what Anisthe was doing. The war mage took one slow pace backward, glancing at them. Another slow step.

Another flash of a rifle's firing lit the room. A rifle-ball skidded sideways in the air. Anisthe turned and jumped out the broken window and landed, crouched on the path.

They ran for the nearby hedge. Fifteen feet and they were under cover. Ten. Five.

"Shielding!" Nagarath's eyes flashed.

"Better than. Now shush," Anisthe whispered.

No. Liara fought the instinct to run, to ignore the man. He was untrustworthy. He would betray them. It was a trap. Still, she did not move, save for a brief shuddering as her feet tried to disobey the order to stand.

Nagarath appeared to have the same difficulties as the palace soldiers ran out into the night towards them. And past. Confused and angry cursing drifted into the quiet hedge.

"Now stop your spell, Nagarath, or you'll give us away to whatever spellpiercers might be among them." Anisthe cast a meaningful eye towards Nagarath's injury.

"And then what? Let me bleed to death?"

"I'll heal you." Even in the dark of the newly fallen night, Liara could see Anisthe roll his eyes. "With magick the king's bloodhounds cannot sense."

"How is it that—?"

"His servant is an oriaurant." Liara winced and looked away.

"Hush. Yes." Anisthe inspected Nagarath's wound. Sticky with half-congealed blood, the coat and vest had shifted so as to hide the entry point for the bullet. The war mage hissed through his teeth, "This will hurt."

In the dark, Liara felt Nagarath slip his hand into hers. He gripped it tightly through Anisthe's spellwork. But he did not cry out lest he give their pursuers an easy target.

"You were never really adept at the healing arts, Anisthe." Strain colored Nagarath's complaint.

"Far better at causing pain than removing it, yes. I remember." Anisthe straightened. Eye to eye, the mages stood. Measuring. Judging. "That will probably give you pain for a while. But it will hold until you're safely out of France."

"Until we're—" Nagarath corrected.

"Liara, listen to me." Anisthe turned to Liara, swiftly cupping her cheek in his hand before anyone could protest. He leaned close, whispering, "Find the book. Do not come back."

Anisthe's eyes seemed to shine in what little light the night possessed. Sheer willpower seemed to illuminate him, or perhaps it was his borrowed magick. Liara shied from his touch, hurt without understanding why. Anisthe looked to Nagarath and then her. "Can you see the aura around you? The shield?"

"What are you doing?" She could see his magick, yes. Dark and darting, the aura seemed to still read "invisible" to her expert eyes. What was the mage planning?

"Nagarath, I—" Anisthe paused and shook his head.

He turned and ran from the safety of the hedge, shouting, "Here! They're over here. I saw the two wizards . . ."

"He—!" Liara's move to stop the mage was halted by Nagarath's hand over her mouth and a restraining hand on her arm.

"No. Wait," Nagarath whispered in her ear. "We're still under his spell."

Comprehension dawned. Anisthe pointed back to the palace, wildly gesticulating as he yelled to the scattered guard. He was buying their escape. But to what end? Surely he wasn't sacrificing himself. Not if he truly thought that Liara had a future.

"Amsalla."

Liara heard Nagarath's sharp intake of breath. He saw her, too. Betrayal. Hopes raised and then dashed. "He's in league with her after all."

"Doubtful. His spell still holds. Come." Nagarath grabbed Liara's hand and together they ran, deep into the towering hedge, far from Amsalla and her spellpiercers.

"Here! They're over here. I saw the two wizards . . ." Anisthe ran haphazardly over the open ground of the king's gardens and into danger. He cringed as rifles were leveled at him and prayed he would not have to use any of his magick in front of Amsalla. That was a secret he did not wish her to know just yet.

For there she stood, elegant in the midst of discord. Amsalla DeBouverelle, who would look glorious even upon a battlefield. Save for a handful of the king's soldiers, she was alone.

Domagoj? He tried to voice his silent question to the witch.

She did not appear to notice. Nodding to the man at her right—a captain from the look of things—Amsalla smiled as the noose tightened around Anisthe. "So tell me, why would these men report three vandals, and you assert a different story? A disagreement amongst your fellows?"

"Your men are mistaken." Anisthe swallowed, his mouth suddenly dry. The eyes that glared at him over the tops of musket barrels did not seem the patient sort. He suddenly feared that Amsalla's authority was more in title than actual. "I was caught up in the chase quite by accident—"

"Arrest him." Amsalla's command, though quiet, rang louder than any musket shot.

Rough hands sprang upon Anisthe. Amsalla's men bound his wrists and pinioned his arms. The prisoner secured, Amsalla and her men waited as first one, then another of the guard returned from their search of the palace grounds. Each reported the same. The mages had escaped.

Anisthe hid his smile, content to glare at Amsalla. With viper quickness, her hand struck. A backhanded slap across his face had him seeing stars. Then that same hand grabbed his chin, cruel and uncompromising. She lifted his eyes to hers and through the haze of his pain he heard her speak. "Don't worry, pet. You're safe until my men can get information from you. What they took; where they were heading; what you did to aid them in their escape."

It was time for Anisthe to show his own hand. He smiled. "Oh, you'll have it of me. For what I have to share makes me rather indispensable to you. If I am not much mistaken, my aurenaurae is now the fairest of them all."

Appendices:

The Laws of Magick:

Laws of Magick Creatio

Law The First: Magickal power mimics the Magickal signature of the originating or altering power.

Law The Second: Once the age of twenty has been reached, a subservient power gains autonomy and its signature is fixed.

Law The Third: The destruction of an originating power subsequently destroys the magickal properties of its surrogate. In the case of Magicked Artifacts, the Second Law of Transferre applies.

Laws of Magick Eversio

*Author's note: The following govern the spells of sundering, of unmagicking. Originally taught as Laws alongside those of Creatio and Transferre, over time the Eversio Laws were shown to harbor uniquely exploitable weaknesses and therefore are not applicable as true Laws of Magick. They are, subsequently, no longer actively taught and are considered "hidden" or lost laws.

Law The First of Eversio: Magickal   power given to another retains its originating signature. As this typically results in two signatures co-mingling, the larger portion of the Magick held will exert dominance.

Law The Second of Eversio: The giving of Power is not directly reversible.

Additional guidance on The Laws of Eversio:

The giving of power is only condoned so long as certain conditions are met:

Condition the First: Said Power must be given freely and not coerced.

Condition the Second: Said Power must have clear and unencumbered provenance.

Condition the Third: The purposeful transferring of magick out of a body must be done with the aim of not physically harming said body.

Laws of Magick Transferre

Law The First of Magicked Artifacts: A Magicked Artifact must be sound both physically and magickally in order to function as intended.

Law The Second of Magicked Artifacts: Damage to either the physical or magickal condition of a Magicked Artifact will affect the outcome of Magicks performed through said Artifact

Addendum: It has been found that these atypical results are often of an unpredictable, uncontrollable, and highly undesirable nature. Purposeful damage to a Magicked Artifact for experimental purposes is not recommended.

Dictionary of magick words:

Terminology

Amésos   /ˈə ˌmeɪ soʊs/

A weapon traditionally given alongside a wizard's first wand when apprenticeship begins; a mage's last resort. Mainly symbolic, the gesture has since has fallen out of fashion.

Aurenaurae   /ˈɔ reɪ ˌnɑ reɪ/

The act of copulation between a human and a magickal creature; also the product of such a union when life is conceived. As most such unions are nonviable, a human aurenaurae is exceptionally rare and would be directly subject to the Laws of Magick Creatio.

Einatus   /ˈaɪ neɪ tʌs/

A mage's Art; Wizard's word similar to the Artless word for 'soul'

Incantate   /ˈɪn kæn ˌteɪt/

A mage who has permanently lost his or her magick. While there are some that say that a magick user may regain their Art, these tales are generally dismissed as rumor and wishful thinking.

Oriaurant   /ˈɔɪ ri ˌɑr rɛnt/

The half-fae offspring of a magickal being and that of another race—typically human. Said offspring often carries within them a purer, 'wilder' magick, not easily sensed by spellpiercers or even other mages.

Common examples in history include the product of relations between faerie/human or merfolk/human.

Praecantator   /ˈpreɪ can ˌteɪt ɔr/

Archaic term for Archmage; Latin for poisoner, wizard

Progenaurae   /ˈproʊ dʒɛ ˌnɑ reɪ/

An indirect participant in the act of aurenaurae via their Art; the mage responsible for the creation and control of the magickal being involved. When said copulation results in offspring, the power signatures of both aurenaurae and progenaurae are identical per the Laws of Magick Creatio.

spellpiercer   /ˈspel pɪrs ər/

Art-less human who can sense, and interfere with, magick.

Note: Mages cannot sense whether someone is a spellpiercer or not unless their Art is affected.

zielsor   /ˈzil sɔːr/

The crime of devouring the magick gift of others.

High crime and gross violation of the 'hidden' Eversio Laws.

Green Language*

*Please forgive the lack of pronunciation for these terms. Magick in the wrong hands can be highly dangerous and so by not aiding in proper pronunciation, the author has erred on the side of caution.

ata	you
atsmi'i	I, magus
geshem	rain
gidel	grow command, as applied to the unliving (see tzamach)
goral	fate
h'ayim	life
he'eniq	give / grant
her'ah	show
hm'shiik'	carry
htslah'a	luck
i'shor	follow
levav	heart, mind
maa'ome	flame, light
na sha q 'ue	bind together/kiss
nif'tach	open command
ruwachkan'a	radiate
shinah	change, to be used as a command

sh'lemull	to be complete (Commonly used to check the soundness of magickal artifacts.)
tra'shuk	heart of the travel spell
tsebeta	fly, throw. (A variation on traditional attack form.)
tzamach	grow command, as applied to the living (see gidel)
yal'ad	bring forth, bear

About the Author

M. K. Wiseman has degrees in animation/video and library science–both from the University of Wisconsin-Madison. Today, her office is a clutter of storyboards and half-catalogued collections of too, too many books. (But, really, is there such a thing as too many books?) When she's not mucking about with stories, she's off playing brač or lying in a hammock in the backyard of her Cedarburg home that she shares with her endlessly patient husband.

Other works by M. K. Wiseman:

"Clockwork Ballet" in Mechanized Masterpieces: A Steampunk Anthology (2013)

"Downward Mobility" in Legends and Lore: An Anthology of Mythic Proportions (2014)

"Silver Scams" in Mechanized Masterpieces 2: An American Anthology (2015)

The Bookminder, Book 1 of The Bookminder series (2016)

Website: http://www.mkwisemanauthor.com

Facebook: http://www.facebook.com/faublesfables

Twitter: https://twitter.com/FaublesFables

Pinterest: https://www.pinterest.com/faublesfables

Amazon: http://www.amazon.com/M.-K.-Wiseman/e/B00CMJK19W

Goodreads: http://goodreads.com/MKWiseman

Acknowledgments

To the team of folks who helped make this book happen: To Xchyler Publishing without whom this series would not have continued: Thank you. You knew where this story was going and wanted to see it through. To Penny and MeriLyn and your marathon-level stamina for plot thread unsnarling and "does M. K. really *really* mean to have this word in this place"-ing and pushing me just past my comfort zone to the place where real stories live: Puno hvala. A 120k manuscript peppered with foreign terms and places is a beast to work through. You are amazing. To the ever-talented Egle Zioma, who has twice now given 'my imaginary friends' faces for the world to see. And, again, to all the folks behind the scenes at Xchyler whom I haven't directly interacted with during this process- You have my thanks.

To my author friends D. Lieber and J. D. Spero who've let me bounce turns of phrase, screams of joy, and groans of defeat into the chat window at all hours for months on end.

And to my friends who've been super supportive of my mad mad dream of authorship. Never underestimate the power of "how's the writing going?" at turning my day/week/month around. The process of getting a book together is monstrous and I thank you for not allowing the occasional complaint/cancelled plans/general unavailability to get in the way of our friendship.

To my super supportive husband and family: When writing wonky wizards doing horrible horrible things to one another, it is ever so comforting to have such love around you as I have.

About Xchyler Publishing

Xchyler Publishing, an imprint of Hamilton Springs Press, proudly presents *The Kithseeker*, Book 2 of the *Bookminder* series, by M. K. Wiseman. Xchyler Publishing strives to bring intelligent, engaging speculative fiction from emerging authors to discriminating readers. While we specialize in fantasy, Steampunk, paranormal genres, and speculative fiction, we are also expanding into more general fiction categories, including several manuscripts in the developmental phase. We believe that "family friendly" books don't have to be boring or inane. We exert our best creative efforts to expand the horizons of our readers with imaginative worlds and thought-provoking content.

Other YA series from Xchyler Publishing you may enjoy:

Forte by JD Spero:
Forte, *Concerto*, and *Cadence* (coming winter 2018)
Vivatera by Candace J. Thomas:
Vivatera, *Conjectrix*, *Everstar*
Vanguard Legacy by Joanne Kershaw:
Foretold, *Reflected*, *Fated*

Made in the USA
Lexington, KY
20 July 2018